Praise for *Second Pe*

"Kashua's protagonists struggle, ofte
being both citizens of Israel and the kin of Israel.
ally end up encountering ignorance and bigotry on both sides of
divide, making his narratives more nuanced than some of the other
Arabs writing about the conflict." —*Newsweek*

"Nothing is what it seems in Kashua's look at the subtleties of contemporary life in Jerusalem . . . the plot here is merely the vehicle through which Kashua keenly dissects issues of identity and
class. . . . The themes are universal in a world in which every culture, it seems, has an 'other' against which to play out prejudice,
and feelings of supremacy." —*Los Angeles Times*

"Kashua's writing and insight serve to translate several different, and
conflicting, realities at once . . . [his] work captures the unique and
often painful situation of Israel's Arab citizens, while also opening a
window for the non-Arab reader to better understand this dilemma."
—*Tablet*

"*Second Person Singular* triumphs as a tragicomedy composed of
two suspensefully intertwined stories tracing the lives of two unnamed Arab protagonists, illuminating their fraught condition
as insiders and outsiders and their painful struggle to create a life
of meaning . . . Kashua's razor-sharp wit and irony are on full display . . . [This] is storytelling of the highest order."
—*Jewish Daily Forward*

"Sayed Kashua is a brilliant, funny, humane writer who effortlessly
overturns any and all preconceptions about the Middle East. God,
I love him."

—Gary Shteyngart, author of *Super Sad True Love Story*

"*Second Person Singular* is many things: a psychological mystery reminiscent of Nabokov; a touching examination of what it means to be Arab in a Jewish state . . . a family comedy that involves all sorts of delusions and secrets and lies; a family tragedy about a young, paralyzed, Jewish man; and, finally, a triumphant escape from one identity into another . . . Kashua is an unusually ambitious and gifted writer." —*The Arts Fuse*

"[Kashua] has a gift for taking the small absurdities of everyday existence and the comic humiliations of family life, themselves served up with self-effacing deadpan humor, and making them comment on the bigger, often darker, contradictions of his life and the two cultures in which he lives." —*Jewish Review of Books*

"Kashua's parable deftly examines universal themes of isolation vs. assimilation. A worthy contribution to the increasingly popular works coming out of the Middle East." —*Library Journal*

"A sardonic sense of humor . . . And sometimes this pushes into uncomfortable territory for both characters and readers. But then, questions about identity—questions about the tension between the private and the public selves—aren't intended to reassure. . . . And perspectives—how we view ourselves, how we view that amorphous and often ill-defined entity called the Other, how we want to be viewed by others—give the book concrete shape." —*Jerusalem Post*

"[*Second Person Singular*] resonates with all of us, all strangers and The Other at one time or another in our lives . . . A must-read." —*The New World Review*

"Powerful . . . Kashua shows us the underside of success, with clear-eyed insight into an Israeli society that is becoming ever more tainted by discrimination based on class and money." —*Haaretz*

"[This] story is one of loneliness and reinvention . . . Kashua narrates powerfully, with careful attention to detail."   —*The Jewish Week*

"Kashua explores what it means to be a Palestinian and an Israeli; a father and a working man. The preoccupations of *Second Person Singular* strike me as adult preoccupations, ones many readers will relate to. Kashua has long been seen as Larry David meets Edward Said, but in this novel, he comes into his own. Incomparable."
                    —Randa Jarrar, author of *A Map of Home*

"This novel illuminates just how fluid identity can be, even—or especially—amid the Arab-Israeli tension of Jerusalem . . . A compelling two-sided narrative . . . [Kashua] has sharp insights on the assumptions made about race, religion, ethnicity, and class that shape Israeli identity."   —*Publishers Weekly*

"All of [Kashua's] work is suffused with his satirical wit . . . He's too savvy a writer, too subtle a social critic, to lose control of his language."   —*The Daily Beast*

"These stereotype-busting protagonists force us to reconsider the painful social situation in which Israeli Arabs find themselves as they grapple with issues of personal fulfillment, economic opportunity, and loyalty to both their Palestinian heritage and their adopted country."   —*Tikkun*

"[*Second Person Singular*] is a kind of existential mystery, probing for answers about how one fashions a sense of self under excruciating political and social conditions. . . . His work is not only aesthetically satisfying; in what it represents and the humane point of view it expresses, it has the feeling of something essential."   —*The National*

SECOND
PERSON
SINGULAR

SECOND
PERSON
SINGULAR

Sayed Kashua

Translated from the Hebrew
by Mitch Ginsburg

Grove Press
an imprint of Grove/Atlantic, Inc.
New York

Published simultaneously in Canada
Printed in the United States of America

ISBN 978-0-8021-2120-2
eISBN 978-0-8021-9464-0

Grove Press
an imprint of Grove Atlantic
154 West 14th Street
New York, NY 10011

Distributed by Publishers Group West

www.groveatlantic.com

18 19 20 21   10 9 8 7 6 5

To my parents

PART
ONE

THE BRATZ BEDDING

The moment the lawyer opened his eyes he knew he'd be tired for the rest of the day. He wasn't sure whether he'd heard it on the radio or read it in the newspaper, but he'd come across a specialist who described sleep in terms of cycles. Often the reason people are tired, the specialist explained, was not due to insufficient sleep but rather a sudden awakening before the cycle had run its course. The lawyer did not know anything about these cycles — their duration, their starting point, their ending point — but he did know that this morning, in essence almost every morning, he rose right in the middle of one. Had he ever experienced what must be the wonderful sensation of waking up naturally, at the tail end of a cycle? He wasn't sure. He imagined sleep cycles like the waves of the sea and himself as a surfer upon them, gliding toward shore and then suddenly, violently, being tossed into the water, waking up with a terror he did not fully understand.

The lawyer was internally programmed to wake up early, and yet, when he had to be in court in the morning, he would set the alarm on his cell phone, even though he knew he would jolt awake before it rang.

The sounds of his family's morning routine floated down to his bed. Or rather, his daughter's bed. She was six years old, in first grade, and ever since her birth the lawyer had made a habit of sleeping in her room. As a baby, she woke up often in the middle of the night, in need of nursing, changing, and soothing, and it was at this time that the lawyer first altered the family's sleeping arrangements. The baby slept in a crib in her parents' bedroom, alongside her mother, who tended to her, and he slept alone on the floor of his daughter's room, on a mattress.

At the time, his wife did not begrudge him this arrangement. She knew her husband needed a full night's sleep in order to function properly at work, and she, enjoying a full year of maternity leave, was not saddled with the difficult and demanding work of a young attorney who was just beginning to establish himself as one of Jerusalem's most promising criminal lawyers.

So for two years, the lawyer slept on a thin mattress laid over a Winnie-the-Pooh rug, the bear sailing along in the basket of a hot air balloon, surrounded by four serene, sky-blue, cloud-graced walls and a posse of stuffed animals, some of which were gifts from family and friends, and others, the bulk of the collection, bought by the couple for their firstborn child, who continued to sleep in her parents' bedroom alongside her mother. Ever since their daughter had begun to sleep through the night, the lawyer had been visiting his wife several times a week, staying in their bed until morning. Occasionally, his wife would pay him a visit, but he preferred the former arrangement, because the toys, housed on the shelves and in the drawers—teddy bears, puppies, and innocent dolls in wedding dresses—seemed to peer out at them in fear and astonishment, aghast at the strange ceremony being performed right beneath their noses.

When their daughter turned two, the couple decided it was time for her to make the leap from crib to toddler bed.

She was tall for her age—and still is, even today, looming a full head over the rest of her classmates—but even after buying the new bed, a pink race car that contrasted nicely with the sky-blue walls and the floating clouds, the lawyer continued to sleep in the girl's room and she began to sleep on his side of the queen bed with her mother. The lawyer's life, though, took a turn for the better with this new stage in his daughter's development because the toddler bed came equipped with an orthopedic mattress.

Last year, the couple had a second child, a son. Several weeks after his birth, the couple moved out of their rented apartment and into a duplex that they had built and designed to their specifications. The upper floor consisted of a large living room, a designer kitchen, and two bedrooms, one of which was especially large—the couple enjoyed calling it the master bedroom, a term they'd only recently acquired—and another that had been outfitted for the new baby boy, with sky-blue ceilings and Shrek wallpaper. The girl's room was downstairs. It was airy and cream-colored, with a matching bed, desk, shelves, and a spacious purple-and-cream closet. The bottom floor also had a bathroom, a small storage room, and an office, the lawyer's sanctuary—an antique mahogany desk, a gift from one of his clients, dominated the book-lined room.

The move to the new house did not alter the couple's sleeping habits. Their son was still an infant and his mother preferred that his crib be near her bed, and their daughter, despite all attempts to convince her otherwise, was scared to sleep alone in her room. The lawyer and his wife, sensitive to her fear of being alone on the bottom floor, suggested that she sleep on a mattress in her brother's room. She agreed, but nearly every night she woke up terrified and ran straight to her parents' room. And that is how the lawyer found himself back in his daughter's bed. Not that he minded. At the end of the day, the lawyer preferred sleeping alone.

The lawyer heard his wife's shrill voice ordering their daughter to wash her face and brush her teeth. Her quick and cantankerous steps reverberated through the ceiling. Why does she walk like that? he wondered. It was like she was making a point with her feet. Boom, boom, boom. Red Army soldiers on parade. "How should I know where your hair scrunchies are?" he heard his wife yell. "Maybe next time you should be a little more careful with your things. You're not a baby anymore, you know. Let's go. Quick. Downstairs, get dressed, and make sure you have all your school books. Too bad. No hair scrunchies. You'll make do. Let's go. I don't want to hear another word. I'm late."

The lawyer recognized his daughter's chastened steps on the wooden stairs and the sounds of his wife, blowing her nose in the bathroom and spitting as she brushed her teeth. He thought about his wife, about the noises she made, and wondered if there was a way to tell her how awful it sounded. He was sure that, if she knew, she would change her ways. The toilet seat came down with a thud and his daughter pushed open the door to her room. Her eyes, as he expected, seemed to be seeking shelter from her mother's scolding.

The lawyer smiled at his daughter, peeled off the Bratz blanket, sat up in bed, and motioned to her to come sit beside him — the exact sign she had been waiting for. She wanted to know whose side he had chosen this morning, and the smile and the invitation for a hug reassured her. Who knew, perhaps he'd even criticize his wife, admonish her. "I didn't lose my hair thingies," the girl protested, sitting in her father's lap. "I put them next to the sink yesterday before I went to bed. Why's she yelling at me? Tell her, Daddy, I didn't lose them."

"I'm sure we'll find them soon," the lawyer said, caressing his daughter's hair.

"We'll never find them. And anyway, they're old. I need new ones, lots of new ones, so that if some of them get lost there'll still be more. Okay?"

"Okay," the lawyer said. "Now get dressed. We don't want to be late, all right, sweetheart?"

"I don't have anything to wear," she said, pouting as she peered into her closet. The lawyer smiled at his daughter again and left the room. He considered going into the master bedroom to wish his wife a good morning and then wondered whether she'd come downstairs to greet him, but he did not go in and she did not come down. The lawyer had no tolerance for false gestures. He had heard often, from clients and experts on TV, that the way to ensure quiet on the home front was for the husband to deceive the wife, to compliment and praise her at all times, but that quiet, of the kind they were referring to, he already had aplenty. The lawyer could not contend that his wife henpecked him; on the contrary, she ran the house and took care of the kids with unwavering authority and never complained when he stayed late at the office or refrained from helping around the house. As he went upstairs and into the kitchen to make coffee, he considered these things, satisfied that his wife harbored no complaints.

He heard her cooing to the baby as she dressed him. He could have popped into the bedroom and she could have stopped by the kitchen. Instead he made his way back downstairs with a cup of coffee. He saw that his daughter was getting dressed in her room and then continued on to the study, shutting the door behind him. This was the only smoking room, in accordance with his house rule. This applied to everyone. If any of their guests wanted to smoke, they were welcome to step out onto the patio or to go downstairs. The lawyer's wife did not smoke.

SCHOOL

After checking that his daughter was properly buckled into the backseat of his black Mercedes-Benz, the lawyer looked over at his wife and saw her strapping the baby into her blue Volkswagen Golf. Ordinarily, his wife did the dropping off—their daughter at school and the baby at the nanny's house, a two-minute drive away—but on Thursdays, the last day of the work week for most Israelis, she worried about being late to her staff meetings, which started at eight o'clock sharp. The lawyer was rarely in a rush to get to the office on Thursdays so on this day alone they divided the labor.

The lawyer's wife clicked open the garage door. She came up to the lawyer's car and waved to her daughter. "Bye," she said to her husband, got into her car, and was the first to leave. She turned around and looked back at her husband and waved once again, smiling with gratitude. The lawyer nodded his head and sat down in his car. He felt himself a supportive husband who encouraged his wife's endeavors. True, other than dropping their daughter off on Thursdays he did not do much around the house or on the child-care front, but even small gestures, like taking their daughter to school or on occasion coming home early from work so that she could attend a conference or some work-related social function, were seen, by both of them, as major career sacrifices. They were aware that there was no comparing their salaries, the lawyer's and the social worker's, and though the lawyer never mentioned this to his wife, his friend, who was also his accountant, had told him that if his wife were to quit her job and stay at home, their income would actually rise. As a sole income earner, their tax breaks would amount to more than his wife's annual salary.

Mulling these things over as he drove his daughter to school, the lawyer realized that he did not know exactly what his wife did at work. That is to say, he knew she had a bachelor's degree in social work and that when they first met she had been working at the welfare office in Wadi Joz, in east Jerusalem, and that she had been enrolled in a master's program of some sort. He also knew that she had, over the years, attained an additional master's degree, in something therapy-related. He felt he had always encouraged her to study, always supported her, but he could not say with any degree of certainty what she did at her current welfare job in the south of the city, where she worked part-time, nor did he know whom she treated at the mental health clinic, where she held an additional part-time position. All of a sudden, before flipping on the radio to hear the seven-thirty news flash, the lawyer wanted to know what, for instance, those

Thursday morning staff meetings looked like, the ones she was always nervous about being late for.

He drove slowly through the neighborhood's narrow streets, sunglasses shielding his eyes. Sometimes there was traffic at the main intersection, where hundreds of day laborers waited to be picked up. The young, strong-looking ones were selected early in the day, and by seven thirty in the morning all that remained were the older, weaker men. Contractors who woke up late would have to make do with them. At close to eight in the morning, when the lawyer generally crossed through the intersection, there was only a smattering of lonely workers. The sight always stung. What did the locals think of him? What did they make of Arabs like him, citizens of the state? With their luxury cars and their ostentatious lifestyles, the ones like him, who came here for college and stayed for financial reasons, immigrants in their own land. The Israeli Arabs with independent careers are the ones who avoid beating a track back to the villages of the Galilee and the Triangle. They are frequently lawyers, like him, or accountants or doctors. Some are academics. They are the only ones who can afford to stay and live in a city where the cost of living, even in the Arab neighborhoods, is many times higher than in any village in the Galilee or the Triangle.

Lawyers, accountants, tax advisors, and doctors— brokers between the noncitizen Arabs and the Israeli authorities, a few thousand people, living within Jerusalem but divorced from the locals among whom they reside. They will always be seen as strangers, somewhat suspicious, but wholly indispensable. Without them who would represent the residents of east Jerusalem and the surrounding villages in the Hebrew-speaking courts and tax authorities, against the insurance companies and the hospitals? Not that there is any great lack of doctors, lawyers, or economists among the east Jerusalem Arabs, but what can be done if, more often than not, the Israeli authorities do not accept their credentials? A higher education from somewhere in the West Bank or from another part of the Arab world does not suffice in Israel; a whole slew of supplementary material and a battery of tests, the vast majority of which are in Hebrew, are required. A few of the east Jerusalemites actually push through the grueling Israeli accreditation process, but the lawyer also knew that many of the locals preferred to be represented by someone who was a citizen of the state of Israel. He, so the lawyer felt they thought, was surely more familiar with the workings of the Jewish mind and soul. He, they believed, could not have attained his position in life without connections, kosher or otherwise. Somehow, in the eyes of the locals, the Arab citizens of Israel were considered to be half-Jewish.

The lawyer pulled his luxury sedan into the parking lot of the Jewish-Arab school, which had been founded by Arabs like him. They did not want their children educated in the east Jerusalemites' schools, public institutions infamous for their physical and pedagogical decay. The Israeli-Arab immigrants in Jerusalem wanted their children to study as they had, in other words in a school under the auspices of the Israeli Ministry of Education, a place that issued matriculation certificates that were recognized in Israel and internationally, as opposed to the east Jerusalem system, where, until recently, they had followed the Jordanian system, and, more recently, since the founding of the Palestinian

Authority, the dictates of the Palestinian Ministry of Education. But even they, citizens of the state, educated people in positions of power, knew that they had no chance of setting up a school for their children without coming up with a novel idea. An immigrant from the Galilee, a PhD in education, found the solution: mixed bilingual education. He founded an NGO, called it Jews and Arabs Study Together in Jerusalem, and easily raised the money from European and American philanthropists seeking to promote peace in the Middle East.

The mostly Arab school board, with the assistance of the parent-teacher association, did all they could to ensure that only the children of the Arab citizens of Israel—these immigrants-in-their-own-land—would study in the school alongside the Jewish students, but they were unable to completely bar the acceptance of local Arabs. The board voiced their objections in nationalist terms, stating that the joint Arab-Jewish educational venture was meant for the Arab citizens of the state and not the Jerusalemites, who were part of the occupied West Bank. They argued that inclusion of the local children would violate their political beliefs, according to which, Israel must withdraw from the West Bank and Gaza, and east Jerusalem must be liberated from Israeli occupation and crowned as the capital of Palestine.

But these convictions could not be brought before the municipality of Jerusalem and certainly not before the Israeli Department of Education, which insisted on seeing Jerusalem as the united and eternal capital of the Jewish people. Voicing these types of concerns before the Israeli authorities would put the school in danger of being closed down and the parents charged with heresy and political treason. Therefore, and due to the fact that the immigrants' children were too few in number to fill the class quotas for Arabic speakers—the school mandate called for thirty students per class, half Arabs and half Jews—they were forced by the department of education and the municipality to accept several local kids.

It's so easy to differentiate between the Jewish and the Arab cars, the lawyer thought as he walked from the parking lot to the entrance of the school, holding his daughter's hand. The Jews' cars were modest, affordable, generally products of Japan or Korea. The Arabs' cars were expensive and German, with massive engines under the gleaming hoods and dashboards full of accessories; many of them were luxury SUVs. Not that the parents of the Jewish kids earned less—the lawyer could swear to the contrary—but as opposed to the Arab parents, the Jewish parents were not in competition, none of them felt they had to prove their success to their peers, and certainly not by upgrading their cars annually. Judging by the parents of the kids in his daughter's class, the lawyer surmised that the Jews worked in a variety of fields. There were high-tech employees, several senior public servants from the foreign, finance, and justice ministries, a few professors, and two artists. A wide range of professions when compared with the Arab children, who had at least one parent, usually the husband, in law, accounting, or medicine. Most of the Arab mothers were teachers, generally senior staff—they were far more likely to rise up through the ranks of Jerusalem's educational system than the local Arabs—but still, just teachers.

The lawyer, for his part, would have been happy to forgo the Mercedes and make do with a cheaper car. He had considered a top-of-the-line Mazda, but he knew he could not afford that. Even during the tough days after the purchase of the duplex, he knew that if he did not upgrade his car to a model that surpassed what the competition was driving, it would be seen as a retreat. He had to do everything in his power to ensure that he would remain, in the eyes of the public, the number one Arab criminal defense lawyer in the city, and a fancy black Mercedes was an integral part of that campaign. If one of his competitors bought a BMW with a V6 and three hundred horsepower, then he had to get the Benz with the V8 and a few hundred more horses under the hood. If the competition had optical sensors all around the car, he had to have DVD players built into the headrests. Not that the lawyer was having trouble paying back the loan he had taken to finance the car, but he certainly would have felt a little less pressure and would have had the luxury of being a bit more selective in the cases he took on if he had made do without the Mercedes. But he could not.

KING GEORGE

Five years ago the lawyer had moved his offices from Salah al-Din Street, the major thoroughfare in east Jerusalem, to King George Street, the main drag in the western half of the city. Aside from a few Jews, his clientele was based in east Jerusalem and the West Bank, and so on the face of things it made more sense for him to stay where he was, but the lawyer suspected that the east Jerusalemites, despite everything, had more esteem for a lawyer whose offices were located in a Jewish neighborhood. Forgoing his colleagues' advice, he went with his gut feeling, and found, in a matter of months, that the move to King George Street, which entailed a tripling of the rent, was financially sound. In a year he had doubled his clientele and his income.

Not long after his move to the western part of the city, the lawyer realized that in addition to a permanent secretary and a rotating student intern, he also needed another lawyer to help with the caseload. One year after the move to King George Street, he offered the position to a former intern, Tarik, whom he liked and who reminded him of himself back in the day. He knew he could trust him and soon enough he managed to convince Tarik to abandon his plans of returning to the Galilee, where he had intended to open an office of his own.

"Why go back? Just so your dad can see the shingle on the door?" the lawyer had said to Tarik. "You want to spend your life working for the village car thieves, or deal with the real thing down here?" In order to show to Tarik what the real thing was, he sent the twenty-three-year-old lawyer, fresh from the bar exam, which he had aced, to file an appeal at the High Court of Justice in Jerusalem. Upon return, Tarik, feeling victorious, with an interim injunction in hand, agreed to the terms the lawyer had laid out, a monthly salary plus 10 percent of all income from the cases he handled.

The office secretary, Samah Mansour, had worked for the lawyer for eight years, ever since the lawyer had opened his private practice in the eastern part of the city. At first he had hired her part-time, but after a year he was able to offer her a full-time position. Samah, who was thirty years old, had graduated from law school in Amman and was looking for a law office where she could learn the language and the system, in hopes that she could one day gain entry to the Israel Bar Association. She had come to the interview accompanied by her fiancé. The lawyer knew that the woman seated before him was the daughter of one of the senior Fatah officials in Jerusalem, and he decided to give her a job even though she didn't speak a word of Hebrew. He never would have admitted it but her father was the main reason he had hired her, especially since in those days he could hardly afford to pay her salary. But as a young criminal lawyer, he needed the seal of approval of a man like Mr. Mansour, Samah's father.

Samah's father ran for office in the first Palestinian parliamentary elections, was elected, and became, before long, a confidant of those in the upper echelons of the Palestinian government. Samah married her fiancé, a Kuwait-educated city planner, who had been working as a successful contractor ever since his return to Jerusalem. The couple had three children. By now she had a firm command of Hebrew, ran the office with a high hand, and seemed to have made her peace with her position, perhaps even deriving some satisfaction from it. Nonetheless, she took the bar exam every year and though she failed it close to a dozen times, she still insisted on trying her luck each year.

The lawyer pulled his car into the lot near his office and greeted the old guard with a hearty good morning. As usual, the man was busy brewing strong mint tea. The lawyer parked in one of the five spots he had rented—one for himself, one each for Samah and Tarik, whose cars were already in place, and two for important clients.

The old guard, black *kippah* on his head, waddled over toward the lawyer's car, tea in hand. "Will you do me the honor of having a glass of tea with me?" he asked. The lawyer got out of his car and smiled. "Thank you very much, Mr. Yehezkel, but today I'm in a hurry," he said, handing the guard the keys, as he did every Thursday, so that he could clean the vehicle. "You're always in a hurry," the guard said, adding in thick Kurdish-accented Arabic, "haste is from the devil." The guard laughed a hearty laugh that ended in a cough.

"Good morning, Samah," the lawyer said into his cell phone as he walked up King George Street. "They aren't here yet, are they?" He knew that the clients scheduled to arrive this morning were not known for their punctuality and, furthermore, he had seen that the parking spots reserved for his clients were both still open. "Okay, so I'll be downstairs in the café. Let me know when they come. Thanks." He hung up the phone, tucked it into his jacket pocket, straightened his tie, and turned away from his office.

The lawyer liked starting his day with a double cappuccino at Oved's Café but all too often he had to take it to go. Usually he'd find himself sipping his coffee out of a paper cup in his office. On especially busy days, he would very cordially ask Samah to do him a favor and get him some coffee from Oved, adding, of course, that she should get one for herself and whoever else was in the office. But Thursdays were different. They were quiet, practically dead compared to the rest of the week. The lawyer always made sure not to schedule court appearances on Thursdays. If something unforeseen arose, he sent Tarik. The majority of the day was devoted to paperwork.

"Good morning, Mr. Attorney," Oved said as he brought a brass canister of milk to a steaming spout. "Good morning," the lawyer responded, looking around the café, making sure he recognized all the faces. He didn't know them all by name, and he certainly didn't know them by profession, but Oved's customers were loyal, and he nodded in their direction. Once he'd gotten some form of recognition in return, he sat down on one of the three bar stools. "For here?" Oved asked from behind the bar. "Yeah, you believe that?" the lawyer responded, nodding, stretching the skin on his forehead and raising his eyebrows.

Oved knew how his regulars took their coffee—how much milk, how many shots of espresso, how much foam, if any, and how much sugar. "You want something with that?" he asked as he began making the lawyer's coffee. "Yes, thank you," the lawyer answered, even though he didn't want any-thing but coffee at this hour of the morning. Decorum, and the fact that he was occupying a seat in the café, compelled him to show some generosity and so he tacked a pastry onto the bill. "A croissant, please," he said, nodding.

The lawyer liked Oved and felt that Oved responded in kind. He was the owner of one of the only independent cafés downtown and had also been one of the first people to welcome the lawyer to his new surroundings five years earlier. He was outwardly kind and jovial toward him and somehow the lawyer felt that it was on account of, and not despite, his being an Arab. At first the lawyer thought that Oved was another one of those Kurdish Jews, a Sephardic store owner whose tongue and heart were not in the same place, but soon enough he found that Oved's political analyses were in line with his own. Occasionally, he even picked up on traces of bigotry that the lawyer had missed. Oved was the last of the socialists in the center of town or, as one of his regulars, an arts editor at a local paper, referred to him, "the one and only communist Kurd in Jerusalem."

Morning was the café's busiest time. Most of the customers, like the lawyer, worked in the area, and they took their plastic-lidded coffees with them to the clothing stores, shoe stores, hairdressers, travel agencies, insurance agencies, real estate agencies, law offices, and doctors' offices. Oved was too busy for conversation with the lawyer, who sipped slowly and looked around often. The skinny journalist was there with a cigarette in her hand and a small computer screen flickering in front of her face. The art history professor, known to the lawyer mostly from his appearances on TV, sat before an open book. The real estate agent sat with a client, speaking loudly about soccer, and an elderly couple shared breakfast without exchanging a word. I wonder what I look like, the lawyer thought to himself as he examined his skewed reflection on the polished chrome coffee machine. Afterward, once again offhandedly, he looked down and checked his shirt and tie.

"Nice tie, Mr. Attorney," Oved said. "What is it, Versace?"

"Thanks," the lawyer said, slightly embarrassed. "Not really sure what it is," even though he knew full well it was Ralph Lauren.

There was once a time when the lawyer knew he looked like an Arab. In fact, it wasn't that long ago. His first year in university was the toughest of all as far as that was concerned. He was nineteen years old when he left his village in the Triangle and came to the university in Jerusalem. For all intents and purposes it was the first time he had left his parents' home. He was stopped practically every time he boarded a bus—whenever he left the Mount Scopus dorms and headed toward the Old City, and again upon return. Nothing awful ever happened during those routine checks of his papers but standing there in front of the policeman or the soldier was always annoying, grating, constraining. But unlike other students in those days, who resisted the security checks, refusing to hand over their papers, butting heads with the policemen and the soldiers, charging them with discrimination and racism—assuming their stories were accurate and not mere bravado—the lawyer always forked over his papers with a smile. He was always courteous, wanting the policemen and the soldiers to know that he understood that they were just doing their jobs. The lawyer had always known that he was no hero and that he was not made for clashes, certainly not ones that could be avoided.

As his financial situation improved, he found he was stopped less. During his second year of school he got a job working at the law library and spent most of his paycheck on the kind of clothes the Jewish students wore. After he graduated, during his internship at the public defender's office, he made a little more money and the security checks grew ever rarer. Then he passed the bar exam, opened his own office, moved to King George Street, and, for the entire five years of working there, had not been stopped once. Not by the police, not by the security guards who worked for the bus company, and not by the border policemen who patrolled the downtown day and night.

By now the lawyer understood that it had nothing to do with the way a person looked, his accent or his mustache. It had taken him some time, but he had finally figured out that the border police, the security guards, and the police officers, all of whom generally hail from the lower socioeconomic classes of Israeli society, will never stop anyone dressed in clothes that seem more expensive than their own.

SUSHI

The lawyer failed to notice how late it was until his wife called. He had been going over his notes as he constructed the defense plea for a member of the Popular Front for the Liberation of Palestine who was charged with taking part in the shooting of an Israeli car on one of the Territories' many bypass roads. The lawyer was fastidious with the details, just as he had been during the trial itself, even though he knew full well, as did the accused and his family, that the man would be sentenced to multiple life sentences and that his only chance of release would be in a prisoner exchange with the Israelis. The lawyer thought these seemingly unwinnable cases were the most interesting. His task, in essence, was to do his utmost to ensure that the verdict allowed his client the chance of being included in a future prisoner exchange. The details — had he seen his victims? Had he hit his target?

Had he inflicted the fatal wounds?—would have virtually no bearing on the severity of his client's sentence but they could prove critical when the Israelis went over the names of the incarcerated and decided, based on the quality and quantity of blood on each prisoner's hands, who was eligible for inclusion.

The lawyer's cell phone rang. HOME appeared on the screen. Only then did he realize that it was seven in the evening.

"Are you still at the office?" his wife asked. He got out of his seat and began packing his bag, telling his wife that no, he had already left.

"Did you swing by Sakura?" she asked, and again the lawyer lied, saying he had placed the order, that they had called to say it was ready, and that he was on his way to pick it up. "Okay," his wife said. He heard her open and shut the oven door. "We need some white wine, too. You know how Samir is, he'll get all bent out of shape if we don't have any. Oh, and did you invite Tarik?" she asked just as he walked out of his office and through Samah's empty reception area. "Just a second," he said as knocked on Tarik's door and opened it without waiting for a response. Tarik was seated at his desk and the lawyer twisted his face and smiled as he spoke with his wife. "What did you say? I didn't catch that? Did I invite Tarik to come to dinner at our place at eight thirty?" the lawyer said, nodding and looking to Tarik for an answer. Tarik nodded back and the lawyer winked at him and said to his wife, "Of course I invited Tarik. He's coming. I'll be home in an hour at the latest. Okay? Bye." He hung up and put the phone in his pocket. "Sorry, Tarik, I completely forgot we're having dinner at our house tonight." Tarik laughed. He seemed to enjoy the lawyer's absentmindedness.

"No problem," Tarik said, looking at his watch. "I'll close up here in a little while. What time did you say, eight thirty? I'll go home first, take a shower, and then come over."

For three years now the lawyer and his wife had been part of a group, along with three other couples, that met on the first Thursday of every month for dinner and a salon discussion. The topic was set in advance, usually a movie, a book, or a sociopolitical affair. The discussions opened on an intellectual note and deteriorated quickly. The men wound up talking about money and real estate—who bought, who loaned, who owed—while the women talked about the teachers and the parents in their children's school.

The group was meeting at the lawyer and his wife's house and since it was customary for the hosts to invite another couple or two, the kind of people whom they deemed worthy of inclusion, the lawyer and his wife—well, mostly his wife—had decided to invite Tarik. Not that they thought he was the perfect fit for the group or that he was eager to join them. They wanted him to come because they wanted to introduce him to their guests in hopes that one of them, particularly one of the women—and especially the wife of Anton the accountant, who was a faculty member at one of the teachers' colleges in Jerusalem where the vast majority of the student body was young, female, and from one of the villages of the Galilee and the Triangle—would find a good match for the twenty-eight-year-old bachelor.

The lawyer and his wife never even considered inviting Samah and her husband. They were well-educated and well-off, more so than anyone else in the group, but were

ineligible on account of their status. These meetings were
for immigrant families alone. They believed that some things
simply could not be shared with the locals, regardless of
their material and intellectual wealth.

Sakura, the lawyer reminded himself as he skimmed
down the stairs and out onto King George Street, pointing
himself in the direction of the Ben Yehuda pedestrian mall.
It was evening, and the early-September sun had not yet
set over Jerusalem. A pleasant breeze had brought people
out onto the street. It was back-to-school season, before
Rosh Hashanah and the Jewish holidays, and several street
musicians performed along the length of the cobblestone
walkway. The lawyer fished around in his pocket and came
up with the list his wife had left for him in the morning. The
first item brought a smile to his lips—one inside-out maki
roll—and for a moment he forgot the crowds around him
in the center of town. He knew the maki roll was for his
daughter and he got a kick out of the fact that his six-year-
old knew exactly what kind of sushi she liked, especially
since he'd only heard of sushi in law school and had tasted
it for the first time two years ago, on his thirtieth birthday.
And here he was on the way to Sakura, the most expensive
sushi bar in the city. His wife had decided to serve a first
course of sushi and the lawyer knew, as did his wife, that
when the wife of Samir the gynecologist asked, while holding a soy-capped cone, "Where's the sushi from?" there was
only one acceptable response.

The thought of the gynecologist's wife biting into a cone
of sushi instead of a stuffed eggplant amused the lawyer for
an instant, but the feeling passed with a dark thought, one
that surfaced every now and again, that his life was a mirage,

that all of it could suddenly melt away. What business did he have eating sushi? Why was he spending his evenings with these people, friends whose company he wasn't even sure he enjoyed? Dinner would cost half a teacher's monthly wage. He thought of his older brother, a high school teacher in the village, and imagined him sitting down to dinner with his parents, and he knew that no matter what his mother made, even if it was only scrambled eggs with green onions, it would be better than what he was about to order.

He looked at his watch as he walked through Zion Square, hoping he wouldn't be late. He wished he had ordered in advance, as he'd told his wife. He turned right on Jaffa Road and walked to Feingold Court. The owner of the restaurant smiled at him as he walked in. The lawyer handed him the note with the order and very politely mentioned that he was in somewhat of a rush. He looked at his watch again and saw that he would be on time. "Oh, and add two bottles of white wine, please," he told the owner, even though he knew he'd be paying double.

BOOKSTORE

"Don't worry," the lawyer told his wife, when she called again, a touch more anxiety in her voice. "I'll be home on time."

She gets so uptight before these meetings, he thought to himself. There was so much tension and unspoken competition between her and the other women in the group. Maybe she, like him, saw the monthly meetings as a kind of burden, the type of thing that was required of immigrants

like themselves. He imagined his wife getting dressed in
the bedroom. She had probably parked their daughter in
front of a movie, and their son, if he wasn't asleep, in the
playpen, and then spent the better part of an hour deciding
what to wear. Ordinarily she didn't spend much time on
her clothes, throwing on a simple shirt and a pair of slacks
before going to work. As far as he could tell she also didn't
wear makeup, and she definitely wasn't one of those women
who spent hours putting on their faces in the morning. But
when it came to the monthly meetings, she couldn't afford
to look rumpled or even ordinary. Perhaps she had gone out
and bought something for the occasion. "Look at Faten,"
he remembered her saying about Anton's wife. "I've never
seen her wear the same thing twice."

His wife frequently took offense at things said by the
other women in the group, especially on the matter of their
children. Faten, for instance, had once noted that her daughter knew both the Hebrew and Arabic alphabets, and that
she, along with other kids from the class, had been going
to something called First Grade Prep, an initiative that the
lawyer's wife had not been told about.

The lawyer smiled to himself as he remembered how his
wife had, for months afterward, begun spelling and penman-
ship lessons the second their daughter came home. "Anton's
kids are no smarter than yours," he remembered her telling
him when he tried to calm her down.

The lawyer looked at his watch and saw that it was only
seven thirty. He slung his briefcase over his shoulder, picked
up the brown paper bags with the sushi, and turned back

up Jaffa Road, toward King George Street and his favorite bookstore. The place, located behind the Mashbir department store and a few feet from his parking lot, closed at eight in the evening. He went there once a week, whenever he was able to leave the office in time.

He pushed open the glass door, stirring the metallic wind chime.

"Hello," the saleswoman said, looking up from her book and smiling at the lawyer.

"Hi, Meirav, how are you?"

She nodded, returning to her book, knowing that the lawyer would follow his usual browsing route and that he would find the still unshelved new arrivals.

He breathed in deeply, basking in the singular smell of used books. Oved, the café owner, a fervent supporter of independently owned businesses, had first recommended the new-and-used bookstore. The art critic, one of the regulars at the café, cited the owner's personal touch and his ability to get all sorts of rare books.

The lawyer first came to the store three years ago, in preparation for the monthly meeting. Anton, his accountant and college friend, had invited them all over to his house for dinner and a discussion of the best seller *Who Moved My Cheese?*

Placing his bag and his sushi next to the counter, the lawyer remembered how mortified he had been when he brought his selection to the old saleswoman. Standing at the register, he hated Anton for making him buy the book, hated the saleswoman for her sneer and for making him feel the way he did, and, predominantly, hated himself for the many things he wanted to know but did not.

That saleswoman was replaced by the helpful and polite Meirav, at least in the Thursday evening slot, his preferred time of arrival. Ever since the *Cheese* incident he had decided to bolster his literary education and, in order to ensure that he would not be embarrassed again, he made a point of reading the Wednesday book review in *Haaretz*, the highbrow Hebrew paper he subscribed to. Accordingly, he usually knew what book he would buy before he even walked into the store. This had started three years ago, and since then he had been buying, and reading, a book a week—a task complicated by the fact that he allowed himself only non-work-related texts before bed.

The lawyer knew he had no reason to browse upstairs, where the English and Jewish Studies books were housed. Mostly he bought fiction, modern fiction to be exact, for the simple reason that that was what was reviewed in the paper. The lawyer actually very much wanted to read the classics and he would have been happy to familiarize himself with the great works, those that were known in name even to nonreaders. He wanted to know what Dostoevsky had said, what *Anna Karenina* and *War and Peace* were about, and he wanted to read Kafka and Chekhov and even Chaim Nachman Bialik, but it was hard to do, almost impossible. How could he pull it off? If he brought those books to the register then Meirav, who had once told him "I wish all our customers were like you" when he purchased all three books in Italo Calvino's historical fantasy trilogy, would realize how mistaken she had been. He would never forget how good her remark had made him feel, even though he had bought the books only because a young author had said, in an interview that appeared in the book review, that they had

had a great influence on him. The feeling of elation in the store that day had surpassed anything he had felt at work, even after the acquittal of a client. He did not tell Meirav that he had not managed to get past the first thirty pages of the first much-praised book—and that those pages had nearly driven him to give up reading entirely.

Sometimes, when he could not overcome his curiosity, he would take one of the classics off the shelf and ask Meirav to gift wrap it. *Lolita, Crime and Punishment,* and *Anna Karenina* were all taken home in festive wrapping because, more than anything else, the lawyer wanted to read the great works, the ones that all his Jewish peers had read.

He looked at his watch and saw that the store would be closing in ten minutes. He already knew which book he was going to buy: he had seen it reviewed in that week's paper, had spotted it on the shelf, and knew that after a quick walk through the classics he would return to it. As he browsed, *The Kreutzer Sonata* caught his eye and he remembered that his wife had asked him once, as the resident expert on books, whether he'd ever read the novella by Tolstoy. The lawyer had been surprised by her sudden interest in books and she explained that *The Kreutzer Sonata* came up in class whenever her professor discussed Freud. He pulled the book off the shelf and walked over to the new-books section, where he picked up Haruki Murakami's most recent novel.

"I'd like this one gift wrapped, please," he said, handing Meirav the used copy of *The Kreutzer Sonata,* adding, "my wife's studying psychology and she's been nagging me forever to get her this book."

Meirav nodded. "All the Freudians are crazy about it. But it's a great book no matter how you read it. We just got it today," she said, pointing at a stack of book cartons in the corner. "I only had time to unpack one of the boxes but there are some gems in there."

"Great," the lawyer said, putting Murakami in a plastic bag, "in that case, I'll be back soon."

DINNER

Anton-the-accountant and his wife, Faten, the instructor at the teachers' college in Jerusalem, were the first to arrive.

The lawyer had met Anton in university, back when he was a nineteen-year-old freshman and Anton was in his final year of accounting and economics, but the two only became friends after the lawyer had branched out on his own and needed someone to handle the office finances. Anton had already made a name for himself in east Jerusalem, where he still had his office, on Salah al-Din Street, not far from the lawyer's old place.

Anton and his wife had first come over to the lawyer's house after his daughter was born but the two couples became closer when the lawyer's daughter and the accountant's son, their third child, started going to the same day care center, at age three. It was then that the accountant invited the lawyer and his wife to join the group's monthly meetings.

The lawyer found it difficult to describe his relationship with Anton as a friendship, even though he liked the accountant and was quite sure that the accountant liked him. Anton and his wife were the only Christians in the group and the only ones who lived in the northeast neighborhood of Beit Hanina, unlike the lawyer and everyone else, who lived in Beit Safafa, the southernmost enclave of east Jerusalem, just within walking distance of the locked gates of Bethlehem.

Tarik was next to arrive, at a few minutes to nine. Samir, the gynecologist, and his wife, Nili, the principal of a girls' school in the eastern half of the city, arrived along with Nabil, the civil lawyer, and his wife, Sonya, who had once been a nurse at Shaare Zedek Medical Center but had opted, quite a few years earlier, to devote herself to the rearing of their four children. Aside from Tarik, the lawyer was the youngest of the group. The oldest was the civil lawyer, whose daughter would be graduating from the Anglican International High School in Jerusalem later that year.

The lawyer's wife exchanged kisses with the other women, introduced Tarik to the guests, and then said, "Welcome, *tefaðlu*," her hands stretched toward the table. She was wearing gray pinstriped pants and a black tunic that came down to her hips. She looks great, the lawyer thought, imagining the struggle it must have taken to wiggle her bottom and hips into the girdle she wore.

"Where's the sushi from?" asked Nili, the gynecologist's wife.

"From Sakura," the lawyer's wife said, ready.

"Really?" the gynecologist's wife asked, dropping a slab of raw salmon from the clasp of her chopsticks, "that's weird, usually their sashimi is a lot fresher."

"Would you like a fork?" the lawyer's wife shot back.

The gynecologist, a senior faculty member at Hadassah Medical Center, intervened. "Did you hear the gunshots yesterday?" he asked.

"Oh, my God, yes, they were terrifying," his wife said. "Right opposite our house. And did you see how many policemen showed up? Must have been half the district."

Tarik exchanged a look with the lawyer and understood that although the lawyer was quite familiar with the details of the case, he would not be saying anything.

"Beit Safafa," Nabil said mournfully. "Two shootings in the last six months. That's never happened here before."

Beit Safafa is the neighborhood of choice for the immigrants from the north. It stands apart from the rest of east Jerusalem and is a short drive from the center of town. The Israelis consider the neighborhood to be friendly. A few isolated incidents notwithstanding, the residents barely participated in the first intifada and didn't stage a single protest march during the second one.

Most of the village only came under Israeli control in 1967, meaning that those born in the village, unlike the lawyer and his ilk, were given resident status rather than full citizenship. For them, political passivity has paid off; Beit Safafa is the best neighborhood in east Jerusalem. It's relatively uncrowded and up until recently it was thought to be virtually crime-free. Over the past several years, rent and real estate prices skyrocketed. Nabil, the civil lawyer, the point man for the local real estate trade, was the one who approached the criminal lawyer with a legal and newly available plot of land. The lawyer bought it and built his house. "In two years' time," Nabil had told the lawyer, "these properties are going to double in value." And he was right.

The immigrants from the north were largely responsible for the rise in prices. To the locals, the immigrants were rich, exploitable foreigners who could be made to pay the kind of prices they had previously been able to extract only from Jews. And the influx of people with money brought inflation to more than just the real estate market: meat, milk, and vegetables became more expensive and the neighborhood bakery had adopted two sets of prices — one for the locals and one for the foreigners. Price hikes aside, the locals liked the immigrants. They knew that the immigrants were far better than the rest of the riffraff that were apartment hunting around there — Palestinian collaborators who had been relocated to east Jerusalem by the Israeli security services. The collaborators had money but, as far as the locals were concerned, they were traitors. The Arab-Israeli immigrants, on the other hand, were well-educated and politically savvy and the locals respected the achievements of their brethren from the Galilee, hoping that their academic and economic success would trickle down to the rest of the village. The trouble was that the sudden rise in real estate values sparked feuds within clans and families, with cousins and brothers quarreling over every square inch of land.

"What was it all about?" the gynecologist asked, looking at the lawyer. "Or are you going to tell me they didn't come to you with their problems?" he added, chuckling.

The lawyer smiled and nodded his head in affirmation, but it was clear he had no interest in discussing what had happened. The lawyer's wife, sensing this, got up from her chair and announced that it was time for the next course.

The lawyer rose and began collecting the guests' sushi plates. He poured what remained of the white and red wines into the appropriate glasses and brought new bottles to the table. His wife served an arugula salad with a balsamic dressing, pumpkin ravioli, and entrecôte steaks in a cream and mushroom sauce, along with a potato pastry.

"So you're not telling?" the gynecologist tried again. "Come on, these are my neighbors, don't I deserve to know why my neighbors are shooting each other?"

The lawyer offered him another smile and tried to treat his demands as a joke. "No, not a word, Samir, especially because I see how badly you want to know."

The lawyer's response drew a few laughs. Nabil, the civil lawyer, felt an allegiance toward his colleague and said, "You're right, let him stew in his own curiosity. Don't say another word."

Samir, of course, was correct. Both sides had turned to the lawyer for representation. He, though, had to pick one party, and he picked the stronger one, not out of greed but because, on the contrary, he knew he would have a better chance of pushing the stronger side toward reconciliation. At the end of the day, it was his neighborhood, too, and if the two biggest clans became locked into a blood feud his life would be affected.

The situation had begun with a fight at the local high school. One student, a member of the stronger clan, the one the lawyer had decided to represent, supposedly used his cell phone to snap a picture of one of the girls in the class. When word of this treachery reached her male cousins, who went to the same school, they assaulted the alleged cameraman, and sent him home bleeding and bruised. The parents and brothers of the kid, who swore he had never taken any such picture, set out for revenge. They mobbed the house of the boys who had attacked their kin, pelted it with rocks, and demanded that the perpetrators come out and show their faces. The head of the household had drawn an unlicensed weapon and begun shooting in the air, summoning, with great alacrity, the police and border police, who do not tolerate armed feuds in the eastern part of the city. The security forces dispersed the mob and arrested five family members from each clan. The gun, however, was not found.

The lawyer chose to represent the stronger clan, hoping to reach a compromise out of court. If he could get them to agree, there was no doubt that the weaker one would consent, too. In the meantime, he spoke to the head of the household of the stronger clan and convinced him that the feud was not worth the arrest of the youths and the damage that could be done by dragging this matter through the Israeli courts. The patriarch agreed to try and settle the problem with the help of the village *mukhtars* and peacemakers. "But only on one condition," he said to the lawyer, "that the head of the other family comes and personally asks for my forgiveness." The lawyer nodded and immediately sent Samah's father, the Fatah official, to go and make peace between the two hawks.

"The steaks are delicious," Faten said, and her husband, Anton, agreed.

"Everything is excellent," Nabil said to the lawyer's wife. "You were blessed with hands of gold."

Only Samir and his wife were silent. "What's wrong, Samir," a chuckling Nabil asked the gynecologist. "The food isn't good enough for you?"

"I won't pay her any compliments until her husband tells me why there were people shooting guns right outside my house," he said, laughing, and everyone understood that the matter of the gunfire in the neighborhood had been brought to a close.

DISCUSSION

Tarik snorted cigarette smoke out of his nose and chuckled when he learned from the lawyer that they were about to join a salon discussion on a predetermined topic. "Are you kidding me?" he asked.

"Relax," the lawyer said, "there'll be exactly five minutes of discussion before the conversation goes off on a tangent."

"Well, what's the discussion supposed to be about?" Tarik asked.

"You think I know?" the lawyer said, and Tarik covered his mouth so that his laughter wouldn't carry from the office downstairs to the guests seated upstairs in the living room.

"What's going on," Samir's voice boomed, "you still smoking down there? We've got important matters to discuss up here."

The lawyer put his cigarette out in the ashtray and Tarik prepared to do the same but the lawyer signaled to him to take his time. Tarik took several long drags as the lawyer ripped open his gift-wrapped book. *"The Kreutzer Sonata?"* Tarik read, mispronouncing the name. "You know what, I'm really jealous that you can find time to read."

"I don't," the lawyer said, yearning to see his guests filing out of his house.

Faten, the accountant's wife who was also an assistant professor at the teachers' college, sat on a separate couch, poised to lead the discussion.

"I want to begin by wishing everyone a good evening," she said. "We're so happy you're all here and so glad to finally meet . . ." and the lawyer's wife stepped in, "Tarik."

"Yes, of course, Tarik, sorry," she said. "Our topic tonight is nationalist education and the absence of a Palestinian narrative within the Israeli ministry of education's curricula for the Arab citizens of Israel."

The lawyer recalled that this was what they had agreed to discuss while sitting at the last meeting, at the gynecologist and his wife's house. It also happened to be the topic of Faten's PhD thesis at Hebrew University, where she had been studying for quite some time now.

For many long minutes Faten relayed the findings of her research and compared the ministry's guidelines for Jewish and Arab elementary school children in the following subjects: homeland studies, geography, history, and civics. She spoke of methodology, of ideology, and of her work within the ministry, where, she explained, the collective history of the Arab citizens of this state was erased, the Palestinian narrative was trampled, and the Arab students were force-fed the Zionist version of events. The other people present had very little to add. They conveyed their agreement with silent nods. She carried on, speaking about the intentional blurring of identity and the cultural, social, and moral crisis within the Arab student body—a crisis rooted in the tireless attempts to strip the Arab citizens of Israel of their true sense of national belonging.

The lawyer noticed that all present, but particularly the males, were looking fatigued by the all-too-familiar lecture. He got up every now and again, apologized, and went to the freezer to replenish the ice supply, which was being used with the whiskey at this stage of the evening. Two bottles sat on the table, one Chivas and one Johnnie Walker Black—the whiskies of the rich Arab.

The lawyer glanced at his watch as casually as possible and saw that the discussion had been going on for longer than usual. Faten, armed with all sorts of facts and figures, had not yet run out of steam. Had the discussion adhered to what the group had initially intended—a cultural dialogue—it would have gone stone-cold long ago.

The lawyer knew, as did everyone present, that they all merely gave the impression of being educated. They had come a long way, each in their own field, but in their hearts they knew that they were lacking in comparison to their Jewish colleagues. There was no changing the fact that they were all members of the first generation of educated Arabs in Israel. Their parents, like most of the Palestinian population that remained in the land after the War of Independence, were soil tillers, *fellahin*, who, if they were lucky, and their village had had a school, had perhaps attained a high school education. The parents of all those

present, although uneducated, understood the importance
of education and did all they could to ensure that their
children went to university and succeeded. The dream
of every Arab mother in Israel is for her son to become a
lawyer or a doctor. The Arab students that are accepted
to those faculties are as revered in their communities as
the flight school cadets among Jewish Israelis. But academic achievements were one thing and a firm knowledge
of the essentials of Western culture quite another. When in
school, the lawyer had frequently cringed at his own lack
of familiarity with contemporary music, literature, theater,
and film. Like all now present, he, too, consoled himself
with the thought that the Jewish students were certainly
ignorant of Arab culture, its singers, movies, and plays, but
he had to admit that most of that culture was frankly not
worthy of being called art. There were several impressive
classical musicians, but in so far as theater and film were
concerned, most of which came from Egypt, the lawyer
knew there was nothing to be proud of.

The lawyer was certain that the other members of the
group had also been made aware of their shortcomings and
that they realized that they, too, had to close the gap. If they
were unable, then they had to ensure that their children were
given the tools to do so. After all, the decision to found a mixed
school, to send their children off to study with Jews, the lawyer thought, was not borne of shared ideals or a dedication to
coexistence, as the brochures claimed and the philanthropists
believed; the Arab parents simply wanted their children to
soak up Western culture, for their children to learn from the
Jews that which they themselves could not provide. All of a

sudden the lawyer started to feel that they were sending their
children like spies into the heart of a foreign culture. It will be
interesting to see what type of insights they come back with,
he thought, whether they return as double agents.

He shook himself free of his thoughts and tried to follow the twists and turns of the discussion, which had veered
into the nature of the curriculum at the school that many of
their kids attended. "We have to look really closely at the
kind of values that are being instilled there," Nili, the gynecologist's wife, said. "All week long my son's been singing
'On Rosh Hashanah, On Rosh Hashanah.'"

"What's wrong with that?" the gynecologist asked,
turning to his wife. "It's a good song." Everyone laughed,
and then Anton, who was on the school's steering committee, said, "We're working on that, though," adding that the
school administration had been told in no uncertain terms to
beef up the Palestinian nationalist dimension of the studies,
which, he conceded, was lacking in comparison to that of
the Zionist Israeli narrative.

"It's true," Nili said. "I see that the kids are constantly
singing about the Land of Israel and Hanukkah and Passover, but other than that one poem by Mahmoud Darwish
they haven't learned a thing that qualifies as Palestinian.
There has to be equality. It can't go on like this. We have
to do something."

"Why is that?" Tarik asked, drawing all the eyes in the
room. "I'm sorry. I don't really know anything about this
and I don't have kids yet, but why exactly do they need to
strengthen their Palestinian nationalism?"

Tarik's question was met with silence and an edgy
bewilderment.

"What do you mean, *why*?" Samir asked. "Because they're Palestinians. A child needs to grow up with a sense of national and cultural awareness. Look at the Jewish kids, from age six they know all about the wars and have a good sense of where they want to serve in the army when the time comes."

"Yes, I know," Tarik said, somewhat bashfully, feeling as though he had butted into a conversation that did not include him. "But when you see that kind of an Israeli kid, how does it make you feel?"

"Bad," Samir spat, earning nods all around. "Because they don't teach them about *us*. They purposely pave over the Palestinian side of the story. They learn the Israeli narrative, as viewed through the lens of the Zionist industry."

"Yes, I understand that. But why respect either side of the story?" Tarik inquired, plodding on even though his face showed that he already regretted it.

"What do you mean, that's the history of our people you're talking about. Our roots, our culture. Children have to understand and internalize these things, otherwise how will they plot their own futures?"

"That's true," Tarik said, preferring to avoid an argument. "You're right."

The lawyer knew where Tarik had been headed. He had worked with him for long enough and he regretted that Tarik felt too shy to continue to make his case.

"You know what," the lawyer said, quoting a line he'd heard from Tarik, "I also don't buy catchphrases like, *He who has no past, has no future.*"

"How can we raise a proud generation," the gynecologist's wife asked, "if we don't teach them to be proud of their forefathers, their history, their people? I don't get it."

"I don't know," the lawyer said. "It just seems to me sometimes that we—not just us Arabs, but all of us—don't have that much to be proud of in terms of our pasts."

"That's nonsense," the gynecologist said, gathering a fistful of cashews. "Honestly, I'm surprised at you. What's a man worth without his roots? It's just like a tree, how can it grow without strong roots? It's the same with kids, with nations."

"Well, that's the thing," the lawyer said, smiling as he distributed more ice and whiskey. "Sometimes I think a tree is a tree and a man is a man."

BED

"Tarik can forget about Faten finding him a match," the lawyer's wife whispered, mindful of the baby in the nearby crib. She was sitting on the edge of the bed, rubbing cream into her hands while the lawyer took off his clothes, stripping down to his boxer shorts. "What was that about?" she asked her husband, "I thought Tarik was a nationalist."

"He's all right," the lawyer said. "They just didn't get what he was saying."

"What do you mean?"

"He's a bit of an anarchist," the lawyer said, knowing his wife wouldn't understand him. "He doesn't buy into the system. He's not willing to play the nationalist game."

"Maybe, but I don't think they liked him."

"It's probably better that way," the lawyer said, heading into the bathroom to brush his teeth. He had known all along that the assistant professor at the teachers' college would not be the one to find Tarik a bride. He knew Tarik well, and he knew that he was in a tight spot as an Arab-Israeli bachelor in Jerusalem, where there were few matches to be found for those no longer in school, and Tarik had been out of school for five years. Nor was he in the habit of frequenting the humanities department cafeteria, as the lawyer's wife had advised. Which all explained why, when the lawyer saw that three of the best candidates for the internship in his office were female, he had immediately hoped they were pretty and decided that he'd hire the one who seemed most suitable for Tarik.

"Are you coming to bed?" his wife asked as he left the bathroom. The lawyer was expecting the question, even though he was hoping, on account of his exhaustion and the book that awaited him downstairs, that he would be given an exemption. But it had been two weeks since they'd been together, and the wine she'd drunk during dinner was surely having its effect.

The lawyer shut the bedroom door, fearing that their daughter would wake up and stumble in, and then slid under the covers beside his wife. He knew that she was embarrassed about her body and that even on the hottest summer nights she preferred to conceal it beneath the blankets. They kissed quickly and without passion, and the lawyer set himself to the task at hand.

It would be wrong to say that the lawyer did not enjoy sex, but there was something about it that always bothered him. He found the whole thing to be more of a burden than a pleasure, a situation he knew to be perverse.

He recalled the early days after their marriage, during their honeymoon. He had been twenty-five but it was the first time he had come into physical contact with a woman. He remembered the feeling of shame at the speed with which it had all happened. He knew that something was wrong, and that his wife had not been fully satisfied. She never mentioned it, never said a word about it, but he knew that this was not how it was supposed to be. He remembered his apprehension at the time, the articles he had combed through, the sex-advice columns. After thoroughly researching the matter of premature ejaculation, he had tried to put the techniques to use, relaxing his muscles, pulling his testicles back, dulling his senses with alcohol, even smoking marijuana before coming to bed, but none of it helped. In some articles it said that sexual partners had to learn one another, give their bodies time to get acquainted, to achieve a natural harmony, but the lawyer blamed himself. After a few months of failed attempts, he tried to increase his endurance by summoning sad images from his youth. This worked, and he could tell by his wife's moaning that some progress had been made. It didn't happen all at once but he felt, at last, that he was moving in the right direction.

The first time he was sure that his wife had been fully satisfied was after he had screened the footage of his grandfather's funeral in his mind. The lawyer was eight years old when he saw his grandfather's dead body. Years later, he lay on top of his wife, thrusting gently, eyes wide open, trying not to be distracted by the sounds of her pleasure. He recalled how the entire family had shown up at his parents' house and how the body had arrived on the back of an orange pickup truck. He recalled how he had stood off to the side while the adults washed his grandfather's corpse, which lay prone on an elevated wooden plank. He thought about the prayers the sheikh had intoned and the way the men had shaved the pallid body. And he remembered his grandfather's wrinkled, flaccid penis and the white sheets with which the men wrapped him as they called out "Allahu Akbar." He saw himself running in order to keep up with the brisk pace of the funeral procession, saw them raise the coffin up in the air, saw the opening on one side and the way it was tilted down till his grandfather's white-robed body slid into the grave. He recalled the sound the body had made upon impact, and realized that he had just given his wife her first orgasm. She clawed his back and planted warm kisses on his face while he remained above the grave, aware that he would never again be the boy he had been.

LETTER

In his office, the lawyer found a pack of cigarettes. He lit one just as the baby began to wail. His wife's measured steps moved toward the crib. The crying subsided. He took a few long drags, then ground the cigarette out in the ashtray and, after a moment's hesitation, poured water over the blackened stub. Satisfied that no gust of wind would come through the open window and breathe life into the dead ashes, he took a long gulp of water, picked up *The Kreutzer Sonata,* and left the room.

The lawyer didn't like getting out of bed once he was settled for the night, which was why he went to the bathroom

even though he didn't have to, and tried, without success,
to urinate. Then he went to his daughter's room, stacked
two pillows up against the headboard, turned on the pink
bunny lamp, and lay down in her bed, cradling the book.

Although it was a used copy and had likely been passed
from hand to hand, the book was in good condition, practically new. This, the lawyer felt, spoke to the character of its
previous owners. Clearly they valued it, protected it. The
lawyer also knew how to care for a book. He never dog-
eared a page, never wrote in the margins, never broke the
spine. He looked at the rather ugly cover. Two thick black
lines dissected it into three unequal parts. The uppermost
part was yellow and bore the author's name, Tolstoy. The
lower, green section was home to the title, *The Kreutzer Sonata,* and the middle one featured an ugly pastel illustration.
On the right side of the drawing there was a man with fiery
eyes, a hooked nose, and a set mouth. His hand was balled
around the handle of a dagger. On the other side of the
drawing was a faceless woman whose body was curled and
indistinct, her hand feebly raised before the murderer. Had
he not known who the author was, the lawyer thought to
himself, he would never have bought this book.

He flipped to the front page, where the author's full
name was written, Leo Nikolayevich Tolstoy. He went over
the name several times, embarrassed that he hadn't known
it, imagining himself as a contestant on a game show, "What
are the first and middle names of the famous Russian author
Tolstoy?"

On the contents page, he was pleasantly surprised to
find that the book consisted of four stories and not just one,
as the cover seemed to imply. Other than the first story,

"The Kreutzer Sonata," there was also "The Devil," "The Forged Coupon," and "After the Ball." The lawyer had an aversion to long books, both because he didn't have time and because he liked to check off the boxes on the long list of books he felt he should read.

In the upper left corner of the page he saw the name *Yonatan*, delicately printed in blue ink. The previous owner's handwriting gave the lawyer pause. Many used books had someone's name printed on the inside flap but for some reason this name, or rather this man's handwriting, soft and feminine, begging for help, almost like the cowering woman on the cover, caught his attention. Never mind, he said to himself, start reading. He knew he didn't have much time. The guests had kept him up late and the wine was taking its toll.

The lawyer read the quote on the first page of the book. "But I say unto you, That whosoever looketh on a woman to lust after her hath committed adultery with her already in his heart." (Matthew 5:28) He chuckled to himself. If that was the case, he was the undisputed king of adulterers, even though he hadn't had sex with anyone besides the woman whose bed he had just left. The quote took him elsewhere. He hadn't even started to read the book and already he found himself transported. He was back in the café on King George Street, reviewing all the women he had seen—young, old, secular, religious, Ashkenazi, Sephardic, Arab, and Jewish. He recalled how he had looked the women up and down, the ones coming toward him, the ones beside him, and the ones in front of him, how he had sized up their behinds, evaluated them in pants and in skirts, how he had examined their thighs, imagined their precise shape, and how he had known that no one was onto him, that he was not the kind of person who got caught ogling—he was quick about it, and yet none of the details evaded him. In a few split seconds he could attain all of the pertinent information. His eyes were trained to spot cleavage, panty lines, bra straps. He registered the way they walked, the way they moved their bottoms, the size and sway of their breasts. The lawyer had no intention of acting on this information. More than anything else, he was trying to figure out his own taste. He knew that his wife, widely considered to be a good-looking woman, did not attract him the way he would have liked, and this he attributed to the shape of her body, her stout thighs, and the stretch marks along her abdomen, which had appeared once their son was born. At times the lawyer felt he was attracted to all women aside from the one he was married to. And at times, while walking behind a woman on King George Street, watching her and lusting for her, he realized that her body was remarkably similar to his wife's.

The lawyer shook his head free of these thoughts. He tried to go back to the book, but knew that his eyes would not stay open for more than a few minutes. No sense in starting, he decided. He was too tired. It would be better to begin reading the next day. Before turning off the light, he checked to see how long the title story was. He flipped through the pages, taking pleasure in the gentle breeze and the familiar scent they produced. He reached page 102, where the story ended, and just as he was about to shut the book a small white note fell from the pages. The lawyer started to smile as he read the note, written in his wife's hand, in Arabic. *I waited for you, but you didn't come. I hope everything's all right. I wanted to thank you for last night. It was wonderful. Call me tomorrow?*

KNIFE

The lawyer leaped out of his daughter's bed to kill his wife. He'd stab the bitch, cut her throat, gouge out her eyes, butcher her body. Or maybe he'd strangle her. He'd sit on her stomach, straddle her, pin her to the bed, and wrap his fingers around her throat, thumbs pushing deep into the flesh. He saw her writhing, gasping, her eyes popping out of her head, and saw himself staring at her, meeting her pleading and fear with furious derision. He'd throttle her while she tried to resist him, her fingers scratching at his arms as he clamped down on her windpipe, squeezing even harder, puncturing the skin of her neck, soaking his fingers with her blood, keeping up the pressure long after her body had gone slack.

He bounded up the stairs. A fog moved through his mind. He saw an image of his wife, stark naked, laughing uproariously beside a strange, faceless man — a lowlife, the lawyer was sure, a petty criminal, perhaps the man on the cover of the book, the one with the dagger. In his mind's eye, he saw her as he had never seen her before, moaning, kneading her own suddenly shapely thighs, clinging to the stranger, who lay on top of her, his face filled with scorn and malicious mirth, maybe it was someone he knew after all. His wife's eyes shone with a passion he had never seen, scratching the man's back with nails she didn't have and whispering words of love as she arched up toward him.

The lawyer felt like he was choking. Pain ripped through his head. His heart thumped. His breath was short. Quick. He could not draw enough air. He'd kill her. He'd wake her up without saying a word and he'd kill her, or maybe he'd wake her up, tell her that he knew everything, and then kill her. He turned toward the kitchen, opened a drawer, and looked for the right knife. He grabbed the biggest one, wrapped his right hand around the handle, and headed for the bedroom.

His wife lay on her stomach, a thin summer blanket covering one leg, the other stretched diagonally across the length of the bed, completely bare. She looked at ease, her breathing rhythmic and calm. She was wearing green panties and a simple white tank top. Her face was turned to the right, covered by her hair, which fell across her ear and cheek. This was not the woman he wanted to murder. This was a different woman, one who had a one-year-old baby by her side.

The lawyer's muscles relaxed. The hand that wielded the knife fell to his side, his head slumped forward, and he began to sob softly at the foot of the bed, realizing that his wife would not have dared were she not so certain of his cowardice.

He moved the pillow that his wife had placed alongside the baby. He'd told her a thousand times to stop doing that. The pillow would not stop the baby from falling out of bed if he rolled over in his sleep. On ordinary nights, when the lawyer woke up in a terror and raced to see that his children were safe, he would pick the baby up and carry him over to his crib, but on this night he was scared of rousing him. He placed another pillow on the floor, where he imagined his son's head might strike if he fell out of bed. Then he tucked his son back in. *His* son? A flash of pain surged through his chest.

What would he do now? Wake her quietly so that the baby would stay asleep and tell her to come downstairs, where he'd confront her with the note? Shove it in her face and demand an explanation? What would he do if she said the handwriting wasn't hers? And maybe she'd be right, maybe it really wasn't. The lawyer tried to cling to his former life. Of course it was her hand that had written the note. He knew it was. And anyway, what was he expecting, that his wife, who up until a few minutes ago had seemed faithful, almost foolishly so, would just burst into tears and come clean? After all, he reminded himself, he had no idea who she really was. They'd been living together for years and only now did he realize that he did not know her. What if she did admit her guilt? Would she cry, accept responsibility, beg for her life? Promise that she'd melt away without so much as a single demand? The whore.

And what would he do? The coward. The despicable coward. If only he could do the deed. But what about the kids? He couldn't live with the notion that his kids would see their mother's lifeless body sprawled before them. He'd get them out of the house. He'd kill her when they were away. Then he'd call the police. And what about him? What would he do? Sit in jail? Commit suicide? He should have killed her right away. He should have done it before he started thinking. But how would he do it? And what about the kids? They'd grow up with no mother and a father behind bars, living with his parents, maybe hers? Oh, God, what had she done?

No matter what, he'd be the laughingstock of his peers and his village. Even if he killed her. He winced at the thought of being ridiculed behind his back. He imagined his friends, including the ones who had been over for dinner, smirking at him, the fancy lawyer laid low. He saw the man to whom his wife had written the note, imagined him sitting with his buddies and regaling them with the tales. Oh, God, what had she done? The bitch. She'd trampled him. Made him a character in one of those stories he was constantly hearing from his clients, about naive husbands who let their wives run rampant. Again he saw clusters of men convulsing with laughter. The lowlife that his wife had taken to bed was sitting with his buddies and telling, precisely, what she had been like, detailing all the things she had done to him, things that far exceeded what the lawyer had thought his wife was capable. It was clear that the fornicator did not hold his newest conquest in high esteem. Or did he? Maybe they were in love? Maybe they planned to live together? How old was the guy anyway? Did he know him? And how long had this been going on?

The lawyer left the bedroom. Once a coward, always a coward he thought. He put the knife back in the kitchen drawer and went to his daughter. She'd tossed off her blanket but he didn't cover her. It wasn't cold. It was hot. Stifling. Sweat beaded up over his body.

He went downstairs, looked for the note in the bed, and didn't find it. He searched furiously through the folds in the blanket. For a second he entertained the notion that he had been mistaken, that he had imagined the whole thing, that fatigue had authored the note. He flipped through the book again, thinking that perhaps he had tucked it back where he had found it, but it wasn't there.

Then he saw it beside the bed. He picked it up, wedged it deep inside the pages of the book, and took the evidence to his study. He eased the door closed behind him, lit a cigarette, and tried to organize his thoughts. He took a long drag, then exhaled slowly. He might be a coward, but a chump was something he had never been. And he definitely did not plan on being her chump. Who the hell did she think she was? He didn't even know her. That had to be the basis of his plan, that he did not know her. In the end he would kill her, that much was clear. Maybe not with his own hands, because he had no intention of paying the price for her crimes, but he would bring about her death, of that there was no doubt. At the end of the day, the husband was not responsible for the wife's honor. Her family members — father, brothers, cousins — were the keepers of the family's honor; it was their blood, and it was on them alone that the dishonor would rest if they did not take it upon themselves to obliterate it. Not on him, not by any means.

He shivered, put out the cigarette, and opened the book. There was something he wanted to check. Up on the top left-hand side of the contents page he found it again, written in a thin delicate hand, in blue ink, the name: *Yonatan*.

PART
TWO

ELECTRIC RADIATOR

Yonatan is dead. I buried him last Thursday. I paid two Arab teenagers to carry the coffin. Aside from me, no one else came to the funeral. No one was invited. He was a twenty-eight-year-old man, just like me.

"He could die at any moment"—that's what I was told when I first laid eyes on him. That was six years ago. I had just graduated from Hebrew University with a degree in social work and gotten a job at the east Jerusalem bureau for outpatient substance abuse treatment run by the Ministry of Social Affairs. I knew the place well; it was where I'd done my internship during my final year of school.

I was twenty-two years old and had spent the last three years living in the student dorms. After graduation, I managed to stay on for three more months, but in late October, when the new students started to arrive, I was forced to find someplace else to live. I took a number off a notice that had been posted outside the dorms — SEEKING THIRD ROOMMATE, it said in Arabic — and called from a public phone.

That evening I turned my keys in to the dorm monitor and made my way to the Nusseibah housing projects, in Beit Hanina row 3, building 1, apartment 2.

"You're right on time," Wassim said. "I have to go to work. I got a friend to cover me until six. I'm leaving you a key, but make your own copy, okay? My shift's over at nine and I'll be home by nine thirty, so if you have to go out or anything leave me the key in the electrical cabinet downstairs."

"I'm not going anywhere."

"Okay," he said. "Welcome."

The sun was setting and it was freezing in the apartment. I'd come with all my belongings. They were stuffed into three bags: one backpack, which had been used for school and then for work, and two identical gym bags with the emblem of the German national soccer team. They were the bags my mother had bought for me when I first left home.

In the bedroom, a neon light flickered continuously without ever coming to life. There was a damp, moldy smell, but I didn't dare open the window. I buttoned my coat all the way up and tucked my head into the collar. It seemed like it was colder inside than out, and winter was just beginning.

The metal-framed bed groaned when I put my bags on it. Wassim had made sure there was a mattress for me, just as he'd promised over the phone, but it was smaller than the frame of the bed and it was very thin, the kind Arabs use for divans. I switched on the hot water heater outside the shower. The toilet looked as though someone had tried to clean it but it was still dirty and the water at the bottom of the bowl was black. I made a note to myself: get sodium chloride. From our phone conversation I had learned that Wassim lived in the apartment with his cousin Majdi, that they were both from Jat, that Wassim was a special-ed teacher, and that Majdi was in the middle of his internship at a law office. What kind of special-ed classes was Wassim teaching at this hour, I wondered.

There was a small heater in the living room, the kind with a screen and two electric coils. As soon as I plugged it in the lights in the apartment dimmed. The heater made a sizzling sound. I brought the heater with me and sat down on the wicker couch. The coils burned a pale yellow and I had to practically sit on top of it to feel any heat. I put my hands in front of the metal screen, which was blackened with dust and charred pita. The coffeepot on the table was flanked by two dirty glasses and the contents were cold. In the dorms at least there were radiators.

I did not call my mother. I'll talk to her tomorrow, I thought. That was the longest the conversation could be put off. And anyway there was no phone in the house, and for all I knew no pay phones at all in Beit Hanina. Tomorrow, I told myself, I'll call her from work.

Once I'd warmed up a bit, I went into my room and started to unpack my clothes. I didn't have much, and most of what I had was dirty. It had been more than three weeks since I'd last been home and if I didn't go back over the coming weekend, I'd have to find a laundry. There had to be one somewhere in the neighborhood.

I put the clothes in the closet without sorting them and went back to the electric heater. Once I'd warmed up, I returned to the room and unpacked my kitchenware: one plate, one cup, a tablespoon, a teaspoon, a fork, a knife, and a frying pan. I set it all out on the plastic table in the bedroom. Then I took out my sheets and the heavy comforter that my mother had insisted on buying for me. I hoped it would get me through the first night in the apartment. The next day, I decided, I'd buy an electric radiator. Call Mom, then buy radiator.

An hour after I'd turned on the boiler, I went to check for hot water. I tried the faucet with the red sticker, gave it some time, and then tried the other one. Nothing. I figured the water heater must need a little more time. In the meanwhile I took off my shoes, left my jacket on, and crawled under the covers. I shivered for a while but then felt the heat begin to spread through my body and my eyes begin to close.

I was startled awake by the sound of a door slamming and it took me a few seconds to remember that I was in the new apartment. I sat up in bed. A head and shoulders poked through the doorway.

"Hi, did I wake you? I saw the light was on and . . ."

"No, no, I was just taking a little rest."

"Nice to meet you," he said, still standing in the doorway. "I'm Majdi."

I got out of bed and walked over to him, feeling the cold rise up from the floor, seeping through my socks and into my feet. I introduced myself and shook my roommate's hand.

"Wow," Majdi said, "I can't believe we let you freeze in here like this. He didn't tell you we have a heater?"

"Sure, I turned it on in the living room."

"Not that one," Majdi said, turning around and motioning me to follow. He walked through the kitchen and out to a little box of a balcony. "We've got an amazing kerosene heater. I can't believe Wassim didn't tell you."

"He was in a rush to get to his shift," I said, "and I got here late."

"How did you survive in this cold? The house is freezing! We keep the heater on the balcony because it emits toxic fumes when you shut it off." Majdi pulled a lighter from his coat pocket, leaned over the heater, unscrewed a little domelike lid, removed it, and then threaded his hand in from the bottom and lit the wick. "We'll let it burn for a little while out here. It's only really dangerous when you light it and extinguish it, that's why we always do it on the balcony. This window stays open, too. Anyway, how are you doing?"

I nodded and Majdi pulled out a pack of cigarettes from his coat and offered me one.

"I don't smoke, but it doesn't bother me," I said. He lit one for himself and looked over toward the bathroom. "What, he fixed the boiler?" The red light was still on.

"I don't know," I said. "I turned it on at around six and an hour later there was still no hot water."

"Motherffff . . ." Majdi started to say, walking into the bathroom. He turned the faucet on, let the water run, and then put his hand in to check the temperature. "That bastard," he said, striding toward the door. I heard him knocking somewhere upstairs, and then the sound of his angry voice and the soothing tone of an elderly man.

Majdi came back to the apartment, still pissed off and still smoking the cigarette. "That son of a bitch said he was going to fix it today. For the last week we've been heating water the way they used to twenty years ago, on the stovetop." He walked through the kitchen to the living room and returned with the kerosene heater. "I can't believe you sat here without this thing. You must have been freezing."

"No, I was fine."

"By the way, the guy I just spoke to is the landlord. Have you met him?"

"No."

"The asshole lives on the top floor. He owns a few apartments in the building. He tried to tell me he didn't know it hadn't been fixed and that first thing tomorrow he was going to have a talk with his handyman. In the meantime, do you still have your hundred dollars for the rent?"

"Yeah, of course," I said, reaching for my wallet.

"Good. Keep it. Don't give him a cent. I told him that if tomorrow morning the boiler isn't working, we're going out to buy a new one with the next month's rent. If he asks you for it, don't pay him, okay?"

"Okay, sure."

Majdi put out the cigarette and went into the kitchen. I heard the refrigerator door open. "Don't tell me you didn't eat anything either," he yelled from the kitchen.

"No, I wasn't hungry."

"What, are you crazy? It's after nine at night. You were just being polite. *Ayouni,*" he said. "Make yourself at home, what kind of place do you think this is? I'm making dinner right now. Wassim will be back any minute, and then we're sitting down to eat."

THE COMMUTE

We used to leave the house together at seven fifteen. Those early-morning hours were pretty much the only times I saw my roommates. Majdi interned at the law office until the afternoon and from there he went to the Sheraton, where he worked as a cashier until nine or ten in the evening. Wassim taught in the morning, came home, and then headed out again at four thirty for his other job, as director of a hostel for the mentally ill in Shuafat. Sometimes I got home from the clinic in time to see him, but usually he had left the apartment before I got back.

I was the first one up in the morning, but Wassim was first to get out of bed. He'd boil water for coffee before even going to the bathroom. Then I'd get up and use the bathroom. Only when the coffee was ready did Wassim go back and wake Majdi. They were the same age but it seemed that Wassim was the responsible adult, a kind of older brother to his cousin Majdi, who, unlike him, had managed to get into law school.

Majdi was the last one into the bathroom and the last one dressed, but he was never late. Probably thanks to Wassim's badgering. "Come on, are you up?" he'd say. "Let's go, the coffee's getting cold." Or, "Come on, no time for a whole cigarette, we're late, smoke on the way to the bus, *yallah*, let's go."

I liked those guys better than my old dorm roommates, and was glad to be rooming with them. Each morning we'd walk up the path through the projects and out onto the main road that linked Jerusalem and Ramallah, looking for a ride heading south. Our apartment was on the right side of the checkpoint that was within municipal Jerusalem.

Wassím and I liked the Ford Transit share-taxis. They were faster than the buses. But if they pulled over and only had a spot or two then we waited for whatever came next, van or bus. Majdi preferred the buses, liked their color and their ambience. They were old clunkers that the Israeli bus company had retired. The Palestinians bought them, painted a coat of blue over the red, and turned them into the main source of public transportation in the eastern part of the city. I thought they were awful. Loud and slow, unheated in winter and uncooled in summer. There were hardly any seats that weren't broken, wobbly, or with springs jutting out. But Majdi loved them. As soon as he got on and paid the driver, he lit a cigarette. "It's an experience," he'd say. "Not only can you smoke, but the driver's usually too busy lighting up his own cigarette to take your fare."

Nearly all the men smoked on the bus. It was a sort of ceremony. The windows were always open, winter and summer, and hands would dangle out, cigarettes clasped between their fingers. "Palestinians," Majdi used to say, "smoke more than any other people in the world."

It's not far from Beit Hanina to downtown east Jerusalem but the traffic in the morning was some of the most brutal in the country. The cars inched forward. A five-minute drive took half an hour, and that was on regular days, when there were no surprise checkpoints.

Majdi used to say that the green signal at the traffic light for the Arab cars from Beit Hanina and Shuafat was the shortest in the city. The settlers' cars got five minutes of green for every half minute they gave us. One hundred thousand people waiting in line for a few settlers from Ma'ale Adumim, Neve Yaakov, and Pisgat Ze'ev. Each morning Majdi used to swear that the first thing he was going to do when he passed the bar was file an appeal against that fucking traffic light in the High Court of Justice. "It's a sure win," he'd say. "They'll cover it everywhere in the Arab press. All I need is a good suit for the cameras and I'll be the number-one lawyer in east Jerusalem. You'll see. *If you will it, it is no dream.*"

Majdi was first off the bus, at the Sheikh Jarrah stop. From there he took an Israeli bus to the center of town. I got off right after him, at the district court on Salah al-Din Street, and walked from there to the welfare office in Wadi Joz. Wassim took the bus all the way to the last stop, Damascus Gate, and from there he took a share-taxi to the school in Jabel Mukaber.

METHADONE

I was conscientious about getting to work on time. I always punched in before eight, even though the only other person in the office at that hour was the janitor. In general, there was not much to do at the office. I'd been far busier and far more stimulated as an intern. There were hundreds of addicts who had opened files in our office but only a handful of them were "active" cases, users who actually wanted to kick their habits. The rest just showed up to collect their income support, which they were eligible for only if they could prove that they were in treatment. And we did not make it difficult for them. We filed our reports to the Ministry of Social Affairs, renewing the welfare payments and the income support even if they didn't come to a single meeting. It was the path of least resistance.

One year earlier, as a student intern, I'd come to the office twice a week. In order to get my BSW from Hebrew University I'd had to handle a minimum of four cases a year and the office manager, who was my supervisor, made sure that I met the requirement. Now I was a full-time employee, and four cases a year was too much to hope for. Full days passed with nothing to do. I had one active case, a forty-year-old addict who had seemed to want treatment but even he was starting to show the usual signs. It turned out that he was only going through the motions because his parole officer had insisted on seeing results.

The addicts mostly followed the same route: they came in, filled out a few questionnaires, talked to a social worker, took a urine test, and opened a file. They'd come back once a week and the few who actually seemed interested in rehab would be invited to a special advisory meeting attended by a social worker from the office, a municipal psychologist, and a district supervisor.

The addict would be sent to a methadone clinic and told to wait for an opening at the rehab center in Lifta, where there was only one bed allocated for the Arab residents of the city. When it became available, he'd be sent there for a two-month stay, with the main objectives being detox and the twelve-step program. They always came out of there happy and drug-free, swearing that they were new men, kissing the social workers and treating them like the parents they never had. Over the following weeks they would continue to come to the NA meetings, which were held downtown, and then, within a few months, they'd be using again. The sole success story, one that had achieved mythic status, was of a father of five, a fifty-year-old man who managed to stay clean for nearly a year. Aside from him, the east Jerusalem office had not managed to keep a single addict clean for any significant period of time in its fifteen-year history.

My colleagues came to work at ten, except on the rare Thursday when the special advisory meeting took place. On those days they came in at eight. Sometimes they'd even get there before me. Walid, the department head, was usually the second one in. He was also the first to leave, always before four, the official closing time. "I have to make a house call," he would announce, "and then I'll just head home from there." The right-hand column of his time card was lined with his handwriting, *house call*.

Walid was joined by Khalil, who had taken on a sum total of zero cases since I'd arrived. Other than his job with social services, he held two other part-time positions, shuttling between them in his squeaky clean, bright red Peugeot 205, a CD of his beloved Gypsy Kings spinning from the rearview mirror. He and Walid were the only ones with a car. Shadi, who was one year older than me, used to come to work in jeans and designer T-shirts. He wore a gold chain around his neck with the first letter of his girlfriend's name hanging off the end. He was always talking about a club—the Underground—and about how he had befriended the security guard, who let him in every Thursday. Sometimes he'd shut the office door and show us some of his new moves.

Like everyone else at the office, Shadi hated being a social worker. He used to say that he aspired to other things, that he'd studied social work by mistake, and that the college entrance exam, "the psychometric," was engineered to screw Arabs. He had just enrolled in an accounting program at a private college, and showed up for work with his new textbooks, and that was pretty much all he ever did at the office.

Not that that was a problem. With the caseload being as it was, all employees were free to pursue other endeavors. They would show up at the office, sit down at their desks, and swivel the chairs toward the center of the room, sipping coffee and gossiping, mostly about girls they had known in college. I hadn't heard of any of the girls they talked about, all notorious, all Arab, all sluts who had slept with half the guys on campus.

Hebrew University remained central to my colleagues' lives. It was the reason they had left their villages and come to Jerusalem, and it was the reason that they had stayed. Aside from me, they were all somehow tied to the university. Walid was a teacher's assistant at the School for Social Work, and was looking for a PhD thesis advisor. Khalil, whose grades were too poor to continue on in social work, had just begun a master's in criminology, which made no difference at all to him, because "an MA in criminology gets you the exact same three-hundred-shekel raise." Shadi, not wanting to waste money on rent, had settled on the floor of his cousin's dorm room, splitting the rent three ways with him and his roommate.

At eleven, they'd each hand me ten shekels and send me to get them hummus from Abu-Ali on Salah al-Din Street, a five-minute walk from the office. I was more than happy to run the errand, pleased to get out of that wretched office, and I made the journey to Abu-Ali a little like a tourist, taking in the stone houses, the shops, the trees on the side of the road as though seeing them for the first time.

Soon enough, I didn't have to say a word to Abu-Ali. Once we'd exchanged pleasantries, he'd make the usual — three orders of hummus with fava beans, one with chickpeas and spicy sauce; one plate of sliced tomato, cucumber, onion, green pepper, and pickles; one plate of falafel balls; and four glass bottles of Coke. He'd arrange it all on a brass tray and I'd carry it back to the office. When we were done eating, they'd all make fun of me for having to bring it back. What

they didn't know was that Abu-Ali always offered to send
one of his boys to deliver the food and pick it up, but that
I refused, cherishing my few minutes away from the office
every day. That was why I also volunteered to go out again
at two thirty to get schnitzel sandwiches in a pita from Abu-
Ilaz's stand near the Orient House. I ate mine alone, taking
little bites as I walked, ever so slowly, back to the office.

ROTARY TELEPHONE

After lunch was over, Walid left on his so-called house
call, and everyone else left soon after. I closed the door, sat
down at Walid's desk, picked up the old yellow receiver,
and dialed. I waited for a few rings and then she picked up.

"Mom."

"Hi, *ya habibi*, how are you? *Inshallah*, everything is
okay. Please, tell me, how are things?"

"I'm fine. How are you?"

"I miss you. I've been waiting for days for you to call.
I was really worried about you, *habibi*. *Inshallah*, everything
is okay? Did you get your grades yet?"

It had been two weeks since I'd last called home. During our last conversation I had told her that I was waiting
for a final grade on a term paper and that once I got it I
could start working as a social worker. She knew nothing of
the new apartment; as far as she was concerned, I still lived
in the dorms. The last time I had been home, more than a
month prior, I had told her that I was going to stay in the
dorms during exams.

"*Alhamdulillah*," I said. "Everything's fine, I got the degree."

"Congratulations, congratulations," she said, her voice rising with excitement. "And the grades, with God's help, they were good?"

"Fine."

"So you're happy?" That was her standard question. Are you happy? Are you content? Are you doing well?

"Absolutely, Mom," I said.

"Congratulations, congratulations."

I cut her short because I knew what was coming—her asking me when I was coming home. And I knew that, having moved into a new apartment, I had no choice but to disappoint her. Above all else my mother wanted me to graduate and to come home, to live with her so that we could wage our battles together.

"Mom, listen. My grades were really good. My average was up above ninety, which means that I made Dean's List and they're going to announce that at the graduation," I said, preparing her. I could hear the excitement in her voice and I knew that she was already planning to tell all the people she knew about her son's grades. *I am successful,* she would be saying. Despite all, *I raised a successful son.* Up to that point, I'd told the truth. "Mom, listen. One of my teachers, the one I wrote the term paper for, a professor, took me aside this week and suggested that with my grades I should continue on toward a master's."

"That sounds great."

"Yeah, I was really happy. If I do that, I'll be able to advance much faster and who knows, maybe I'll even keep on going with the studies from there."

"Wonderful, I am so happy."

"Yeah, me, too, but the thing is, this master's, it's a prestigious track, one that will allow me to treat patients privately, too, but in order to be accepted I need experience, not just grades. I mean, I have no problem in terms of grades, but I need work experience, too."

"How much experience do you need?"

"With my grades, I only need two years. But the professor said he'd make sure that they counted my internship as one year, so I'll be eligible already next year."

"Great. You know you'll find work right away in the village. I already spoke to some people and from what I understand there's a constant shortage of social workers around here. I talked to someone from the local council and she said you could probably start right away."

"That's the thing, Mom. I thought the same thing, but when I spoke to the professor, he said that I had to have two years in the same field, in the same place. If I work for the local council in the village then I'd have to do two full years, and I was thinking . . ."

She went quiet and I felt a weight on my chest on account of what I was doing. But I continued on with the same false optimism, fawning over the professor and the make-believe master's degree, which I had no intention of pursuing. "So, Mom, I actually spoke with the head of the east Jerusalem office, the guy I did the internship with, and he was really happy because he needs someone and he said he could get me a position right away and that they would count the internship as a year of experience, which means I'd get a higher salary."

She remained silent. What I was telling her was that not only was I not coming home, but that I was staying in

Jerusalem for three more years at least, which made it twice as long as she had originally thought. And even back when I finished high school, she had begged me to study in Tel Aviv or at Bar Ilan University so that I could sleep at home every night, and then, too, I had sold her some story about talking to people in the field who said that a degree from Hebrew University was worth far more.

"But I'm not entirely sure," I said, trying to cheer her up. "I really wanted to come home already. I'm sick of this city. I also want to rest a little after all this studying. I mean, I'm really happy I got these offers, but I haven't made up my mind yet. I'll come home for the holiday, Mom, and then we'll talk. In the meantime, I'll do some thinking on my own. The truth is, I'm really kind of tired. We'll see, all right?"

I tried to keep myself busy till four. I went over my notes from my conversation with Daud Abu-Ramila, my addict, and then filed some papers in a tan folder and flipped through the many case histories in the long-dormant files. Testimonies from addicts, their wives, their social workers, reports from house calls, descriptions of violence and neglect. What interested me most were the reports about the welfare of the children. Were they in school? Were they working? Had they been sent away to foster homes? During those last hours of the workday the office was completely silent. At exactly four, I punched my time card and walked out, saying *good night* to the janitor, who pushed his mop across the outdoor steps and looked at me with a gaze both supportive and pitying—he knew exactly what went on in the office.

I strode through Wadi Joz to Salah al-Din Street. Dark clouds drifted to the east and I hoped it would rain. Joining a throng of people waiting for a ride, I managed to get on the third Transit that came past. There was one spot available, next to a pretty girl. Taking my seat, I looked over at her briefly, feigning nonchalance, and then didn't dare to look her way again. I usually tried not to sit next to young women. The best option was to sit next to a man and if that wasn't possible then an older woman. I pulled my body in so that the sleeves of my coat wouldn't touch her arms. I pressed my legs close to one another and laid my black bag on my lap. For the duration of the ride I made sure not to let my gaze stray far from the window and soon enough I forgot all about the girl beside me. Instead I immersed myself in my favorite hobby, peering into homes, looking for lit rooms in otherwise dark buildings, for the glow of television sets, and wondering about the people inside—were their rooms warm, were they surrounded by children who had come home from school, were they doing homework together, watching cartoons, enmeshed in family life?

"Excuse me," the girl's voice pulled me back to the taxi. The old Transit had pulled up next to the mosque in Shuafat and she wanted to get off. I didn't want her to have to squeeze past me, for her legs to brush up against mine, so I opened the taxi door and got out, clearing the way for her. She didn't say thank you and I sat back down in my seat and hoped that Wassim had not yet left for his second job. I just wanted to chat with him, hear how his day had gone and touch base, if only for a moment.

SODIUM CHLORIDE

During my first weeks at the Nusseibah housing projects I hardly left the building, aside from daily trips to work and the occasional trip to the grocery. I shopped for the three of us and after a while Majdi started calling me the Minister of Shopping. I'd get receipts for the things we shared—bread, eggs, sausages, cheese—and we'd split the cost three ways, even though I'd frequently get a fancier cheese or a more expensive sausage and ask the grocer to put it on a separate bill. "Ever since you arrived we have cleaning supplies in our apartment," Majdi would say, laughing at the sight of floor cleaning liquid or dish soap.

I took charge of the actual cleaning also. That meant scouring surfaces that hadn't been touched since the day the cousins moved in. My first mission was the refrigerator. Majdi and Wassim were shocked to learn that its interior could be cleaned and that the shelves could be made white again. The bathroom was no easier. It took an entire bottle of sodium chloride and a bottle of bleach to make the sink, bathtub, and toilet somewhat acceptable. I'm not sure if I cleaned because I wanted to combat the filth or simply because I wanted something to do with myself, a way to pass the time until Wassim and Majdi came home. They arrived one after another, at just before nine thirty.

Other than late in the evening, it was rare for the three of us to be awake and together in the apartment at the same time. Wassim and Majdi worked whenever they could, even on the weekends, trying to earn a little extra cash. Those were the worst times for me. I tried to entertain myself with the small TV and the old newspapers that Majdi brought home from the hotel. Every once in a while I'd treat myself to a cup of coffee. Those dead hours alone were dreadful enough to make me miss the office, and when I knew I'd have to spend an entire weekend alone in the apartment, I'd photocopy a few files, the thickest ones I could find, and shove them into my bag so that at least I'd have something entertaining to read.

The weekends that we spent together, on the other hand, were glorious. When Wassim and Majdi were off and hadn't gone home to visit their families, we'd take the bus or a share-taxi down to Damascus Gate and go to Lina for hummus with fava beans. Then we'd meander through the old market, shuffling in and out of the human traffic while Majdi shopped for what he called "hilarious" music, asking the shop owners to play him a track from, say, Egyptian pop star Ahmad Adawiya's newest album and then bursting out laughing. He liked Sheikh Imam, Ziad Rahbani, Michel Halifa, and a Palestinian band called Sabarin, which he talked about constantly. Wassim, whom Majdi called a hopeless conservative, liked the classics, always on the look-out for el-Halim, Farid al-Atrash, Sabah Fakhri, and Fairuz. I didn't buy cassettes. I didn't own a single tape of my own. Nor did I have a stereo. But I was fine with whatever they played at home. All-out wars would erupt over which music was to be played during what we called our narghile nights.

Majdi was the master of the narghile. Like an artist at work he would shape the tobacco in his hands — the flavor of choice was usually apple — then he'd cover the tobacco with aluminum foil and punch strategic holes with a toothpick,

laying the heated coals over the aluminum tent. He'd sit
with the rubber hose in his hand and take monumental pulls
from the water pipe. The king of nonsense, Wassim would
say. The two of them passed the hose from mouth to mouth,
exhaling long plumes of smoke toward the ceiling. I tried
the pipe a few times, but I couldn't really figure out what
to do with the smoke once it was in my mouth. In the end I
gave up trying, but still very much loved the narghile nights.
Especially the tea, a weak brew with sharp mint leaves and
tons of sugar—three teaspoons in each little glass.

On most narghile nights the main topic of conversation was girls. Majdi, who loved all kinds of girls, was full
of stories about those he met at the hotel, at work, and on
the bus. He liked talking about girls, especially the pretty
Russian ones who worked with him at the hotel and the
tourists who made eyes at him over their dinners. Wassim
contended that he made it all up, that every single detail
was false and that from what he could tell Majdi was on the
fast track to becoming the most flagrantly lying lawyer in
the country and that God should have mercy on his clients.
Wassim, for his part, had a girlfriend. Or at least a sort of
girlfriend. She was from their village, had studied education
in school, and had gone back home after college. Wassim
had never spent a minute alone with her, nor could he call
her, because her parents or brother might answer the phone.
But they loved each other, and it was clear that they would
soon be engaged to be married.

"You're missing out on life," Majdi would say to him,
"you should get the most out of the city before you lock yourself up in the village." His advice, of course, was not heeded.
Wassim was the exact kind of guy who would stay true to his

love and marry the honest, shy girl from the village whom he had never so much as touched. "So long as her parents don't give me too much grief," he would say. "Her father is very rich. He has an electronic appliance store. And what am I? A teacher . . ." Without a house in the village, there was no point in even discussing marriage. That was one of the reasons Wassim was still in Jerusalem. He wanted to save as much as he could before heading back home. That was also why every cent of the rent was painful for him to cough up. He managed to put away a salary and a half, but neither of them was substantial.

Majdi was more of a high roller. He earned a lot less than Wassim—interns got minimum wage—but he treated himself to new jeans and new shirts, and the money he did put away was earmarked for a new car. That was the other topic of conversation—cars. A BMW was the ultimate vehicle. It's not the most expensive, Majdi would say, but it's a beast on the road. In the meantime, he had his sights on a Volkswagen Golf, an '84 or an '85.

"Maybe you should get a second job," Wassim said to me one night, the night that led me to Yonatan. "Maybe you should get a girl," Majdi added, but Wassim ignored him. "There's this one job," he went on, "I don't know if it's still available but if it is, it would be perfect for you. The shifts are evening and nights, I think." Wassim told me about Ayub, a teacher in his school who was about to get married and would have to give up the night shift. I remember Wassim saying, "You don't have to do a thing, absolutely nothing. He takes care of a kid, in the kid's house. The kid has some kind of problem, I'm not exactly sure what the technical name for it is, but if you want, I could ask Ayub tomorrow.

All I know is that Ayub works nights and he doesn't lift a finger. He says he sleeps better there than he does at home."

"Okay, sounds good," I said, not meaning it at all.

SCOUT

I waited for Ayub at exactly six p.m. at the bus station opposite Damascus Gate, just as Wassim had told me. Ayub showed up at six fifteen. I spotted him as he darted across the street that divides east from west. He was wearing a thick gray sweater and a heavy jean jacket that was lined with fake sheepskin. A backpack hung off one shoulder. "You're the guy?" he asked before extending a hand. "Sorry I'm late. The road was backed up, some kind of accident or something, but don't worry, we'll make it on time."

Ayub said that he usually took a share-taxi from Issawiya, where he lived, to Damascus Gate and that from there he walked down to Jaffa Road, some ten minutes away, and took the 27 bus or the 18, which went down Herzl Boulevard, leaving a short walk to Scout Street. But since it was really cold he suggested we take the bus to Jaffa Road. "I don't mind walking," I said, but Ayub said he didn't want to be late, and just as he said that a bus nosed into the stop.

I got on ahead of him and bought two fares. The bus was practically empty. We sat toward the back and Ayub started telling me about himself and about the job. He said he was a special-ed teacher and that he had studied at the David Yellin College, which was no simple feat because he had a Jordanian matriculation certificate. "But I played it right, because I knew that the only thing I'd be able to do with a teaching degree from the West Bank was to wipe my ass, so I spent the year after college working on my Hebrew, then I took a prep course and got in to David Yellin. Of course, Birzeit and Bethlehem Universities are a thousand times better than David Yellin, but what's a Jerusalem resident going to do with a degree from there? Everything here's Israeli."

When he decided he needed someone to take his night shift, he considered offering it to his cousins. They sat at home all day long and did nothing, but Wassim had recommended me really strongly, and Wassim's a hard person to say no to. "Wassim's a great guy," he said. "He's got a heart of gold. It's hard to find people like him these days. Anyway, he told me a lot about you." He also knew they wouldn't take just anyone for the job. "They want a quality person, someone who knows Hebrew, too, and someone who has some kind of background. Someone who studied special-ed or nursing, but social work is good, too. It's different, but it's still about caring for others." And anyway, he explained, there's a registered nurse there all day long. "We'll meet her in a second. She's a good person, precise, goes by the books, but good. Her name's Osnat."

We got off the bus on Jaffa Road. Ayub waved me into a run as he sprinted toward the 27 bus, which was already at the stop. The bus was packed and there was nowhere to sit. There was barely anywhere to stand. Ayub, who up until then had been speaking in Arabic, switched to Hebrew — which he spoke with a heavy Hebron accent — and he did it naturally, as though it were the most obvious thing in the world. I didn't know how to respond, in Hebrew or

Arabic, so I held my silence. "The most important thing," he
said to me, "is to show her that you care about people. Be
sympathetic. You know, interested. And don't get freaked
out when you see the kid. Just treat him like a normal person. He's handicapped, but he's still a person. His name's
Yonatan."

Ayub told me that Yonatan was twenty-one or maybe,
now that he thought about it, twenty-two, because more than
a year had gone by since he started working there. Before
that he'd worked at a home for mentally disabled adults,
in addition to his job as a teacher. The home was where he
met Osnat, the nurse, who came once a week to instruct the
caregivers on how to treat the residents. The two of them
got along well and one day she asked Ayub if he would be
willing to take the night shift with Yonatan. "Working at the
home was so different," he said. "This job's a breeze. You
don't have to do a thing. Yonatan sleeps through the night.
All you have to do is rotate him a little bit every two hours.
Turn him onto his back, his right side, his left side. That's
it. The rest of the time all you do is sleep, and no one cares.
The mother's out to lunch, doesn't know what's going on.
Poor thing, she's a good person, too. All she has is Yonatan.
She lost her husband, not sure how, but he's gone. Maybe
she's a widow or a divorcée, I'm not really sure what her
story is. The best thing is not to ask. Why complicate things,
that's what I say."

Ruchaleh, the mother, was some kind of doctor. Maybe
of sociology. She worked up at Hebrew U and was a real
lefty. So Osnat had told him. And Osnat, Ayub said, was
also in favor of some kind of peace deal, which meant that
the two of us should get along.

"We get off at the next stop," he said all of a sudden, still in Hebrew, as he pushed the bell. When we stepped off the bus, he switched back to Arabic. "Remember this stop," he said. "Right next to the pizzeria on Herzl. One minute from here and you're at work."

I followed Ayub down a small side street in the Beit Hakerem neighborhood. This is Scout Street, he said, then filled me in on more details about the job. "The shift starts at seven in the evening and ends at seven in the morning. It's okay to sleep while on duty—there's even a couch there for that purpose—but don't say anything about it in the interview. Say you don't plan on sleeping. Even though Osnat knows you will. She does, too. It's fine. All you have to do is set your alarm for every two hours. I don't even really need to wake up to rotate him. I just do it and go straight back to sleep. In the morning I'm refreshed, I sleep better than at home," he said, laughing. He stopped outside one of the houses and pushed open a small gate. I followed him through a modest little garden. It was a stand-alone house, two stories. "Remember," he said before sliding the key into the lock, "Scout Street, number thirty-five."

JELLY

A week later I made my way to Beit Hakerem for my first night shift with Yonatan.

"I hope you're always this early," Osnat said, opening the door for me. She was alone, which is to say just she and Yonatan were home. I followed her down the hall and flicked a glance to the right, toward the book-filled living room. She led me up the narrow wooden stairs to the attic, where Yonatan lay.

"Hi, Yonatan," Osnat said as we walked into the room. A strong smell hit me, the smell of unventilated air, medicine, and hospital food. "Look who's here," she said in a loud voice, as though the increase in volume would heighten his perception. "He's going to spend the night with you, okay, Yonatan?"

Yonatan lay on his back. I looked at him, nodded in his direction, and offered a mute hello. I had spent two or three hours a day with him the week before, learning how to do the job, and I wasn't sure if he recognized me or not, if he was even capable of such a thing. His eyes were open, fixed on the ceiling. I steered my eyes away from him, so it wouldn't look like I was staring.

Osnat shouldered her bag. "Oh, I nearly forgot," she said, walking over to what she called the staff closet, "there are sheets and blankets here for you. Everything's been washed, so make yourself at home. Ruchaleh will probably be back soon and she knows it's your first night. If you need anything, I'll be home in half an hour and my home number's on the board. Feel free to call till around midnight, okay? See you tomorrow morning at seven. Good night. Have a good shift." She wrapped herself in a heavy wool coat, walked toward the door, and said, "'Bye, Yonatan, good night." Then she left.

I heard the door slam shut below and immediately threw open the attic window. Shoving my head out, I breathed in the crisp air. Then I slid the window back along its track till it was just barely open. The radiator was working full steam and Yonatan was tucked under a blanket that had been pulled up to his chin.

He was positioned in the middle of the room, on a large bed, on what Osnat called an electric egg-carton mattress. It was connected to a machine that sent waves through the mattress, preventing bedsores. *Bedsores* —that was the word I heard most from Osnat, so much so that it seemed to me that my main goal at work was to keep them at bay.

There was nothing for me to do with Yonatan until eight, when I would feed him his dinner. The food was in a jar in a small refrigerator in the corner of the attic and once he had eaten it I was supposed to give him a small container of jelly, instead of water, which he couldn't swallow.

I sat down on the recliner and stole a few glances at Yonatan, just to make sure that the blanket was rising and falling with the rhythm of his breathing. His wide eyes were fixed on the ceiling, his face expressionless. Osnat had said that Yonatan's condition was defined as vegetative and that the cause was an accident. Ayub said it was a car accident, but he wasn't 100 percent sure. I got up and looked for figures in the lit windows of the high-rises on Herzl Boulevard, thinking of how jealous I had always been of people who live in big buildings looking over crowded streets. They would never be bored, they could always just look out the window and see people. They'd never feel like they were alone.

A substantial amount of space had been set aside for Yonatan. The attic was built like a studio, with a large bathroom and a grand desk. There was an old computer monitor on the desk and shelves full of books above it. There was

also a sleek and powerful-looking stereo. The speakers, on
either side of the desk, faced the bed and alongside one of
them were two tall racks of CDs.

I ran my eyes down the long column of discs and found
that I did not know a single one of them. I'd never had a CD
player. At my mother's house and in the apartment in Beit
Hanina we only used a tape deck and cassettes. I looked
over the books and some of the titles seemed familiar, even
though I'd never read any of them. The truth is that back
then the only books I'd ever read were the young adult books
my mother used to bring back from the school where she
taught in Jaljulia. She talked a lot about how important it
was to read, even though she never did it herself, and there
were few books at home. At one point she bought me a set
of encyclopedias — the school principal was a salesman — and
I read from them pretty often. They, for instance, taught me
about the reproductive system. I spent many a long hour
in front of the strange genitalia illustrations, especially the
female ones. I had read the chapter called "The Human
Body" close to a million times.

I was sure that prior to the accident Yonatan had been
a musician. There was a hard black guitar case in the room
and a black box that looked like an amp. There were posters
of what must have been his favorite bands up on the walls.
One stretch of wall was decorated with framed photos, but
they weren't family pictures or anything like that, they were
just photos, not always clear, sometimes shadowy and blurry,
all in black and white. I thought to myself that it would have
been interesting to hear him play, this Yonatan.

I was jealous of people who could play music. When I
was a kid I really wanted to learn how to play an instrument,

and for a while my wish came true. An engineer who lived in the village had gone to study in Russia and had come home with a music teacher for a wife. The engineer had not found work and his Russian wife, who was known in the village as Sweeta, started offering piano lessons to the kids in the village. My mother sent me to her house every Wednesday and for six months I had a weekly one-hour lesson. Sweeta was happy with my progress and said that if I wanted to continue to develop I had to have a piano at home. It could be a used one, she said, or an organ would be okay, too, but I had to have something to practice on. Mom went to Petach Tikva especially and bought me a battery-operated keyboard. When I brought it over to Sweeta's house, she said that it wasn't an instrument at all, that it was a toy. She showed me how it played nursery rhymes. And it only had eight keys, which was useless, because I needed to practice playing with two hands. That was my last lesson. I told my mother, who didn't understand why I had given up the piano, that the teacher had said I wasn't good enough.

LIQUID FOOD

I took the jar of food out of the fridge and placed it on the bedside table. Pressing the button, I raised Yonatan's bed to what I thought was a suitable angle. His expression never wavered, and his stare, which had been set on the ceiling, was now leveled at the desk opposite his bed. I brought a chair over to the side of the bed and looked at the clock. In a minute it would be eight p.m.

The procedure sounded so simple and natural when Osnat explained it. But when I touched his inert body, a shiver went through me. Maybe it really would have been easier if I had spoken to him, as Osnat had recommended, but back then I was not able to relate to that thing at all. I wasn't sure if he could even hear or see. While pulling down his blanket I tried to avoid all bodily contact. I stretched my arms to their full length, keeping my distance, and with unsteady hands tried to tuck the paper napkin into the neck of his pajamas. I felt the heat of his body and my hands jerked back as if I'd touched a poisonous snake.

"You can't know what they know," Osnat had told me. "You can't know what he feels. But we have to be as humane as possible and treat him as though he were fully aware of everything around him. You shouldn't mention his condition and you shouldn't say things like 'poor thing' or 'he'll never get better.'" I reminded myself to act naturally and, inhaling through my mouth, I straightened the napkin under his chin.

I scooped up a flat teaspoon of the gelatinous purple food, just as Osnat had shown me, and tried putting the spoon into his mouth. Nothing. He did not open his mouth at all and I wound up smearing the food across his lips and down his chin. I took a napkin from the drawer and cleaned his face. Then I put some more food on the spoon and tried to pry his mouth open with my other hand, using a thumb and finger on either side of his jaw, feeling his teeth through his skin, but his mouth remained shut. I was scared that he'd suddenly open his mouth and clamp down on my fingers but I reminded myself that if he bit me it would be considered a medical miracle and that everyone would be glad.

Using a lot more strength than I had anticipated, I finally managed to open his mouth and guide the spoon inside, but nothing happened. The food stayed on the spoon. I turned it over in his mouth and shook the food off onto his tongue. "Slide it all the way back," Osnat had said. There was no movement whatsoever, no sign of swallowing. I pried his mouth farther open and looked inside. Just as I had thought. All the food remained exactly where I had left it. Nothing had been swallowed. What do you do with this thing?

I knew this was not for me. I should have refused the job. But I hadn't, and now I had no choice. I was alone and there were tasks that had to be done. I slid the long spoon back into his mouth and moved the food back toward his throat. With my other hand I raised his chin in the air, forcing his head back in a movement that reminded me of my grandmother and the way she used to feed her chicks. I wondered if something had gone wrong, if his situation had somehow changed since I had arrived. Otherwise Osnat and Ayub would have told me that feeding him is one of the most difficult chores. I tried my system again — squeeze open his mouth, insert the spoon, deposit the food, raise his chin — and then again. It wasn't easy or fast, but it worked. When the food was consumed, I moved on to the water substitute, employing the same technique. By the time the meal was over I realized that I had touched him without so much as a second thought and that a full hour had passed.

I removed the napkin and wiped his face with two wet cloths. Then I used the button on his bed to return him to a prone position. That was it. All I had left to do was to rotate him every few hours and to watch him fall asleep. "He goes to sleep right after the meal," Osnat had said, "and he stays asleep till morning."

But Yonatan did not fall asleep. His eyes remained open and fixed on the ceiling. I decided to flip him onto his side. It wasn't difficult: with one hand on his shoulder and another on his hip, I tugged once and he was on his side, staring me in the face. I should have flipped him the other way, I thought, so that I wouldn't have that incomprehensible look staring me in the face. I could have moved my chair over to the other side of the bed, but that wouldn't have looked good. You have to be mindful of his feelings, I reminded myself. I stayed put, doing whatever I could to avoid his gaze. Every once in a while I looked back at him to see whether his eyes were still open. They were, hauntingly so, but more than anything else they simply testified to the fact that he was not asleep.

A sharp smell filled the room. It was nothing like the unventilated, medicinal scent I had encountered when I first came up to the attic. No one had mentioned this to me. Not Osnat and definitely not Ayub, that son of a bitch. I went over to the window and opened it all the way, trying to overcome my nausea and cursing myself and Wassim and Ayub and Osnat. Yonatan, there was no longer any doubt, had defecated in his bed. I considered calling Osnat and telling her that I was very sorry but that I would be leaving right away. Instead I found myself on the phone apologizing for bothering her at this hour and asking all too politely how I should handle the situation. "It's very simple," she said. "You take off the diaper, clean him up with some wipes, and put on a new diaper. Strange, that almost never happens at night."

I tried to work on autopilot. I marched over to the bed and pulled down his blanket. His body was surprisingly robust and athletic, considering, and he wore what looked like rather expensive pajamas. I decided on two things: I would get this done, and I would quit. This would be a one-time thing. I'd stay through till the end of this awful night and then go back to my life in Beit Hanina. At this hour, Majdi and Wassim were probably home. What I wouldn't give to be with them.

The excrement had stained the waistband of his pajamas. Without thinking, I pulled his pajama pants down. It was worse than I had imagined. The excrement was smeared across his back and legs. I tried not to breathe. I flipped him on his back, undid the diaper tabs, and pulled. Then his bottom half was bare and for a moment I felt sorry for him, wondering if he could tell what I was doing and how it made him feel, if he felt anything at all. The situation was ghastly: most of his body and the bedding were covered in shit. Wipes were not going to be of any use. I remembered what Osnat had said about showering him, even though, as she put it, "this is hardly relevant because I give him a shower in the morning," and I decided to put him in the special showering wheelchair, the one with the hole in the seat. I decided that there was no other way. A shower was what he needed.

I raised Yonatan's head and tucked my arms under his armpits. He was far heavier than I had anticipated. My hands were wrapped across his chest. The special wheelchair was positioned alongside the bed. I pulled him as hard as I could and smeared shit all across the sheets. With considerable effort, I managed to get his uncooperative body into the wheelchair. According to the explanations I had received, this was all supposed to be relatively simple. He was to be placed in the chair and then tied in for support. Only there was no way to keep him steady and tie him in at the same time. Each time I took one hand off him he started to slide out of the chair.

You have to act as though you're under fire, I told myself. I summoned every ounce of strength I had and in the end was able to press his heavy body into the chair and tie the straps around him. I took the sheets off the bed and threw them into the washing machine in the bathroom. Then I pushed the wheelchair into the bathroom and turned on the shower, waiting for it to get warm. What does this person, this thing, even know? If he felt anything at all, it must be hatred for me. Yonatan probably hates me more than anything else in the world, I thought. I'll get this over with, deal with the rest of the night, and never see him again.

Later that night I wasn't able to fall asleep. I lay down on the sofa, closed my eyes, and tried to think of soccer moves, a drill that usually put me to sleep. Instead I found myself practicing my conversation with Osnat, accusing her of lying about the nature of the job, and telling her that I would not be continuing. "By eight he's usually asleep" . . . Is that right? Well, why was he wide awake till midnight then? And yes, this was after I'd showered him, washed his hair, and wrestled him into his new diaper and pajamas.

In the morning I was supposed to take a shower myself, change clothes, and go straight to the office, "feeling fresh and well-rested," as Ayub put it. I passed on the shower. It made me nauseous to think that I might have to stand naked and barefoot in the exact spot where the filth had poured off Yonatan the previous night. All thoughts of the previous night were revolting. I had washed my face, brushed my teeth, and used a towel from the staff closet, but I had been sorry that I had not brought my own.

Osnat arrived at five past seven. She had her own key.

"Good morning," she whispered. Yonatan was still asleep.

"Good morning."

"So, is everything all right? He seems to be sleeping nicely," she said, yawning.

"Everything's all right," I heard myself say.

I took the undershirt, the T-shirt, and the pants I was supposed to wear that day and stashed them in the staff closet. I moved my toiletries kit there, too. "Have a good shift," I told Osnat and hurried down the stairs. Why hadn't I said anything? What am I going to do now? I thought. I was angry with myself and I felt my face flush.

Waiting at the bus stop on Herzl Boulevard, I imagined Wassim making coffee and hurrying Majdi out of bed. This was my first time leaving for work without them. Why the hell had I not said anything to Osnat? Maybe I'll just disappear, I thought, without saying anything. What could possibly happen if I don't show up tonight at seven? It would be a little awkward, and Osnat would definitely talk to Ayub, who would talk to Wassim, but all of that could easily be explained. I could also call her as soon as I got to the office and tell her that I would not be coming back. Some things have to be handled in that way. A clean cut. I decided that's what I would do. So I'd lose a shirt and a pair of pants. It was a small price to pay.

The 23 bus was stuck at a red light before the stop. It didn't run often but it was the best bus for me, as it went straight to the courthouse and from there it was just a two-minute walk to work. I counted the coins in my hand. I always tried to have exact change because I hated making the drivers do the extra work. A white car veered into the bus stop. I hated drivers who pulled in to bus stops.

"Excuse me," I heard a voice call out. I swiveled my head. "I'm Ruchaleh, Yonatan's mother. Where are you headed?"

I leaned forward and looked through the open window at the driver of the car.

"Wadi Joz."

"Okay, get in, it's on my way."

I looked back one more time at the 23, which was pulling up to the stop, and then opened the car door and hurried in.

I made sure to look straight ahead and tried to breathe quietly.

"I'm headed to Mount Scopus. Wadi Joz is on my way," she said in a tone that reminded me of her son's expressionless stare.

"Thank you very much."

"I saw you on the way down the stairs this morning. I was sitting in the kitchen."

I nodded in silence and only then realized that there had been someone else in the house during that night of sleeplessness. At no point did I feel or hear her presence, there had been no shutting of doors and no footfalls. No sign of life at all.

"It was a rough night last night," she said, and I wasn't sure if she was asking or telling. "I came upstairs to say hi when I got home but I saw that you were busy with Yonatan in the shower and I didn't want to bother you."

I nodded bashfully. She had been there, and she knew what I had been through.

"I know this will sound strange to you," she said, "but he was testing you last night. That's why I didn't get involved."

I didn't respond, and the two of us stayed silent. The roads were full of traffic and we moved along slowly from light to light. I looked over at the cars trapped beside us and tried to guess where they were all headed.

"Where do you need to go in Wadi Joz?" she asked when we reached Route 1.

"Right by the district court would be perfect," I said, because I knew that it was on her way to the university and that most Jews didn't like driving deep into Arab neighborhoods.

"That's where you live?"

"No, that's where I work, at the bureau of social services."

"But that's not near the courthouse," she said.

"No, but it's a two-minute walk from there."

She drove past the courthouse, turned right, and then left into Wadi Joz, stopping right in front of the office.

"See you tonight," she said, without a trace of a question mark.

MARLBORO LIGHT

Daud Abu-Ramila, my only active case, was waiting for me outside the office. He sat on the floor, hugging a big bag. "I'm clean today," he said, adding with a laugh, "got the rehab started already." This was the day I was to take him to the clinic in Lifta. He had already been through the committee, met all the requirements, and been told that the bed for the Arab residents was now available.

I punched in and made coffee for the two of us. He was excited, his movements sharp and quick. "I won't let you down, you'll see. I'm dying to get there already," he said. "I'll never forget what you did for me. Never. You saved me." Once we'd finished our coffees, I called a cab and we prepared to head out to wait for the driver.

"Is this the outpatient center?" a woman's voice breathed behind me as I was shutting the door.

"Yes." I turned around and looked at the skinny, curly-haired girl before me. She was chewing gum and trying to catch her breath at the same time.

"Hi," she said, extending a hand. "I'm Leila, the new intern. Sorry I'm late, I got a little lost. Walid told you I was coming, right?"

The cab driver announced himself with a honk. "Tell him to wait a second," I told Daud, who pulled his eyes off Leila and set off at a run.

"Walid's my supervisor for this internship and he asked that I accompany you to Lifta. He didn't tell you?"

Walid hadn't told me a thing about a new intern and certainly not about her accompanying me anywhere.

"All right, let's go," I said, shutting the door and leading her toward the taxi. Abu-Ramila had already taken the front seat. Leila and I sat in the back.

"Daud, meet . . . Leila?" I said, making sure I had the name right. She nodded, "Leila."

Without turning around Daud began to sing my praises. "He's the best guy here, I'm telling you, this is the man that saved my life. I would do anything in the world for him." His comments irritated me and drew the early signs of a smile on Leila's face.

Why had Walid told her to join me on the trip to Lifta? What was I, her supervisor? Why didn't he do it himself? I remembered that Walid had said he wasn't going to mentor any student-interns this year. Of course he was going to dump her on me. I was the only one in the office with an active case.

"Did you hear what happened in the southern district office?" Leila asked.

"No."

"You don't know? The whole world's talking about it."

"Yeah, *Allah istor*," Daud's voice came from the front seat. "How many got killed there, three?"

"Two, and several injured," Leila said.

Only then did I remember that I had heard something about the incident a few days earlier, either in the office or over the radio while on the bus, but I hadn't really paid it any attention. In those days I didn't follow the news, didn't listen to the radio, and didn't read the papers, aside from the old magazines that Majdi brought back from the hotel.

Leila said that one of the addicts came in one day and just started stabbing people. A secretary and a social worker were killed on the spot. One of the wounded was Leila's previous supervisor. She couldn't believe it when she heard the story. It was so awful, terrifying. Luckily it hadn't happened on a day that she went into the office. After the incident, the social work department decided to repost her to a different bureau,

to Walid, even though she didn't want to work in the Arab
sector—not because she had anything against her own kind,
God forbid, but because of the budget constraints. "I wanted
to do a real internship, not one of these half-baked ones," she
said. At any rate, she was happy they found her an alternative
because there was no way she was going back to the southern
district and she definitely didn't want to waste a whole year.

At the clinic we pushed the intercom and waited for
the director, who said he would be right down. "This place
is nice," Leila said. "What is it?" She looked over at the
abandoned stone houses clustered at the foot of the hill.

"You never heard of Lifta?" Daud asked, getting more
and more agitated, shifting his bag from hand to hand, waiting for the door to be opened. There were several addicts
on the balcony, Styrofoam cups of coffee in their hands,
sucking on their cigarettes. They had to be the veterans.
The newcomers spent the first few days of rehab in their
rooms, confined to their beds.

The director introduced himself to Daud and shook
hands with everyone. I introduced him to Leila and he gave
us a tour of the building, proudly showing her the office,
the group therapy room, the inpatient rooms, the kitchen,
and the dining area. He offered us coffee but we declined.
I put a hand out to part with Daud but he pulled me in for
a hug. Tears spilled out of his eyes. I told him again that I
would come visit and that if he needed anything he should
tell the social worker and that she would pass it on to me.

When I walked back into the office, Khalil called out, "Oh,
just in time. I thought we were going to starve to death in

here." Leila came in behind me and the room fell silent. They knew she was coming. Walid had already been in and let them know. My colleagues were unusually polite. They stood, said hi, shook her hand, and looked her over. She smiled and repeated their names to make sure that she had gotten them right. Shadi, his confident gaze locking on her eyes, told her that Walid had gone down to city hall and that he would be back soon. "Sit here in the meantime," he said, offering her his chair and moving over to Walid's.

"Too bad for you," Khalil said as he handed me the breakfast money. "If we would've gotten a male intern he would've switched you up with the food delivery." Everyone laughed. "Allow me," Shadi said to Leila, handing me an extra twenty shekels.

"When did you get so generous?" Khalil asked, looking over at Leila and smiling.

"No, thank you," she said, smiling. "I've eaten already. But thank you very much."

"Come on," Shadi said, but when she didn't change her mind he turned to me and said, "okay, so get me a pack of Marlboro Lights."

When I got up to go, Leila jumped out of her chair and asked, "Can I come with you?"

PISTOLS

After a month with Yonatan, Osnat felt I could handle the day shift and she agreed to switch one of my nights for one of her days, either Friday or Saturday. More than two months had passed since I'd last seen my mother—the longest I'd ever been away from home—and since the Festival of the Sacrifice was coming up, during which the office was closed and my roommates would be returning to their villages, I decided that it would be the best time to go home.

Back when I was in grade school, I would spend the first two days of the holiday in Tira, with my grandmother from my father's side. All the kids in Tira ran around during the holiday with toy guns and each year um-Bassem would hunt around Jaljulia and find me the best pistol money could buy. The guns um-Bassem got me were better than anything my uncles got for their kids and better even than the ones um-Bassem's grandkids got from their parents. I don't remember exactly when, maybe in kindergarten or first grade, but one year I went to um-Bassem's house in my holiday clothes to get that year's pistol and I heard Aunt Maryam ask her why she spent all that money on me. "It is written in the Koran," um-Bassem answered. "The orphan must be honored."

I liked being in Tira on the Festival of the Sacrifice because each year my uncles would roast a sheep, sometimes even a calf, in my grandmother's yard. I liked it also because I got to play with my cousins, who had the same last name as me. In Jaljulia there was no one with my name. Usually there were around four people in every class with the same last name and I was the only one in my grade—and later, I learned, in the school and the entire village—with a strange last name. Sometimes I signed my homework and tests with a different name, usually um-Bassem's. Her grandchildren called her *Siti,* Grandma, just like me, so why shouldn't I have her name, too? But the teachers were never fooled, not even the new ones, and whenever it happened they told my mother and she sat me down and explained that um-Bassem was an *honorary* grandmother, not a real one. I knew that. I wasn't an idiot. My notebooks and report cards carried my real last name, from Tira, but when the kids in school asked for my family name I gave them um-Bassem's.

I was a stranger in school, a stranger in the village with a weird last name just like all the other strangers in Jaljulia. Everyone knew that the strangers came to the village because of a blood feud, and that the police had brought them there. That's what they used to say then, but I didn't really understand what it meant. I did know that something was wrong with the strangers, that their fathers were in jail, and that I shouldn't hang out with them. Some of the strangers were called *collaborators*, and they were the most hated of all. There were never any of the collaborators' children in my class, because I was in the A class and none of the children of the people that the police had brought to the village were in the A class. Our teachers would warn us about them and criticize the government for carting all of the country's trash to Jaljulia. It's true that I was also a stranger, but I was a different kind of stranger: a stranger in the A class, a stranger that the teachers liked, a stranger with good grades, a stranger with a mother who taught at the school. My mother told me that the police had not moved us to Jaljulia but that she had come in order to work in the school. I knew full well, though, that that was not true and that the police had brought us to Jaljulia just like the rest of the trash, just like the children of the blood feuds and the collaborators.

I remember that one time my father's mother insisted that I remain in Tira after the holiday and not go back to my mother in Jaljulia. She yelled at my uncle that she would never speak to him again if he took me back. The holiday ended and I stayed in Tira. My cousins went to school and I stayed alone at home with Grandma. A few days later, my mother showed up at Grandma's house in a police jeep. She got out of the backseat accompanied by two policemen. They were dressed in blue uniforms that looked like the costume um-Bassem got me in Mecca when she went for the *haj*. My mother was crying. She yanked my arm and then picked me up and ran back to the police jeep while my grandmother stood there and yelled, "You whore, you killed our son and now you're taking his son. You whore, you should kill yourself. It would be better for you, you bitch."

I packed a bag at the apartment and saw Wassim and Majdi as they were heading home to their village. When I finally got home for the Festival of the Sacrifice, I squeezed my mother's hand and she squeezed mine. I could see in her face that she wanted to hug me, but she knew it was best to resist that urge. Instead her eyes glazed over. Me and my mother did not hug or kiss. At times I would try to imagine what that kind of touch might feel like. I was sure she had held me and cuddled me when I was a baby, at the very least in order to feed me, and I tried to imagine that feeling but couldn't. Perhaps, I used to think, if I had a picture of her holding me as a baby it would help.

"Eight weeks," she said, trying to break the awkwardness. "What did you do with all your clothes?"

"What I always do. I washed my underwear in the sink. No problem."

"Are you hungry?" she asked, putting my bags back in the house.

"Soon."

"Do you need to use the bathroom?" she asked, then started sorting the clothes and throwing them into the washing machine in the bathroom.

I shook my head.

"Mom, I'm going to go say hi to um-Bassem," I said, and went outside into the courtyard.

Um-Bassem's door was open. "*Siti,*" I called out before going in.

"Come, welcome," I heard her say.

She was on a prayer mat in the living room. The radio played verses from the Koran. It would soon be time for the afternoon prayer and um-Bassem could no longer hear the village muezzin's call to prayer so she used a radio station from Jordan to know when to pray — precisely one minute after the radio, because that, she had decided, was the time difference between Amman and Jaljulia.

Standing at the door with the light at my back, she couldn't recognize me. She brought a hand up to her face to shield her eyes and started to get up off the mat. "Stay where you are, Siti, it's me," I said as I walked toward her.

"*Ahalan, ahalan, ahalan,*" she said, opening her arms. I bent over to hug her and she kissed me on the cheeks and the head. "How are you, *ya habibi*?" she beamed. "What kind of evil have you been up to? Fifty-four days and we hear nothing from you. How are you? Is everything okay?"

"I'm fine, Siti, how are you?"

"*Alhamdulillah.* I'm waiting to pray, but the radio keeps coming in and out. These Jordanians can't sit still. I find them and then they disappear. It's not prayer time yet, is it?"

"Not yet. Soon."

"When did you come? Now?"

"Just now."

"So go eat first, and I'll pray. I want to talk to you. This is how you treat your mother? What did she ever do to you?" As I was about to leave, she fished around under the couch and pulled out an envelope. "This is *halaweh,* for the good grades and the tests. Your mother told me you're all set to be a social worker now. May God be with you always. Allah, every prayer I mention you and ask Him to keep you safe." I took the envelope and kissed her on the cheek.

"Allah be with you, I'll come soon."

I knew that there was money in the envelope and that there was no way I'd be able to refuse it. She gave me a present at the end of every school year. "*Halaweh* for your grades," she would say. When I was young I liked her envelopes a lot more than the good grades. I'd run over to her house with my report card, knowing that she wouldn't be able to read it and that the envelope was waiting for me anyway, because she knew I got the best grades in the class. "Bassem was the same way," she would say. "He was smart like you. Always top of the class. Now he's in Italy, a big doctor."

I remember the first time Bassem came to visit Jaljulia. He had a fair-skinned wife who couldn't speak. Um-Bassem decorated the courtyard and we helped her hang balloons and a poster board on which I'd written, IN HONOR OF

DOCTOR BASSEM ABU-RAS. Early in the morning um-Bassem's four daughters, Bassem's sisters, showed up with their children and began to wait for him. He arrived and kissed his mother and his sisters, who introduced him to their children. He hugged and kissed each one of them and gave them each a little plane with blinking lights. I remember waiting for my hug and my plane and Bassem asked, "Who's this little guy, whose son is he?" and one of the aunts said that we were just renting an apartment. "That's my grandson," um-Bassem said. "As dear to me as a son." Afterward she took me inside and told me in a whisper that Bassem had gotten me the best plane of all but that she was keeping it with her because she didn't want the other children to get jealous. It was a long time before I understood that she had gone out the next day to Petach Tikva to buy me the remote-control airplane.

Mom and I had lived with um-Bassem ever since we left Tira. The unit we lived in was a little apartment that um-Bassem had built for her son when he left for Italy to study medicine but he had never returned to live in it. I was one year old when we moved into um-Bassem's place. My mother ran away from Tira the year after my father's death, when I was less than one month old. After the mourning period was over, my father's family and my mother's father, who was actually my father's uncle, demanded that she marry my uncle, my father's younger brother, to preserve her honor.

Even now I don't know exactly what happened, but I do know that my mother refused to marry my uncle and that she ran away from the village to Jaljulia. She left my father's house, left everything behind, taking only me and a small bag of clothes. The family never forgave her. They cut her off. Her family did the same. My uncles on my father's side and my only uncle on my mother's side never once came to visit us, not even on holidays when it's commanded that you visit the women of the family. I remember my mother crying inconsolably when they told her over the phone that her father had died. My uncle came to get me for the funeral but my mother stayed in Jaljulia.

There were five hundred shekels in um-Bassem's envelope.

"Mom, that's too much. I feel bad."

"Just don't disappoint her," my mother said, lighting a cigarette. My mother was always bashful when she smoked in front of me. She never smoked outside, only at home. Her eyes would ask permission before she picked a cigarette out of the pack. She was forty-five, but she looked older. She was skinny and her face was furrowed. There was something especially old about her face, about that unchanging look, a look that seemed to be forever apologizing.

My mother had bought meat and charcoal, as she did every year. On every Festival of the Sacrifice, she tried for us to be like everyone else, with smoke and the smell of grilling meat swirling out of the courtyard. "Will you light the fire?" she asked before going inside to prepare the meat and the salads. "Yes," I said, heading out to the yard. Small children played with cap guns and loud music bellowed out of aimlessly wandering cars. I dumped the charcoal into the grill and my mother came out with the matches and a few blocks of fire starter. "Use this, it's better," she said. "The lighter fluid leaves a bad taste on the meat."

Back when I was little, it was always me and my mother, just us, eating the meat of the Festival of the Sacrifice. We never roasted a lamb because "Who's going to slaughter it?" as she always asked when I wanted to have the same thing the other kids in the class had.

Now, fire leaped up from the starter blocks and I took the tongs and began building a cone of charcoal, taking the wind direction into account, leaving deliberate air vents in the construction. I used to like that, being in charge of the charcoal. I had to. "On the Festival of the Sacrifice," I heard my religious studies teacher intoning, "not everyone can afford to buy a lamb, not everyone can afford to buy meat. A true Muslim is considerate of his neighbors, considerate of others, those who do not have. A good Muslim gives meat to his hungry neighbors and does not think only of his own stomach." I remember wanting to be a good Muslim but I remember, more forcefully, wanting not to be the hungry neighbor on the Festival of the Sacrifice.

Um-Bassem left her house and shuffled, with the help of her cane, toward me.

"Let me help you." I said, approaching her.

"No strength left," she said, "you see what humans are?" She leaned on my left arm, the one I had extended to her, and hobbled over to a plastic chair in the courtyard near our house. She panted and wiped sweat from her brow with a white handkerchief. My mother came outside with a brass tray full of skewered lamb and kebab.

"You must eat with us, um-Bassem," my mother said, knowing that that would never happen. It never had and it never would. The orphan's food, it says in the Koran, is not to be devoured.

"I wish I could," she said, "but you know what my stomach is like these days. I can't eat a thing beside yogurt."

"We have that, too," I said, and um-Bassem laughed.

"Thanks, I just had two cups at home."

Mom sat on a chair next to um-Bassem. I flattened out the mound of charcoal, set down the grill, and rubbed it with a half onion that had been dipped in olive oil.

"So," um-Bassem said, "months go by and you don't visit?"

"I'm really busy," I said.

"Spare me," um-Bassem said. My mother sat up straight in her chair. "You think that I don't know?"

"Know what?"

"There's only one thing that keeps a man away from his mother," she said.

I said nothing.

"Come on, come out with it already, is she pretty? She must be pretty. You are a good-looking man and you will take yourself a pretty woman."

I started with the kebab. I lay them down on the grill and a cloud of smoke wafted up into the air. I placed a tomato-and-onion skewer on the side.

"What are you embarrassed about?" um-Bassem asked, "There are no strangers here."

"No," I said, "I really have been busy."

"So there's no girl? I don't believe it."

All I did was shake my head and flip the kebab and the vegetable skewer.

Um-Bassem exchanged looks with my mother, inhaled deeply, and started again. "Now that you've finished school and you have a profession it's time to find the right bride, no?" She directed the question at my mother, who nodded impatiently.

Soon it would all start again. Um-Bassem would voice the words that my mother could not say, make the requests my mother could not make. Bride, home, land—for how long will you continue to surrender to your father's family? When will you demand what is rightfully yours? How will you ever marry without land? Who would ever agree to marry someone who has no home? You lack for nothing and you deserve the very best. What are you worried about? It's your father's land.

"I think the kebab is ready," I said, and my mother rushed over with a plate.

"How long will this go on?" um-Bassem asked and did not wait for an answer. "It's time you demand what's rightfully yours."

"Nothing's rightfully mine."

"It most certainly is," she said, raising her voice. "It's yours and it's also your mother's."

"My mother can demand what's hers on her own."

"Me," my mother said. "Why would they listen to me?"

"You should have thought about that twenty years ago," I said and immediately regretted it but did not apologize, making do with an apologetic look toward my mother, who was quiet, staring into the fire. Um-Bassem mumbled a prayer. After that it was silent. A round of fireworks exploded in the skies above the village.

I set the lamb skewers on the grill, spacing them evenly, knowing that they would not be touched. The thick smell of burning fat filled the courtyard. The wind changed directions and the smoke blew straight into my eyes.

CLEAN DIAPER

I went from being the roommate who spent too much time at home to the invisible roommate. Most days I came home from work at around four thirty, took a shower, got dressed, got my bag together, and left at around six fifteen for Yonatan's. My time with Wassim and Majdi was cut down to the rare weekends when they were off and didn't go home, which happened around once every two months.

Occasionally, I still considered quitting on Yonatan. I didn't really need the money. My social worker salary was enough to live on and the caretaker money went completely untouched. I did not feel the need to save up at the time, though. I had no plans for the future. The thought of the long hours alone in the apartment, waiting for Majdi and Wassim to come back from work, was what convinced me not to quit.

Also, I started to really enjoy my time there, up in that attic on Scout Street. The physical part of the job got easier, much more like what Ayub and Osnat had described: quick dinner for Yonatan, jelly hydration, and a long deep sleep, generally till the morning.

Osnat asked me every once in a while to switch with her on the weekend, or to come in a bit early, at six or even at five, and I was always happy to oblige. Sometimes it worked out that I would spend twenty-four hours straight with Yonatan. Osnat probably thought I agreed so readily because I wanted to work longer hours, to make a little more money, but the truth is that I was willing to take her place because I had nothing else to do and I preferred spending time with Yonatan in his warm room to being alone in the cold, empty apartment in Beit Hanina.

The day shift with Yonatan was not particularly tricky either. After breakfast, which consisted of the same jar of food and shot of jelly, I would put Yonatan in the shower, which was never easy but had gotten significantly less difficult, and wash him with liquid soap and a soft sponge, hitting spots that I don't even touch on my own body. Lifting his head and cleaning his neck, cleaning behind his ears, in his crotch. I would even bend over and meticulously clean his bottom through the hole in the chair. I'd wash his hair with baby shampoo. Then I'd pat him down with a towel until he was completely dry because Osnat told me that anything less would guarantee bedsores and all sorts of funguses. I dried him everywhere, even tugging the towel back and forth between his toes. When he was good and dry, I would rub a special cream on his body, occasionally massaging his muscles as I had seen Osnat do.

Then I'd transfer him to the bed, diaper him, dress him in clean pajamas, put him in the wheelchair with the headrest, and move him over to the window. Sometimes I'd turn on the radio to Galgalatz, which offered a constant medley of popular music and traffic reports.

Soon enough I realized that Yonatan had more than one frozen expression — sometimes he smiled, or did something that looked like a smile with his lips, and sometimes he made noises. I could tell by the sounds he made when he was pleased or upset. When he was tired of sitting by the window, I knew it, and I moved him back to the bed, and when he was tired of his position, I rotated him.

Even though it wasn't easy, I learned how to change his diaper and keep the bed clean. He had to be pushed over onto his side with one hand, held in place so that he wouldn't flop back down, and then with the other hand you had to take off the diaper, wipe him, sprinkle talc on his bottom, and then lay the new diaper out so that the straps were open and ready, and only then allow him to flop back down on his back. Then you could close the diaper, inserting two fingers to make sure that it was not too tight or too loose.

All this was done with latex gloves and immediately afterward I washed my hands with soap. Still, when Yonatan went to sleep I would go back into the bathroom, scrub myself up to my elbows, dig my fingernails into the bar of soap, and disinfect my hands for a very long time under a stream of hot water.

The thing I tried to avoid most was Yonatan's stare. I liked it better when his eyes were shut. There was something scary about them when they were open. Everything about this limp creature seemed so healthy: his straight, light brown hair, which was cut every two weeks by a barber who came to the house; his smooth, pale face, electrically shaved by Osnat once every three days; and those wet brown eyes. Everything was as it should be. Yonatan was a good-looking guy.

Sometimes, after he went to sleep, I'd sit down at his desk, turn on the lamp, and leaf through his books and CDs. There was a big white yearbook that said Jerusalem High School for the Arts. Several years had passed since his picture was taken, but Yonatan hadn't changed. He even had the same serious expression on his face. The big somber eyes that never really focused anywhere. The only difference was that in the picture he was standing on his feet and there was a camera hanging around his neck, held in his right hand. You could see that he had used his index finger to take a picture of himself in the mirror. Under the picture, in a sloping sprawl, it said, *Yonatan, we looked everywhere, but couldn't find a better photographer to take your picture. Stay safe and good luck taking pictures for the army, you jobnik. Lots of love! P.S. Don't be so serious all the time—it's okay to smile for the camera every once in a while.*

Sometimes I'd sit at his desk and halfway expect to find him leaning over my shoulder, looking down at me as I touched his things. It seemed to me that he was completely capable of getting up and that he was deceiving everyone, lying in bed, aware of everything, not actually felled by infirmity. His body bore no sign of illness, no scratch or scar that spoke of an accident. He looked exactly like the picture in the yearbook on the shelf.

The main problem up in the attic was figuring out how to pass the time from when Yonatan fell asleep till I got tired enough to go to bed. I'd try my mother's technique, shutting my eyes and initiating yawns, but I was never able to go to sleep before midnight. I had five hours to burn in that attic. After getting the okay from Osnat, I started listening to Yonatan's music. Aside from the stereo he also had a separate CD player with small Sony earphones. "I don't know if you'll like his music, though," she said, "he has really weird taste."

I didn't know any of the albums that he had, so I decided to start from the top of the stack and work my way down. At first it had nothing to do with enjoyment; I listened to Yonatan's music in order to pass the time. I sat on the couch, opposite Yonatan, with an album cover in my hands and listened, trying to remember the name of the band and the song. When the album cover came with the lyrics, I tried to read along. Osnat was right—he really did have weird taste. The music he liked was nothing like what I had listened to up until then, and I don't mean Wassim's and Majdi's music or the Egyptian pop my dorm mate used to play. His CDs were nothing like what I used to hear over the radio on the Israeli buses, either.

The first album I listened to was by a band called Sonic Youth and their songs, the first time around, sounded like they'd been recorded in a carpenter's workshop. But I listened to it all the way through, and then again, and then I felt tired and was able to fall asleep.

SPOON, LEMON WEDGE, LIGHTER

Walid didn't waste any time getting Leila an active case and he asked me to accompany her on her first house call, to the Old City. At the time the Old City was one of the main drug centers in Jerusalem. All by itself it could have kept two outpatient clinics in business, but no one wanted to work there and only a few of the addicts actually wanted anything aside from their income support.

Leila showed up on time, at exactly eight thirty, half an hour after me. I tried to cover the awkwardness by rifling through the paperwork and shoving a sheaf of papers that I hadn't really looked at into a folder. I kept my head down and said, "Okay, if you're ready to go, we should head out."

I knew I felt something when I was with Leila. I didn't know if it was the same tension and shyness that I felt around all Arab girls or if it was something different. Either way, I tried to stifle it. I didn't want to be like all those other men I knew, drooling over every woman they saw. That's not who I am, girls don't even really interest me, I told myself, and I knew that it was precisely the other way around.

"You're walking too fast," Leila said. "We're not late, are we?"

"Sorry," I said, turning around. I hesitated for a moment, my eyes focusing in the general vicinity of her face, and then looked her straight in the eye. I blushed and felt my face burn and hated myself for it, wanting to run away.

"You're so shy," Leila said, smiling.

Where the hell did she get that from? I thought to myself. But I liked it. I saw it as a kind of understanding, a sense of trust, a lack of fear. Sometimes, when I heard my colleagues or even Majdi talk about girls, I was sure that if I was a girl I would be terrified of every man in the world. I walked slower, but still one step ahead of Leila so that no one would think we were together. I could've led us through the side streets and alleys that link Wadi Joz to the Old City but I chose to take the main road so that there'd be witnesses, so that we wouldn't be alone. We got to Salah al-Din Street and from there to Musrara. I tried walking slowly, at her pace. As we prepared to cross the street from Musrara to Damascus Gate, we stood close to one another and she said, "You're different from all of the rest of the guys in the office."

I crossed the street fast and Leila ran after me.

There were faces that I recognized at the entrance to Damascus Gate but I lowered my gaze and ignored them. Some of them were selling toys and perfume and others were just leaning against the stone walls. As we entered the Old City, I drew close to Leila and said, in a professional whisper, "Damascus Gate is one of the biggest drug-dealing zones in the city." It was a Wednesday, still early in the morning, and the foot traffic in the market was thin.

"How long will it take us to get there?" she asked, looking at her watch.

"Five minutes."

"Then we have some time," she said. "Do you think we could go to Lina? I haven't been there in a long time."

Lina's ground-floor seating area was full. The waiter pointed us upstairs and we found a table for two. I shouldn't have agreed to this, I thought. Leila flashed her smile, which I saw out of the corner of my eye. For some reason it seemed to me that I was making her laugh. The big city girl from the Galilee must've thought that I was a walking stereotype from a small village in the Triangle: the kind of guy who is embarrassed by the presence of girls. After all, she didn't know how they talked behind her back. I still remember a joke about a guy from the Triangle who asks a Christian girl from the Galilee if she'd like to dance, and she says, "Your name's Muhammad, you're from the Triangle, and

you want to dance with me?" For some reason I was sure
that Leila was a Christian, even though, as opposed to the
other Christian students I had met, she did not wear a cross.
Many of the Christian students wore one over their clothes,
displaying it so that everyone would know: I'm not a Muslim,
not really an Arab.

We both ordered our hummus plain, no chickpeas, no
fava beans. "Mmm, I love Lina," Leila said, scooping the
hummus out of her bowl with a pita. I watched her hands
work: she was not one of those girls who patted some hummus on a pita with a fork. She held the pita and she shoveled
the hummus into her mouth. Holding an onion wedge, she
asked "Do you mind?" and took a big bite. "What are you
doing?" she asked. "Why aren't you eating?"

"I'm not hungry," I lied. The truth is I didn't eat because
it seemed to me at that moment that it was embarrassing,
beastly, the kind of thing that should be done alone, behind
closed doors. Definitely not in front of a girl and definitely
not in front of a girl for whom I already knew I felt something, despite my best efforts to keep that feeling at bay.

"I'm not hungry, but I'll have a little," I said, and I
tore off a modest piece of pita and dipped it into the deep
bowl. I bowed my head and put it in my mouth, chewing
carefully, with my mouth shut, trying not to make any eating noises.And I immediately took a napkin and mopped
up around my mouth. When I eat, it always seems to me
that the food is smeared all over my cheeks and across my
whole face.

Skinny, curly-haired Leila with her small delicate face
finished her hummus fast and asked, "So, are you going to
eat all of yours?" and when I shook my head no, she pulled

my bowl over and ate it, too, this time with a fork and no pita. When we were done we paid separately.

Our destination was the Aluwad neighborhood, the home of Shareef Abu-Siam, Leila's addict.

"Where are the Abu-Siams?" I asked an old salesman who was sitting in a wicker chair in front of the neighborhood grocery store. He pointed at a green gate, behind which we could hear an entire clan of children. Ten children met us at the entrance and an elderly woman, whose hands were busy with her hair covering, shooed them off and asked, "Are you from social services? Welcome." The small courtyard was trapped between rooms and walls, and cement stairs descended from the upper floor in all directions and seemingly without any logic. Some of the rooms on the upper floors were unpainted and unfinished and the windows and doors were wide open. "Coffee or tea?" the old woman asked.

"No, thank you," Leila said. "Are you Shareef's mother?"

"Yes," the woman said, and immediately called out three names. "These are his kids," she said as the children clustered around her. "Two boys and one girl, and the infant's in his mother's arms." The woman pointed to one of the doors. "That's Shareef's house. He's not home, just his wife's around. God only knows where he is. He was once as strong as a convoy camel. *Inshallah* you will be able to help, my children," she said.

A young woman opened the door to Shareef's house. "Please," she said, "come in. It's cold outside. Son," she added, "go bring chairs." Her son ran downstairs and came back with white plastic stools from the courtyard and set them down in the small room, under the light of a single bare bulb. A kerosene heater burned in the middle of the room. Mattresses were stacked in the corner and, on a small pallet near the stove, the baby slept.

Shareef's wife looked to be less than thirty. She was wearing loose green sweatpants and an old sweater, and she sat opposite Leila, answering her questions with tired eyes. Shareef leaves early each morning. It's not clear where he goes. He says he's going to work, but he never comes home with money. He comes home at all hours. And he only comes home when he's high and has another hit for the morning. Sometimes he pulls out a spoon, a lemon wedge, and a lighter right in front of the kids and starts preparing his hit. He'll tie off and stick the needle in right in front of the kids. The young woman held a napkin in her hand and dabbed at her eyes and nose as she spoke. Leila sat before her with a pen and paper and nodded her head. She asked more and more questions, mostly about the kids, with surprising proficiency, unrattled by the tears, speaking softly but without pity.

The children don't go to school anymore, Shareef's wife explained. They weren't even enrolled this year. Why should I sign them up? Last year I did but they never went to class, just spent all their time roaming around the Old City. According to the neighbors, her eldest had been seen begging near Jaffa Gate, where the tourists congregated, and outside the mosque. Might as well stay at home, she said, it's better than having them out on the street. The oldest one was arrested for trying to steal a tourist's bag and that was before he even started third grade. The younger ones try to do what he does, they copy him. According to her friends, there are boarding schools for kids like hers and she used to think it was impossible for a mother to send her children away and not see them every day, but now she knows it's the only thing that will save them. "As long as they're put in a good place," she said. "At least that way they'll have a clean bed, food, and an education. Maybe they'll even learn a trade or something. If they stay here they'll end up just like their father, who's never ever going to stop using." Her husband's older brothers had locked him up in his room several times, keeping him there for days on end, swearing they wouldn't let him out till he kicked the habit, and he would yell, beg, and cry like a baby but they didn't give in—till they got tired of the whole routine. Then they'd let him go and soon enough he'd disappear again, returning home a day or two later, high as a kite.

Shareef was the youngest of five brothers, his wife said. All of the brothers had left the neighborhood. They owned houses in Dahiyat al-Bareed or in a-Ram, and lived there with their families. Shareef was the only one who had stayed on in his mother's house after he got married. Her mother-in-law, said Shareef's wife, lived in one room and they had the run of the other three. But the new residency law brought all the brothers back to their mother's house. None of them wanted to risk losing their national health insurance, their free educations, their blue identity cards. So they came back with their families and now all we have is one room, she told Leila, and then because they didn't have enough space they built two extra rooms upstairs and now the city says it will demolish the rooms because they were built without a permit, so now we have a whole legal battle, a whole other mess. In the morning, she said, blowing her nose, I stack the mattresses, and in the evening I lay them back out. Everyone lives in this one room, just like this.

Leila walked back to the office with her head bowed. She said nothing. When we got there, she asked me to remind her of the clerk's name at the welfare bureau and before leaving the room she asked me which boarding school was considered the best for at-risk kids.

CORDUROYS

I recall the smell of Yonatan's clothes. Somehow they held on to the good smell of the fabric softener and not the medicinal scent of the attic.

I showed up at Scout Street an hour before the beginning of my shift and hesitantly asked Osnat if it would be okay to come a little late the following evening.

"What time will you be able to come?" she asked.

"I'm not sure, but no later than midnight. Is that okay?"

She smiled. "It's only okay if it's because of a girl."

I blushed and let a stupid grin creep across my face.

"*Sakhtein,*" she said, turning to Yonatan and raising her voice, "at long last our shy friend has found someone. See!" then she turned back to me and asked for details.

"An intern at the office," I said.

"How old?"

"Twenty-one."

"Name?"

"Leila."

"Pretty?"

I nodded.

"You're so cute. Where are you going?"

"To a party . . . at the Hyatt . . ."

"And what are you going to wear?"

I shrugged. "I'm going like this," I said, pointing to the clothes I had on.

Osnat shook her head. "No, you're not. I hope you don't take this the wrong way, but you're not going like that. You'll scare her away."

I had never thought about clothes before. I had never bought anything for myself aside from underwear and socks, and those I had gotten at the flea market outside Damascus Gate. Every once in a while I'd come home and find that my mother had bought me a new pair of jeans or a shirt or some sweatpants. Before I left for college, she bought me a new wardrobe, clothes that were suitable for the cold Jerusalem winters.

Osnat opened Yonatan's closet and said, "Let's see what we can find here for you," and I was flabbergasted by the sheer volume of clothing. I had never opened that closet before and somehow I had figured that it held nothing but additional sets of pajamas. Instead, there were dozens of ironed, bright-colored shirts on hangers and alongside them a dozen pair of pants. The shelves were covered with stacks of T-shirts, arranged by color, and everything was clean and straight, not a single shirt out of place.

"You're Yonatan's size," Osnat said. "He has so many beautiful clothes. Don't you, Yonatan?" she continued, looking over toward his bed. "And you don't mind loaning a few things to our friend here for a date with his girl, do you?" She's not really my girl, I thought, all she did was invite me to come to the Arab students' spring semester party. On the other hand, it was going to be the first time I would see her outside work. A part of me was excited by the prospect, but most of me was scared.

Osnat flipped through the shirts and chose a black one with a starched collar. "Black will work well with your pale skin," she said. "Now, let's see what else we need . . . no, no jeans, I'm sure she's pretty sick of seeing you in the same jeans every day . . . Oh, here, this could work." She pulled a pair of corduroy pants out of the closet. They were what she called "off-white" and they had a matching jacket with brown leather patches on the elbows.

"Come on," she said, "try it on. I want to see how it fits."

"No way!"

"Shut up and change. Go, put it on, I'm in a rush."

The pants were a perfect fit. They were just right in the waist and length. I tucked the shirt in and put on the jacket. Osnat smiled from ear to ear when I came out in Yonatan's clothes. She turned me this way and that, walked over to the closet, and returned with a brown leather belt with a wide rectangular buckle. I threaded it through the belt loops of the pants and while I did that, Osnat went back to the closet and pulled out a pair of brown leather shoes. I saw five pairs of dress shoes and three pairs of sneakers. "These are about a thousand times better than your white sneakers," she said, pointing at the new-looking shoes. She looked me up and down and then pressed the tip of her thumb to the tip of her index finger, drawing a circle with her fingers and announcing, "Perfect."

"This isn't me," I said. I felt like I'd been stuffed into a costume.

"It is *totally* you. This is what you're wearing to the party. You look great. There's no reason for you to put those work clothes back on." I liked hearing that I looked good. The things Osnat said gave me some hope and for a moment I really did feel like someone else, just what I'd always wanted to be.

"You know," she said, "it's not just that you're the same size as Yonatan. As soon as you came in with Ayub I felt this kind of tightening in my heart, felt at ease with you, as though I'd known you for years and only later did I realize why. You look like him, did you know that? The two of you are practically identical. Don't you think, Yonatan?" She took her bag, wished me a good shift, and said good-bye to the two of us.

THE SOLES OF OUR SHOES

I got back early from the party. By about ten thirty I was on Scout Street, opening the door to the house and trying to walk on my tiptoes so that Yonatan's thick-soled leather shoes wouldn't make any noise. I froze when I saw Ruchaleh out of the corner of my eye. She was sitting in the dining room. Sometimes I forgot she even existed. My heart thumped wildly as I stood there, in an outfit that belonged, in its entirety, to her paralyzed son.

"Good evening," I managed to say to her, stuck to my spot on the floor. She was sitting at the dining room table, surrounded by folders and papers and an open bottle of liquor. I saw her look me over from top to bottom. She nodded, said nothing, refilled her glass, and went back to her paperwork. I went up the stairs, still trying not to make noise, to Yonatan's room.

Osnat was sitting on the couch reading a book. She looked at me and then back at her watch.

"What happened?" she whispered. Yonatan was asleep.

"Nothing," I said. "Everything's fine."

"You sure? You don't look so great."

"Ruchaleh is downstairs. She saw me in Yonatan's clothes."

"So what," Osnat said. "She doesn't care. Besides, at this hour, with her drinking, she doesn't notice a thing. Relax. And if it makes you feel better I'll talk to her and tell her it was all my idea. Even though it's totally unnecessary. Believe me. She's a good person. She understands. Do you know how many years she spent protesting with the Women in Black?"

As soon as Osnat left, I took off the clothes, shoved them into the washing machine, and put on the T-shirt and sweat-pants I'd left in the staff closet. I stood in front of Yonatan's CD collection, which I had begun to enjoy more with each shift, and decided on Lou Reed's *Berlin*. I slid the disc in and fast-forwarded to the song about the mother whose kids are taken away, the one that ends with the sound of wailing babies. I flipped Yonatan over on his side so that he was facing me. I lay down on the recliner and listened to the music. Then I took Tolstoy's *The Kreutzer Sonata* off the shelf and tried to focus on the text. I didn't want to remember any part of the party.

Leila had worn a long black dress and a wool jacket, high heels, and just a touch of makeup. The only thing I'd seen before were her hoop earrings, which she'd worn once to the office. She breezed past the guard outside the dorms and smiled at me. I think she was a little bit shy about her outfit, maybe as much as I was about mine.

"Hey."

"Hey."

We walked down the road together, toward the club at the Hyatt—it was called the Orient Express—maintaining a safe distance between one another, not saying a word. The only conversation between us was the clack of her heels and the squeak of Yonatan's leather shoes. Her scent wafted toward me. I looked down, trying to quiet the unrecognizable feelings inside me. What is she feeling right now? I wondered. Does she feel regret, like I do? Why is she not the same easygoing, funny Leila, the rambling Leila I hung out with yesterday in the office?

"Leila," I said, realizing it was the first time I had said her name aloud. I didn't even know why I said it, maybe I just wanted to speak her name.

"What?" she asked, turning to me. I shook my head, showing I didn't really have anything to say, and I looked back down at the sidewalk.

Leila insisted on reimbursing me for the tickets but she let me buy her an orange juice. I got myself a Coke. We were among the first people to arrive at the club. The music of Wadih El Safi played in the background but no one danced. We sat next to each other and still said nothing. Breaking her usual habit, Leila did her best to avoid my gaze. A considerable amount of time passed before she spoke.

"I'm sorry that I'm acting this way, but you have no idea what kind of interrogation my roommate put me through when she heard I was going to the party. She acts like a police officer, watching my every move, listening to everything I say, and reporting back to my parents afterward. She's disgusting. I can't stand her. 'Are you going alone? Who are you going with? Why are you going, anyway? Don't you have work to do? What are you wearing?' It's my first college party, I bought the clothes today. I went to the mall and got the dress. I'm twenty-one years old, can't I get some clothes and go to a party? Who does she think she is?"

The club started to fill up. Compared to what the students were wearing, I started to feel underdressed. I had never seen this side of campus life. I didn't know anyone other than my roommates when I went to the university. Leila's mood improved, she smiled and started talking more. "I just hope my roommate doesn't come in here looking for me with her *hijab*," she said, laughing. I felt good. The place was crowded and loud and the music started to get more rhythmic. More and more couples moved onto the dance floor. It started with Shadi Jamil, classic high-country stuff, then Sabah Fakhri, and from there to some very danceable Egyptian pop. It was obvious to me that Leila wanted to dance. She was moving to the music and singing along. I didn't recognize most of the songs, which surprised Leila. "What, you don't know who Amr Diyab is?" she asked.

I don't know how to dance. I've been to very few weddings, and that's where everyone learns to dance. In Jaljulia no one knew us well enough to invite us to any weddings, and in Tira we were simply not invited. I stood on the dance floor, not moving a muscle, while Leila moved gracefully before me. She smiled the whole time and it did not seem that she minded that her partner was just standing there like a lump of clay. Slowly I managed to convince myself that no one was watching me, that everyone there had something better to do than watch me dance, and I began to move my body. I imitated what the men around me were doing and I kept a safe distance from Leila, reminding myself that she was a colleague. All of a sudden I froze, realizing that someone was watching me. The guy next to me moved, and past him I saw Khalil. He raised a bottle of beer, offering me a silent cheer, and then burst out laughing. Shadi and Walid were sitting beside him. I didn't move. I could just hear their comments and their sniggering. I could read the ridicule in their eyes. Leila noticed that something was bothering me, looked over at their table, and then turned back to me, still dancing, and made a *who cares?* shrug with her shoulders and a scrunching up of her face. She tried smiling again and went on dancing but she realized that I was no longer there, on the dance floor at the Orient Express. Five minutes later I told Leila I was leaving, and did not wait for a response.

Leaving Yonatan's place and walking toward the bus stop on Herzl Boulevard, everything became clear. Enough. This

cannot go on. I'll put an end to it today. I had a clear vision
of exactly how I was going to change my life. Images of the
revolution played in my mind. I was done turning the other
cheek. Why should I let those jerks dominate me? How had
I let myself be so stupid, leaving Leila like that?

Ruchaleh's white car pulled into the bus stop. "You
going to the office?" she asked.

"Yes, thank you," I said and got in.

If she says anything about the clothes, I won't so much
as apologize, I told myself. I'm done being scared. Completely done. If she says one word, I'll get out of the car
and never come back to her son's stinking attic. I don't need
this crappy job.

But Ruchaleh did not mention clothes. She said nothing
the entire time. She drove quietly, as always, her face very
much like Yonatan's, her gaze, like his, fixed nowhere and
everywhere. In my head I heard Metallica's slashing gui-
tars, my soundtrack for the morning's revolution. I imagined
myself in the office, standing tall, head and shoulders above
everyone else, yelling, putting them back in their places,
and they, my colleagues, cowering, silent, the smiles wiped
off their faces, understanding that their days of toying with
me were over. Or maybe I should forget the office and go
straight to Leila's dorm? I'll buy flowers and wait for her
by the entrance to the building. I'll stand there for all to
see, even her roommate with the *hijab* and I'll give her the
flowers and I won't even whisper when I say, "I love you."

"Thank you," I said to Ruchaleh as she pulled the car
up to the front of the building. I walked differently. I could
feel it in my feet and hear it in the sounds of my shoes.
I felt like a new man, strong, proud, unafraid, marching

toward a revolution with a spade in one hand and a rifle in the other.

It was eight in the morning and I had a solid two hours before anyone would come into the office. I imagined Khalil coming in first, smiling at me and saying, "What, just like that you leave a girl hanging?" I won't say a thing to him. Not a word. I'll wait for everyone to show up, wait for them to start their day, their usual gossip and sniggering, and then, when they pull out their change for the breakfast run, I'll throw it back in their faces and launch my attack. I won't be defensive in any way. I'll stay on the attack, my face burning with rage. I'll show them who's a wimp. I'll show them how lame it is to think every girl in the world is just a pair of legs and an ass. I don't care if Walid's there or not. I won't yell at him, but I've got no problem letting him hear what I think of my colleagues. I could see them sinking into their chairs and me going back to work as though nothing had happened, my chest threatening to burst with pride.

"A battle," I heard my mother's voice say, just as she did whenever I stood before her, bruised but not crying, and she knew I had been beaten up again on the way back from school. "A battle," I could hear her say, "is like when two people bite each other's fingers. It hurts both of them but the loser is the one who admits it first." (Only later did I learn that she had been quoting from some Vietcong revolutionary whose book she had on her shelf.)

I remembered that sentence well, even though it had never been relevant to me. I never felt like I was biting anyone's finger; it was only my finger in my adversary's mouth and I never thought there was any chance that he would cry out before me. I never fought back. I just tried to deflect the blows as best I could and then run away. Just like my mother, who ran away, too, years before I ever had to, and who explained that she had done it because of me, for me, because she didn't want me to suffer, to feel unwanted and alienated. Later she told me that she didn't run away so much as sneak me away, just as she did again in the middle of the school year in elementary school when she heard that I was being picked on, this time smuggling me into a Jewish school in Petach Tikva, using every last one of her connections with the teachers union. I went to that school for two years and I liked it a whole lot better. No one told me that my father had murdered anybody or that I was the son of a collaborator. The kids simply did not speak to me and I did not speak to them. I was good in school, though, and soon enough I learned the language, learned to speak like them, and even started writing better than most of them.

When Mom made me go back to Jaljulia for junior high, I started to cry, but she said it wasn't up to her, that the school guidance counselor had said that I wasn't getting along in Petach Tikva, that it was not the right place for me. In junior high and in high school I was no longer beaten up, because my mother was a teacher at the school and she kept a close eye on me. Twice a day at least she would come into class and ask how I was doing. That's when I started to keep my distance from her and today I regret that I can't so much as imagine a hug from her.

Five minutes after I arrived at the office, the images of the revolution started to fade. I remembered that it was Leila's day to come into the office and that she would be in soon. I left the room, locked the door, told the janitor that I wasn't feeling well, and asked him to tell Walid that I had gone to the doctor. I punched my card and left. That evening I left for Scout Street half an hour early. I got off the bus near the courthouse and walked in the dark to the empty office, holding an envelope and a printed letter. The text was short. Beneath the date and the subject I had written, *I quit,* and beneath that I had scribbled my signature. I knew that no one would come looking for me. I pushed the envelope into Walid's mailbox.

In my box I saw a small piece of paper. It said, *I waited for you, but you didn't come. I hope everything's all right. I wanted to thank you for last night. It was wonderful. Call me tomorrow?*

PART THREE

VANITY CASE

The lawyer put out his cigarette, opened the study door, and crept up the stairs. His wife's cell phone was charging on a table in the living room. The lawyer went into the bedroom where his wife and son slept. Out of habit, he held his breath, listening for the sounds of his son's respiration. By the foot of the bed he found his wife's leather attaché case, the one he had bought her for her twenty-seventh birthday. Of course, it was on the floor. She always peeled off her clothes, kicked off her shoes, and dumped her bag on the floor, a habit that the lawyer had attributed to carelessness or the permanent frenzy of a woman returning from work to a house full of children. Now, though, as he lifted the bag, he realized that her behavior, the scattering of her belongings despite his protestations, was a sort of revolt, a statement, a piece of writing on the wall that any clear-eyed person would've understood.

The lawyer went back downstairs, cradling his wife's attaché case and her telephone. There was no chance that she would wake up at night, and even if she did she'd never look for her bag or her phone. She was a woman who constantly misplaced her things, running around the house looking for her bag only to remember that she had left it in the car, or worse, at work. The telephone was even more elusive and on most mornings she had to hunt it down by calling it from the landline.

The lawyer took her appointment book out of the bag, a thin blue notebook embossed with the seal of the union of social workers in Israel, given to their members as an annual Rosh Hashanah present. He flipped it open, looking for a sample of her handwriting, hoping, in a dimly lit part of his brain, that he had only imagined the similarity. He reread the note and felt a sharp pain at the sight of the words, *I waited for you, but you didn't come* . . . The appointment book was filled with telephone numbers, random notes, and what looked like patients' names. He slid the book back into the attaché case and found a bunch of loose paper, notes that she had kept, most of them old. Why does she keep these things? he wondered, angered again at her disorder. He examined the notes, hoping to find something suspicious, a smoking gun. But what exactly did he think he'd discover? Another love letter? A doodle of an arrow-pierced heart with her and her lover's names? Every sentence, every line, roused his suspicion, but he did not find any hard evidence in his wife's briefcase. He then looked through the main compartment of her bag, where he found patient files and academic articles.

The lawyer decided to comb through her cell phone, too. First, he checked the in-box, where he found several unfamiliar names, and even though the names were mostly female, or at least listed as such, and the messages seemed benign, he wrote them down. The lawyer knew that he no longer had the privilege of assuming that everything was as it seemed. The note itself already proved how devious she was: she had neither addressed nor signed her procla-mation of love. Only now did he realize that the woman he had always believed to be disorganized and blundering was actually a cautious and deliberate plotter who left no trail. By the time he went through her sent messages, the lawyer no longer expected to find any incriminating evidence, and, in fact, most of the messages he saw had been sent to him, undoubtedly because she had erased the rest, knowing that the day would come when her husband's suspicions would be aroused.

The lawyer shut off her phone—which was listed under his name, for tax purposes—and decided to order an itemized bill from the phone company. He'd go over the statements, looking for long calls and unidentified numbers.

The act of investigation took the edge off the lawyer's pain. Now that he was involved in the assembly of evidence, the betrayal was just another case, details that had to be amassed and marshaled to form a convincing argument, but that sense of relief faded when he opened a pocket in his wife's briefcase and found her compact. He felt his jaw lock. She, who always ridiculed women who spent hours in front of the mirror, carried a compact to work. Just like the women he eyed during his daily commute, the ones who applied their makeup at red lights, and he thought of her flipping down the sun visor on the car he'd bought for her, examining her face in the small mirror, pulling out her compact, pursing her lips, putting on lipstick, tousling her hair, consulting with the mirror again, and then painting her eyelashes, powdering her nose. The whore. The bitch.

Why didn't she wear makeup at home? Why did she criticize those women and then do the exact same thing? At least they were open about their vanity. They did not hide their daily routines from their husbands. And it turned out that she, who complained mightily before every event that demanded makeup, hid a compact in her own bag, and not just any old compact, but one that he had bought for her several years earlier, because the lawyer liked women who wore makeup and had hoped that his wife would follow their example, arousing, in that way, his dwindling passion. And she, ever so cruelly, kept from him what she happily gave to others. He envisioned her in the bathroom at work, taking off her makeup before coming home to him, even though he was never around when she returned.

Again the lawyer was furious. Again he felt the same quickening of his heartbeat, the same desire to slit her throat, to tear open the veins of her neck. With trembling hands he lit another cigarette, trying to make order of his thoughts. After all, he had a plan, and an alternate plan. He was a criminal lawyer and though he had never handled any divorce cases, he knew the difference between Israeli family court and Sharia court. He knew that whoever filed first decided where the case would be held, and he knew, as did every Muslim man, that he would be better off in the Sharia courts, where a man, if he can prove his wife's infidelity, can strip her of everything she has. What's more, barring any unusual circumstances, the kids stay with the father. If he was able to prove to the judges that she had cheated on him, she'd never see her kids again. The letter he'd found was insufficient, but he'd find other evidence, incontrovertible, and as soon as he did, he'd rush to the Sharia court in east Jerusalem. In the meantime, she had to remain completely unaware. She could not have even the slightest sense of his suspicions, because if she realized what he was up to and filed first—in an Israeli family court—she'd get it all: alimony, the house, the kids.

The lawyer put out the cigarette. He took a piece of paper with his wife's handwriting in Arabic and the incriminating note and placed them in his briefcase, clicking the combination lock shut. She can't have the slightest indication, he thought, and immediately shoved the damned *Kreutzer Sonata* back into the briefcase, too. He padded out of the study and climbed the stairs, putting her phone back in its place and her bag by the foot of the bed. He listened to his son's breathing and cast an involuntary glance at his wife, saw her sleeping on her side, her legs bare to the thigh, and felt a surge of passion that he had been sure he had long since lost.

ALARM

The lawyer left the house at five in the morning. He wasn't sure if he wanted his wife to be aware of this or not, but still he slammed the door behind him. On the one hand, he'd already decided that he should act as though all was normal. On the other hand, he wanted to vent, to express his rage, for her to know just how much he hated her. Walking toward his car, he hoped that she had been jolted awake, that she was in the process of fumbling toward the door and would come chasing after him, wondering why he had decided to leave so early. That didn't happen. Instead, he sat down in the cold driver's seat, started the car, and pressed hard on the accelerator, hoping the growl of the engine would wake her. Maybe it did, and maybe she had decided it was best not to pursue him and not to ask too many questions. It was rare for him to go into the office on a Friday and rarer still for him to go in this early. Throughout the commute to work he waited for her call, eager to hear the tremor of worry in her voice, but his phone did not ring.

He parked in the usual spot. The lot was empty and the guard had not yet arrived. He walked down the steps to King George Street. A police car, lights flickering in silence, coasted down the empty street and a municipal sanitation crew picked up the stray garbage. Cartons of bread and boxes of vegetables were stacked against closed restaurant doors. Weekend editions of the papers, lashed into knee-high cubes, waited outside convenience stores. Milk crates were parked in front of cafés. The scene was pleasing to the lawyer, who walked down the street in a short-sleeved shirt holding a black leather attaché case in his right hand, the morning chill toying with the hair on his arms, and he shivered once in pleasure.

Friday was a day off at the office. Most of the businesses downtown worked a half day on Friday but the lawyer, whose clients were generally Arabs, decided to keep his office closed on the Muslim holy day, not least because on Fridays the security forces tightened the ring around Jerusalem, keeping worshippers from the West Bank away from the al-Aqsa Mosque, making it that much harder for his clients to sneak into the city. The old stone office building was dark and he turned on the light and went up the stairs to the first floor. A few seconds later he heard the alarm spring to life. For a moment he was nervous because he had no clear recollection of the code, but without thinking he punched in five digits and the alarm stopped. He flipped the lights on in the office and had the feeling that he was not alone. He walked toward the conference room, opened the door hesitantly, and peered in, looking at the oval hardwood table, the couches, and the long decorative rows of law books that were never opened.

The lawyer peeked into Tarik's office and knocked on the bathroom door. Then, just to make sure, he looked inside. He unlocked his own office and scanned the room. He checked the windows to see if they had been broken and whether the security bars were still in place. Once he was sure that he was alone, he laid his briefcase on the table and went to make himself a cup of coffee. He had been in the same office for five years and even though it had never been broken into he was sure that the first burglary was imminent. The offices and businesses in the area were frequently burglarized, and he, as an outsider, was sure he was being targeted. He'd already had to replace the Hebrew, Arabic, and English brass sign outside the building several times because his name, and later Tarik's, too, had been spray painted over, a thick black stripe through the Arabic.

It was five thirty. Why was she not calling? He was pretty sure that this was when his son started to wake up. Had she gotten up at all when he left the house or had she slept through the whole thing? She had been tired last night. The guests had left late and she, of course, had to put the dishes in the dishwasher, tidy up the living room, and mop the kitchen floor. She must be exhausted, the lawyer told himself, looking at his watch and deciding to give her a little more time.

He opened his briefcase, took out *The Kreutzer Sonata*, and felt another stab of pain. He felt like an idiot waiting for her call, thinking that if only he heard some worry in her voice then everything would be all right. Nothing would be all right. Nothing would be as it was. His hand trembled as it held the note written by his wife. He reminded himself that he had to remain calm, to give her no indication, but he didn't know how he could do it. How would he temper his rage, stifle the urge to harm her, and still plot her ruination? Because that is precisely what she had done to him, ruined his world. He had to be calm and collected, and he reminded himself that he had always been a reserved and calculating individual, the kind of strategist who plotted his each and every move.

The lawyer considered himself someone who was always prepared for the worst. He was prepared for the death of his parents, even though both were in good health. At first, as a child, the notion that they might die was awful, unbearable, until, with time, the expectation of their deaths became somewhat more tolerable and, perhaps once he became a father, even inconsequential. The lawyer went so far as to envision losing his children, preparing himself for that eventuality, too. He imagined what would happen if one of his children was struck by disease, or SIDS, or an accident at school. The thought of enduring such a thing was particularly gruesome, rather like his childhood thoughts about the loss of his parents, but he knew he had to be prepared. Of course, he had devoted some thought to the death of his wife as well, and to be perfectly honest that thought was not as painful as the other ones, the wound was of a far more tolerable variety, the kind that can be overcome, but when he screened those images in his mind, there was no escaping the image of his children weeping for their lost mother, and so, at this stage, when the loss of either parent

would be a debilitating blow to the children, he hoped that
they would both retain their health. That said, he had an
unformed feeling, from somewhere deep inside, that once
his children reached an age where the loss of their parents
would not be that awful, he would consider the loss of his
wife to be a desirable eventuality. Even when their relationship seemed solid he would occasionally, perhaps before
sleep, imagine a brighter future without her. And now, for
the first time, he was shaken by the understanding that she
apparently felt likewise. Before sleep, she, too, longed for
the death of her husband.

How had it come to pass that he, who prepared himself
for every scenario, had not even considered the possibility
that his wife might cheat on him? He'd heard innumerable
stories about infidelity but had always thought that such
behavior was the domain of a certain kind of woman and
that it could only happen to men who were nothing like him.
How naive and idiotic. The lawyer was sorry he had not
heeded the advice of his sister, who had actually introduced
him to his future wife, though not intentionally. He recalled
how his sister had then tried to do everything in her power
to scare him off, but he, like a fool, cast it all aside. Not so
much because he felt an unwavering love for the woman
who was to be his wife but because he was committed to
the idea of marrying a woman that in no way reminded him
of his sister or his mother or the rest of his highly conservative family. The lawyer wanted something different, and he
thought he was smarter than everyone else.

His parents would never have sent their daughter to
study at the university in Jerusalem, to sleep in the dorms
without the knowledge that he, her brother, who had just

finished his internship at the time, was around and could be the *muhram*, the first-degree relative that could safeguard and vouch for her honor. "She's studying along with her brother in Jerusalem," his mother would always say to relatives and neighbors. The lawyer's sister had been wearing the *hijab* since high school and she wore it all through her bachelor's degree in education. It was patently clear that she would go back to the village as soon as she graduated, and try to secure a teaching position.

During those days the lawyer would visit his sister at least once a week but he never met her roommate because his sister believed that he, an unrelated male, should not be allowed to spend time in the company of her female roommate. The lawyer first met the roommate, the woman who would be his wife, on a night when she had gone to a student party and was not supposed to be back before midnight. The lawyer had accepted his sister's invitation to come by the dorm room with two mixed-grill sandwiches, which she loved, but the roommate came home early, just before ten. He recalled the moment: a thin girl with curly hair and a sad look in her eyes. He recalled the elegant black dress, the way it accentuated her body. He got up to leave as soon as she came in but his sister was compelled to show that she was not spending time with random men, and so, with little enthusiasm, she introduced them. "This is my brother," she had said, before he left the room.

The lawyer, a native of the Triangle, had always wanted to wed a girl from the Galilee. The Galileans tended to think of themselves as superior to the natives of the Triangle, and the lawyer tended to agree with them. He had been painfully aware of his crude country accent and upon arrival at the university in Jerusalem he adopted the more refined, less threatening accent of the Galileans. They seemed more enlightened, more educated, better dressed, better off, the products of superior schools.

The lawyer had known that it was high time he got married. He had just passed the bar and was working at the public defender's office, where he had done his internship, and was planning his next move: the opening of his own practice in east Jerusalem. He knew that he should get married or at the very least engaged before starting out on his own. The east Jerusalemites did not trust bachelors. They were considered less serious, less trustworthy, and, more importantly, completely off-limits to any Arab woman. Even for the purposes of business, no Arab woman would step foot in a bachelor's office. There'd be too much gossip. And women, he'd learned during his internship, were a slice of the market that he could not afford to lose—not so much as clients, but as the wives, mothers, and sisters of prisoners who sought his counsel. Palestinian families often sent a woman to Jerusalem to find a lawyer: they had a far better chance of getting through the checkpoints without the proper paperwork.

He liked her immediately. She was beautiful, he recalled, and now an unbidden thought set in: perhaps most people would still consider her to be so. The lawyer remembered how angry his sister had been when he called her the next day and asked whether her roommate had a boyfriend. She stammered and said, "Brother, she's not for you. She's not like us." She had no idea that that was exactly what he was looking for, someone *not like us*. He learned from his sister that the roommate was not in a relationship, at least not one she knew of. No boys came to visit the roommate in the dorm, but his sister made clear that it was possible that none came because of the restrictions that she, his sister, imposed. She went on to say that this girl wore short sleeves and tight jeans, that she went to parties and cafés, and each word only spurred the lawyer on further.

The lawyer was bashful. He was nearly twenty-five at the time and had never had a girlfriend. He had been attracted to many of the Arab students while in school, but he never struck up a conversation, making due with heartache and wistful thoughts before bed. The lawyer had no sense of how he looked. No one had ever told him if he looked good or bad and he himself was not a good judge. He always felt that different mirrors, on different days, provided different perspectives. Photographs didn't help, either. Like the mirrors, they showed something different each time. Sometimes he felt he looked good, but most of the time he was sure he looked bad. He was not too skinny or too fat. He felt his body was average, normal, not muscular—after all he never worked out—but not flabby, either. His height was average and he wished he was a bit taller, and his skin, like everyone in his family, was light, at least for an Arab. He liked being light-skinned but, much like with his height, he wished he was a bit lighter-skinned, and he would have been happy to have blond hair, or at least chestnut-colored.

Either way, he wasn't very much preoccupied with his looks: the lawyer knew that his profession, and his success in that profession, would determine who he would marry. He did not have much money and he had bought a used Fiat Punto with the little money he did have, but having graduated at the top of his class, from the best law school in the land, his potential earning power was unquestioned.

One week after their chance encounter, the lawyer went back to the Mount Scopus dorms. It was the middle of the afternoon and the lawyer knew that his sister didn't get out of class until six. He knocked on her door and no one answered. He decided to wait and walked around among the buildings. Within minutes he saw the room-mate walking alone from the bus stop to the dorms. She was wearing blue jeans and a white shirt with some kind of flower design on the front. There was a bag slung over her shoulder and it hung down to her knees. Her hair was long and curly and she was small, about five foot four, which was exactly what he liked. In those clothes, as opposed to the semiformal dress, she looked boyish. He saw her go into the building and decided to smoke a cigarette before going up to knock on her door. While smoking, he rehearsed his lines and tried to imagine her responses. They started out as charming and then got increasingly more barbed. He almost called the whole thing off but in the end he ground out the cigarette and bounded up the stairs with his heart racing.

"Who is it?" she asked from the other side of the door. He said his name and identified himself as her roommate's brother. She opened the door a crack and looked at him.

"She's not here," she said. "She doesn't get back till six today."

"I know," the lawyer said, flustered, stripped of all of his rehearsed lines. "Please," he said, pushing a bar of chocolate through the barely open door. She took the chocolate from his hand and said, "No problem, I'll give it to her."

"No," the lawyer said, shaken by the sound of his own voice. "It's for you."

He still recalled the scorn he had seen in her eyes. She stood behind the door, did not invite him in, and said she was not interested in receiving anything from him. "If you want me to give it to your sister, I will, but if you don't, please take this back and go away. I don't know you." She extended the chocolate bar in his direction, but the lawyer just nodded his head and hurried out of the building.

He berated himself all night long. He went back to his rented apartment in the Sheikh Jarrah neighborhood and waited for the call that was sure to come from his sister. He had nothing but contempt for himself. What had he been thinking? That he would offer her chocolate and she would invite him in for coffee and then fall head over heels for his charms? What charm? He was such an idiot. What a miserable decision, one that would make him look ridiculous in front of his little sister. He, the collected, deliberate one, how had he dared do something so dumb? He chain-smoked, tried to distract himself by watching TV, then by reading, then by looking through his casework, but his mind was trained on the sound of the soon-to-ring phone. He envisioned his sister coming home after class, walking into her room, and hearing from her roommate, as she waved the incriminating bar of chocolate in her hand, that her rude nymphomaniac brother had come by unannounced earlier that afternoon. When the call failed to arrive, he figured that either his sister had not yet returned to her room or that her roommate had left before she came back. At close to ten at night he decided he couldn't wait any longer and called his sister, expecting the worst. But she sounded natural, asked how he was doing, and said nothing about the events of earlier that day.

"Are you alone in the room?" he got up the nerve to ask, trying to verify whether the roommates had seen each other.

"No," his sister answered, and he could hear the sound of her door opening and he understood that she had walked out so that they could continue the conversation in private. But she said nothing about chocolate or her roommate.

"I've been thinking about coming to visit you," he said, feeling things out.

"Too bad you didn't," she said. "Maybe you could come tomorrow. My roommate's in class till eight. You want to come at six?"

The next day, at seven in the evening, the lawyer showed up at his sister's place. He was intentionally late, because he never spent more than an hour in his sister's room and he didn't want her to know that something was up. They sat on his sister's bed and talked, and his sister ate the meal he had brought for her. He, unable to eat, pored over the photos hanging above her roommate's bed. Some of them, he decided, were taken in the courtyard of her family home and the others in the living room. Her parents seemed rather old and she appeared to be their youngest. Judging by the furniture and the state of the house, their financial situation seemed standard small-town Arab. Her mother wore a flower-embroidered head covering, as women her age did. If all of her siblings were in the photos then there were three sisters and two brothers, and a few little ones, perhaps nephews.

The lawyer looked around for the bar of chocolate but did not see it anywhere. Maybe she'd hid it and maybe she'd eaten it. For a moment he grimaced at the thought of her throwing it out.

Just before eight, he parted with his sister and walked toward the gate outside the dorm.

The roommate was coming up the walk. She approached along with another girl and the lawyer feared saying anything to her in front of her friend. He sat stone still on the wooden bench and watched her come toward him. He looked down when he saw that she had noticed him. When he looked back up she was standing above him with her friend by her side. His face flushed a deep red. He had no idea what to expect.

"Are you here to visit your sister?" she asked. The lawyer got to his feet, looked bashfully at her friend, and nodded.

"I'll be there in a second," she told her friend, who said good-bye and left.

"What do you want?" she asked him when they were alone. The lawyer managed to draw a deep breath and stay focused. He decided not to get sidetracked this time and to act according to his original plan. Just as he did in court.

"I came to ask what your response would be if I were to tell you that I want to ask your father for your hand," the lawyer said. He wanted to make clear that he was not looking for a fling. He did not have time to waste and, as always, he had decided it would be best to be straightforward.

"What?" she snapped. "My response would be a resounding *no*, that's what my response would be."

The lawyer let the insult wash over him. He nodded.

"Okay," he said, "if that's the case then I'm sorry if my behavior has in any way been offensive to you." He wanted to leave as soon as possible.

"Are you out of your mind?" she asked.

"I apologize," he said, begging to be set free, allowed to return to his room to process the humiliation.

"What do you have to apologize for?" she asked. "I don't even know you. I met you for two seconds and then you come over and say you want to ask for my hand in marriage? What do you think this is, the Stone Age?"

"I brought you chocolate," the lawyer said.

"Wonderful," she said, smiling.

"Did you throw it away?"

"No, it's good Belgian chocolate. What do you think I am, an idiot?"

"So, what did you do with it?"

"I ate some and I hid the rest from your sister."

"You didn't even offer her a piece?"

"No! Your sister is a nightmare."

"You see," the lawyer said, starting to feel slightly optimistic, "that's already a good sign."

"What's good about it?" she asked.

"You already hate my sister. All women hate their sisters-in-law."

She laughed, a wonderful and uplifting sound.

One month later the lawyer went to her village, Tamra, along with his father and mother, and asked for her hand. During their engagement, she finished her studies and her internship and later, once they'd gotten married, they moved into a rented apartment in Beit Safafa.

XEROX MACHINE

By six thirty in the morning the lawyer was already starting to regret not staying home. He chain-smoked, and drank three cups of coffee in an hour. His thoughts were fractured and visions of his wife flashed through his mind; she seemed happy, smiling, beautiful, and attractive. Why doesn't she call? He pounded the table with his fist. Enough, he couldn't go on like this anymore. He'd call her father, tell him about the note, and politely ask that he come and remove his filth from the lawyer's home. But the lawyer was not sure how her father would react to that type of charge. Perhaps he would stand behind his daughter. Perhaps he would prove himself to be more of a slave to avarice than a guardian of the family's honor. The lawyer had no way of knowing. He had never forged any serious ties with her family. The Galilean family of his dreams, educated and rich, turned out to be far more modest in wealth and education than any of the ones he knew in the Triangle. Her father was a construction worker, her mother a housewife, and she was the only member of the family to have gone to college.

And why had she not yet called, the whore? There was no way she was still asleep. Was he so insignificant as to not be worth a phone call? But there was really no reason for her not to call. No reason at all for her to be suspicious, unless she had woken up while he rifled through her date book and her cell phone—but there was no chance of that. She had been asleep. He'd made sure of it. There was no reason that he could think of for her to be suspicious of him. Maybe the fact that he left the house on his day off and at such an early hour was enough to make her think that something dreadful had happened. Maybe she had left the house, taken the kids, and run away to the village of her birth. That notion troubled him, and he became certain that that was what she had done. He began dialing her number, sure she would ignore his call, imagining her in her new car, fleeing from him. And maybe she would answer, throwing the truth in his face as she drove. Her words would drip with derision and his children, seated in the backseat, would hear just what their beloved mother thought of their father. They were capable of believing her, the lawyer thought, shaking his head.

"Hello," she answered, and her voice revealed that she had been up. "Where are you?"

The lawyer was glad that she had answered. Her tone soothed him.

"Are you awake?" he asked, trying to hide the tremor in his voice.

"Yes," she said, "why, have your kids ever let me sleep in? What's going on, why are you calling?"

"What do you mean?" he asked.

"I mean, why are you calling me from downstairs," she asked, chuckling. "Why don't you just come up?"

"I'm in the office."

"What? Why? Is something wrong?"

"No, nothing, I just woke up early and I have a ton of work."

"Oh, wow, I'm such an idiot. I thought you were asleep," she said, laughing. "I've been shushing the kids all morning."

"Ha," the lawyer grunted, trying to join her laughter.

"Will you be stuck in the office for a long time?"

"I'm not sure. I can't really tell yet."

"Oh, God, now we're not going to see you on Fridays, either? Enough! You're killing yourself! You're coming for lunch, though, right?"

"What? Ah, I'll see when I'm done here."

The lawyer relaxed. It was clear she really had thought he had been sleeping downstairs. Of all the possible scenarios, he had forgotten to take the most logical one into account. After all, he always stayed in bed on his days off, until long after the house had come to life. Why should his wife have thought that this day was any different?

"Don't be late, okay?" she asked, her tone convincing. "And also, don't forget that I'm going over to Diana's tonight."

"I won't," the lawyer said, lying, having totally forgotten that she was supposed to go out with a few friends from work to see one of their colleagues and her one-month-old baby. Again he felt the gloom cloud his mind. The visit now seemed like a thin and feeble cover story.

"All right," he said, feeling his voice shake, "I should get going. I'll talk to you later. I'm not sure how long I'll have to stay here." He realized that this was the night to catch her in the act.

The lawyer hurried over to the Xerox machine and made copies of the note he'd found in the book and the sample of her handwriting from her bag. He went over to Samah's desk, took a sheet of stationery with the office letterhead on it, and wrote out a request for an analysis from the graphologist. He made clear that he did not need an official report, as he sometimes did, but merely a verdict on whether the two notes were written by the same hand. The lawyer added that the matter was urgent and that he would like the results ASAP, and then he underlined ASAP twice and left his cell phone number just in case. Standing by the fax machine, waiting for it to start to ring, he looked at his watch and knew he was sending it off to an empty office. It was not yet seven in the morning.

The lawyer walked back to his office and stashed the two notes in his attaché case. He prayed that the graphologist would rule that the two samples did not match. He imagined the man telling him that one of the notes was a forgery or that the two samples were remarkably similar but in no way the same. His heart would be flooded with warmth and he'd run out of the office and buy his wife the most expensive present he'd ever bought her and then go home and kiss her and hug her and whisper the kind of sweet nothings he had not uttered in a long while.

He stood by the window and looked out at King George Street. A supply truck rumbled down the empty street. Jewish men in white shirts and black hats walked past under the window, clutching their tefillin in velvet bags that looked like black pillows, adorned with gold and silver thread. All of a sudden the lawyer was sorry he had left the house without saying good-bye to his kids, without kissing his daughter and tickling his little son's stomach until he laughed the way only babies do. He sat down at his desk, looked at his computer, and scrolled through the morning's headlines on one of the many news sites. Then he went to Google and asked it to search for *why women cheat*.

The lawyer read through the results avidly, attaching scientific importance to the most superficial of claims, even the ones that appeared in the glossiest, most shallow publications. He was furious when he found out that women cheat nearly as often as men. The rationale was different: they wanted attention, empathy, and support, and when the husband did not provide those things, they sought them elsewhere. According to one article, women seek sexual satisfaction outside the house because their husbands are often tired and uninterested, just as their own sexuality hits full stride. A sexologist said that her years of therapy had taught her that women want to feel attractive and desirable and that all too often their husbands see them differently, as caretakers of the children and the home. Other women sought wealth — gourmet restaurants, diamonds, invitations to glittering parties. Private eyes weighed in on the matter, too, and said that from their experience female adulterers were far more cautious than their male counterparts. Marriage counselors agreed: women are more discreet, and they are better liars.

The lawyer fit all of these facts to his own situation. He went from site to site, feeling more humiliated than ever before. Going back to the search page, he typed in the word *hymen* and soon enough realized that his assumption that his wife had been a virgin when they got married was utterly baseless. He read all about hymenoplasties and how immensely simple and popular the procedure had become. He read about blood capsules that could be surgically inserted so as to satisfy the groom's mother, too, on the wedding night. The notion that she had fooled him from day one was more painful than the subsequent betrayal. The lawyer had never thought that the matter of his wife's virginity was important to him, but now he learned that it was, more so than anything else in the world. He remembered how he'd always told his friends that he pitied all those Arab men who said they would never date a girl who had a boyfriend. What an idiot he had been then, during those conversations, and what an idiot he was now. Only recently he had sat with a friend, the accountant, and laughed at him for saying that he was worried about the Arab-Jewish education he was giving his daughter because he was afraid that as she approached puberty she would think, like the Jews, that it was only natural to have sex before marriage. The lawyer could not say why his opinions and beliefs, the things he had thought to be a result of his nature, had changed so rapidly. Experience had taught him that he was a conservative. Yes, a conservative, and from now on he would not be apologetic about it. What an idiot he had been when he spoke out, time and again, against the treatment of women in the Arab world, saying that it was widespread misogyny that held those societies back. What an idiot he had been, quoting Israeli writers and leaders. It was not the financial situation, he had said, parroting those public intellectuals, not the occupation, not the rotten education system, but simply the treatment of women. Only now did he realize that their goal had been to bring ruin to Arab society. Only now, for the first time in his life, did he understand what honor meant. He, who spoke out against and even lectured now and again about honor killings, he, who opposed the phenomenon and labeled it barbaric, only now saw the error of his ways. He wished someone from her family would kill her. But who would do it? Which of her married brothers would risk arrest and a life of destitution for his children? He wished she was dead. But what about the kids, he wondered, and his heart broke at the thought of them mourning their mother.

STRUDEL

The lawyer walked along King George Street as it came slowly to life. The buses whooshed past with greater regularity, but were still half-full. The sidewalks were crowded with people, though mostly those belonging to the lower class: construction workers, sanitation workers, dishwashers, security guards, and saleswomen. "What's up?" a security guard asked him near a bus stop, and the lawyer, who knew that the security guards checked the Hebrew of passersby, and who always answered crisply and with a generous smile, now merely nodded, but that, too, sufficed. The guard did not ask to see his papers.

The lawyer knew that the bookstore would probably be closed at this hour, but still decided to try his luck. He stood before the locked door and read the store's hours. Looking at his watch, seeing that the store would open in fifteen minutes, he decided not to go back to the office but to get a cup of coffee and then return to the bookstore.

"Good morning," Oved chimed as the lawyer walked into the empty café.

"Good morning," the lawyer said, sitting down at the bar.

"Coffee will be ready soon," Oved said, and the lawyer nodded and looked over at Oved and the Arab worker as they got the café ready for the day. Oved pulled a tray of apple walnut strudels from the oven and slid in a tray of cheese *bourekas* in its place. The Arab worker transferred the strudels onto a glass tray and separated them with a spatula. "The machine will be up and running in a second," Oved apologized and the lawyer said it was fine, he was not in a rush, and that he would wait if he wasn't in the way.

"Not at all," Oved said, "make yourself at home."

The lawyer tried flipping through the weekend edition of the papers. He turned the pages and stared at the headlines, but made no attempt to try and understand what the articles were about, his eyes bouncing from picture to picture and from paper to paper.

"So, everything all right with you?" Oved asked, setting a cup of coffee in front of the lawyer.

"Sure, everything's fine," he sighed, making Oved laugh.

"You can smoke," he said. "It's fine so long as no one's in yet."

The lawyer's phone rang and he pulled it out of his pants pocket and answered. Seeing that the call was from the graphologist's office, he walked out of the café as he spoke. No, he told the graphologist, there was no need for an official report. Yes, the bill should be sent to the office as always. He knew there had been no need for an expert's opinion, yet hearing the man tell him that the two notes were identical and surely from the same hand only intensified his pain. Up until then he had been able to tell himself that the whole thing was just a figment of his imagination.

He walked back into the café with a fallen face, and Oved, who noticed his expression, kept silent. The lawyer drank his coffee quietly while his thoughts bounced around inside his head. He put out his cigarette when he saw Sara, one of the elderly regulars, enter the café along with her Filipina caretaker, her constant companion.

The lawyer thanked Oved, paid his bill, and left the café. More than anything else he wanted to go home and kick his wife out of the house, drag her out by the hair as he'd seen them do time after time in Egyptian movies.

The bookstore was still closed but the lawyer could see the saleswoman straightening up around the register. He smoked another cigarette and waited for her to come to the door and flip the sign over. When she did, the lawyer nodded a greeting at the saleswoman, whom he'd never seen before. "Meirav's not in today?" he asked, partly to show that he was a regular and partly so that she wouldn't suspect him of anything, even though there was no reason for her to be suspicious.

"No," she said, "she's not working today."

The lawyer went over to the area where he had found the novella. The books were still stacked on top of each other, unsorted, and the lawyer picked one up and winced when he saw the name, *Yonatan,* in the same spiky handwriting on the top left-hand corner of the page. He picked up another book and saw it again, *Yonatan.*

"Those just came in yesterday," the saleswoman said. She walked over to him and pointed to four boxes on the floor in the corner of the store. "They only unpacked two of the boxes so far. I think there's some great stuff in there. I'm going to unpack them and put them out today."

"Can I look at them?" the lawyer asked.

"Sure," the saleswoman said after a pause, "but I wouldn't know what to charge if you wanted something."

"You know what," the saleswoman said, slicing open the boxes with a penknife, "look through them, and if you find something you like I'll just call the owner and ask him how much I should sell it for."

The lawyer bent over the first box and picked up a

book, opening it slowly as though weighing its merits. He found the same name, in the same hand, on the same place in each of the books.

"There really are some great books in here," the lawyer said without bothering to so much as read the titles. "They all from the same guy?"

"Yes," she said, "it was a liquidation sale."

"What does that mean?"

"It's when someone sells their whole collection."

"Does that happen often?" the lawyer asked, trying to smile and leave the impression of someone faintly interested.

"Absolutely," she said, happy to talk about the book business. "Most of the books in this store are from liquidation sales, usually heirs who have no interest in keeping all of someone's books. They call the owner of the store and he comes to the house and gives them a price for the entire collection and then they decide if they want to sell the whole thing at once or not."

"Wow. So what you're saying is that I'm browsing through a dead man's library?"

"No, no, not necessarily," she said, giggling. "A lot of people also sell before a big move."

"Okay," the lawyer said, checking the name on yet another book, "so now I'm dying to know who all these books belonged to."

"I don't know," the saleswoman said, shrugging. "They came in during Meirav's shift."

"Oh," the lawyer said, disappointed. "There really are some amazing things here." He was trying to set the groundwork for what would be a substantial purchase. He wasn't sure how many he could buy without making her suspicious. He wanted to tell her that he would take the whole thing, to go ahead and call the owner and ask him his price for the whole lot of them. He figured there were around two hundred books here with Yonatan's signature and he wanted them all. He was sure that a careful inspection would reveal more of his wife's love letters and he felt scared and yet compelled to read every one of them. He burrowed through the books, pretended to sort them, flipping through the pages and looking for more notes. At random he chose the ones he would buy and set them down on the floor and placed the others back in the box. Then he looked at the titles. Most of the volumes were prose and the rest were about drawing and photography, filled with black-and-white photographs and coal drawings. The lawyer's heart thumped. He did not want to leave any of Yonatan's books in the store. At any moment someone could come in, buy them, find a note written in his wife's hand, and throw it out, thinking nothing of it.

The lawyer decided to take ten books now and come back on Sunday for ten more. By then, though, the volumes would be dispersed throughout the store, sorted by language, topic, and name of the author.

PSYCHOANALYSIS

The lawyer was hunched over his desk, boring into the ten books he had bought. He found nothing. Maybe the notes had stuck to the pages, he thought, and flipped through them again, more carefully, caressing each page with the palm of his hand, looking for little slips of paper.

His wife called in the middle of the day and the lawyer, hunting for evidence, answered her as he always did
when he was immersed in a client's case. "No, no," he said
in response to her questions, "I'm really busy right now and
I won't make it home for lunch. I don't know when I'll be
back. No, not late. Okay, 'bye."

Who is this Yonatan, the lawyer wondered, leaning back
in his large leather chair, and why would she be writing to
him in Arabic? The chances of a Jew knowing how to speak
Arabic were slim, and the chances of him reading and writing the language were even slimmer. What's more, there was
not a single book in Arabic among those boxes. Yonatan was
probably one of those Jews who chose to major in Arabic in
high school so that he could get into a top intelligence unit in
the army. But he knew it was still more likely that she would
have written to him in Hebrew, since her Hebrew was perfect
and there was no reason for her to make it difficult for him
with her swirling, calligraphic Arabic. Unless, of course, it
was part of their attraction, one of the games they played
with each other, the lawyer thought, and just like that the
evidence before him became personal. Maybe Yonatan is one
of those Jews who's always saying he wants to learn Arabic,
and his wife, Yonatan's lover, had decided to teach it to him
the hard way. If he wanted to understand the depths of her
love, he'd have to learn her mother tongue. Maybe it was a
sort of seduction. Maybe they both wanted to be loved by
the proverbial Other. Just a few hours earlier, the lawyer had
read that thrill seeking was one of the chief causes of infidelity.

For some reason the notion that his wife's lover was
Jewish was a relief to the lawyer. A lover from a different
world, who would not talk behind their backs to anyone

they might know—there was no doubt that this mitigated the crime of her betrayal. A Jew, especially an Ashkenazi Jew, would just be cheating, not trampling the lawyer's honor. A Jewish lover seemed like his wife's problem; an Arab lover was a disgrace. "He only stole from Jews"—that was a sentence he heard often in his line of work. That's what relatives would say when trying to prove that the arrested man was moral, because the Jews had a different set of laws and it wasn't really theft when the property belonged to them. It didn't even mean that much to the Jews, they said, because they were covered, they had insurance, they had savings accounts. Stealing a car from a Jew was more of a loan or a return to the original owners than a real sin that demanded punishment.

But it was also possible that her lover was an Arab like him, one who frequented used bookstores, and that he, too, had bought a book that had been signed by the same Yonatan. Or maybe it was the other way around, maybe the Jew, Yonatan, had bought a used book with no name in it and he had signed his name into a book sold to the store by the Arab lover. After all, other than the one note he had found in *The Kreutzer Sonata* the lawyer had not seen any evidence of correspondence. This seemed like the most likely scenario. His wife had gone out of her way to tell him about *The Kreutzer Sonata*. Why that book? She didn't care about literature at all. She had said that all of her classmates in the supplementary course about psychoanalytic theory were crazy about the book, but maybe she had just said that to cover up for a slip of the tongue. Maybe, the lawyer thought, *The Kreutzer Sonata* had just been a favorite of her lover's. He regretted not knowing who she had studied with, whether there were other Arabs in the class or not. The details of her professional and academic life had never seemed interesting to him and, judging by the income they generated, they had seemed more like a game than a career, a hobby that he encouraged so that she would have other things in her life aside from the house and the kids. It had to be an Arab classmate, the lawyer decided, a classmate who had heard about the book and then sold it to the bookstore, where Yonatan bought it and took it home without knowing that it held an Arabic love letter between its pages. Maybe Yonatan took the little slip of paper with the hieroglyphic letters and used it as a bookmark.

And maybe the Arab was not a classmate but a professor, an intellectual who wooed his wife with his knowledge and the fraudulent sensitivity that is second nature to psychoanalysts. Perhaps part of the seduction had been his instructing her which books to read, putting *The Kreutzer Sonata* on his short list. But why would a professor, who certainly made an adequate salary, sell his book secondhand? Maybe it was a fellow student after all.

Ideally it would be a Jew, the lawyer thought again. Aside from the shame and the fear that his wife's betrayal would become the topic of the day among his peers, the lawyer hated the fact that his wife was cheating on him with someone who read books. The ancient smell of the pages told him that while he had read *The Kreutzer Sonata* by chance, her lover, whomever he might be, had read it long before. The lover, who had seemed like a bloodthirsty wolf seeking nothing but the lawyer's humiliation, now seemed bookish, bespectacled, sensitive, and gentle, the kind of man who listened carefully to the lawyer's wife, understood her, supported her, embraced her. The lawyer no longer saw her in the middle of wild unabashed lovemaking. Instead she ran to her lover and took refuge in his arms while he stroked her back.

The lawyer, unable to remember the last time he'd felt tears on his cheeks, cried himself to sleep on his desk.

TUNA SANDWICH

He woke up to the sound of the phone. The office was dark and it took him a few moments to figure out where he was. He turned on the reading lamp above his desk, looked at the clock on the wall, and saw that it was already after six.

"I don't believe it," his wife said, when he answered the phone. "Are you still at work?"

"I fell asleep," he said. "I still have some more work to do."

"It's Friday. The kids have been asking for you all day. Enough with the work, you're killing yourself."

"Okay," the lawyer said. "I'll be home soon."

"Soon doesn't matter," she said, "I'm late. I'm going to send the kids over to Nili's, all right?"

"Okay," he said. "I'll pick them up if I get home before you. How long do you think you're going to be at Diana's?"

"No more than an hour," she said. "I'll call and see where you are when I'm done there, okay?"

"Sure," he said. "Sounds good."

"Have you eaten?"

"Yes," the lawyer said, recalling that since the previous night's dinner he hadn't had a thing besides coffee.

He went to the bathroom, relieved himself, then washed his hands and face. He went back to his office and, in addition to *The Kreutzer Sonata* and his wife's note, he chose two of the new books and shoved them in his briefcase. The other eight he put in a drawer and locked it. He shut off the light, turned on the alarm, locked the office, and left the building.

The lawyer knew where Diana lived. If his wife was really going to leave the kids with Nili, the gynecologist's wife, then it would take her half an hour to get to Diana's place in Sheikh Jarrah. He walked down to the Nahalat Shiv'a pedestrian mall, to the only café that he knew would be open on the eve of Shabbat. The downtown area was filled with freshly showered young men and women in festive Shabbat clothes walking toward the Great Synagogue on King George Street. The men had trimmed beards and wore white shirts and knitted yarmulkes; the girls wore their hair up, with skirts that fell below the knee. The lawyer thought they looked provocative for religious girls. He was jealous of these teenagers on their way to Shabbat prayers, noticing the bashful, virginal glances that the girls cast in the direction of the young men, all of whom seemed to be bursting with self-confidence. He thought of the guys all the girls wanted and of the ones they didn't, the ones who knew they'd have to make do with the leftovers, the ones who knew they'd have to bank on their parents' wealth, or their education—or, more likely, the fact that all of the best guys were already spoken for—in order to find love, start a family, build a home. The lawyer had never felt as repulsive as he did at that minute. He dragged his feet along in shame and hoped that none of the passersby noticed him. He had nothing but disdain for himself and his dwindling conviction that his success—his car and his salary—made him desirable. For years he had considered his wife lucky because she got to share her life with him, could reap the fruits of his sharp mind and his uncompromising diligence. But now he disdained himself to such an extent that for a moment he was even able to understand her betrayal. She, he remembered, was one of the more desirable girls, and he shivered at the thought that she might still be.

The café was empty. The lawyer sat outside and ordered a tuna sandwich and a cappuccino. Soft Israeli music flowed from the army radio station. The lawyer smoked, sipped his coffee, and, even though he wasn't hungry, he ate fast and wondered if he should get himself an additional sandwich. He looked at his watch again and again, but couldn't have said what time it was. He was checking only to see how much time he had left.

He paid, leaving a generous tip for the young waiter, and walked back up to King George Street, surprised by the silence that the sabbath brought. The only crack in the quiet was the clicking sound at the crosswalks, the signal for the blind. The lawyer's stride fell into rhythm with the clicking sound, tick, tick, tick, tick, tick. He looked at his watch again and although he thought he might still be early, he set off for the eastern part of the city, driving smoothly and without music, as though trying to avoid desecrating the sabbath.

In the eastern part of the city, Friday at dusk is the busiest time of the week. But as the eastern part of the city would shut down, the west would come to life, the neon lights beckoning the secular partiers, mostly soldiers on weekend leave.

The lawyer drove slowly, quietly, his heart racing as he entered the Sheikh Jarrah neighborhood and turned onto Diana's street, looking for his wife's blue car. Maybe I'm early, he thought, trying to console himself in advance, in case he didn't find her car in front of the new mother's house. The street was lined with parked cars on either side and the lawyer drove slowly, swiveling his head left and right, searching. Not finding it, he decided to call his wife and ask her where she was. If she said she was at her friend's house, then he would know for certain that his suspicious were correct. He continued to ease the car down the street as he tapped the buttons on his phone. The lawyer imagined how she would lie, looking at the screen of her cell phone, shushing her lover, inhaling, and answering him in the most casual way.

Before she even answered the phone he saw a blue car turning onto the road.

"Hello," he heard his wife say as he punched the gas.

"Hey," he said, "are you there yet?"

"I'm just looking for parking," she said. "The baby bawled when I left. Where are you?"

"I'm on my way home," the lawyer said, relieved. "I just wanted to let you know. Five minutes and I'll be there."

"Great," she said. "Get the kids. At least the baby. He broke my heart. I almost didn't go, he was crying so hard."

The lawyer drove home. Radio Ramallah played an upbeat song and even though he only knew a few of the words, he sang along, practically happy.

EGON SCHIELE

The lawyer's daughter fell asleep on the couch while watching TV. His son seemed also about to fall asleep, his pacifier bobbing in his mouth as he opened and closed his eyes. The lawyer looked at his son's face and decided that they had the same nose, not long and somewhat flat. Many people told him that his son looked just like him. He tried to remember some of the people but couldn't come up with any names. He looked at his son's big toe on his right foot. He had once heard that the big toe was one of the clear indicators of paternity, but he couldn't remember if that had been said in jest or not. He took off his shoes and compared big toes with his son, but was unable to say whether they were alike. By this time his son had fallen asleep, but he knew that he had to hold him for a while longer, until he fell deeper into sleep, otherwise he would wake up while being transferred to the crib.

The lawyer looked at the cherrywood-and-wire-framed clock on the wall, a housewarming gift from the accountant and his wife. His wife had said she'd be home in an hour. Or maybe that she'd leave Diana's place in an hour. He wasn't sure. As far as he could tell, though, an hour had passed. If she was leaving now, she'd be home in fifteen minutes.

The lawyer got up off the leather couch, moving as slowly and smoothly as possible, trying to limit his body's movements to the bare minimum and checking that his son's eyes remained closed. Treading lightly, he walked through the living room to the bedroom and, supporting his son's neck, lay his head on the pillow in the crib and then let the rest of his body follow. The baby opened his eyes for an instant and then shut them again, and the lawyer covered him with a thin blanket and returned to the living room to transfer his daughter to her brother's room.

"In the name of Allah, the most merciful and compassionate," he found himself mumbling, as his mother did, as all Muslim women do when they lift a child in their arms.

The notion that his wife would come home to a house of sleeping children was satisfying to the lawyer. She'd come home and smile and when she realized she didn't have to put the kids to sleep, she'd give him a little kiss. After that they'd have a glass of wine and climb into bed. Maybe they'd even shower together, like they used to do, long ago.

He took his briefcase and went down to the study. He lit a cigarette and knew his wife would be home before he had the chance to finish it. Would he hear her coming in? He was tense. He didn't want to miss the expression on her face when she realized that they'd have the night to themselves. But even if he didn't hear her come in, she'd definitely come down to the study to find him, kissing him in his office chair.

The lawyer did not want to open the briefcase. He did not want to see that damned note or *The Kreutzer Sonata* or any of Yonatan's books. He exhaled a long plume of smoke. The whole thing was probably just an awful misunderstanding. When she got home, he'd show her the note and she'd laugh and say, "Where did you get that thing?" and tell him the whole ridiculous truth. But the lawyer couldn't really imagine an explanation that would put him at ease. Maybe she had written it for him and somehow it had wound up in the pages of Tolstoy's novella. "Oh, my God!" he heard her laugh like a little girl, holding the note in two hands like a scroll, reading it and then remembering the circumstances under which it had been written. An honest reaction that would leave no room for doubt. Maybe something like, "Wow, I wrote this to you back when I was still in school and as soon as I wrote it, your sister came into the library, so I shoved it into the first book I found. How did you find it? I looked for the book forever. The librarian must have come by with that little wagon and taken all the books off the table."

That was not a likely scenario. Maybe she'd have a different explanation. Perhaps Yonatan was a colleague who had asked her to translate the sentence into Arabic for him. Or maybe she had written it to someone else before the lawyer had met her. But the notion of her having an Arab boyfriend before they met made the lawyer wince and ruined his peace of mind. He breathed deeply and tried to remember all the conversations he'd had with his friends, in which he bragged how enlightened he was and how he would not mind marrying an Arab girl who'd been in a prior relationship. He even remembered exactly what he had said to his friends, most of whom had always said they would never marry a nonvirgin, even though some of them had spent years together with Arab girls whom they called girlfriends, but who were clearly only playthings because, as they said, she who had relinquished her honor once would relinquish it over and over again.

At the time he had disdained those friends, particularly because they hid the fact from their girlfriends, sometimes for years, that there would come a time that they would unceremoniously dump them. What are you going to do, they would say, we weren't the ones who popped the cherry.

But if she'd had a prior relationship, why hadn't she told him? He would have forgiven her. But would I have? he wondered. Yes, if she had been straight with me, then yes. But she had not been. And what kind of relationship had it been? Had she slept with him and then had her hymen restored before the wedding? Had she faked the blood on their wedding night? And if she hadn't slept with the other guy, what would he think? If all they did was kiss? Or hold hands? Or write each other love letters?

The lawyer shook himself free of those thoughts and tried to restore the calm he had felt when he learned that she had in fact gone to her friend's house. He decided that when she came home he'd simply give her the note and see how she reacted, see if her explanation seemed plausible. After all, he knew his wife and he knew there was no way she had cheated on him. No way.

The lawyer put his cigarette out in the ashtray. He thought he heard a noise coming from the upper floor. He rolled his chair over to the door, opened it a crack, and listened. "Leila," he said softly, but there was no response. She hadn't come home yet. He considered taking a shower, perhaps even getting out before she made it home, but didn't like leaving the kids alone, especially the little one. He could wake up at any second and start howling and no one would hear him. But mostly he didn't want to miss the moment when his wife came home. More than anything else he wanted to see that smile, the one that would explain it all away, promising that everything was okay, that nothing had changed.

According to his calculations she should have been home already. But the lawyer figured that once she'd heard that he had picked up the kids she had decided it was all right to stick around at Diana's, chatting a little more with her friends. He would not call her. He did not want to be one of those men that are always checking up on their wives and are stingy with their free time. She'd be home any minute. Even though he'd sworn he wasn't going to look at the briefcase, the books, or the note, he couldn't resist. Just the books, he told himself. The first was a book of drawings by an artist named Egon Schiele. The lawyer flipped through the book and looked at the crooked, distorted coal drawings of nudes. He went through it quickly and wondered if the artist was someone serious or just some unimportant fringe painter. How does one tell? The lawyer didn't like the drawings much but he knew he didn't know anything about art and as he browsed he felt a familiar ache. He Googled the artist and saw that he was an important figure. I wonder what Yonatan does for a living, he thought, and then tried to impose the artist's name on his memory. Egon Schiele, Egon Schiele. Another scrap of information that could help him fill the glaring gaps in his education, especially in so far as art was concerned. He recalled how a colleague had once said to him in court, "Don't tell me you don't know who Chekhov was?" And that recollection led him to another earlier but no less painful one, from back in his college days, when a Jewish student had discovered that he had never heard of the Rolling Stones. He, of course, resorted to the technique he had learned from other Arab students, who employed it often, and responded with a question that was meant to underscore the cultural divide, "Why, how many Fairuz songs do you know? Do you have any idea what Al-Mutanabbi wrote?" And yet he had felt a sharp twinge of inferiority.

He looked at the signature on the first page of the art book again, *Yonatan,* and only then turned his attention to the other book. It was *One Hundred Years of Solitude,* by Gabriel García Márquez. The lawyer had heard of the author and the book. Maybe this was his chance to read it. He flipped through the pages. He stopped for a moment and made sure that the sounds he heard were not coming from the upper floor of the house and then looked at the signature again before closing the book. He went back to the Egon Schiele book and opened it to the signature page. Something didn't add up. The same word was written in the same place, in a similar style, but the lawyer felt that the signatures were different. He left both books open to the signature page and took *The Kreutzer Sonata* out of his briefcase. The signature on that one was more like the one on *One Hundred Years of Solitude.* Those signatures were written in bigger letters and, though they were written with different pens, he was sure that they were identical. Something must have been bothering Yonatan when he penned his name in the Schiele book, the lawyer thought.

When he called his wife he hoped to hear the ring of her phone from just outside, but no one answered. She must be driving, he thought, or maybe she was really close to home. She never answered when she was nearby. Instead, she'd park and come into the house and say, "I was right outside when you called." He looked out through the living room window. First toward the garage and then down the block, but saw no approaching lights. He decided to call again after he smoked a cigarette, but he called after two drags and got her answering machine again. This time he didn't even put the phone down, just immediately redialed. Why wouldn't she answer the phone, the whore. He exhaled in bursts and kept the telephone in his hand. He punched her number in again and again and kept getting her voicemail. The lawyer slammed his hand down on the table. He inhaled sharply on his cigarette and his chest began to constrict. Again he saw his wife frolicking in bed like one of those sluts in the movies, casting a sideways glance at her phone and ignoring his calls without any remorse. Or maybe she was sitting in the car he had bought her, and her lover, who now seemed to be the most manly of men, with wide shoulders and a chiseled face, was slipping his tongue into her willing mouth, and she playfully bit his lips and then licked her own. Her lover's lips moved down to her neck and she stretched up toward him, arching her back and moaning as his lips reached her chest. He could see this lover sliding his hands under her dress. When the hell did she start wearing dresses anyway?

The lawyer knew he had to do something. He thought he might take the car and go out and look for her and beat the two of them to death. He was capable of that, he knew he was. No man, no matter how strong, could stop him now. But the lawyer couldn't leave the kids alone.

He raced up the stairs, his heart pounding, hands balled up into a fists, fingernails digging into the skin of his palms. He knew she was late, knew there was no way she had stayed at her friend's this long. Where could she have gone? And why wasn't she answering the phone? He knew the answer. The lawyer went into the bedroom and opened her side of the closet. She had taken the better side, the one with more shelves and bigger drawers, the one with more space, and still she always complained that she didn't have enough room for all her things. He shoved both hands into the closet and starting clearing the shelves, flinging her clothes to the floor. Pants, shirts, nightgowns, gym clothes, underwear, all of it landing in a pile on the floor. He pulled dresses and jackets off their hangers, yanked open drawers and shook them free of their contents but making sure to do it in silence so as not to wake up the baby in the crib. He stomped down to the kitchen to find scissors, there had to be scissors! The lawyer whipped open the kitchen drawers, which opened with a smooth European efficiency, and rifled through the implements, settling on the kitchen knife.

"What are you doing?" he heard her ask, and spun around.

"Where were you?"

"What's wrong? What are you doing?"

The lawyer wanted to pummel her and yell at the top of his lungs, but he would not raise his voice, not if it meant the neighbors would know what was happening inside his house. So he shrieked softly, tightening every muscle in his body, "Where were you? Where?"

"What do you mean where was I? I was at Diana's. What's wrong? Is something wrong? You're scaring me. Are the kids okay?"

"You're a liar."

"What? Why are you talking to me this way?" She'd never seen him act like this before. "What did I do?"

"You're a liar. Why didn't you answer the phone?"

"What? When did you call?" she said, bending down toward the bag she had already tossed on the floor. She pulled out the phone. "You called? I didn't hear a thing. Look, my battery's dead," she said, showing him the phone.

"Stop lying and tell me where you were."

"What do you want from me?" she said, bursting into tears. "I told you I was at Diana's." She covered her face with her hands and ran to the bedroom. The lawyer wasn't buying her act. He ran after her. The pile of clothes on the floor added a decibel to her crying and the lawyer saw true fear in her face, the fear of a cornered animal.

"What is this? What happened?" she started backing away toward the wall, looking for shelter, fearing her husband as if he were some unknown creature.

"Why are you pretending to be scared? Just tell me where you were," he said, and she just sobbed. She curled into herself and raised her hands to shield her face from an expected blow, even though the lawyer had never hit her. He looked over at the crib to make sure that his son was sleeping through this. Not being able to punch her in the face, to crack the cartilage of her nose, made him feel weak and lowly. Someone like her could interpret his behavior as helplessness.

"Who were you with? I want you to tell me who you were with."

"What do you want from me?" And then more sobs.

"I know that you weren't at your friend's house," the lawyer said, shifting tactics. For some reason he felt at ease and in charge. "So tell me where you were."

She sobbed. "I swear I was at her house. Ask her."

"I did," the lawyer said coolly. "I called her and she said you left over an hour ago." The lawyer turned to her, full of confidence. He hoped to see true bewilderment in her face, for her to accuse him, or Diana, of lying and for her to insist that he call her back this instant. But his wife did not react in that manner and a listless, melancholy feeling began to spread through him, replacing the rage of earlier, when she said, "I went out with Faten for coffee at Iskandinia. She wanted to discuss something about work. So what? So what?"

The lawyer saw her fear morph into defensiveness and he knew that he had lost. He walked slowly down to the study and lit a cigarette, but he couldn't focus. He should have restrained himself, and now he hated himself for his impulsiveness. He had lost this battle, perhaps the war, but that wasn't what was on his mind just then. Actually nothing was on his mind, because what did it matter if he got half their property or custody over the kids. He smoked leisurely and felt his heart rate relax. He did not respond when she knocked on the study door. She opened it and stood there with eyes swollen from crying. There was no trace of the earlier fear. He looked her way and then turned to watch the cigarette smoke curl out of the open window.

"Can you please tell me what all of that was about?" she asked. He kept his head down so that she wouldn't see the failure on his face. "I'm sorry," the lawyer said softly, then reached into his briefcase and handed her the note. He did not look at her and he did not expect an adequate response.

"What is this?" she asked after reading the note. "What is this thing?"

"I thought that was your handwriting."

"Mine? No," she said, shoving the note away, the way children do, thinking that once you've hidden the evidence it ceases to exist.

PART
FOUR

FRIED SAUSAGES

For the first few weeks after quitting the outpatient clinic, I hardly ever got out of bed before noon. After the night shift with Yonatan I'd take the bus to Musrara and get hummus with fava beans at Akramawi's hole in the wall and then take a share-taxi back to the apartment in Beit Hanina and crawl straight into bed. Majdi and Wassim were already at work so the place was empty and quiet. Sometimes I'd go straight to sleep and sometimes I'd read one of the books I'd borrowed from Yonatan's library until my eyes closed. I'd wake up at some point, drink some water, go to the bathroom, and then crawl back into bed.

Wassim would come back at three in the afternoon. If he hadn't eaten anything on the way home, we'd fry up some sausage and eggs or make some tuna and cream cheese and eat together. After that he'd rest for an hour before his evening shift at the hostel. Majdi, I barely saw.

I stopped sleeping during the night shift, remaining awake until Osnat showed up in the morning. Ever since I told her that I had left the social services job and that I didn't mind if she came in a little late, she started showing up at eight in the morning. She was very happy with the new arrangement, even said that her husband was going to buy me a present because he wasn't in charge of getting the kids off to school in the morning anymore. "We almost got divorced over it," she said, laughing.

I spent the sleepless nights listening to music and reading Yonatan's books. There were 156 books on the shelves and 98 CDs on the racks, 70 in English and 28 in Hebrew. Yonatan had written his name on the inside jacket of his discs, too. He had nice handwriting, very delicate, like a good student or a pretty girl.

On one of the top shelves he had a fine collection of hardcover art books. Most of them were photography-related. They looked old, filled with black-and-white photos. I looked through the photos occasionally, but mostly I was interested in the Hebrew fiction. I must have averaged a book every three shifts. Some I liked more than others, but I made a point of reading each one all the way through.

There was nothing for me in Jerusalem. I was an unemployed social worker. The night shift with Yonatan wasn't really a job and the salary I got barely covered the rent for my little room in Beit Hanina. I knew I wouldn't be able to spend much more time in this city, and each night I would decide that it was time to go back to the village, to my mother, but when the sun came up and the shift was over, I'd delay my return by another day. Sometimes I'd lean on the windowsill of the open attic window and take in giant gulps of fresh air, telling myself that everything would work out, that a new job was waiting for me right around the corner. After all, there was always a lack of social workers. I'd go to the social services' main branch, show them my diploma, and ask for a position, this time in the western half of the city. I'd show them that my Hebrew was as good as any native speaker's and I'd tell them that the problem with the outpatient clinic in the Arab part of town was my colleagues' miserable work ethic. I'd speak disparagingly of Arabs and the Jewish interviewer would nod; he knew what went on down there. This guy came to social work as a calling, he'd think to himself, not like the rest of the Arabs who studied it just because it was the only department that they could get in to. Everyone knows that Arabs study a trade in university. Everyone knows they want to be doctors or lawyers or accountants or at least registered nurses, and that their fallback options are education and social work. The university application gives you six department options and the Arab applications are all identical. My application had also had medicine on top and education on the bottom.

Once I finish charming the interviewer from social services, I'll go straight to the Mount Scopus dorms and knock on Leila's door and apologize for disappearing. I'll tell her everything I told the interviewer. She'll definitely identify with what I have to say and will understand how disgusted I was with the outpatient clinic. She's not like them, she's different—for some reason I had the feeling that she must have put social work first on her application. I'll tell her that I love her, that I'm starting my master's, that I'll definitely get a PhD and that it won't take me long to become a professor. I have the grades. I'll get a faculty position and be able to support her and she'll be proud of me and won't be ashamed to take me to her parents and their faces will shine when they learn that their daughter has snagged herself a professor. I'll tell her that I'm rich, not me personally, but that my family owns lots of land, and that will not be a lie but a statement of fact. Her parents could ask anyone in the Triangle about my father's family and they'd hear that they were the biggest landowners in the region. True, I'm not in contact with them, but I am a legal heir and any court of law would give me my father's land. I am the only heir and I could be rich. All I have to do is demand what is rightfully mine. "How long will you sit around idly," I have heard my mother say, over and over. "It's your future, your land."

Tomorrow—that was the conclusion I drew from all of those nighttime thoughts, not now, tomorrow. Tomorrow I'll go to social services main branch. Tomorrow I'll go home and start to wage my war against my family. Tomorrow I'll launch the campaign to restore my mother's pride. Tonight I'll finish the chapter of this book I'm holding and then I'll go back to the apartment to be alone.

PASSPORT PHOTO

I learned everything there was to know about Yonatan during those sleepless nights. I read every scrap of paper, every note, and every document that I found in the drawers.

Yonatan was born in 1979. Just like me. In his small, square ID photo he made a point of looking serious, not smiling, and in his eyes I saw a melancholic look that I interpreted as sixteen-year-old sincerity. Mother's name: Ruchaleh. Father's name: Yakov. Address: Same. Nationality: Jewish.

That was the first time I'd seen a Jew's identity card. I had thought that the nationality article on the IDs was something only Arabs had, so they could be separated from the pack, but it turned out that Jews had to be categorized, too.

In one of the lower drawers there were drawings that looked like they might be relics from Yonatan's kindergarten days. Blue, black, and red lines and a few attempts at circles. His report cards from first through twelfth grade, his class pictures. It was always fun looking for his face in the pictures and once I found it I'd look carefully at the other kids. They were all white and they almost all had European names, some of them Hebraized. Yonatan had gone to the local public school until sixth grade and then transferred to the elite Leyada School on the Givat Ram campus of Hebrew University. He had pretty much straight As all through school. I could see from the report cards that the Jews had a different system than we did. Instead of Arabic they had Hebrew and in third grade they started English; in junior high he took Jewish history and Bible instead of Koran. He also had art and computers, while in the village we had a few subjects that were not on Yonatan's transcripts, like carpentry and metalwork and Islamic religious studies.

He went to the Jerusalem High School for the Arts and majored in photography. There were shoe boxes in some of the drawers with black-and-white photos and, based on his grades and the comments his teachers left on his work, it was clear that he had done exceptionally well. For his foreign language requirement, he took French.

On one of the top shelves in his closet I found a padded black case that looked like it might hold some kind of medical equipment. I got up on a chair and coaxed the box out. As I shimmied it free, I felt that Yonatan had turned his head and was watching me, as though he'd caught me in the act. But Yonatan was in the same position, face and eyes turned the other way, always away from me, especially when I went through his things and invaded his privacy. The case held Yonatan's camera. A big camera, the kind journalists had, nothing like the little ones I'd seen at home. I put it on the table, sat with my back to Yonatan, and pulled the camera out of the main compartment. It was heavier than I expected. Alongside it, in their own compartments, were a few different lenses and a few rolls of film. I took one of the round lenses out of the case and tried to fit it onto the camera, cautiously, slowly, till I heard it click into place. I picked up the camera, looked through the viewfinder, and saw nothing but blackness. I checked the lens and saw that I hadn't removed the cap, and then I looked back through the viewfinder and saw before me a blurry, out-of-focus world.

BLUE LIGHTER

That night, while watching Yonatan, I smoked my first cigarette. On the way from Beit Hanina to Beit Hakerem I stopped in at a little convenience store in Musrara and bought a pack of Marlboro Lights, which was what Majdi smoked. A few seconds later I went back in and asked for a lighter. The shopkeeper took out a clear blue one and sparked it to show me that it worked.

That afternoon Wassim had told me he had decided to go back to the village. He'd gotten a job as a special-ed teacher in a school near Jat and he'd decided to go home, get engaged, build a house alongside his parents, and get married.

"If I stay in the city I'll never really be able to save up," he said, and back home he'd have no expenditures at all. Majdi was staying in Jerusalem for the time being, but not in the same apartment. He said he'd rather rent a place in Wadi Joz or Sheikh Jarrah, as close as possible to the courthouse and the office.

"If you want," Wassim said, "Majdi could find something that would work for both of you."

I nodded and said nothing. I knew that if something didn't give soon, I wouldn't be able to afford the rent much longer. But the knowledge that in two weeks' time I would no longer have a place didn't bother me; on the contrary, it was calming, liberating. I knew I could always sleep on the sofa bed beside Yonatan.

I got to Yonatan's an hour early. Osnat opened the door and told me that I was early and that she had finally talked to Ruchaleh about splitting the work into three shifts. She couldn't go on not seeing her daughter from seven in the morning until seven at night.

"We're just going to have to find one more caretaker, Yonatan," she said, caressing his hair before leaving.

I sat on the windowsill in front of the open window and took out a cigarette. I put it between my lips and lit it with the blue lighter. The cigarette went out. I lit it again, and again it went out. I didn't understand how Majdi and the rest of the smokers in the world managed to burn a cigarette into ash. My first one was just blackened.

I rotated Yonatan in his bed and returned to *The Notebook*, which I had started the night before. The book was about twin brothers whose mother hides them in their grandmother's small village during the Second World War. I was completely drawn in by the novel. It was one of the best I'd read and I knew that the night would fly by. The problem was that the book was too thin, too short, and even though I tried to read it as slowly as possible, I finished it within two hours. I rotated Yonatan again and then tried my luck with the cigarettes. I was sure the nights would be easier if I smoked.

I put another cigarette in my mouth and brought the flame close to the tip and when it touched the paper and tobacco, I inhaled deeply. This time it worked and I started to choke. I smothered my cough and felt my eyes water and threaten to pop out of their sockets. I ran into the bathroom, shut the door, and coughed hard until I was able to breathe normally again. I came out of the bathroom with my face washed and saw Ruchaleh waiting for me by the door.

"Is everything okay?" she asked, looking up at the ceiling and then directly at me.

I froze. She did not usually come up to the attic at night.

"Yes, everything's fine," I said.

"I don't want you smoking next to Yonatan," she said. "Not in the room."

"I, I'm, ah . . ." I stammered, "I'm not really smoking, I mean I . . ."

"Doesn't matter," she said. "If you want to smoke just go outside to the garden or come down to the living room or the kitchen." She shut the door behind her and left.

My face was flushed with shame and my attempts to smother another cough. I stood by the window and tried to breathe regularly, gingerly at first and then heartily, taking pleasure in the clean air now being drawn into my lungs. What did she mean, you can smoke in the living room? Where would she be while I was smoking in the living room? What was I supposed to do, go down there and smoke with her? I thought of how she never even really looked at Yonatan. She treated him as though he were transparent, looking over, under, and through him. What did she care if I smoked in his room or not? How was it that she was never by his side, that she preferred to spend money on round-the-clock care so that she didn't have to spend any time with him.

It was a little past midnight and I was not having any luck putting myself to sleep. I opened Yonatan's closet and carefully took out the camera. Soon enough I was able to click the lens into place. I looked through the viewfinder and tried to bring the items in the room into focus. When I spotted Yonatan, lying in bed with his back to me, I hit the shutter release and heard it click. The noise scared me. What the hell did I do that for? I looked at the door, waited for Ruchaleh to storm in and throw me out of the house. I quickly took off the lens, laid it back in the case, put the whole thing in the closet, sat down on the sofa, and listened to a long and undisturbed silence.

I tried to start another book, I counted cars passing below, and I listened to one of his Ministry albums twice, but it was still only three in the morning. I have to change my sleeping patterns, I thought. I have to be active during the days and sleep at night. It must be easier to be up during the day than at night. The thoughts that come and assault you during the day seem gentler and less scary than the ones that come at night. What's the big deal? Why am I not allowed to use the camera and yet allowed to read the books and use the bathroom?

I turned my attention back to the camera and tried convincing myself that there was nothing wrong with what

I was doing. Let Ruchaleh come in, who cares? She should be thankful that I'm here doing her job, taking care of her kid for her. She should be grateful that for a few nickels and dimes I come here every night, all night, and that I always come on time, even early. I looked through the viewfinder again, this time toward the street, the Jerusalem landscape at night, and pushed the button. There was no click. I looked at the camera. A little knob showed the number 22 and I realized that that was probably the number of pictures that had been taken. But I'd only taken one, so someone had used this camera before me. I hit the button again, without pointing the camera anywhere in particular, but it did not respond. I remembered that with our old camera at home you had to turn a little plastic wheel each time you took a picture, but there was nothing like that on Yonatan's camera. I touched all the buttons and in the end decided to pull a lever alongside the knob. I heard the film advance and saw the number 23 on the knob. I pushed the button again and this time it clicked. I pointed the camera at the bookshelf, brought it into focus, and shot. Then I did that again and again until I hit 36 and could no longer pull the lever.

BUS PASS

I didn't have much to move. The schoolwork, the folders, and all my papers went into the big garbage can outside our apartment building in Beit Hanina. The clothes came with me. I took them little by little in my gym bag, each day another installment, straight up to the attic in Beit Hakerem. I made some room for my things on the top shelf of Yonatan's closet, up above the camera. I had to stand on a chair to reach my stuff. Within a week all my clothes were in Yonatan's room. It was embarrassing to see how little I had when compared to the wardrobe of the immobile man I cared for.

At the end of the month, Wassim left the city and moved back to his hometown village and Majdi moved into a place in Wadi Joz along with another lawyer. I was left with no place of my own, but with a pull-out sofa alongside Yonatan's egg mattress. At first I tried forcing myself to get some sleep during the night shift, knowing that I had no bed to sleep on during the day. I told Osnat that as far as I was concerned she could show up at ten, but she said that would be unprofessional.

I bought a monthly bus pass and spent a lot of the time going from bus to bus, equipped with Yonatan's Discman and the CDs I chose each morning. They were my company until the next shift.

Sometimes I'd fall asleep on the bus and the drivers would wake me up at the last stop. I always apologized, got off the bus, and waited for another one. Most mornings I was in the Old City, where I'd eat a late breakfast of hummus and fava beans. After that I'd take a bus to Sacher Park and sit down with my book under a tree, passing the hot hours of the day in the shade. Sometimes I'd fall asleep, but not usually. Then I'd walk up to the nearby Nachlaot neighborhood, take a walk through the marketplace, go up King George, down Ben Yehuda, and around to Nahalat Shiv'a. About an hour before my shift started, I'd get a falafel sandwich or two. Half an hour later, I'd take a bus from downtown to Beit Hakerem.

A week of endless wandering was enough. I realized there was no way I could go on like that. This was in early September and I knew that soon Jerusalem would start to get cold. What would I do then? What would I do when it rained? At first I thought I'd just go to the university and spend my time in the library, but I didn't want to run into old acquaintances from school or the guys from the office or, least of all, Leila. At some point during the day I always thought about going back to my mother's house, but that notion retreated under inspection.

It didn't take me long to get back in the habit of sleeping at night. At first for just an hour or two, but within a week I was up to four hours a night. The rest of the time I soothed myself with music, books, and, especially, the camera. I wished I hadn't burned through all the film on the first night and that I could see the pictures I had taken. I played with the camera every night, putting pictures into focus and pushing the button even though I knew nothing would happen. I wasn't sure what you did with the film that was already spent, how you took it out and got it developed. One morning, though, feeling audacious, I snuck the camera into my bag and took it out of the apartment for the first time.

"Wow," said the shopkeeper in the Armenian Quarter as he sipped his coffee, "this is an excellent camera. Japanese. They don't make them like this anymore." He gripped the camera, looked through the viewfinder, and started to mess with the lens and a few other dials. "There's nothing like a 50mm lens," he said, "it's the best. No zoom, no nonsense, just like in real life." I told him I had bought the camera from some Jewish guy and that I was still trying to figure

it all out. "Does it still have film in it?" he asked, looking at
the knob and the numbers.

"Yes," I said, nodding.

"Do you know how to take it out?"

"No," I said, trying to smile. "I mean, I didn't want to
ruin it."

"Here, look," the Armenian said, pushing a button on
the left side of the the camera and swiveling a little handle.
"You have to keep this pressed the whole time," he said,
showing me the button, "and you swivel this all the way
till the end. Here, listen." We both stayed quiet and waited
to hear the sound of the film safely back in its roll. Then
he pulled a little lever and the back of the camera popped
open, the roll of film visible. "That's it. You take it out like
this. This roll's black and white. You want it developed?"

"Yes," I said, and the Armenian popped the roll into
an envelope and wrote my name on it.

"It'll be ready tomorrow," he said, to my great disappointment. I had thought it would be just a matter of minutes.

"You want a new roll?" the Armenian asked.

"What? Oh, yes, yes, thank you," I said, consoled by
the prospect of taking more pictures.

"Black and white?"

"Yes," I said, "black and white."

"What ISO speed?"

"Excuse me?"

"The ISO speed relates to the film's sensitivity to light.
The higher the number the faster it responds. There's one
hundred, four hundred, and more. Do you shoot at night,
too?"

"Yes," I said.

"Take the four hundred then," he said, grabbing a roll off one of the shelves. "Do you know how to load it?" he asked, and without waiting for an answer he popped open the back again, made sure I was paying attention to what his hands were doing, and put the film in the chamber. He fed the front end into a spool and hit the shutter-release button.

"The first two or three frames are goners as soon as the film is exposed to the light so just advance right on through them."

The film cost fifteen shekels and the Armenian, who saw the surprise on my face, said, "I gave you the highest quality stuff." I put the camera around my neck and headed out to the Old City.

EIGHTEEN SHEKELS

"Each picture's a shekel," the Armenian told me with a smile the next morning, and I cursed my new hobby under my breath. "All told, it's eighteen shekels," he said, handing me a bright yellow envelope. It took a moment until I understood.

"Eighteen? Why eighteen?

"Because all the other ones were overexposed," he said. I knew right away that the eighteen that survived were the ones someone else had taken before me. The little wheel had been on the number 21 and I already knew that the first three shots couldn't be counted. I was crestfallen and the Armenian made a gesture with his hand for the camera.

"Do you know what an aperture ring is?" he asked and all I did was shake my head. "You took a picture in the dark and didn't compensate by slowing your shutter speed," he said, watching to see by my response if I had any idea what he was talking about.

"Look through the viewfinder," he instructed me, putting the camera near my face. "You see that little needle moving left and right?"

"Yes."

"That's the aperture. When it's in the middle it means you won't over- or underexpose a picture. Where is it now? Closer to the minus or the plus side?"

"The minus," I said, and I wondered how I hadn't noticed those signs staring at me from deep within the viewfinder.

"That means there isn't enough light. You either didn't open the aperture wide enough or you put the shutter speed on too fast a setting. You have to learn how to play with these things. Here, let me show you."

The Armenian took the camera and started tinkering with a button I hadn't seen before.

"This is the aperture," he said. "You can open or close it depending on how much light you want to let in."

He toyed with the ring of the lens, with something that said f-stop on it, and showed me how the small numbers let in a lot of light and the big ones blocked it out almost entirely. Then he put his finger on a button, the one that determines the shutter speed, and went on and on about how you have to balance the two of them, walking me in and out of the store to see the difference between natural light, electric light, and darkness. In the end I paid him eighteen shekels for pictures I didn't really want and left the store. I was pretty sure that the day before I had already managed to overexpose five shots.

Not hungry, I walked east, out of the Armenian Quarter and toward the square outside the al-Aqsa Mosque. The Armenian had said that the wide open square caught the early morning light and was an ideal spot to learn how to play with the aperture and the shutter speed. "I guarantee you," the Armenian said with a smile as I left his store, "that you won't overexpose more than two more rolls of film."

On the way to the mosque I did the calculations: I could afford five rolls of film a month, no more. The film would cost 75 shekels a month; the development of 33 photos per roll would add another 165 on to the bill. Back then 240 shekels a month was a fortune. My salary was only 2,500 shekels a month, but at that time my attraction to the camera was stronger than anything else. At first I thought it was just some unemployed man's hobby, the kind of thing that would pass with one more roll of overexposed film. But I had this real desire to take pictures and, especially, to see the pictures I'd taken once they were developed. Nights, I went through Yonatan's boxes of photos and noticed things I'd never seen before. Yonatan mostly took pictures of people. Before I'd found the camera, I would just flip through the pictures and try to guess if they were taken at a family event or on a class trip. But what had been rather dull was now fascinating. Yonatan did not take pictures at events or weddings or birthday parties. He photographed people and their expressions, freezing and preserving moments of sadness, fear, contemplation, happiness, and worry.

I arrived at the square outside the mosque and knew that I had no intention of photographing old domes and other tourist attractions. People, that's what I wanted to capture on film. I wanted to see if I could be as precise and knowing as Yonatan, if I could also take the kind of sharp, detailed pictures that revealed the entire world of the stranger on the other end of the lens.

The guards at the entrance to the square asked to see identification and let me in only once they'd verified that I was a Muslim. It was early, and between prayer times, so the square, which was usually full of careening kids who had nowhere else to play, was nearly empty.

A few beggars asked for spare change and I ignored them, knowing that if I coughed up a single cent I'd be hounded all the way out of the Old City, followed by their outstretched hands and sorry eyes.

"Excuse me," a bearded man said, striding toward me with a walkie-talkie. "Wait," he commanded and I stopped. "Are you a Muslim?"

"Yes," I answered.

"Muslim," he said, raising his radio to his mouth. "I'm sorry, your appearance was misleading. The camera made me think that maybe . . . where are you from?"

"Jaljulia."

"Welcome," he said, bringing his palm to his chest.

I sat down on the stairs that led from the al-Aqsa square to the Mosque of Omar. I looked around and saw there was nothing that I really wanted to photograph. I opened the yellow envelope the Armenian had given me and took out the eighteen pictures from the previous roll of film.

I saw Yonatan, an eighteen-year-old Yonatan, standing on his own two feet. In the first photo, he held the camera that

I now had around my neck. He had held it down around his waist and taken a picture of himself in the mirror in the attic bathroom, a sealed, sharp expression on his face. I flipped to the next picture: Yonatan, standing by the side of the bed. He held a release cable in his hand, the kind that lets you operate the camera from afar. The cable, I thought, wasn't in the photo by chance. He knew what he wanted in his frames. In the third photo, he was standing on a chair in the middle of the room. In the next one, he threaded a rope through an anchor for the light fixture in the ceiling. I started breathing quickly, racing through the photos. He was in all of them. He tied the noose. He took a shot of himself from below. He moved the camera away and took a picture of himself testing the rope. And always the same expression, cold, emotionless, remote. He had taken a few different shots of himself, from various angles, with his neck in the noose. I felt starved for air. I stood up and tried to inhale properly, but still I could feel myself shaking. Yonatan stood on the back of the chair and in the last photo, number 18, I saw him push the chair away with his feet. Behind him, very vividly, I could see the bed and the pictures on the wall, but the center of the frame, where the body hung, was blurry, the neck, stomach, hands, and feet were all elongated, and I knew that he had used a slow shutter speed and a long exposure.

THE CARDBOARD BOX

I showed up half an hour early. There were two girls in the waiting room. Each had a big square art bag and they were chatting. They stopped their conversation for a second when I showed up, looked me over, and nodded in my direction. I nodded back, then lowered my eyes and went to check out the list of names on the door. I was number five.

"What time did they call you for?" one of the girls asked. She was skinny, with blonde hair that had been dyed purple.

"Eleven thirty," I said.

"They're running ridiculously late. The ten o'clock just went in now. How far down the list are you?"

"I'm fifth."

"Cool, I'm fourth."

"I'm sixth," the other girl said softly. "After you." She was more filled out than her friend and she wore a Ministry T-shirt. She noticed that I was staring at her shirt and lowered her eyes, and I, fearing she would think I was looking at her chest, said, "I have the same shirt." She nodded and smiled. Her breasts were round and full and I could see the shape of her nipples through the fabric.

Each applicant had a half hour slot, and if the skinny one was right and the third on the list had only gone in now, then I had at least an hour until it was my turn. My first thought was to flee, to give up; what were the chances of me being accepted to the Bezalel Academy of Arts and Design? Knowing I didn't belong, I sat down on the floor and leaned my back against the wall, opposite the girls.

"If the whole point of photography is to capture a single moment in time, I figured why not go for it, you know?" the skinny girl said. "I figured I'll just go for it. I'll photograph time. Or what time means to me."

She picked up her portfolio, laid it on her knees, and started taking out photographs in black matte frames. I couldn't see the photos she passed along to the other girl, one after another, carefully, as though handling the pages of a holy book. Every once in a while she blew dust off the surface of a photo and carried on with her presentation.

"To me this represents the passing of time, and here I tried to understand and conceptualize the meaning of the present, and here at the end I tried to capture the future as I see it, in other words, within the infinite space of time."

The girl with the Ministry T-shirt seemed to find the skinny girl's presentation interesting, and I knew there was no way I could carry on like that about time, and what's more I realized that I had not framed any of my photographs. It was a mistake to come. I had no idea how I had ever made it through the first stage of the application process, but I knew for sure that I was not an artist. The Ministry girl glanced up for a moment and caught me looking at her. She smiled at me and I smiled back.

"And this is my self-portrait," the skinny one said. "A woman with no head and no limbs."

I made a face and just at that moment the Ministry girl looked up at me and burst out laughing.

"I'm sorry," she said, trying to keep her poise. "I'm really sorry. He's just making me laugh," she said, pointing at me.

Several long minutes later the door opened and a young dark-skinned guy with long curly hair emerged. He was well-dressed, clothed from head to toe in designer apparel. He inhaled deeply and shut the door. The skinny girl hopped up.

"Well, what did they ask?" she clamored.

"You know, just questions about my work, where I'm from, why I want to study here, that kind of thing," he said in Nazareth-accented Hebrew. The door opened again and a woman with a file in her hand summoned the skinny girl.

"Good luck," the cute one said, and I mumbled after her, "Good luck."

Just before the woman shut the door, the guy from Nazareth asked when he could expect results and she said within a month and then closed the door.

He was bursting with confidence. He said he had also applied to the department of architecture and that if he got in there he would definitely go, but that if he didn't, he'd do a year of photography and then reapply to architecture at the end of the year.

"He definitely got in," the Ministry girl said when we were left alone in the waiting room. "To photography *and* to architecture. They'll probably fight over who gets him."

"You know him?" I asked.

"No," she said, shrugging, "but this is Bezalel. They'd kill to have an Arab in the program."

"Maybe he has competition in the department of architecture," I said, smiling.

"You're right," she said. "I hadn't thought of that. Two Arabs is already too much."

The skinny one walked out with a big smile on her face.

"How'd it go?" number six asked her halfheartedly.

"Hard, stressful, but I think it went well."

"Yonatan, Yonatan Forschmidt," the woman with the file said and I jumped up from the floor and straightened out. "That's me," I said.

"Good luck, Yonatan," number six said.

Yonatan Forschmidt. That's the name I'd put down on the application, the name I'd used for the psychometric exam, the name that had appeared on the sheet in the waiting room. For the previous six months I had been walking around with Yonatan's ID in my pocket, or rather, to be exact, with two IDs—his, which I'd found in the attic, and mine.

I remember how scared I was the first time I'd identified myself as a Jew. It was in a café on Ben Yehuda Street, the fifth one I'd gone to in search of a job. The boss looked at Yonatan's ID, eyed his old picture, and then filled in his personal details on the application without any hint of suspicion. In all of the other cafés, where I'd identified myself as an Arab, the bosses suddenly didn't have waitering positions available, despite the WAITSTAFF WANTED sign on the door. Either that or they offered me a job as a dishwasher. I agreed to that once. It was called chef's assistant, but all I was asked to do was wash dishes, clean the bathrooms, bring in the supplies, and take out the garbage. I had to come in at seven thirty in the morning and stay until six in the evening and my pay was minimum wage. I knew that the waiters worked less and made more. All of the waitstaff were Jewish and all of the kitchen workers were Arabs: the ones the customers didn't see were always Arabs.

Once I'd gotten the job by posing as a Jew, I felt embarrassed by what I'd done and decided I wouldn't show up for my first shift. But I needed the money and I convinced myself that I had not done anything wrong. Just a little hoax so I could get a reasonable job. The first week was training and throughout that period I focused on not answering the kitchen staff in my native tongue when they said good morning in Arabic or asked if I'd like something to eat. The training went well and the owner saw that I could be trusted. I always showed up on time, didn't ask for days off, didn't come in tired, and was generous with the customers, even the most difficult ones.

The kitchen staff consisted of Muhammad, whom everyone called Mukhi; Rafik, whom everyone called Rafi; and Suleiman, who preferred to be called Soli. All three of them were from east Jerusalem, and all three of them smoked, prayed, and talked about girls all the time.

As opposed to the waitstaff, who were given their shifts in advance, Mukhi, Rafi, and Soli worked all day every day, from seven in the morning until midnight, except for Fridays, which were short days, and Saturdays, when the café was closed.

My relationship with the owner, the kitchen workers, and the other waiters was polite, nothing more. I didn't let anyone get too close to me, especially not Dana, a young waitress who, like me, preferred the morning shift—she had Bagrut matriculation courses in the afternoon. She was a pretty, smart girl who had dropped out of high school because she couldn't stand the teachers, the other kids, and the material that was being taught. Nor could she stand the sleazeballs and bimbos who went to the Bagrut courses in the afternoon instead of high school, but she had no choice. She wanted to go to college, probably to study psychology or art history; she wasn't sure. She invited me over to her place in the Nachlaot neighborhood for Saturday brunch but I had to restrain myself and say no. Back then, I couldn't imagine lying to other people about my identity, although, after spending a night practicing the signature he'd left in his books, I had opened a bank account in Yonatan's name. I told myself that my lie was solely for the purposes of work, and it could not be allowed to spread to my personal life, even though I wasn't sure I had one of those.

"Your portfolio, please," the woman with the file said, and I already regretted coming. I opened my bag and took out a cardboard box, my portfolio. The three members of the admissions committee sat around a round table: the chair of the department, an instructor, and a fourth-year student. They looked over the paperwork in front of them and waited for me to take out my work.

The applicants who had made it through the first two stages of the application process were asked, for the final stage, to do three things: a story in ten pictures, a self-portrait, and three pictures of your choosing. I gave the secretary my box.

"What's this," asked the instructor. "Store-developed photos?"

"Yes," I said. He started looking through the first photos, my story in ten pictures. In contrast to those of the skinny girl from the waiting room, my pictures were all standard size. The Armenian had developed them for me and I had not even thought of blowing them up or framing them.

"When did you start taking photographs?" he asked.

"A year ago, about a year ago."

"Did you study anywhere?" he asked, without taking his eyes off the photos.

"No, I studied alone. I mean, someone showed me the basics and I read some books," I said, and the instructor passed the ten photos to the head of the department.

"So you didn't study photography in high school or anywhere else?" the instructor continued.

"No," I said, and I felt myself blush. I hated myself for having the gall to come to this place, for listening to Osnat and Dana, who said I would get into Bezalel with my eyes closed.

"Do you have your camera with you now?" the head of the department asked, spreading the photos out on the table so the student could see, too.

"Yes," I said. "I have it here."

"Let me see it, please," the department head said, and I opened the camera bag, which had almost always been on my shoulder during the past year and a half.

"Wow, a Pentax," he said, when I handed it to him. "Do they still make these?" The department head held the camera in both hands and passed the rest of the pictures over to the instructor.

My portfolio consisted of portraits. I asked permission and I photographed people. Yonatan had focused on portraits and I studied his work at night, tried to understand what it was about his photos that drew me in. I also studied his books, which dealt only with the art of portraiture, and I looked over each and every photograph under the lamp in the attic for hours. Since I'd learned how to use the camera, I'd been taking pictures of people, especially in the Old City.

Ruchaleh had split the caretaking work into three shifts and I took the afternoon and night, back to back, and that, along with the waitering, left me a lot more money for photography. After a few weeks at the café I worked up to asking the owner if I could take pictures, and I started shooting on the premises, taking pictures of the employees once they'd given me their permission. I used those for my story in ten pictures. They were portraits of the kitchen workers, from the moment they were given an order until they slid the dish out from under the window in the wall that divided the café and the kitchen and hit the bell. I had also been taking pictures of the café regulars, the ones who came each morning, and for the category of three pictures of my choosing, I picked Sara, who, so long as she wasn't in the hospital, came to the café each morning along with her Filipina caretaker. In the picture I submitted, she was holding a cup of tea in both hands and smiling with her eyes. The other two shots were from the Old City: one of the Armenian laughing, a gold tooth glinting in his open mouth, and the other of a border policeman smiling as he checked my ID, which is to say Yonatan's.

"Hold on," the department head said, sifting through the pictures on the table, "I'm missing the self-portrait."

P.O. BOX

I hurried out to check the mail the next day to see whether I'd gotten an answer. After applying as Yonatan I'd also gotten myself a post office box with his name. You had to have a mailing address to put on the application form and I remembered from back when I was a student that some of those who didn't have a permanent address rented a post office box. Before mailing the application off to Bezalel, I rented a box for a few dozen shekels at the King George Street post office, near the café where I worked. Each morning, on the way from Beit Hakerem to the café, I stopped in at the post office and checked my box. Sometimes I found advertisements or mail with someone else's name, but now an entire month had passed since the interview and I had not heard a word from the Bezalel Academy of Arts and Design.

Before the interview I had not been sure I even wanted to go there and I was pretty sure that even if I did want to there was no way I'd dare embark on a four-year degree with a stolen identity. But once I'd gone to the interview there was nothing I wanted more than the piece of paper that said I had been accepted. I wanted to know that I had convinced the panel that my photographs were good enough to continue on in the field. I just wanted to be told that I was good. I constantly imagined myself reading from a piece of paper embossed with the Bezalel seal, "We are pleased to inform you . . ." During those days of waiting I was extremely sorry I had not completed the third assignment, the self-portrait, even though the head of the department had smiled forgivingly when I offered my explanation for its absence: "It hasn't come into focus yet."

By the fourth week of waiting, I had convinced myself that applying to Bezalel's school of photography had been a terrible mistake. Sure I loved photography more than anything else, but I was a naive idiot, believing that a few months of tinkering would get me into the most prestigious art school in the country, one that only took a handful of students each year, all of whom had studied art in school, not learned it on their own in an attic that reeked of medicine and having their pictures developed in an old machine in a crummy store in the middle of the Armenian Quarter.

School was set to start in a couple of months and I knew that the acceptance letters must have been sent long ago. Clearly I had not gotten in. Two months was too little time, especially for out-of-town students who had to find a place to live and get settled in Jerusalem before the school year started. Nonetheless I continued to check the post office box every morning and afternoon. In the middle of the week, when the café was relatively empty, I'd head out and check the box compulsively — sometimes five times in a single shift. During those days I started to get the feeling that someone was onto me, that they'd discovered my true identity, because even if I'd been rejected I should still have been given notice of some kind. Maybe someone who'd known Yonatan in school or someone who knew the Forschmidt family, or someone who knew me, who picked up the foreign intonation and had his suspicions had turned me in. The criminal implications of what I'd done, the theft of Yonatan's identity, suddenly became clear and in my mind I no longer saw myself reading an acceptance letter but began to envision police officers arriving at the house in Beit Hakerem or at the café, or, worse, at my mother's place, looking for the imposter. All I wanted was some word from Bezalel, preferably a rejection letter, so I could put the whole affair behind me and get rid of all the stress.

I tried convincing myself that I'd get a pretty lenient sentence. I'd be arrested, no doubt about that, and I'd have a criminal record, but since the identity theft had not been for the purpose of fraud—the pictures were truly mine—I probably wouldn't have to do time, at least not a lot of time. I had been asked to provide a Bagrut certificate and I had given them Yonatan's, but I had one of my own and mine was just as good as his. My assumed identity for the purpose of work at the café didn't seem like the kind of crime you did time for, either.

"Your Honor," I imagined myself saying from the stand, "all I did was provide a different name than my own. Ask the owner, though, I was his best worker. Ask the clients. My sole intent was to get a job as a waiter and not a kitchen worker."

The prosecution's attempts to attribute a nationalistic element to the crime, to say that my goal had been to harm Israelis, would surely be discredited by the brilliant young lawyer, Majdi, whom I would have to contact even though I had no idea how I would explain my actions to him. It would be easy to show that I was not politically active. I'd never been in a rally, never voted for the Knesset, never voted in the local council elections, never even voted in the elections for Arab student council or in the general elections on campus.

"A waiter, Your Honor," I imagined myself concluding my argument. "All I wanted to be was a waiter."

I used to spend the afternoons, on my way from the café to the house, thinking about an immediate escape. I practiced the lines I would use on Osnat. "Please tell Ruchaleh that there's been a family emergency." Or, "I have to go home and be with my mother." Or, "There's a bit of trouble in the village." All lines that were tailor-made for Osnat and Ruchaleh, spiced with a dash of mysterious Oriental drama so they wouldn't ask too many questions, merely accept that a situation had arisen that required my immediate attention. I had to be with my mother, and they would understand that I had no choice but to leave and they would find someone else on very short notice to pick up the shifts. But what if they didn't forgive me for leaving like that? What if they were offended? Well, screw them, I thought to myself. True, they didn't ridicule me or underestimate me, but the salary they had been paying me was a joke. The monthly salary did not correlate at all to the sixteen hours a day that I worked, and the only reason I was able to get by was because I had no rent to pay and I made do with a fold-out couch for a bed.

They can both go to hell, the two of them and the guy with the frozen gaze. Tonight is the night I bail. I'll call Osnat from the central bus station and tell her I'm leaving Jerusalem and then hang up. She could shove it. Neither she nor Ruchaleh would come looking for me. Why would they? What good would they get out of it? I hadn't violated any agreement, there was no contract, and they couldn't demand anything of me just as I wasn't demanding anything of them. Unlike Osnat, I had no benefits — no sick days, no vacations, no worker's insurance. Nothing. A defenseless day laborer. Just as they could boot me out whenever they saw fit so, too, could I leave whenever I felt like it. They'd find another Arab to take my place. He'd be happy to have the job, no questions asked. Same goes for the café owner. I wouldn't even call him. Screw him and the way he talked about the kitchen workers behind their backs, patting them on the shoulders and then talking about them like scum. So proud of the few words he knew in Arabic, the greetings and the curses, which he used as if they were a joke, waxing on about the techniques he'd developed to tame his Arab workers to make them follow his commands.

"You have to constantly remind them who's boss," he told me once, letting me in on the tricks of his trade. "If you let your guard down even the littlest bit, they'll eat you alive."

During one of those days, while I was bracing myself for arrest and planning my escape from Jerusalem, I heard a girl's voice call me from behind. I had just finished up at the café and was on my way to the bus stop on King George Street. I didn't turn around. "Yonatan," she called again, this time from closer. I turned around, scared, and I saw number six smiling at me and plucking little earphones out of her ears.

"You don't remember me?"

"I do," I said. "Number six."

"Noa," she said, shaking my hand. The soft touch of her long fingers in my palm made me withdraw my hand quickly.

"You looking for an apartment?"

"No, I live here."

"Oh, you're a Jerusalemite?"

"Yes," I said. "I work over at the café down the block. What about you?"

"I don't know the area at all. And I don't really understand what a school like Bezalel is doing in the middle of this city. Just the thought of four years in this place weirds me out."

"You're looking for an apartment?"

"Yes, I've been to this fucking city every day. Sorry. I must have seen five or six places already, but you have no idea what kind of rat holes they rent around here for five hundred dollars!"

"I know. The prices are crazy."

"I found something nice today, though. In Nachlaot. I figure if it's going to be Jerusalem, I might as well go all the way."

"Yeah, all the Bezalel students live there."

"This goes to the central bus station, right?" she asked, pointing with her chin toward an approaching bus.

"Yes," I said.

"Good seeing you. I'll see you in school, right?"

"I didn't get in."

"What?" she yelled, and I heard her say, "No way!" as the bus closed its doors.

I'm glad that just happened, I thought as I waited for the bus to Beit Hakerem. I'm glad it happened now. I needed that wake-up call, that smack in the face from Bezalel. I am a social worker, with a degree from Hebrew University, with good grades and the ability to get a good job. Why have I been wasting my time with photography? Why have I been wasting my time in an attic redolent of medicine and excrement?

LETTER

I fed Yonatan, brushed his teeth, changed his diaper, put him in his pajamas, moisturized his hands and feet, and got

him ready for bed. I'd put my escape off until tomorrow.
In the morning, I thought to myself, tomorrow morning, as
soon as Osnat shows up, I'll tell her that I'm leaving. I won't
even demand my salary for the days I worked in August.
I'll just disappear.

When Yonatan's eyes closed, I took down the camera
from the top shelf. I hadn't taken a single shot since that
cursed day when I went to the Bezalel interview. During
the six months before that, I had shot about half a roll a day,
about three rolls a week, but since that day, nothing. The
thrill was gone. During the first week after the interview I
still kept the camera slung over my shoulder, but after that I
put it back in the closet. Now I took off the lens and looked
through it, aiming at the farthest point of light outside the
window, then I turned it toward Yonatan and tried to focus
on his half-closed eyes.

I almost dropped the camera when I heard knocking
on the attic door. "Just a second," I yelled as I stuffed the
camera back in its box and up on the shelf. I tried catching
my breath as I opened the door. I didn't know that Ruchaleh
was home. Ordinarily I kept very close tabs on what was
happening on the floor below me, listening to the jingle of
keys as she returned home, following her steps and the sound
of the keys hitting the wood of the dining room table. The
faucet, the opening of the fridge, the bottles, the clink of
the plates, the lights. I could always tell when she was in the
living room and when she was in the bedroom. That night,
maybe because she had come home earlier, while I was still
in the bathroom with Yonatan, I hadn't heard her come in.

"I think someone meant to send this to you," she said,
handing me an envelope and then leaving, shutting the attic

door behind her. It was from Bezalel. I recognized the logo on the front of the envelope, next to the sticker that bore my name, which is to say Yonatan's, and the address of the house in Beit Hakerem.

"I'm really sorry," I said to Ruchaleh. She was sitting on the couch in the living room reading a book. I had never before started a conversation with her, but it was clear that she knew I had been using her son's identity. She had not opened the envelope.

"I didn't mean to," I said, begging her forgiveness, avoiding her eyes. "I really don't know what came over me."

"Sit down," she said, but I remained standing, eyes downcast.

"Again," I said, "I'm really sorry, ma'am. It was just a game. I really don't know why I decided to write your son's name down and not my own." I really didn't know if the whole thing had happened because Yonatan had been a photographer or because the camera belonged to him or because I had learned everything I knew from his books, his pictures. Maybe it was just a game, I don't know. But when I was taking photographs I was someone else, someone unfamiliar, foreign. Holding the camera in my hand I felt like an extension of Yonatan or the continuation of what he had been. I didn't tell her about the post office box or the café or the bank account. She might not understand.

"Ma'am . . ." I started.

"Don't ma'am me," she said. "Sit down. And don't give me this I'm-an-obedient-little-Arab routine." No one had ever called me a little Arab before or spoken to me in that tone.

"You're insulted?" she asked. "Good, I'm glad. Now do me a favor and do yourself a favor and don't talk to me in that groveling slave-at-the-master's-house tone. And sit down already." I sat before her, prepared to fling one of her books in her face. I'm not apologizing anymore. Let her call the police for all I care. I'm not scared of her or of anything else in this world.

"Listen to me, ma'am," I said, this time in a gruff tone. "I know I did something wrong, something that I can't even explain to myself at this point. But I don't intend to study photography using your son's name and I had no good reason to apply as him. As you know, I have a Bagrut certificate and a BSW and my chances of getting into Bezalel, if I really wanted to go there, were far better if I'd applied as an Arab."

"Yes," she chuckled, "I'm familiar with Bezalel's system. They take every Arab that applies. Maybe that's what led you to apply with a Jewish name?"

"No, not that."

"Then why? I can understand the desire to want to be judged for who you are and what you've done and not your nationality or your ethnicity. That's a very reasonable thing to do."

"I don't think that's why."

"No? You applied with a Jewish name, an Ashkenazi one, the kind that has no chance at affirmative action. I think you probably didn't want to feel like someone was doing you a favor."

"I don't really know why I did it," I said again, realizing that she wasn't interested in chastising me or charging me with an offense. "Maybe it was because I knew that Yonatan wanted to go there," I said without thinking, and I saw her expression change. Perhaps only now was she realizing that I had been looking through all of his things.

"I know," she said.

"I'm really, really sorry. I didn't mean to offend you."

"You didn't," she said, and then added, "Well, don't leave us hanging."

"What do you mean?"

"The letter," she said. "What does it say? Did you get in?"

PART
FIVE

TRANCE

The lawyer leaned against the wall and tried not to collapse onto the filthy tiles of the bathroom floor. The thump of the speakers pounded his eardrums. Feeling like someone on the deck of a bucking ship, he tried to take a deep breath and scatter the collage of nauseating images. He leaned against the wall, legs weak and untrustworthy, and stuck his hand out for some toilet paper but felt only metal. Looking out of the corner of his eye, which took considerable effort, he saw that there was no toilet paper to be had. There was a thick roll of paper towels on top of the toilet and he spread his legs out, anchoring himself on the wet, filthy floor, and reached for them. He palmed the wall behind the toilet as he reached forward and in that way managed not to fall. Once he felt his body was adequately prepared, he let go of the wall and, with the sleight of hand known only to three-card monte players and expert pickpockets, snatched the roll of paper. He ripped off a big piece, put it on the floor near the toilet and with his foot began mopping away some of the mud and grime. Placing more paper on the floor, he felt a wave of relief as he dropped to his knees in front of the toilet. He wrapped a long length of paper around his hands, fashioning a pair of paper mittens, and held on to the sides of the toilet bowl as he brought his face close to the foul water at the bottom. He thought he could see the shimmering reflection of his face.

The main door to the bathroom opened and a blast of awful techno music burst in and was promptly muffled by the closing of the door.

"Come on," he heard someone say, banging on the door, "how long you going to be in there?" This meant he'd have to wait again, until the man gave up and went back outside, because the lawyer did not want anyone to hear him vomit.

As soon as he left the house, the lawyer felt he had made a mistake. Leaving his crying wife in the room as she retrieved her clothes from the floor, he stood outside the door for a moment. She had asked where he was going, asked him not to leave, repeated again and again that she had no idea what was going on, begged that he explain it all to her, but he had taken his attaché case and left without saying a word. He had to show her that he meant business. She had to understand that something had been broken. But as soon as he left the house, he wanted to return, and if she had come out after him maybe he would have gone back in. All the lawyer really wanted was to have his old life back again and he tried to find a reasonable explanation for her actions, something that would set his mind at ease, something he could live with. He refused to believe the worst and began thinking of possible alibis for her.

Starting up the car, he hoped she would not flee. The lawyer was scared that when he came back home, in an hour or two, he'd find that she was no longer there. That she'd taken the kids and some clothes and gone to her parents' house. Maybe her lover would drive them. Now that she knew her illicit love had been exposed, what was to stop her from calling her lover? Maybe that's exactly what she was doing at this moment, talking to him on the phone, bawling, but also reveling in the drama, feeling like her life had finally started to look like those Egyptian, Syrian, and Lebanese soap operas she loved. And he—being just as stupid as she—would speak the kinds of syrupy words that were supposed to calm her, promising to take care of her, to watch out for her, to lay his life down on the line for her. Let her go off with whoever she wants, the lawyer said to himself, wondering about the complex character of this lover who was learned in art and literature and Egyptian sap.

Before even pulling out of the garage, the lawyer called his wife. Not to talk, but to make sure that her line was not busy. He let it ring twice and hung up. It wasn't busy. Then he thought she might be talking to her lover on the landline and he called that number, too, waited for it to ring once, then hung up and pulled out. She called right back, undoubtedly having seen his missed call. But he, of course, did not answer.

He drove slowly and tried to piece together the chain of events. The moment she came home, the look on her face when she told him about the battery on her phone. Had she planned everything? Was she that devious? He'd known her for seven years and had never noticed anything that would lead him to believe that she could plot her steps so cunningly. He recalled social events that she attended alone, parties she had said were work-related, visits to friends' houses. Those were a weekly occurrence. But prior to the discovery of her love letter, the lawyer had never suspected they were anything beyond social calls. Maybe she really was telling the truth. Maybe the battery really had died and maybe she really had gone out with Faten for a cup of coffee and some gossip, as they often did?

The lawyer breathed deeply before dialing Faten's number. It wasn't late at night and he knew he could call the accountant's house.

"Hello," Faten answered. There was a trace of surprise in her voice, not on account of the hour or the identity of the caller, but because hardly anyone besides unsolicited callers used the landlines these days.

"Good evening," the lawyer said, trying to make sure his voice didn't waver.

"Good evening," Faten said, her voice more playful.

"So that's how it is, ah?" he said, trying to keep his voice as light and friendly as possible. "The two of you leave us at home and go out to cafés?" His heart was pounding.

"Half an hour is too much for you guys?" Faten said playfully and the lawyer's body melted with relief.

"Who is it?" he heard Anton ask.

"Hold on a second. I'm putting Anton on," she said, passing the phone to her husband.

The lawyer had to come up with something. "I was thinking that if the girls can go out for coffee, maybe we could do the same. What are your thoughts on a beer at the Ambassador?" he said, praying that Anton would refuse.

"I wish," Anton said, "I just came home now with the kids. I took them out to eat. My dear wife is so busy she didn't have time to make anything."

"I knew I couldn't count on you," the lawyer said. "Never mind, we'll do it next time. *Yallah,* good night."

So she did meet up with Faten. There was no way she would ask one of her friends to lie on her behalf. The lawyer nearly turned his car around and went home, but he still couldn't come up with a good explanation as to why she had lied about the letter. He drove out of the village and onto the wider streets of the main road, the one that had once linked Jerusalem and Bethlehem. He called Tarik and then realized that Tarik was actually the only person he wanted to see that night. The lawyer knew Tarik would not refuse. He detected a note of happiness in the young lawyer's voice when he asked him, over the noise of Tarik's television, "So, where do you usually go to drink?" Once they'd decided the where and the when, the lawyer hit the gas and flew through the empty streets, trying to remember just when it was that the gates to Bethlehem had been locked.

THE FUTON

The lawyer opened his eyes and was saddened by the fact that he'd lost the ability to cry. He wanted to go back to the village, to his parents' house, his real home, not the rentals he'd lived in in Jerusalem and not the house he owned in Beit Safafa, which he had never called home, as though he had been doing nothing but sojourning in the city. He wanted to go back to his old room, the cold room he had shared with his three brothers, the thin mattress and the sheepskin that his mother would put under it for insulation during the winter. He missed the crispness of morning, the walk to school bursting with confidence, the knowledge that his homework was perfect and that it had been written out in elegant handwriting, the kind that made his parents proud. Too bad he hadn't gone back to the village after school, too bad he hadn't listened to his father, who begged him to return home.

The lawyer's eyes fluttered open and then closed again. Lying in Tarik's bedroom, he drifted in and out of sleep and thought that the first thing he would do when he gained control of his consciousness would be to send Tarik home, to his village. If it comes down to it, I'll fire him, and make sure no lawyer in the city takes him on. He was sorry he had stood in Tarik's way, that he'd convinced him to stay in the city and not go home, and he knew he'd done it in order to prove to himself that he had not been mistaken, that he'd been right to stay in Jerusalem. The lawyer recalled that Tarik had driven him in the lawyer's car after the long night of drinking and that he'd wanted to take the lawyer back to his house but that he had refused. He did not recall how it happened that Tarik had given him his bed, but he imagined that the young lawyer had insisted that his boss take it, saying that he would sleep on the couch in the hall.

The lawyer's throat felt sandy, his head striped with pain. Specific memories of the night dissolved in a murk of shame. He knew he had acted like a complete fool. He had drunk like he never had before and it was very likely he had embarrassed himself like never before, too. Certainly he'd never exposed Tarik to this kind of behavior. But what most concerned him was whether he had let anything slip about his wife's letter, her lies, the book, and the real reason he had not wanted to go back to his house. The lawyer tried hard to remember the night, and he was able to summon many things, fragments and entire conversations from earlier in the evening, and he was pretty sure he had not said anything specific about his wife, and so he was inclined to let himself off the hook. He remembered picking Tarik up at his house and driving to a pub called Ha'sira and that Tarik had said it was his favorite place on the western side of the city. He also remembered how surprised he had been and the way he had laughed when Tarik led him into the place, which looked less like a nightspot and more like a storage room that stank of beer, sweat, and cigarettes.

Tarik had apologized and said, "I warned you. I told you it wasn't your style."

Tarik had suggested going to a different place, "somewhere a little cleaner," but the lawyer insisted on staying. They sat in the corner, around a heavy wood table near the little square of a dance floor, which was still empty because it wasn't yet ten, and started off the evening with two pints of Taybeh. Tarik said that Ha'sira, the Boat, was one of the strongholds of the young Jerusalem left-wing crowd, and that most of the patrons were students at the city's art schools—Bezalel, Nissan Nativ, and Sam Spiegel. They sold Palestinian beer on principle.

"Arab students come here, too." He said. "Not many, but they come."

"Arab girls, too?" the lawyer remembered asking, and Tarik had nodded.

"Yeah, not a lot, but some," Tarik said, turning his head toward the door and the young couple that had just entered.

"Looking for someone?" the lawyer asked, smiling at his friend.

"Not sure," Tarik said, and it seemed to the lawyer like he was a little embarrassed by the question, since the two of them had never before discussed personal affairs. But personal affairs were all that mattered to the lawyer at this point and that was why he had called Tarik. He felt blind, or like a deaf man at a loud wedding, as the Arab saying goes, and he wanted to know what it was like for young Arabs these days, especially the girls, what had changed since his days in university. Even then he had felt that a new, accursed wind of sexual freedom was blowing through the campus. The lawyer never partook in any of that, had never slept with an Arab girl other than his wife, even though the university was seemingly beyond the reach of parental and societal restraints, a place where different rules applied and he could have done as he pleased. There was an unwritten rule on campus whereby what happened on campus stayed on campus, and as soon as school was over all was forgotten and returned to its earlier state.

The pub began to fill up and the lawyer got them each another beer and offered to buy them a round of fine whiskey, but the pub did not have anything that matched that definition. There were no single malts, no malt whiskey at all, and the two of them had to make do with Johnnie Walker Red.

After the whiskey the lawyer asked Tarik what he thought of marrying a girl who'd had previous sexual partners, and Tarik had responded with a shrug, "I don't have any problem with it."

"I used to think the same way," the lawyer said.

"And then what happened?" Tarik asked.

"I don't know. I really don't know what I think these days."

"You know what," Tarik said, draining his whiskey and seeming on the verge of a proclamation. "Not only do

I not have a problem marrying a nonvirgin, I have a serious problem marrying a girl who is one."

"What do you mean?" the lawyer asked, trying to smile encouragingly at Tarik.

"I want to marry an Arab girl who, for all I care, has fucked half the guys in the city. But only of her own free will. Someone who has used those Arab boys for her own means, slept with them and then dumped them. A wild girl, that's what I want. That way I'll know she picked me because she wanted me and not because it was the best of the choices she was offered or because I was the most socially acceptable option. I want to know that this girl chose me after rejecting all the other options."

The lawyer, lying in Tarik's bed now, deep under his comforter, didn't attach much significance to what Tarik had said. He'd been able to say those things because there was nothing serious in the works, but he knew his parents would hang him by the balls if he did anything that tainted their honor. He remembered also that he had continued to drink whiskey while Tarik had made do with beer. At some point the pub had filled up entirely and everyone there seemed young and attractive to the lawyer. It was around then that his inhibitions drifted off entirely and he became convinced that he was as young and beautiful as they were, and with that knowledge he sauntered onto the dance floor. With all of his heart and soul the lawyer wanted to get a girl. Acting on information he'd amassed while watching television, he knew that the key was in the eyes, and with several long glances he told the girls around him exactly what he was after. On this night he would do what he had never before done. He would cheat on his wife. He'd take whichever woman fell for him to the most expensive hotel in the city. To the King David.

He looked at the women dancing nearby and got to thinking about how he'd find the perfect one, smart and beautiful and full of life, and already he began planning their lives together. He'd divorce his wife, and no one would say it was because she had an illicit affair. They'd say he was a creep, a skirt chaser, and they'd talk about how he had run off with a girl ten years younger than him. Yes, that's what he would do, that would be respectable. And if she was the kind of young and bold Arab girl Tarik had talked about, all the better. A girl who'd fucked around, who'd used Arab men like socks, trying them on and tossing them aside. The important thing was that she not lie, he thought, that she be forthright.

None of the girls around him seemed like the type he was looking for and he waited for her to come through the door and for her to realize at first sight that he was the one, and for her to choose to come dance with him, to choose to get into bed with him, to choose to sleep with him, and he would be an amazing lover, using his trick—lying on top of her, or perhaps the other way around—recalling each and every check he had deposited that month, moving in and out of her as he worked out all of the bank charges, the VAT and the payments to the income tax authorities. And the next morning, when she told him he was the one and only, his friends would be stunned and jealous, especially his wife, the whore. He continued to look around at the girls, feeling he had found what he was looking for and then changing his mind, until he realized that his stares were not being well-received. He remembered now how his confidence had crumbled and how disgust and humiliation had taken its place and how his rooster dance had turned into a tremor in his knees. It was then that he felt his way to the bathroom to vomit his guts out.

The lawyer moved his head left and right and saw his pants and shirt on the chair in Tarik's room, alongside the big futon. He jumped out of bed, clad only in his boxers, and his head spun. His leather attaché case was on the chair, too, and he opened it and looked for his phone while making sure not to let his eyes rest on the book or the rest of the evidence. The screen on the phone said that the time was eight in the morning and that he had missed twenty calls, all from his wife. The last one had been made just after two in the morning. The notion that she had been worried was comforting, but the comfort soon turned to fear when he wondered where the calls had been made from and whether she had gone back to her parents' house. Maybe it wasn't concern or remorse that had driven her to call but rather the urge to let him know that she had taken the kids and left, and that she just wanted to let him know that she did not want to see him again and that she thought he was a nothing, always had. Maybe she wanted to say that she had been an idiot, spending her best years with a creep like him, that he made her sick, or maybe she'd just hit him over the head with the truth, tell him about her true love, her unblemished lover, his support and devotion. Now that she held all the cards, she could tell him whatever she wanted. What a mistake he had made, the lawyer thought; he, the cold and calculating lawyer, had thrown half his net worth away in one moment of recklessness. By letting his guard down for one moment he had robbed himself of the chance to leave her penniless, to strip her of everything she had, to take away the children. All he had to do was wait one more day, until Sunday, when the Sharia courts opened, and file for divorce. His only hope was to get up and wait outside the Sharia courts and file for divorce before she made it to the civil court. But she had surely already consulted with her parents and family and was certainly at this very moment seated before some lowly lawyer from the Galilee with a crude accent and together they were, at this moment, wording her plea. Who knew what she might accuse him of? For a moment he really was curious about the nature of her accusations. Perhaps verbal violence, neglect of the children, oppressiveness toward her; perhaps even a charge of physical violence. The closet incident of last night would surely loom large in her allegations, along with jealousy, feverish suspicion, and baseless accusations.

The lawyer fished around in his pants pocket for a cigarette. His head was still spinning and he was thirsty. But he did not leave the bedroom because he knew that outside, in the hall, Tarik was asleep on the couch and he didn't want to wake him up this early. He'd done more than enough by giving up his bed and who knew what kind of things he'd endured while hauling his boss up the stairs. The lawyer hoped that at least he had not been noisy and that none of the neighbors had woken up. He opened the bedroom window and saw that the view was of a neighbor's balcony and that there was an old man sitting out there smoking a cigarette and having a cup of coffee. The neighbor was looking back at the lawyer. The lawyer snapped the curtain closed and pushed his legs into his pants and his arms into his shirt. As he buttoned his pants, he heard the harsh ring of a doorbell. After a moment of silence he heard the hoarse doorbell again, followed by Tarik, who, just woken, grumbled, "Just a second," and then a confused "Who is it?"

The lawyer went to the bedroom door and practically put his ear to the wood in his attempt to hear what was going on. The key turned in the lock, the door creaked, and then he heard his wife.

"Good morning, Tarik, where's the man of the hour?"

The lawyer was about to get up and greet her when he got his bearings back and sat down on the edge of the bed and shoved the extinguished cigarette between his lips, assuming a foul expression. Soon enough there were soft knocks on the bedroom door, followed by a gentle swiveling of the doorknob. His wife stood before him, smiling, and he could tell that she was going out of her way to keep the smile fixed on her face.

"Well, well," she said to Tarik. "Here's our man, all dressed and awake."

The lawyer was silent, and Tarik, who stood somewhere in the hall, called out a "Good morning."

"Good morning, Tarik," the lawyer said, "could you do me a favor and get me a glass of water, please?"

His wife remained next to the door, fighting back tears, staring at her husband. How attractive she was now. He wanted to take her by the hand, pull her over to the bed, rip off her clothes, kiss her neck, feel her writhe beneath him on the hard futon. Don't give in, he reminded himself, you have a plan and you have to stick to it. Don't be weak; don't let her control you. Don't let her sad eyes trick you. Remember, he told himself, this is war and your adversary is a woman that you hardly even know.

His wife took the bottle of water and the two glasses from Tarik and smiled.

"Thank you," she said. "Sorry for the inconvenience."

"No, not at all," Tarik said in a voice that was gruff with sleeplessness and the residue of alcohol. "I'm going to head out in a second. There's a café around the corner. Boss, I know what you want. A cappuccino, right?" he asked from the hall, still not visible to the lawyer.

"Yes, two shots, please."

"And for the lady?" Tarik asked, referring to her as he always did. If only he knew the kind of things this lady was capable of, the lawyer thought.

"No, nothing, thank you. We'll be leaving soon anyway, won't we?" she said, looking at her husband and waiting for an answer that did not come.

"Okay, so two cappuccinos it is," Tarik said and headed out.

The lawyer's wife put the bottle of water and the glasses at the foot of the futon. "Would you please tell me what all this is about?" she asked. The lawyer sent her a combative glance and then drank long and hard from the bottle. Let her wait. Then he set it back down on the floor and looked her in the face.

"Where are the kids?"

"With Nili."

"What did you tell her? That your husband got drunk and that you went out looking for him?"

"No, don't worry. I didn't say a thing. That's what you're always worried about, what they'll think, what the neighbors will say."

"Yes," the lawyer said, "that's what I'm worried about. What they'll say is precisely what worries me, so lower your voice, please, there are neighbors here, too."

"Okay."

"So what did you tell Nili?"

"Relax," she said, her voice sharp and challenging. "I didn't tell her anything. I told her something had come up in the village. That you'd gone home and that I was heading up after you."

"What kind of something?"

"I don't know, I didn't specify."

"And she didn't ask?"

"No, she didn't ask. I've done a million favors for her over the years. So just relax, okay, no one knows anything. No one knows that you weren't home last night and that you acted like a maniac."

"Me?"

"Yes, you. And I'd like an explanation, too. Because I won't live like this, not a chance," she said, and she burst into tears and shut the bedroom door, which until then had been half open.

"Enough, cut the crap," the lawyer said as his wife mopped the tears from her face.

"You're insane," she said, her face recomposed and fresh. "You are totally insane."

"Lower your voice," the lawyer commanded.

"What did I ever do to you? What did I do? You know what?" she said, holding on to the door knob, "you can take all your little conspiracies and shove them."

"You're a liar and an adulterer," he said, trying to score some points. But again he felt that she had gotten the better of him, and with ease. All she'd done was pretend to turn her back and he had lost his cool.

"What did you say?" she asked, letting go of the doorknob.

"I said you are a liar," the lawyer said, retracting part of his earlier statement.

"Why, exactly, am I a liar?" she asked, even though she had heard the other charge, too.

"I think you know well enough yourself."

"No, I don't. Please be so kind as to point out where and when I lied."

"Listen, my love," he said, trying to sound as belittling as he could, "we both know you lied. So why don't we stop with the games, okay?"

"What, when did I lie? You don't believe me that I went out for coffee with Faten?" she said, pulling out her telephone. "Then go ahead and call her. Ask her yourself."

"No," the lawyer said, the blood pounding in his veins. "Not Faten. You know full well when you lied." He ground his teeth and wasn't able to keep in the scream. "Enough. I'm not a little kid. You lied to me and you know it."

"What? The note?" she cried. "That's what all this shit is about?" She sat down and put her head in her hands, and the lawyer knew from experience that a confession was on the way. The question and the crying were the classic precursors to disclosure.

"Where did you even find that thing?" she asked, but didn't wait for an answer. "Who gave it to you? Who's the bastard who gave it to you? You think I even remember that I once wrote that? I recognize my handwriting but I really don't remember writing it. What is it? It's my handwriting, I recognize it, but what is it? Where did you find it? That's what this whole thing is about? A note that I must have written a million years ago? Where did it come from?"

"What does that have to do with anything?" the lawyer groaned. "Why do you care how I got it or who gave it to me? You lied to me, that's what matters."

"How did I lie to you? You think I remembered that thing? I spent the entire night trying to remember what it was, when it was from."

"And?"

"And I remember." Her mouth was twisted into a sneer. "And you know what? If that's what interests you, if this is the kind of thing that makes you act the way you did, then I'm the asshole for living with you for all these years." She wiped at her tears. "Do whatever the hell you want," she said, throwing open the door.

The lawyer jumped off the futon and grabbed her arm. "Where are you going?"

"I can't live like this."

"What will you do?"

"If this is what you think of me, I'll do whatever you want, okay? You want me to go back to my parents? You want to separate? Whatever you want. Whatever you say."

"So," the lawyer said, tightening his grip on her arm as she tried to wriggle free and leave, "you're using this as an alibi to go and run off with him."

"With who?" she yelled. "You maniac, with who?"

"Lower your voice, please."

"No."

"Are these the kinds of power games you play with him, too? Does he like these kinds of games?" The lawyer envisioned them together, his wife moaning with the kind of pleasure he had never inspired, and on top of her this man, smiling with the slyest of smiles.

"You're crazy," she cried, her body slumping, no longer straining to get free. "You think I even remember what he looks like?"

"You remember, you remember," he said softly, as though speaking to a little girl. He took her hands and lowered them from her face. He smiled at her, while his hands held on to hers and lowered them to her waist and suddenly he wanted to hug her, but instead of hugging her he raised his right hand and, had he not heard Tarik come in, would have smacked her across the face, sending her flying onto the bed. That was the language she understood, just like in her Egyptian melodramas, he thought, breathing heavily, his chest rising and falling, the thumping bass of the previous night pounding in his ears.

TWO CARS

Samah was not surprised to hear the lawyer on the phone on a Saturday.

"Good morning," she said over her squealing kids and the high-pitched sounds of the cartoons. Once every few weeks the lawyer would call her on a Saturday with a favor, asking that she look into something, so long as it wasn't too much of an inconvenience, and she, so long as none of her boys were sick and she had not gone out on a family outing, always had time to do the lawyer a favor.

"I'm looking for someone," he said, and his voice wavered when he realized that he was including her in a matter of grave importance. "All I know is that he's an Arab-Israeli, around twenty-eight years old. I need to get ahold of him, put him on the stand. He's a social worker. Here's the telephone number of the head of social services in east Jerusalem. According to the information I have, he worked at their substance abuse outpatient clinic six or seven years ago and then just disappeared. I know this is not very specific information, but for now it's all I have. All I need is his name, unless, of course, you can also find where he works. That's it. Nothing else."

He read Samah the number for the head of social services, whom he knew personally, and then said, "By the way, Samah, if they ask who it's for, say it's for a law firm but don't say which one. Say it has to do with an inheritance and that we can't find a current address, okay? Thank you, and I'm really sorry to bother you with this, it's just that it's urgent, and please send regards to your husband."

The lawyer snapped open his desk drawer, looking for something that would help his headache, sure that he'd find some kind of aspirin. His head throbbed, but he had preferred to go to the office rather than the house. "I have some work that I need to take care of," he had told his wife, even though she had not asked for an explanation.

He got up to make himself a glass of Turkish coffee in the kitchenette and drank some water, in little sips, so that it would be readily accepted by his body, not big gulps that could be shocking to the system, as he'd read online. He heaped two tall teaspoons of finely ground coffee into a glass, poured steaming water over them, and stirred. Although the lawyer had read online that coffee only exacerbated a hangover, he knew he needed to be alert, to take care of business and to avoid mistakes. Over the past two days, he'd certainly made his share.

"I don't remember his name," his wife had said about the guy to whom she'd written the note. This, of course, was a lie. She'd told him the whole story and the lawyer had felt that while she described this man whose name she supposedly didn't remember, there was compassion, even love, in her voice.

The lawyer sipped the coffee, scalding his tongue, and sat down in his chair. Again he wondered about the appearance of the man with whom he had shared his wife. Because even if she had been telling the truth and the man was really just a colleague, a downtrodden kid who had never so much as touched her — even if all that was true, the lawyer knew that love had blossomed between them. What an idiot he had been. He never even considered the possibility that his wife might have loved someone else before him, and now he wasn't even sure if she'd ever loved him at all.

"What's the big deal about the note? What did I say — that I'd had a nice evening and that he should call? That's it," his wife had said, after they'd supposedly made up, a reconciliation that began as soon as Tarik returned to the apartment. The lawyer had come to his senses, apologized, and said he believed her, and she had apologized too, saying again that she had forgotten that she'd ever written that note. She said that the whole thing had happened many years before, while she interned at the outpatient clinic. She'd written the note to another social worker, perhaps the strangest person she'd ever met.

"He was like a kid. And everyone took advantage of him. He was totally helpless," she said, and the lawyer had a hard time bottling up the rage that the description evoked.

So it wasn't a tough guy, a skirt chaser, but a sensitive guy, the kind who may well have read all the books that the lawyer had acquired at the used bookstore. But why *Yonatan*? the lawyer wondered. Why would an Arab sign the name *Yonatan* in all of his books?

"What was I supposed to think?" the lawyer had forced himself to say with a smile. He knew that temporary reconciliation was the only way to avoid defeat.

"Out of nowhere I find this letter, which I could tell you wrote, and I asked myself how is it possible that Leila, the person closest to me in the world, wrote this? I spent an entire day trying to find an explanation and when I couldn't, I was hoping that you would give me one, but when you lied, I let the worst of my imagination run wild. As you can tell, I went out drinking, got terribly drunk, wanted to die. All because of a note you wrote a million years ago. Why didn't you tell me?" he asked, and then without waiting for an answer he asked again, "Why didn't you tell me?"

His wife laughed when he told her about the book. "Can you believe it?" he said and pulled out *The Kreutzer Sonata*. "Here I am putting the kids to bed, waiting for you to come home from your friend's house, and I take out this book that I got at the used bookstore and the next thing I know I'm reading a love letter. At first I thought you had written it and put it in my book so I'd find it. But then . . . I mean, how did you expect me to act? You should be happy all I did was throw your clothes out of the closet. I was thinking about burning them."

His wife laughed, seemingly convinced. "I don't believe it," she said, turning the book over like someone
examining a piece of evidence for the first time. "How did
the note wind up in here?" and her question seemed genuine to the lawyer. "Well," she said, "he was the strangest
guy I ever met. He just disappeared one day. Everyone
laughed at him, poor thing." And that phrase, and the
way she said it, only sharpened the sadness in the lawyer's chest. "I guess you've always had a thing for strange
people," he said, giving her shoulders a squeeze.

They both thanked Tarik, and the lawyer apologized
for the imposition and promised to make it up to him. Then
he and his wife went out to their cars. She was going to pick
up the kids and he said he was going home to shower.

"I don't want the kids to see me like this. Did they ask
about me?" he questioned her before getting into his car.

"I told them you were at work," she said.

"Listen, wait, hold on just a second . . . shut up, will you,"
he heard Samah yell at her kids.

"Okay, I'm shutting up," the lawyer said, and Samah
laughed. "Hold on, I'm moving to the bedroom, I can't get
a word in here."

"Okay, let's hear it," the lawyer said when she got back
on the line.

"The name I got is Amir Lahab, that's him."

"You sure?" The lawyer wrote the name down on a
piece of paper. Amir Lahab; he mumbled the name to himself
and then lit a cigarette and tossed the lighter onto the desk.
"Who gave you his name? The head of social services?"

"Yeah, I called him and he told me right away. He just burst out laughing as soon as I told him that I was looking for a guy who had worked there and then disappeared. 'There's a blast from the past,' he said, laughing the whole time. Turns out that this Amir worked under him and that he'd been Amir's supervisor during his internship. He made a good impression, apparently, and was a good kid, a little weird, but he did his job well and he kept to himself. He started working there right after he graduated. Worked for a few months and then one day he left a resignation letter and disappeared."

"Disappeared? But that was many years ago."

"Right. Several years ago," Samah said. "That's what the guy said. He said he hopes I'm able to find him and that after he left his job they looked for him for a while but he never turned up. He told me to send regards if I found him."

"And then?"

"And then I asked if, by any chance, he had an old address or something and he said he'd look in his file and he found an address in Jaljulia, an old telephone number, and an ID number."

"Oh, really? What's his ID number?" the lawyer asked, practically leaping out of his chair.

"I wrote it down in the kitchen. I'll text it to you in a second."

"Great, Samah, thank you so much," the lawyer said. "And please apologize again to your husband. Tell him I've got some cigars here with his name on them."

So that's his name, *Amir Lahab*. The man his wife had been with—and who knew what they had done—on the night that he, the lawyer, had fallen in love with her. He recalled how she had surprised him and his sister when she came home early from the student party. She had probably been out dancing with Amir Lahab, the lawyer thought, remembering her black dress and the expression on her face when she came back to the dorm. Her face had looked sad, and he, the idiot, had loved her all the more for it. Later that night he had been unable to fall asleep. He kept seeing her at the entrance to the room, in that dress, radiant, and all he could think of was how he could make her his. She, too, probably hadn't been able to sleep that night, but not on account of him. Probably all she could think about was Amir Lahab and the wild night she had had with him, which led to the letter, which was not a letter you write to just any old colleague—of that the lawyer was certain. It was a love letter. He disappeared, she had told him, she wrote him that note and he disappeared. She swore she hadn't seen him since and that she couldn't even remember what he looked like.

"If I saw him on the street, I wouldn't recognize him," she had said, and the lawyer knew you did not have to recognize someone in order to love them. The lawyer realized that she had settled—for him. What would have happened had this Amir not run off? He remembered the early weeks of their courtship and felt humiliated. She wasn't thinking about me at all, he thought, she was waiting for someone else. She was stimulated not by my presence, but by his absence.

Amir Lahab, the lawyer typed into the search engine, at first in Hebrew, which read it as *Lahav*, and he found thousands of links. Designers, lawyers, carpenters—there was a long list. He typed it in along with the words *social worker* and got nothing relevant. Still, he clicked on several links and was surprised to find that all of the Amir Lahavs were Jews.

Then he typed the name in Arabic and found that most of the results were from different countries. The ones that were from Israel did not seem remotely related to social work.

The lawyer reverted to the tried-and-true method of locating an Arab in Israel — using the family name. He typed *Lahab* into the Yellow Pages search engine and found that they were a big family in Tira, not in Jaljulia as Samah had said. In Jaljulia there were no Lahabs at all. Both villages are in the Triangle, and Tira was very close to the lawyer's own hometown. He's from the Triangle? the lawyer wondered. My adversary is a villager? The man who had read more books than he, the one his wife had preferred, was a lousy villager, just like him? The lawyer tried to calm himself. Say she really did love someone before him? Say she had fallen for one of the boys in high school? Would he be jealous then, too? Wasn't he just being primitive? What had happened to his progressive ideas? What happened to women's rights? What about his daughter? Hadn't he promised himself a million times that she would grow up differently? That he would shield her from societal expectations and norms and that he would raise her as a liberated woman?

The problem was that the lawyer knew he was not willing to be different. If it was common, if his friends and family members were married to women who had all had prior relationships, that would be one thing, then he could deal with it. But he was not willing to be the only joker in the group. And anyway, the lawyer wondered, why had she hid this relationship? If she believed she did nothing wrong, then why had she lied? Was she embarrassed of what she'd done, did she feel it was wrong, so wrong that she had hid the truth from her husband, and if that was the case, then why should he accept it now?

The lawyer found no Amir Lahab in the telephone directory. He chose one of the Lahabs in the phone book from Tira and called from the unidentified number in the office. A child, he couldn't tell if it was a boy or a girl, answered the phone.

"Who is this?" the little voice asked. "Who's speaking?"

The lawyer asked to speak with the child's father and the little voice giggled and handed the phone to the mother.

"Hello."

"*Salaam alaikum,*" the lawyer said, and the mother's voice changed when she realized it was not someone she knew.

"*Alaikum a-salaam.* How can I help you?"

"I'm looking for Amir Lahab," the lawyer said.

"Who? There's no one here by that name. I think you have the wrong number."

"I'm a lawyer from Jerusalem, and I thought you might be able to help me find him. Maybe he's a family member?"

"Hold on," the woman said, and she yelled, "There's a lawyer on the line and he says he's looking for someone named Amir Lahab from our family. You know any Amirs?"

The lawyer could hear her husband walking toward her and taking the phone.

"Hello, who's speaking?"

"*Salaam alaikum,*" the lawyer said, using the greeting he always used when he wanted to set someone at ease.

"*Alaikum a-salaam.* Who's speaking, please?"

"I'm a lawyer," the lawyer said, and gave the man a name he had made up on the spot. "I'm handling an inheritance case and I'm looking for someone by the name of Amir Lahab. I thought he might be from your extended family and that perhaps you could help me find him."

"Amir," the husband said. "I know an Amir, but he's a little kid. In first grade."

"No, that wouldn't be right."

"Oh," the husband said, "maybe it's that Amir, the son of . . . wait a second." He called to his wife, "Do you remember what's her name's son, you know, Abu Hasan's daughter, the widow, the one who left, what's her name?"

"Meissar?" he heard the woman say. "I think she had a kid but I don't remember his name."

"It's possible," the husband said. "Might be him. If I'm not mistaken, he doesn't live in Tira anymore. They left when he was a kid, he and his mother, there was a whole big mess and they left. Might be the guy you're looking for."

"I see. So they don't live in Tira?"

"If it's them, I really don't know where they are. I think they may have moved to Jaljulia back in the day, the mother and the son. But I'm not sure."

"To Jaljulia," the lawyer said. "Thank you so much for your help, sir. Thank you." The lawyer hung up the phone and typed *Jaljulia* into the space on the Web directory where it asked for place of residence. He didn't find any Amirs but he did see a listing for a Meissar La'ab. He knew that was the person he was looking for, even though the name was slightly different. The Israeli authorities regularly bastardized Arab names.

The lawyer dialed the number. His heart thumped and he tried to organize his thoughts. What if he'd moved back in with his mother? What if he answered? He decided he'd hang up immediately if he heard a male voice. Maybe he'd ask, "Amir?" and then, if the guy said something like, *Yes, who is this?*, the lawyer would end the conversation.

"Hello," the lawyer said to the voice on the other end of the line, but it was a recorded message: "The number you have reached is no longer in service."

95 OCTANE UNLEADED

What exactly was he planning on doing? What would he do if he found out where Amir Lahab lived? The roads were relatively empty on Shabbat and he could make the drive down to Jaljulia in around half an hour. The lawyer felt the need to make the trip even though he wasn't sure he'd get out of the car. He couldn't stay in the office and he had the feeling that a drive on the open road would do him good. Sometimes driving alone in the new car had a therapeutic effect.

There were only a few cars waiting at the light on the way out of Jerusalem. A picnic Saturday, the lawyer thought, as he looked over at the family in the car to his right. He liked it when drivers eyed his car, liked it when he spotted women looking at him through their sunglasses, trying to guess what the rich man in the luxury car did for a living. But right now all he felt was jealousy for the family to his right. He saw the woman talking away at her husband, maybe even arguing, and he recalled the way his wife would hold her silence for long stretches of time when they were in the car together. She could keep quiet for hours, and it always pissed him off.

"Say something," he'd plead whenever they were on their way to his or her parents or just en route to some fancy hotel with the kids for the weekend. And she'd always respond, "What do you want me to say?"

The lawyer hit the gas and headed away from Jerusalem, leaving the family car far behind. They want a show? He thought to himself, I'll give them a show, and he remembered his first time on the highway with his daughter. She was a month old and his wife was in the back with the baby and the lawyer drove more slowly than he ever had in his life. He was sweating and his sweaty hands grew slippery on the wheel and he was afraid of losing control of the car. He stuck exclusively to the right side of the road and pumped the brakes whenever he had to slow down. He despised the car he had at the time, felt it was not to be trusted, that at any moment a tire could blow out, that the brakes could betray him at any turn, sending him and his family flying off the cliff. The lawyer shook his head free of those thoughts now and played with the buttons on the steering wheel, looking for talk radio, anything but music, anything that would take his mind off the matter at hand. But he found nothing.

What was the point in going to Jaljulia? The lawyer was not sure. Maybe it was his wife's innocence that he sought. Maybe he wanted to know that the woman with whom he had not shared a bed for many years still loved him, even though he was not sure to what extent he loved

her. Maybe he wanted to breathe life into the embers of his
love—he'd read of such things—but he knew that at best
the embers were extinguished and at worst had never been
lit in the first place.

Or maybe he sought to retrieve his own honor. What
was it that he wanted? To know that she'd cheated on him or
to go back to living the way he had before he found the note?
Maybe it was for the best that his life had been disrupted.
Maybe it was a sign from above, he thought, even though he
had never been one for celestial signs. Maybe it was time to
pack his things and go, maybe it was time to stop sleeping
alone in his daughter's bed and start fresh, do everything
differently, pick the kind of woman who would, as he imagined in his most melancholic moments, finally light the fire
of love within him. The lawyer recalled an article he'd come
across in which some important psychologist had said that
love meant loving someone more than you loved yourself.
Someone that completed you. Love is the ability to sacrifice
for the object of your love, was the psychologist's point.
While reading the article, the lawyer had asked himself if
those were his feelings toward his wife, and it pained him to
admit that they were not. She did not complete him. On the
contrary, he felt that married life limited him—financially,
because he had a family to support, and professionally, because without the need to support them he might have gone
back to school and pursued an advanced degree, perhaps a
PhD, and become a professor, as he'd once wanted. At any
rate, he didn't want to sacrifice anything for her, that much
he was sure of. But what did she lack anyway? he asked
himself all of a sudden. After all, I give her whatever she
wants. She has never wanted for anything. He remembered

that the real matter at hand was her love for him, and not his for her. Does she sacrifice for me? the lawyer asked himself, and responded that it was not so.

Maybe at some point he really would come across what they call a soul mate. Maybe now that he was older, more organized, more aware of his wants, more in control of his thoughts, he would be able to discern between temporary lust and sustainable love. Maybe now he would be able to find a woman he could sleep next to every night, maybe he would feel the warmth of her body seeping into his bones, granting him a tranquility he had never known. The lawyer saw before his eyes a faceless woman, but he knew she had the face of an angel and she slept peacefully in his arms, her face smooth, a happy sheen across her cheeks. He imagined them sleeping harmoniously together, completing one another in their sleep, too, wrapped in a comfortable embrace, moving their bodies with complete synchronicity, always fitting together. For a moment he felt a rush of warmth in his heart. Maybe all of those romantic poets were right? Maybe he shouldn't have been so dismissive of their words? Maybe he shouldn't have been so skeptical of what was clearly a sublime sensation?

She, on the other hand, had never been skeptical. She was willing to lie, to live in sin, to risk her good name, the name of her family, the future of her children, all for a love she could not get from her husband. For a fleeting moment the lawyer admired his wife for her courage but the admiration quickly faded into hatred and contempt. His wife — she wasn't smart, the lawyer thought; at best she was a functioning airhead. A miserable little Arab woman whose guides in life were love songs and filth-ridden melodramas. Only the lower classes were capable of falling blindly in love after adolescence, the lawyer thought, only the poor, the uneducated and unenlightened, could fall helplessly in love. Like animals, the lawyer said to himself, acknowledging, not for the first time, that there was no bridging the divide between their backgrounds, between where he came from and where he had found her. You must have to be primitive in order to continue believing in the delusion called love. It's a lot like religion, the lawyer thought, it's easy for them, the down and out, to embrace it.

He surprised himself with these thoughts. If that's how I perceive her, he thought, then she must be aware of it, and for a moment he practically condemned himself for her decision to seek solace in someone else's arms. But that's not how it is, he said to himself, cutting the chain of thought, by God that's not how it is. He might be busy, he might not love her as he used to, but he did not ignore her or forsake her or make her life unduly hard. She was just as preoccupied with life as he was. How could she ever find time to think, strive, desire? Who even had time to cheat?

His wife had a good life, he concluded, and mine isn't too bad either. It had been a little bit boring, but by no means dreadful.

A sign missing a few of its letters in Hebrew and Arabic welcomed him to Jaljulia. The lawyer decided to stop at the gas station at the entrance to the village. He'd never been to Jaljulia but he had known, ever since he had been a kid growing up nearby, that it was even worse off than the surrounding Arab villages, which were the kinds of places he learned later in life to call disenfranchised. In college, for instance, he had never once met a student from Jaljulia.

"Hello," a middle-aged attendant said as he wiped his hands on a towel and walked out of his office. "Ninety-five unleaded?" he asked, and the lawyer nodded and said, "Yes, fill it up please."

"How much does a car like this cost these days?" the attendant asked as he shoved the nozzle into the tank.

"Not sure," the lawyer said. "A lot."

"Great ride, though," the attendant said. "You're not from here, are you?"

"No," the lawyer said, and he found himself adding, without much forethought, "Actually I came down here to look for an old friend from school. I haven't seen him in six or seven years."

"Who?" the attendant asked. "Someone from here? From Jaljulia?"

"Yeah," the lawyer said. "His name's Amir Lahab."

"Lahab?" the attendant asked, screwing up his face. "You sure he's from here? There's no Lahab family in this village. Not that I know of."

"No big deal," the lawyer said. "Could be I got confused. I was just driving past and I thought of him. I might've gotten it wrong. Maybe he's from somewhere else."

"Baher!" the attendant yelled, turning his head toward the office.

"What?" a young man asked, coming out of the office and wiping his mouth with a napkin as he chewed.

"Is there someone named Lahab in this village? Is that what you said, Lahab?"

"Amir."

"You know an Amir Lahab?" the old attendant asked just as the tank was filled.

"Ahh," the young guy said, approaching the car. "Lahab? There's that teacher, you know, the one from Tira, you know who I mean . . ."

"Ah, yeah, yeah," the older man said. "That's her son he's looking for?"

"Could be," the young man said. "She had a kid in school. A few years older than me. He went to college. Could be him."

The lawyer knew it was.

"What could someone like her ever do for someone like you?" the young man asked.

At that, the older attendant erupted. "Shut up and get out of here," he hissed at the young man, then turned to the lawyer, afraid that somehow the young man had gotten them into trouble. "The kid is an idiot. I'm sorry. Don't believe a word he says. I'm telling you, this village, may God forgive its inhabitants, they don't let people live their own lives. I'm telling you that your friend was raised in a very good home. And if anyone in this village wants to tell you differently, then I'm telling you that he's a liar and a son of a liar. No one will tell you that they ever saw that boy's mother do anything wrong."

"I'm sure. He was always a great kid," the lawyer said, "that Amir."

"What did I tell you?" the attendant said, shutting the gas tank. "Anyway, she rents from um-Bassem. Go up the hill," the attendant said, pointing straight ahead, "and take a right by the Maccabi health clinic. There's a sign with a Magen David on it, you'll see it; anyway, take a right there.

Go about a hundred yards more and ask for um-Bassem's house."

All the Arab villages look exactly the same, the lawyer thought to himself as he cruised through the streets. The local councils usually invest money on the entrance to the city and let the rest of the place rot, their main concern that there be a nice place for the head of the council to take his next campaign picture. All Arab villages have some kind of traffic circle near the entrance to the village and there's always a pale-looking palm tree rooted there. The deeper into the village you go, the narrower the streets, until they turn to dirt, thin and dusty in summer and thick and oozing with mud in winter. The lawyer followed the gas attendant's directions, driving slowly, attracting stares from the pedestrians. He stopped alongside a neighborhood convenience store. Two older men sat outside. He took off his sunglasses and opened the window. *"Salaam alaikum,"* he said, playing up his country accent. The lawyer didn't need their help but he figured he'd talk to them to quiet the neighbors' unspoken apprehension and curiosity.

"Alaikum a-salaam," the two elderly men answered in unison.

"I am looking for the home of the *haja* um-Bassem."

"Um-Bassem, may Allah have mercy," one of them answered. The lawyer tried to hide his embarrassment at the fact that he hadn't known he was looking for a dead woman's house.

"Take a right down there," the second one said, pointing at the next turn. "The house is on that dirt road. Not the first, not the second, but the third house. That's hers, Allah have mercy."

"*Ta'ish*," the lawyer said, as though he were a family member accepting condolences.

The lawyer fished through his bag to make sure he still had the book. He'd introduce himself as a lawyer and say he was looking for the person to whom the note had been addressed. Or not. He imagined the man's reaction and was rattled. It could be dangerous. And anyway how would he explain why he was looking for the man? The note didn't even have Amir's name on it. Maybe he should say he was a reporter, at least at first, until he had a better sense of the lover's personality and could gauge how he might react. He could be a reporter who was working on a story about the outpatient clinic in east Jerusalem. Yeah, the lawyer thought, that was the way to go. He was a reporter looking into what seemed like years of corruption at the clinic. And if this Amir character didn't buy it, then he'd just leave, no harm done.

"Who gave you my name?" he would certainly ask, and the lawyer would say he heard about him from a social worker by the name of Leila, and he would appraise the effect of her name on him. That's exactly what he would do, he thought, and he parked the car past the house, out of view, because what kind of journalist drives around in a half-million-shekel car?

The lawyer knocked on the door and took a quick step back. A neighbor hanging laundry on a nearby roof eyed him suspiciously.

The door opened. A fifty-year-old woman looked at the stranger on her doorstep and then furtively at the neighbors.

"Hello," the lawyer said.

"Welcome," the woman said. "How can I help you?"

"Excuse me," the lawyer said. "I was wondering if this was the home of Amir Lahab?"

"Yes," the woman said. "Who are you? Did something happen to him?"

"No, no," the lawyer said. "I just wanted to talk to him about something. Nothing major. I guess he's not home, though."

"No," the woman said, her voice knotted with worry. "He's not home."

"I'm a friend of his," the lawyer blurted out.

"A friend?"

"My name's Mazen. I went to school with him. I was just in the area and was thinking of him and figured I'd swing by and see how he's doing."

"Oh, *ahlan wa sahlan*," she said, looking relaxed. She stepped out of the house and closed the door behind her. "No," she said to the lawyer, "my son, he's not home, he's in Jerusalem," and the lawyer realized that he had not disappeared, as his wife had claimed, had not gone back home like most social workers who couldn't afford to live in the big city on their measly salaries. No, he'd stayed in Jerusalem, for her.

"Do you have his phone number by any chance? We just kind of lost touch and . . ."

"I wish," the mother said. "I don't have anything of the sort. Has it been a long time since you've seen him?"

"God, yeah, it's been years. Since college, you know. How is he? Is he still working in the same field?"

"Yes," the mother said, confiding in the lawyer. "He decided to stay there. I begged him to come home but he didn't want to."

"And you don't have a number where you can reach him? How can that be?" the lawyer asked, chuckling, trying to make light of the situation.

"No, he doesn't have a phone. There's a line at work, so every once in a while, whenever he remembers his mother, he picks up the phone and calls me. Once a week, once every two weeks, he'll do me a favor and ask me how I'm doing."

"Well, you know how he is," the lawyer said. "I miss him."

"What can I say? I miss him more. But if he calls, I'll tell him you came by. What did you say your name was?"

"Mazen," the lawyer said. "Tell him Mazen, from the university, from the dorms."

"I'll tell him when he calls. It's been over a month since he's last been back to visit," she said, visibly distraught, and she gestured for him to sit down at the plastic table outside, and the lawyer knew why she did not invite him in.

"So, has he gotten married? Wife? Kids?" the lawyer asked as he sat down across from the mother.

"I wish," the mother moaned. "Nothing. Nothing. But you guys are to blame, his friends. Couldn't you talk to him, find him a good girl. He doesn't listen to a word I say. He's almost thirty."

"Yeah, wow," the lawyer said, forcing himself to laugh, even though the thought of this bachelor, the man who danced with his wife at a party, made his blood boil.

"Are you also a social worker?" the mother asked.

"No," the lawyer said distractedly. "I'm a lawyer." And immediately he felt that he had made a mistake. One call to his mother and Amir would know that a lawyer whom he'd never met had pretended to be an old friend and one more call to the lawyer's wife and she would already know exactly who it was that had been sniffing around Amir's house.

"A lawyer? Amir has a lawyer friend and he doesn't make use of him?" the mother said.

"Why," the lawyer asked. "Is something wrong?"

"His inheritance," she said. "He's got ten *dunam* of land. Inheritance from his father. And he won't even ask for it. You could easily get him his inheritance. I've already stopped telling him to demand what is legally his. Instead of wandering around and paying rent all over the place he could have sold his land and bought himself a house. It's his, from his father. Why shouldn't he take it?"

"Well," the lawyer said, "I'm happy to help. Just tell him to call me. When do you think you'll hear from him?"

"Huh," the mother said, "probably not for another month. He took the trouble to talk to me yesterday. Gave me a whole half minute of his time. Said he was busy and then hung up. What can I get you to drink?"

"Thank you, I'm fine." The lawyer hesitated for a second before asking permission to use the bathroom.

"Of course, no problem," the mother said. She remained outside and gave him instructions for how to find the bathroom. "My house is your house," she said.

The lawyer strode across the living room and already regretted asking to use the bathroom. He could easily have waited until he got back to the gas station. Head down, protecting the mother's privacy, he walked straight to the bathroom. It was small and clean. The lawyer urinated and when he was done he remembered to put the seat back down. On his way out, he turned his head to the side for a second and saw what he was after, a picture of a young Amir. He felt a jolt of pain. The kid was handsome.

"I'm sorry," the lawyer said as he walked back outside.

"What for, my son?" the woman asked, and the lawyer saw a light go out in her eyes when she said the word *son*. "On the contrary, I'm the one who's sorry, for not being able to host you properly."

"Thank you, Auntie," the lawyer said, and he shook her hand. "Please tell Amir that I came by and was looking for him," he added, raising his voice for the neighbor's benefit. He handed the woman a piece of paper with a fictitious telephone number and left the house.

"A friend of Amir's from Jerusalem," he heard the mother yelling across to the neighbor.

A torrent of conflicting thoughts raced through the lawyer's mind as he sat back down behind the wheel of his car. Why had his wife lied to him again? Why? He had so wanted to believe her, to help and defend her, to prove her innocence in the face of his own accusations. But how could he believe anything she said after this conversation with Amir's mother? How was he supposed to believe that she hadn't seen him since that night if Amir had stayed in Jerusalem and still worked as a social worker in the city? The lawyer knew that Arab social workers in Jerusalem were just like the lawyers—they all knew each other. Thanks to his wife, he even knew most of them.

On the way out of the village, the lawyer lit a cigarette and opened the car window. His phone beeped twice, alerting him to a message. He put the cigarette down in the car's gold-colored ashtray. He hoped it was a message from his wife, but it was Samah, sending him Amir's ID number. The lawyer pulled hard on the cigarette and expelled the smoke out the window. He did not like smoking in the car. It's Saturday, and there's no way for you to check his ID number, he reminded himself. Then he turned on the radio, searching for an upbeat song.

PART
SIX

TRANSPORTER

"Yonatan?" the security guard half asked, half said as I got off the bus at Sirkin Junction near Petach Tikva. "Dude, you got to get yourself a new picture," he said, looking at my ID card and then handing it back.

I walked toward the makeshift share-taxi stand that served the residents of Kfar Kassem and Jaljulia. As I arrived one of the taxis pulled out, leaving two Transporters in line. The two drivers, whose faces I recognized, sat on the curb and smoked.

Back in the day, all of the taxis were Mercedes-Benz sedans that could seat seven, but they don't make those anymore, and since a regular four-door isn't worth the drivers' while, they now drive Volkswagen Transporter vans and never leave until they're entirely full. On Thursday afternoons it's never a problem because Petach Tikva is the hub for the villages of the southern Triangle.

I nodded at the drivers and had to mumble, "*Salaam alaikum.*"

"*Alaikum a-salaam,*" one of them said. "You can put your bag in the car." He pointed to the van with the open door.

"Whose son is that?" I heard one of the drivers ask as I put my bag in the backseat.

"Don't know," the other one answered, and I felt their eyes on me. "Village's gotten big, ah?"

❊   ❊   ❊

I had to go down to Jaljulia. "Um-Bassem's days are num-bered," my mother had blubbered over the phone the last time we talked. "It would be a disgrace if you didn't come and say good-bye to her."

The landlord, the one I called *siti,* or grandmother, her condition had been worsening throughout the year. She did not have any specific disease but she had lost her hearing and then her sight and her connection to the world around her had begun to deteriorate.

"I recognize your smell," she said to me the last time I saw her, and her daughters were astonished that she could recognize me and not them or her grandchildren.

She kissed me, as always, and then said, "I saw you last night, you were with them, right? The soldiers. An army on horseback, planes in the sky. They flew right past my eyes." She pointed ahead. "And I waved to them and said, may Allah be with you, may Allah be with you, and I gave them water and food." Since then I had been back to the village twice and, despite my mother's attempts to guilt and wheedle me into going, I had not been to see um-Bassem.

In less than ten minutes we had our seven passengers in the Transporter. Since all the rest of the passengers were women and kids, I sat next to the driver. I remembered that he who rode shotgun was, by convention, also the cashier. The ride from Petach Tikva to Jaljulia costs fifteen shekels and I started to collect the money and distribute the change. In the end I handed the driver ninety shekels in bills and coins.

"Who hasn't paid yet?" the driver asked, looking in his rearview mirror toward the backseat.

"He's a little kid," an old woman in a colorful head scarf said, pointing to a child of four or so, apparently her grandson.

"Ma'am," the driver said impatiently, "little, big, I don't care. Is he sitting on a seat or not?"

"Fine," she said, pulling the child toward her, "now he's on my lap."

"You see what I have to deal with," the driver muttered in my direction. "That's illegal, ma'am, the child needs to be strapped in. He can't ride like that. You're holding us all up and everyone's in a rush."

"But he's just a child," the woman said.

The driver cut the engine and folded his arms across his chest. "Really? Did you know that a child with no seatbelt is a one-thousand-shekel ticket? Where am I going to get one thousand shekels to pay the state of Israel? There's a patrol car parked right at the entrance to the village."

Slowly, so that no one but the driver saw, I slid two coins into the plastic ashtray. The driver looked at me, started the car, and mumbled, *"La hawal, wa la kuwa, ila b'Allah."* Neither by might, nor by strength, but by God. "These people, they come from their holes in the West Bank and they dump all their troubles on us, as if we didn't have enough of our own. Ma'am, do me a favor, put the kid back in his seat and strap him in tight, okay?"

Oh, how I hated the drive from Petach Tikva to Jaljulia. The sharp smells filtered into my nostrils and spread through my entire body. The scent of bad and irrepressible memories. A scent that only intensified as we approached Jaljulia.

"You from the village?" I heard the driver ask, and when I realized he was talking to me I needed a moment to situate myself in my own life story.

"No," I heard myself say, offering a different, but also true, version of my life. "I'm from Tira."

"Ah, from Tira, great people," the driver said quietly, a smile spreading across his face. "*Yáani* one of us. I said to myself, he looks a little different, but he's got a good face. I said to myself, no way he's part of that garbage they're always dumping on us from the Territories."

"No," I said, "I'm not from the Territories."

"They dumped a lot of collaborators on Tira, too, no?"

"So I hear."

"It's just unbelievable. I'm telling you, they've destroyed our villages. These days a man has to worry about letting his kids out of the house after dark, all because of them. The guns, the drugs, the whores, it's all them. And the police? Nothing. What do they care? As far as they're concerned they can turn our villages into hell, they don't care. Best I can tell it's exactly what they want."

"Yeah," I said to the driver, who was looking in his rearview mirror to make sure that his words hadn't been heard by the wrong pair of ears. "Do you have your ID with you?" he asked all of a sudden.

"What? Yes, why?" I asked, nervous, and the driver pointed ahead with his chin toward the traffic cop and the blinking light-stick he was flicking toward the side of the road. "Looking for illegals."

"How you doing tonight?" the officer asked the driver through the window.

"*Walla,* thank God," the driver said, smiling. "As you see, working."

The policeman looked the passengers over and, seeing that it was all women and children, turned to me and asked for my ID. I looked around in my bag and pulled out the right set of papers.

"You have a good night," the policeman said to the driver, sending us off with a raised and blinking wand of light.

"*Kus okhtuk,*" the driver mumbled, cursing his sister's cunt. "Fucking Druze piece of shit."

PRAYER FOR THE DEAD

"Oh," Ruchaleh said, taking off her glasses, placing her book in her lap, and straightening up on the couch. "You're home early." Before setting off for Jaljulia I told her that I would be leaving right after my shift on Thursday and that I wouldn't be back until Saturday night. She'd booked a different caretaker, the same one she used when we went out, usually on Thursday nights, for a movie and dinner.

"Yeah," I mumbled. "Got back early."

Recognizing that now was not the time for her usual cynicism, she sounded concerned when she asked, "What happened? You look wrecked."

"How's Yonatan?"

"Fine, fine. Sit down."

I took a deep breath, put my bag on the floor, and sat on the couch, head down.

"What happened?" she asked again, and all I did was shake my head slowly and snort.

"You want a drink?" she asked, picking up a bottle of red wine. I nodded and she went to the kitchen for another glass.

"You don't want to tell me what happened?"

"Um-Bassem died," I said, and I filled my mouth with wine.

Um-Bassem died. I knew it as soon as I got out of the share-taxi. There was no doubt. There were men milling around the street, looking for a rock or something to perch on, men obviously called from work for a funeral. From a distance I could still recognize a few of them—the husbands of um-Bassem's daughters who, despite having grown up, were still recognizable by the way they moved.

I walked toward them with my head down, pretending that I had come as they had, after receiving word.

"Allah have mercy on her," I said, and shook the hands of a few men in the street. "*Ta'ish*," they said, as was customary. There were only a few dozen men present. The funerals of the elderly draw only kin.

The women's voices could be heard from within the courtyard but I preferred to stay outside with the men. The separation is very clear in these kinds of affairs—men and women do not mix at all.

"Don't be embarrassed," the husband of um-Bassem's oldest daughter said. "Go on in, put your bag down, wash your face. Don't be embarrassed, there's still no one but family in the house, there's still time."

"When did she pass?" I asked as I followed him to the house and, like him, I bowed my head and did not look at the women.

"Before dawn," he said, looking at his watch. "But we waited for Bassem, may God help him. We've been telling him for a week to come immediately and say good-bye, but he hasn't. What kind of job is it that keeps you from parting with your own mother? He just got here a second ago from the airport."

"Amir," I heard my mother's voice behind me. She came out of um-Bassem's courtyard toward me, her head covered with the colorful scarf she wore when visiting a mourner's tent. Her eyes were puffy and red and she nearly hugged me but the look on my face and the way I shifted my gaze to the men in the road deterred her and she merely stroked my arm.

"Do you have laundry?" she asked, taking my little bag, probably hoping I did so that she could do something for me. "Are you hungry?"

"No," I said, and I followed her into the house.

"How are you?" she asked, once the door closed and the two of us were alone.

"I'm fine."

"Poor um-Bassem. But it's better this way. More rest for her and for her daughters. She didn't eat during these last months. Can I get you anything?"

"No, thank you, I had a falafel in Petach Tikva."

"It's good you came."

"Yeah."

"They've been waiting for Bassem all day. He just showed up now."

"I heard."

"So everything's okay with you? Work?"

"Yeah, everything's fine."

"You have your own washing machine in the apartment?"

"Yes," I said, and I knew she was looking at my shirt, which I hadn't worn in over four years but had picked out of the closet that morning so that I could wear something that wouldn't look strange to my mother and her neighbors.

"Don't worry, Mom," I said, walking toward the bathroom, trying to steady the tremble that had risen up from the balls of my feet to my knees and chest. "I have money."

From the bathroom I could hear the teary voices of the women as they parted with um-Bassem. "Say hi to Daddy," I heard the oldest daughter wail, and I assumed that the washing ceremony had been completed and that the coffin was being walked out of the house in the hands of the men.

"Amir," my mother said, knocking on the bathroom door after a few minutes. "Amir, the funeral procession is leaving."

Several dozen men trailed behind the coffin, which was carried to a nearby mosque on the shoulders of a few young men. The pace was brisk, as though everyone wanted to get this over with. Bassem looked a little tired but he smiled warmly whenever someone shook his hand and consoled him.

"Allah *yirakhma*," I said, too, as I shook his hand.

"*Ta'ish*," he said, and I could tell from his face that he didn't recognize me.

A young man near me answered his phone, which rang with the opening chords of Umm Kulthum's "Enta Omri." "I'm at a funeral right now," he whispered into the phone,

"I'll call you later. Um-Bassem. Yes, Bassem. Died today. *Ta'ish*, 'bye."

A few dozen more men waited at the entrance to the mosque. The worshippers followed the body inside and began to say the prayer for the dead before burial. I stayed outside and tried to keep my eyes on the ground so that I wouldn't see familiar faces.

"Hello, Amir," said Nabil, a former classmate. "How are you?" he said, coming up to me and shaking my hand.

"Good, thanks."

"Where've you been? We never see you around," he said.

"In Jerusalem."

"Oh, why? You still in school?"

"No. I graduated."

"Wow, you were always one of the smart kids, weren't you? So, do you make any money with this college job?"

"*Alhamdulillah*." Thank God.

"So why don't you take your mother with you? Poor thing, I feel bad for her, all alone in the village, isn't it a shame?" He smiled and looked around to see if anyone else had heard him, if anyone else was laughing along with him. "You know, as it says in the Koran, 'show compassion for your parents.'"

"What about you?" I asked in a dry tone, signaling that I really didn't want to hear anything more from him.

"*Walla,* as our Jewish cousins say, blessed be God," he said, kissing the back of his hand and thrusting it up toward the sky.

Nabil graduated elementary school without knowing how to read. Of the forty kids in our grade, there were ten or so who were completely illiterate. The majority just dropped out of school. Some went to trade school, with the best of the bunch learning car mechanics and the rest going into carpentry and metalwork. I couldn't remember which route Nabil had taken, if any at all.

He leaned against the outside wall of the mosque and chatted quietly with his friends, occasionally stealing a glance in my direction. Nothing had changed. They were the same old kids, only larger. I could still see them at recess, sitting on the dilapidated benches and laughing at me.

"You got a hundred only 'cause your mother's been going down on the principal," they'd say. Or, "If your mother wasn't a teacher in this school we would fuck you up bad."

I'd often find notes with similar messages in my school bag, spelling mistakes and all. My mother was a teacher in the village's only junior high. She never taught one of my classes, but that didn't matter. My mother was different from the other teachers at the school. The kids cursed out all of the other teachers, ridiculed them behind their backs, but they would never dare tarnish their honor. My mother's honor, all the kids knew, was free for the taking.

That's how I learned that my mother used to show her tits to all the kids in the class; that my mother wore red bras and short skirts; that my mother was ousted from her village for whoring; that at night, after I went to sleep, my mother hosted all sorts of men in her bed; that she smoked cigarettes and drank alcohol; that she collaborated with the authorities; that she slept with policemen; that she slept with the principal; that they did it in the school library; that she'd been seen dancing at nightclubs in Petach Tikva; that she was sleeping with the math teacher, the history teacher, and the supervisor; that on the class trip she'd been seen peeing in the bushes and that she, for a fact, wore no underwear.

"Don't believe a single word they say," um-Bassem would tell me, even though I never told her what the other kids said. "Your mother is more honorable than all the rest of this trashy village. You must know that."

Then, in junior high, I started to pray. I fasted during Ramadan and went to the religion lessons that our Koran teacher gave at the local mosque. During junior high I didn't miss a single Friday prayer service. I became religious. My mother was a good mother. The proof: her son was a devout Muslim. I begged her to cover her hair, "For me," for her to pray, at least on Friday, to stop smoking, to put in for a transfer to a different school, to transfer me to a different school in a different village. I didn't mind taking the bus every morning or even walking to Kfar Kassem so long as it meant that I wouldn't have to suffer kids like Nabil, leaning against the school walls and laughing at me.

I couldn't figure out how it was that these overgrown kids could still intimidate me. You idiots, you assholes, if only you knew what I know. If only you knew what you look like to people who don't live in these little hole-in-the-wall towns. If only you could see how lame your lives are. If you had even the slightest awareness of your social status, you'd lock yourself up in your house and never come out. The peak achievements of your lives are to be in charge of a construction site or to make your Jewish clients happy. Compassion is what you evoke in me, you and your big cars and your fancy houses. None of you will ever manage to escape from the trap in which you were born; none of you will ever venture beyond the boundaries of your village, boundaries that were drawn by another man's hand. And especially you, the men, who think you're so tough and manly, not scared of a thing, your voices so deep and strong they can stop a whole neighborhood in its tracks, you are the very essence of human trash. Keep on prancing around with your guns, keep on puffing up your chests while you do the Debka dance at weddings, keep on marrying virgins and let them preserve your honor and your male delusions. I know things you will never know; I've seen worlds you will never see. I've gone to places where you and your children will never be wanted. Yeah, me, the son of your whore, I will mock you to your face. I have nothing but disdain for you. Only I know what you're worth.

"What are you smiling about?" I heard Nabil's voice nearby. He stood before me, head cocked to the side.

"What? Oh, me, nothing," I said, and um-Bassem came out of the mosque just in time to save me. "Allah Akbar, Allah Akbar," I mumbled, following the coffin with my head bowed, and I knew then that as soon as the ceremony was over I'd grab my bag and leave.

GUEST ROOM

Over the past four years Yonatan's condition had gotten worse. On the day that Ruchaleh paid my tuition for my freshman year at Bezalel, he was taken to the hospital.

"You'll pay me back in installments," she said when I refused to take the money, and she suggested subtracting five hundred shekels a month from my paycheck, even though we both knew that didn't even cover half of the monthly tuition fees.

That night I hadn't been able to feed Yonatan, or maybe it was as Ruchaleh said later at the hospital, that he refused to eat. He spit up the water substitute and his gelatinous meal, and when I came in to relieve Osnat, she said he had done the same with his breakfast and lunch. If this persists, she said, we'll have to take him to the hospital, even though he doesn't have a fever.

That night something changed in Yonatan. He reacted differently to our attempts to dress him, change him, moisturize him. Strange though it may sound to say about an irresponsive body, I felt that his skin had thickened and his bones and muscles had hardened.

When he didn't ingest a thing during dinner, I told Ruchaleh that I didn't think we should wait any more.

"He's trying to kill himself," Ruchaleh said later that night, in the waiting room outside the ER. That was the first time I saw her cry.

The doctors did blood tests, urine tests, a lung X-ray, and a CT scan and found nothing out of the ordinary.

"So he's in good shape, then?" Ruchaleh quipped, but the Arab resident who'd given her the results didn't laugh. "Arabs aren't too strong on the sense of humor front, are they?" she asked me afterward.

In the small hours of the night Ruchaleh and I returned home. Yonatan remained in the hospital for a few more days, for observation.

On the way back Ruchaleh tried to sing along with the radio but she ended up just shaking her head back and forth.

"Are you sleeping at home?" she asked out of the blue, "or are you going to sleep over at that girl's house?"

Her question shocked me because I had not told her or anyone else about the girl. "What girl? I don't have a girl," I said, and Ruchaleh smiled and again tried to sing along with the radio but she got hooked onto a different song, one that wasn't playing, and all the way home she kept mumbling the lyrics, "Hug me hard, kiss me till it hurts, and the sun won't set."

When we got home, Ruchaleh said she needed a drink and she poured herself a glass of whiskey, neat, and drained it in a single gulp. Then she asked me if I wanted anything to drink.

"Yes," I said, "but something else, if you have." Up until that night the only alcohol I'd ever had was a beer now and again with Majdi, whenever he brought a bottle or two home, and red wine, occasionally, when he was given a bottle from the hotel as a Rosh Hashanah gift.

"I don't have beer," Ruchaleh said, taking a bottle of white wine out of the fridge. "White wine is usually chilled," she said, and she showed me how to pull out the cork. Then she drank two glasses while I struggled with one.

"Do you even know how it happened?" she asked me, pouring herself another whiskey. I was silent and I think she interpreted that as a *no*. We'd never spoken about it. *The accident*, was how Osnat and I referred to it and that was all that Osnat knew. Yonatan had been in an accident.

"One fine day I came home and found him hanging from the ceiling," she said, nodding her head and throwing back her whiskey. "I hugged his feet," she said, demonstrating with her arms. "Then I got up on the bed. I grabbed his legs with one arm and tried to lift him with the other, putting all his weight on me as I tried to free his neck from the noose. Did you know that? Did you know that's what Yonatan did to me?"

She took out a cigarette for herself and offered me one, too. I poured another glass of wine and watched the cigarette shake between her fingers.

"What do you say?" she said, trying to take the edge off the melancholy. "Would you do that to your mother?"

"No," I said, smiling a bit for her benefit. "But I'd do it to myself."

That was the first night I didn't sleep up in the attic. Ruchaleh told me that she hated that room so much she could barely bring herself to walk into it, that she had an involuntary response upon entry, her eyes darting toward the ceiling, where there had been a light fixture, and where she found her son's body, swaying in the air. He had been hospitalized in Israel for six months and was then flown to the United States, Belgium, and Switzerland. They—that is, Ruchaleh and Yakov, Yonatan's father a professor of comparative literature at Berkeley—were never married, but they had lived together while Ruchaleh studied and, later, worked in Berkeley. When Yonatan was three, they split up and she came back to Israel. Yakov was all right, she said. Boring and a bastard, a long story, but nothing terrible. The truth is he really was all right, maybe, she couldn't remember. Back when Yonatan was healthy, he would come visit them in Jerusalem twice a year, on Christmas and Passover, and would stay with them.

"This was his room," Ruchaleh said, opening the door to the room that Osnat and I called the guest room, even though we'd never seen a guest. "You can sleep here to-night," she said, and then pointed at the closet. "There are sheets on the top shelf and, by the way, I'd be happy if you made this your room. When you're not with Yonatan, that is, on your days off from school or whatever. Instead of wandering around the streets like some homeless Arab you could just stay here. And do me a favor," she said before leaving the room, "don't get any big ideas in your head, okay? If you want to hang yourself, do it in your mother's house in Jaljulia."

THE FEEDING TUBE

Yonatan came home from the hospital with a feeding tube, a kind of straw that was anchored to the wall of his stom-ach on one end and dangled out of his right nostril on the other. Osnat gave me a brief tutorial and from that day on we started injecting his food into the tube. I learned how to extract the tube, how to clean it, and how to make sure it was not clogged. I'd shoot a syringe full of air into the tube and put a stethoscope to his stomach, listening for air bubbles.

Yonatan was in and out of the hospital over the next four years. He had infections of the intestines and the lungs, aspirational pneumonia, urinary tract infections, lung fail-ures. Everything became more difficult. For some reason he also started to bleed whenever I shaved him, even with an electric shaver. I had the feeling that he didn't want me touching him. It was around then that Osnat told me she was considering leaving and looking for a different job, one where she could be of more use. "Someplace a little less frustrating," she said, and I asked her to please stay on a little longer, promised her that I would take care of all the more difficult tasks—the showers, the haircuts, the dressing and undressing and diaper changing—and that I'd do it all before she came in or after she went home.

"That doesn't sound fair," she said, but I insisted, explaining that Yonatan had become a friend, an ally, and that I would do anything to make sure that he did not have to part with a loving caretaker like herself, that I would do anything to ease him through his last days.

"Let's make it clear to him that we're not abandoning him," I remember myself saying, and Osnat had no idea that what bothered me about the arrival of a new caretaker was that he or she might start asking questions about my relationship with Ruchaleh and with Yonatan, both of which had long since strayed beyond the ordinary.

The guest room became my room and I no longer slept up in the attic with Yonatan. After classes at Bezalel, I'd rush home by bus and relieve Osnat, who had started taking sociology classes at the Open University, mostly out of boredom.

"I feel completely unnecessary," she said, even though, despite the terms of our unwritten agreement whereby I would do all of the hard chores, she continued to do most of the work herself.

As Yonatan's body began to decay, it became more and more difficult to rotate him on the bed. Putting him on his stomach was never a good idea, certainly not without supervision, and once he was hooked up to the feeding tube it became downright impossible. He could no longer be placed on the special wheelchair for showers and so we began laying out rubber sheets and giving him sponge baths on the bed. Osnat, who had preached the importance of speaking positively around Yonatan and of playing him his favorite music and reading to him from his favorite books, now spoke openly about his dire situation. She stopped greeting him and parting with him each time she came and left the attic and instead spoke only with me, ignoring him entirely. I found her behavior embarrassing and usually after she left I would apologize to Yonatan, sometimes telling him outright and sometimes just letting him know with nothing more than a look.

Aside from the occasional evening when Ruchaleh would have friends over for dinner, the two of us ate together. At first she would come up to the attic and knock on the door and say she didn't want to eat alone, but later she said she was sick of calling me to dinner like a little kid, and so I would come down on my own, unbidden, at the usual time.

"How's it going in school?" she asked me over dinner, around a month into my first semester. I nodded in a way that was supposed to imply that everything was under control, even though I was pretty sure I would not be able to finish the semester. I discovered that there was a lot more to school than going to class. All the other students stayed late after class and used the darkrooms and the computer labs, and when I heard that at the end of the semester we were each supposed to present our work, I was sure that I would not make it to that point. Not only did I hardly have time to take pictures, I had no time to develop the film.

"It isn't easy there, is it?" she said, wiping her mouth with a linen napkin and getting up, motioning for me to follow her.

"Here," she said, pushing open the door to a small storage room in the basement. "I think the bulb might have burned out but it doesn't matter. Yonatan used to buy regular bulbs and then color them red." The light from the hall cut into the darkroom. Ruchaleh pulled a sheet off the top of an enlarger. "I think this thing still works," she said. "Check it out. If it doesn't, I'll call someone to fix it."

In the mornings, she drove me to school, since we were both going to Mount Scopus. We almost always left the house together. We waited for Osnat to arrive and then we left. If there was time we ate some breakfast at home and when there wasn't we'd stop somewhere on the way and she'd tuck a fifty-shekel note into my hand and ask me to get two cups of coffee and a couple of croissants. Over time I learned that Ruchaleh did not always have to be on campus at Hebrew University as early as I did, nor did she have to leave as late. "What am I going to do at home?" she asked, and then said, "What, you think I'm a terrible mother?"

No, I did not think she was a terrible mother but I never said anything either way. She was not looking to be comforted, certainly not with words, and I was never sure what effect my words would have, anyway, whether they'd cheer her up or make her snap and accuse me of kissing up to the Jewish boss lady. Slowly I came to be convinced that what she believed was true: that Yonatan's actions were a form of revenge. He never let up, as though trying to commit suicide each day anew, yet somehow surviving, just like the first time, in order to hurt her, to force her to remember. And ever since I started to use his identity officially, I felt he was doing the same to me, that this man, expiring slowly on his eggshell mattress, was acting rationally, premeditatedly. Sometimes, while we had dinner together or when she came into the darkroom to check out my negatives, during those moments of happiness, I'd feel as though Yonatan might at any minute come through the door, that that hollowed-out frame of a man might suddenly appear at the entrance to the darkroom and glare at us and say, "Just as I always suspected."

But Yonatan did not get up or glare at us and his situation only worsened. He refused to live and he refused to die. The last time he was admitted to the hospital, around six months ago, was when I called an ambulance after checking his pulse and finding it unusually slow and weak. The ICU ambulance arrived immediately and hooked him up to a life-support machine. I rode with him in the ambulance and Ruchaleh followed in her car. That night a senior doctor who had been summoned to the hospital told us that it was unlikely that he would breathe again on his own.

"Some families, at this stage, decide to . . ." he began to say, gingerly, but I cut him off, rejected the notion out of hand. My voice frightened me, the ferocity of it, and especially the notion that Yonatan might just disappear right in the middle of things and leave me all alone.

"I understand," Ruchaleh said, after I apologized to her for my outburst, tears welling up in my eyes, "but I just can't go on."

She hugged me harder than usual and whispered in my ear, "You are going to have to decide."

NUMBER 624

With a shaved head and a five o'clock shadow, wearing a long-sleeved Surfer Rosa T-shirt and green corduroy pants, the camera slung across my chest and round sunglasses on my face; with the old ID card, featuring a sixteen-year-old Yonatan, in my right pocket, and two new photos in my left—that is how I strode, back straight, mustering as much self-confidence as I could, toward the main branch of the Ministry of the Interior in downtown west Jerusalem.

I was in my fourth and final year at Bezalel, one of thirty photography majors. Nothing special. Nothing out of the ordinary. A classic Bezalel student, the kind the school was made for. I was Yonatan Forschmidt: Israeli, white, Ashkenazi, a consumer of Western culture. I was not Sephardic and I was not the token Arab.

Every class needed an Arab. In our freshman year we had the guy from Nazareth, but by our sophomore year he had been accepted at the architecture department and left. In the cafeteria we'd joke that we'd lost our Arab, and one kibbutznik from the Galilee said he'd heard that a class with no Arab was cursed and that we'd never succeed in the Israeli art world without one.

We were saved by the janitor from Silwan. According to the reports in the papers, the guy had been working at

Bezalel for five years when the department head discovered him. It turned out that as soon as the guy was done washing the floor and scrubbing the toilets he would head straight for the darkroom, enlarging and developing the pictures he had taken with one of the department's cameras. Apparently, he had made friends with the photography department's storekeeper and had access to all the equipment he needed.

The discovery had occurred by accident: the head of the department had come back to the school late one evening and caught the Arab in the act, in his janitorial uniform, in the photo lab. At first the Arab had been terrified and had promised that he would never do it again, but the head of the department looked on in wonder at the drying photos that the Arab had taken in his village. The head of the department had offered him, right then and there, a spot in our class. The Arab said no, legend has it, because he had eight kids to support and couldn't forgo his salary as a janitor. But the department head arranged it so that the Arab would get a full ride, would start as a sophomore, and would still receive his full salary in exchange for some minor cleanup work in the afternoon. Too bad I wasn't born an Arab, the kibbutznik said, and everyone around the cafeteria table cracked up.

At Bezalel, I, a left-wing liberal like most of the students, learned that Arabs are horny, that they think with their dicks — mostly about pussy and mostly about preserving the honor of their sisters' pussies. I learned that they can get angry fast and that there is no way to know what might set them off. They're unpredictable and can be aggressive.

Honor is desperately important to them; in fact, it's all that matters to them—personal honor, national honor, religious honor, family honor. Show respect and avoid dishonoring them, and you're on safe ground. Even the ones that seem the most enlightened are still, in some very basic ways, primitive. They think differently, have a different culture, a different logic. Arabs are more impulsive, more animalistic. The only thing they really understand is force, and when they sense weakness, they attack. Like hyenas. It does not mean that we should be occupying them, that is not what it means, but it's such a shame that there's no one you can talk to, such a shame that they don't change, that they can't really be trusted. Otherwise we could just sign a peace treaty, make a border, and make sure the two peoples stay friendly, each on their own side. If only they would just let up, let us live, be reasonable neighbors, get over their instinctive need for revenge, get over their obsession with honor, get over their mosque-fed fantasies of an Islamic empire. If only they could just admit that we were here first, that we are the natural owners of this land; if only they would just say thank you and finally understand how generous we have been.

Which is not to say that we don't have our share of crazies. What about the nut-job settlers who are willing to risk the lives of their children in the name of some divine ideology. Or the ultra-Orthodox, and the Sephardim, who go on and on about ethnic discrimination. If they had any sense they'd come around and thank us for plucking them out of that dark and unenlightened place we found them in.

These things were said in the cafeteria or in the makeshift smoking corner, and they were said for white, cultured Israeli ears alone. The token Arab was always welcomed with open arms at Bezalel, with happiness even, and it never seemed artificial. Nor did the Arabs suffer. It seemed like our Arab enjoyed the whole thing. I think the Arabs felt very welcome at Bezalel and they were invited to virtually all of the events. A lot of girls threw themselves at them, and especially at our janitor, who, word was, could get any Jewish girl he wanted. In the cafeteria and the smoking corners, when we were alone, we, the founders, laughed at those girls and the way they used the Arab to get back at their parents. And we talked about the Arab phallus as art. I didn't say much during those conversations but I laughed, got the joke. I was the quietest person in the class and no one knew that it was because I was afraid that my accent might emerge, even though I knew I sounded just like them, or very close to it. I knew that I had to stay focused at all times, making sure to maintain my crisp Ashkenazi Hebrew. *Monk*, is what the kibbutznik called me, also because I never talked about sex. I knew that there was talk in the department of me being gay or in the closet or, eventually, asexual. I picked up on those rumors while listening in on the Arabs' conversations, who had no idea I understood everything they said. *Loti* means gay and *adim achsas jinsi* means asexual. But I didn't care. I wasn't looking for a social life at Bezalel, even though on account of my ethnicity I had one without trying. During breaks and free periods I always found myself sitting with the coffee drinkers and smoking with the smokers. Still, though, other than my Saturday morning visits to Noa's apartment, I had no social life to speak of. I didn't go to any of the parties, mostly because they were at night, when I was busy with Yonatan, and I didn't go to pubs or over to other people's houses for dinner or to work on group projects.

I loved taking pictures and that is all I wanted to do. My show at the end of sophomore year focused on the kids who work at the Mahane Yehuda market, carrying supplies and cleaning up around the stalls. After that my professor called me "the social photographer," a nickname that I took as a compliment, but many of the other students said that I was stuck, that I wasn't trying to break through the formulaic doctrines of field photography and that I was scared to reach for something that might be more "artistic." But the truth was that I had no desire to do that. People were all that I was interested in. Our year-end show was viewed by members of the faculty and either an artist, a curator, or an art reviewer. My grades and appraisals were some of the best in the class. With a little PR, as Noa said, I could have been one of the protégés, but I steered clear of the faculty. I never went to office hours, never confided in them about my photography-related dilemmas. I insisted on doing things my way, shooting only in black and white, and even though some of the teachers thought my insistence was a sort of handicap, I knew that my work was in no way impaired and that each project I did was better than the one that preceded it.

I always shot with the same film, ASA 400, with the same shutter speed and the same aperture. Aside from the assignments that required it, I never touched a digital camera and I never photoshopped any of my pictures. During the first two years of school, I used Yonatan's Pentax 35mm exclusively, which was considered old-fashioned in comparison to the Canons and the Nikons that the rest of the kids had. And I always used a 50mm lens, no flash, no tripod.

For one of my assignments, the family portrait, I received consent and took pictures of kids and their parents in the center of the Beit Hakerem neighborhood on a Friday afternoon. I also took pictures of kids on their way to school and of a group of Romanian construction workers, who let me photograph them as they sat in the Old City on a Saturday and drank cheap beer. Another project, which got me the top marks in the class, was one I called "First Love," in which I took pictures of girls on the phone, smiling and twirling their hair. Ruchaleh, who always looked over my work before I submitted it, also thought that one was the best. There were tears in her eyes when she looked at the girls.

"They're all in love," she had said, and that's how the project got its name. The next day she went out and got me a new Hasselblad 6x6. "Yonatan always wanted a camera like this," she said.

The old security guard at the entrance to the Ministry of the Interior on Shlomzion Hamalka Street asked me to open my bag and then sent me in with a jerk of his head. It was just after eight in the morning and most of the seats in the waiting room were empty. I went over to the wheel and took a number, 624. I looked up at the digital screen above the clerks' heads, saw it said 617, and sat down at the far end of the back row.

"It's like an organ donation," is what Ruchaleh had said when she found out I was using Yonatan's identity. I realized then that she had known about it for months.

"Why would I have a problem with it?" she said, shrugging. "Maybe the authorities have some issues, but it's no harm done to me or my son."

It took me a long time to understand Ruchaleh, or rather, to trust her. At first I thought it was really strange that my actions, which clearly constituted a crime, did not bother her in the least. How could a bereaved mother not care? Then I thought she might be after some kind of sexual quid pro quo, sex in exchange for silence. The poor weak Arab would fuck his way out of his situation and the forty-five-year-old woman would get to feel that she was setting him free while giving release to the passion that was burning inside him. A good deal for both parties involved. I realized soon enough that that was not the case, but I must admit that during those torrid days the thought of accepting such an offer crossed my mind more than once. Had I agreed, though, it would not have been in exchange for her silence or some type of monetary reward. It would have been because back then there really were times that I desired her.

I remember, for instance, the first time she asked me to join her for a movie at the cinema and dinner at Cielo, her favorite Italian restaurant in the city. Ruchaleh looked beautiful to me that evening—maybe because I saw her smile for the first time and maybe because I saw her cover a laugh with the back of her hand. I think she laughed after I asked her if she was doing all this for me because of her left-wing ideology.

"You know what," she said, and a long while passed before she was able to stop laughing. "You Arabs really are idiots."

That first time out to a restaurant was when Ruchaleh taught me how to lay my napkin on my lap while eating, how to keep my elbows off the table, how to dab at my mouth with a napkin, how to hold a glass of red wine and how to hold a glass of white wine, and how to handle the different cutlery.

"Your plate is not a rowboat," she said when I angled my fork and knife against the sides of the plate, and she showed me how to position the cutlery when taking a break from eating and how to arrange it at the four o'clock position when I was through. "There are some things you just have to know," she said, "if you want to be a part of the family."

Ruchaleh's family was from Germany. They hadn't been through the Holocaust, she said, at least not her parents, who had the brains to immigrate to this stinking country in the early thirties. But she didn't like talking about her parents, because "they're not really your grandmother and grandfather." I gathered from our conversations that she had nothing but scorn for tradition, nationalism, religion, roots, roots trips, and sentences like "He who has no past, has no future." She believed that the Arabs did a bad job of impersonating the Zionists, who did a bad job of impersonating the European nationalists of the early twentieth century. Nor did she believe in identity, certainly not the local nationalistic version of it. She said that man was only smart if he was able to shed his identity.

"Skin color is a little hard to shed," she said, "it's true. But the DNA of your social class is even harder to get rid of."

When I told her at first that I had no intention of applying to Bezalel under her son's name, she laughed and said, "Why not? It's like an organ donation. Around here identity is like one of the organs of the body and yours is faulty. You might as well admit it, being an Arab is not exactly the peak of human aspiration," she said, laughing, and I could tell from the tone of her voice that she had not meant to offend me. "And what you have here," she continued, "is an organ donation that could very well save your life." I don't think Ruchaleh was trying to convince me of anything then. She could already tell how badly I yearned for it. I think all she wanted to do was to make clear that if there was going to be any trouble, it would not be from her.

With a ding the digital screen flipped to number 624. I got up and walked toward the agent just as the bell sounded again and the screen jumped forward to number 625. A woman who had gotten up after me hurried over to the agent, racing me to the window, even though it was clear that she was cutting ahead of me. I was willing to give up my number, perhaps the whole procedure.

"Are you 624?" the agent asked me over the head of the other woman, who had already sat down in the chair and was saying, "But it already switched to 625."

"Ma'am," the agent said. "He's ahead of you."

"Doesn't matter," the woman one booth over said. "I'm free." I sat down in front of her.

"How can I help you?" she asked.

"I'd like to update an old ID card," I said, and I put Yonatan's worn card on the counter.

"These days you can just do that in the mail, you know?"

"No, I didn't know that," I lied. Of course I knew—before coming to the ministry I'd found out everything there was to know about updating ID cards. I knew it could be done through the mail but I wanted to do it in person. I look like Yonatan, dress like Yonatan, and there was no way some clerk in the Interior Ministry was ever going to be suspicious of me, straight out of Beit Hakerem, in expensive clothes that were made to look cheap and a T-shirt with a picture of an obviously hip band she had never heard of. It was much safer than sending it in the mail. What I was afraid of was that the disparity between the two pictures, the wild-haired Yonatan and the short-haired shot of myself from the day before, would be too great to issue an ID card through the mail and that then I would be asked to come in to the ministry in person, already a suspect.

"Yonatan?" the clerk asked.

"Yes."

"I was sure that you weren't Israeli," she said, paralyzing me.

"Why? Is something wrong?"

"There was no reason to be so nice to that lady," she said under her breath, taking one of my passport photos and starting to fill out the details. "People here have no shame. Just say, 'It's my turn.' What, you don't know how to deal with people around here? Only force, that's the only language they understand."

On the way out of the office, with a temporary ID card under the name Yonatan Forschmidt in my pocket, I dropped a renewal application for Amir's ID in the mailbox. Attached to the paperwork were two pictures of Yonatan that I had taken myself and touched up on the computer. Everything would stay the same, only the pictures were swapped.

I left the nationality line blank on Amir's application, as many Arabs did now that it was no longer mandatory.

This had to be done to prove that all citizens of Israel are equal, Arab and Jew alike, but once it went into effect, a new number code was introduced to all official ID documents and it told whoever needed to know the ethnicity of the card-holder. After all, names were not enough: Arabs and Jews sometimes had the same names — Amir, for example — and it had become trendy of late for Arabs to give their kids Jewish names, or "universal names" as they preferred to call them.

I was not worried about updating Amir's ID via the mail. Swapping Yonatan's picture for my own would not arouse anyone's suspicion: even the lowliest clerk at the Ministry of the Interior knows that no one in this country wants to be an Arab.

OXIMETER

Late that same Thursday night I called Noa.

"If you're not working," she said, "then I'm free. It'll be the first time I get to see you after nightfall. I was starting to think you turned into a pumpkin at midnight."

I hailed a cab on Herzl Boulervard and took it to her house on the corner of Agrippas and Nissim Behar in Nach-laot. I went up three flights of stairs to the apartment Noa liked calling "the studio." She'd moved in during the summer between junior and senior year. Before that she'd lived with two roommates in a bigger apartment in the area, but that came to an end when one of the roommates began inviting over a rabbi with a white *kippah* and a pervert's grin. Noa said she hated all the Rainbow and Shantipi crap.

She did not hit the India travel circuit after the army. "Even if I had gone to the army, I wouldn't have gone to India," she said. She had a hard time understanding how it was possible to beat the shit out of Arabs all through army service and then run straight into an ashram and feel all pure. Nor had she gone to South America. After high school she went to Europe, then she spent a month in New York City, and then she started school in Jerusalem.

She hated her hometown, Hod HaSharon. The place is disgusting, she said. Afterward she lived in Ra'anana and she detested it, too, said it was even more disgusting. Her father was a doctor but he didn't work in medicine. He started his own company, importing medical supplies. Her younger brother, the "king of the nerds," as she called him, seemed poised to follow their older sister, who was also a doctor and worked with her father.

"My mother is actually an amazing person," she said, an artist at heart who had worked as a nurse for many years and now also worked in the family business. "What about you?" she would ask now and again. "I don't know a thing about your family."

"I don't have one," I'd say with a smile. "Somewhere out there I've got a mother."

Noa was my girlfriend. At least that's how I used to refer to her in front of Ruchaleh, who used to say, "Come on already, when are you going to bring her over?"

But what exactly was I supposed to say to her? *Noa, this is my boss, we just happen to have the same last name.* And what exactly was I supposed to say about the man in the attic —*Meet my brother, we're twins. Fraternal not identical, and, yes, he was in a terrible accident?*

We'd meet up during the day, usually on Saturday mornings if she hadn't gone back to her parents' house for the weekend. She didn't go there often and she would get angry with her mother whenever she forced her to visit, once every few months. The two of us would go on trips together, take photographs, drink coffee, hug when times were tough, hold hands, exchange CDs, download music, and on Thursdays, half days at Bezalel, we'd shop for records and check out photography exhibits. I liked hanging out at her place and she liked having me there. Sometimes she'd get all worked up, visibly furious, and she'd throw me out of the house.

"I need to be alone for a little while," she'd say, starting to cry, but then she'd calm down, invite me back in, suggest we do something together, maybe a walk around the neighborhood or a stroll through the Old City.

"You look different," I blurted out when she opened the door that evening. I'd never seen her dressed up before. In school and when I came by on Saturday mornings she always wore jeans or cords and a T-shirt. Now she stood in the doorway in a gray skirt, the kind that the lawyers wear on American TV shows. Instead of a funky T-shirt she wore a red sleeveless blouse that buttoned up the front. There was lipstick on her lips and black mascara on her eyelashes. I'd never seen her made up before.

"What do you think?" she asked, her hands trembling. "Kind of like a babushka doll?"

"Kind of," I said, laughing. "I feel bad, I'm in my work clothes."

"Do you want me to change?"

"No, no, not at all . . . it's just . . ." I wasn't sure how to finish the sentence.

"Just what?"

"Nothing."

"Come on, say it, you bastard."

"Say what?"

"That I look beautiful."

"You look beautiful."

"Yeah, thanks a lot."

"No problem."

"Hold on, let me grab a shawl or something," she said and turned back into the house.

"Are we going out?" I asked, and I checked to see how much cash Ruchaleh had stuffed into my wallet.

"Yeah," she said, smiling. "You want me to sit around the house like Little Red Riding Hood in this thing? Of course we're going out. Don't you want to?"

"Yeah, of course. I'd love to."

"Good," she said, and she shut the door behind her.

"Where do you want to go?" I asked as we walked down Nissim Behar.

"Your call."

"Ahhhh," I asked, unprepared. "You hungry?"

"A little bit, not really, maybe a little something."

"Okay," I said and I took her hand and then turned it over and looked at her watch. She smiled and I felt a surge of desire.

"I think Cavalier is still open."

"Cavalier?" she asked.

"It's a great restaurant." It was one of Ruchaleh's favorites.

"What are you talking about?" she asked. "How the hell did you get Cavalier into your head?"

"I don't know, it's in walking distance. If you want to take a cab we could also go to the American Colony. The food there is pretty good, too." I knew that those were two of the most expensive restaurants in the city, the kind students walked into only through the staff entrance. One time, when we went to Arkadia, our waiter was a guy in my class. Ruchaleh didn't hesitate. She shook the guy's hand and said, "Nice to meet you; I'm Yonatan's mother."

I didn't know much about Jerusalem's night life but I wanted to impress Noa. I wanted her to know that I was hiding something, that I wasn't just some loser student, working nights and forgoing any semblance of a social life in order to pay tuition.

"Those are the options you're giving me?" she asked, laughing. "When I said I was a little hungry, I was thinking that, like, maybe we'd order some fries with our beer, not Cavalier."

"You know, I have a feeling you know the city a lot better than I do at this point. You decide."

"Okay," she said. "Follow me." And she took my hand in hers, looked for my response, and when I smiled, she tightened her grip and tugged me down the road, saying again, "Where the hell do you have the cash for Cavalier from?"

I had the cash. Ruchaleh had shoved it into my wallet before throwing me out of the house.

"You can go to a hotel, you can go wherever you want, but you're not staying here," she had said at first when I begged her to let me stay.

That was the first change in the plan. I wasn't sure whether she'd known it all along or if it was something she'd decided on when Yonatan's oximeter started to beep, as it had been doing every night for the past few weeks.

That night, after getting Yonatan ready for bed, we strayed from our usual dinner routine.

"I'm not hungry," I told Ruchaleh, who sat, inanimate, on the couch.

"I want to sell the house," she said, looking up at the ceiling. "I don't want to be in this place anymore."

We must have sat there in silence for something like an hour, until the gauge started to beep. That was my cue to run upstairs to the attic and connect the plastic contraption bulging out of Yonatan's throat to the life-support system. Ruchaleh looked at me. I bowed my head and stayed seated. According to her plan, fifteen minutes would suffice. The beeping bounced off the walls, careened inside my head, pinged against the walls of my skull. I envisioned Yonatan gasping, choking, sputtering, his body convulsing, a shocked expression on his face.

"Where are you going?" she yelled, following me as I ran up the stairs. The oximeter, a small device clipped to his finger, beeped hysterically. I stood at the foot of the bed and stared at Yonatan. He looked exactly the same, lying there with the same placid expression on his face, no apparent convulsions or torment wracking his body. Ruchaleh walked over to her son's side, to the oximeter, and turned down the volume of the beeping.

The plan was that she would wait fifteen minutes and then call an ambulance, pleading, panic-stricken, for a mobile ICU unit. "My son has stopped breathing." That was her line. While she was on the phone, I was supposed to hook him up to the ventilator so that when the crew arrived they'd find him on life support, even though Ruchaleh said that the doctors wouldn't be asking any unnecessary questions.

"Doctors tend to encourage end-of-life decisions on far less severe cases," she said, "but who knows, with our luck, we could get some religious doctor and he could cause trouble."

She was supposed to meet the ambulance crew outside. I was supposed to wait by the side of the bed. Ruchaleh said that an ICU doctor coming to the big house in Beit Hakerem, seeing Yonatan on his eggshell mattress, surrounded by the best life-support system money could buy, would probably issue a death certificate on the spot, without ordering an autopsy or any other kind of investigation. They'd probably skip the CPR, since he was on life support already, and just confirm his death, at which point she'd burst into tears.

"I just hope I'll be able to pull it off," she said.

When the doctor asked whether he should issue the death certificate, she'd dissolve in tears and send me to take care of it.

"By then," she said, when the idea first came up, around a year earlier, "I hope you'll have decided which ID card to give to the doctors."

Ruchaleh said that our plan was virtually risk-free. We've already taken care of the tricky part, she said once—the identity change. We both preferred the words *change* and *update* rather than *theft* when speaking of Yonatan's ID.

"It was written from above," Ruchaleh said once. "You think it's coincidence that your name is Amir Lahav, a kosher *lemahadrin* Jewish name?"

My name, written out in Hebrew, really does sound totally Jewish, but in Arabic it's different — Lahab — meaning *flames*. I remembered from a young age that whenever I went to the doctor's office in Petach Tikva or to see my mother when she was in the hospital, Jews always got my name wrong. The way they pronounced it always made me laugh and I would tell my mother about their mistake. Later, as a teenager, it no longer bothered me and I was actually happy to have my name Hebraized, a phenomenon that saved me many a sideways glance. When I went to college the fact that my name could be read both ways turned into a real bonus: it's how I wound up with a good dorm room at Hebrew University, near campus, unlike the Arabs, who, as freshmen, if they didn't have connections, were housed in the notorious Eleph dorms on the Givat Ram campus. A day before school started, I discovered that my roommate was Jewish, an economics major, a freshman. He couldn't keep the surprise off his face when I introduced myself and made a point of pronouncing my name properly, in Arabic.

"Where are you from?' he asked, the way soldiers do.

"Jaljulia," I said.

"Cool," he said, and a moment later he went out for a smoke. Ten minutes later an administrator showed up. "There was a little bit of a misunderstanding here," she said, explaining that university rules require that, barring written consent to the contrary, Jews and Arabs had to live in separate quarters.

"It's fine with me," I said.

"I see," she said, consulting her clipboard. "I'll be back in a bit."

My Jewish roommate came back to the room a few minutes later and started packing up his things. "Bro, they got the living situation a little confused at the office," he said before leaving.

My new roommate was an Arab from I'billin in the Galilee. I'll never forget the expression on his face and the dance of joy he did when he came into the room. "They told me I was in Eleph. They sent me a letter—Eleph, it said—and here I am up on Mount Scopus," he exclaimed. "My friends over at Eleph are going to die when they see this. A steam radiator, on campus. Do you know what Eleph looks like? It's where they throw all the Arabs. Maybe they started letting Christians get rooms on Mount Scopus. Maybe that's what happened. This is a miracle. I'm telling you, it's the miracle of the Virgin Mary." He kissed his cross, and frowned when he found out I was a Muslim, but he did not leave. "What does it matter—Muslim, Christian? At the end of the day it says Arab next to both of our names."

Before leaving the house that night, Ruchaleh said, "I need one of the ID cards." I took one out and gave it to her. The other one I put in my wallet. She opened up the little blue book, smiled, and tears started to well in her eyes. "Everything's going to work out," she said, and then she hugged me hard. "Go, go," she said, "get out of here," and she shut the door behind me.

GOLDSTAR

I want to be like them. That's the sentence that was bouncing around my head as I followed Noa into the Ha'sira pub. She said "hey" to a few of the people there, exchanged kisses with a few others, introduced me to them. "Guys, this is Yonatan."

She walked over to the DJ booth. The guy looked familiar. He slipped off his headphones and smiled at her, leaned over his turntables and his mixer, and kissed her on the cheek.

"Come here," I read her lips as she motioned me over. "Meet Aviad," she said. "He's third-year, visual media."

I shook his hand.

I want to be like them.

Noa asked what I wanted to drink and smiled when I said red wine, suggesting that I go with beer. I agreed. She preferred sitting at the bar, she said, but we took seats at a little wooden table in the corner because all the bar stools were taken. The DJ played some Radiohead and Noa moved her body to the music, saying that at this hour you could still enjoy the music.

"What do you mean?" I asked.

"You'll see," she said.

The more the place filled up, the faster the music got. Aviad played some soft Underworld, then switched to Plastic Man and then back to faster tracks from Underworld. Noa was a better drinker than I was, but she always waited for me to catch up. I struggled to keep the pace, which she thought was funny. I could see that off to the side of the bar the tiny dance floor was starting to fill up, people moving their bodies gently in front of the DJ, not wanting to be the first ones to really dance. I volunteered to buy the third round, and took my place in the crush around the bar. Noa smiled at me each time someone pushed past me. She wanted to get up and come help me but I signaled to her to stay put and save our seats. I was finally able to get two pints of Goldstar and make it back to the table.

I want to be like them. That's what I thought when Noa said this was the only place she liked to go out in this ghost town of a city. "The nerd-in-disguise hangout," she said.

Most of the people looked like they were students and I recognized many of the faces from the halls of Bezalel. I'd never been in a place like that, and I liked it. I'd been out to pubs before with Ruchaleh, but they were the kind of places that had soft light and cool jazz, nothing like what was happening here. I had to stop myself from shivering when I thought of Ruchaleh. What was she doing at this moment? How did she feel? I should have been with her. I shouldn't have left. If everything was going according to plan, then the ambulance should have already left with Yonatan and taken him to the morgue in Shaare Zedek. They don't check anything there, Ruchaleh had said, it's just a refrigerated storage room where they keep the merchandise until it's picked up. Anyone who asked about the funeral would be told that Yonatan, without her even knowing, had decided back in high school to give his body to science.

"What?" Noa asked. I couldn't hear her.

"Nothing," I mumbled, and I tried to return to her, to the pub, the music. "L'chaim," I said, raising my glass, and she raised hers. "L'chaim," I said again as I brought the glass to my lips and tried to remember that legendary hero from before the days of Islam, a-Zir, who was infamous for his love of women and alcohol. On the night that his father, the head of the tribe, was murdered, they came to the drunk poet and told him the news, to which he said, a pitcher of wine in his hand, *"Ilyom hmar wa'ad amar."* Wine today, action tomorrow. The following day he embarked on one of the most brutal vengeance campaigns in the history of the Arabs.

Beer today, I said to myself and looked around. Today I want to be like them. Today I want to be one of them, to go into the places they're allowed to go, to laugh the way they laugh, to drink without having to think about God. I want to be like them. Free, loose, full of dreams, able to think about love. Like them. Like those who started to fill the dance floor with the knowledge that it was theirs, they who felt no need to apologize for their existence, no need to hide their identity. Like them. Those who never looked for suspicious glances, whose loyalty was never questioned, whose acceptance was always taken for granted. Today I want to be like them without feeling like I'm committing a crime. I want to drink with them, dance with them, without feeling as though I'm trespassing in a foreign culture. To feel like I belong, without feeling guilty or disloyal. And what exactly was I being disloyal to?

"You coming?" Noa asked through the haze of house music.

"I don't know how to dance," I said.

She got out of her chair, leaned over the little table between us, and brought her mouth close to my ear.

"Neither do I," she whispered, and I could feel her breath penetrating my ear, bringing me back to life.

PART
SEVEN

HOT WATER

The lawyer couldn't say definitively whether he was asleep or awake. He heard the morning noises of his wife and kids, as he did every morning, but they seemed to be coming from somewhere else, somewhere foreign and unfamiliar. He opened his eyes and hoped to see his daughter standing in front of him but she was not there. The lawyer tried, unsuccessfully, to put his mind in order, and then he gave up and went back to sleep. When he awoke again he wasn't sure how much time had passed, seconds or hours, before the din of the house reached him again. This time he rose to a familiar world. He knew he was sleeping in a bed, in his daughter's room, in his house, and he heard footfalls on the stairs, coming his way.

"You still sleeping?" his wife asked in a soft voice, laying a hand on his forehead to see if he had a fever. "You're a little warm," she said, even though the lawyer knew he wasn't sick. All he was was tired, exhausted. He had started reading *The Kreutzer Sonata*, sure he would never get past the first line, but he had found himself drawn into the plot, which involved a train, a young man, a woman, talk of love, and a character who murdered his wife and starts to tell his story.

"Mommy," his daughter said, her feet pattering behind her mother.

"I asked you to watch your brother for a second," his wife said, raising her voice.

"I know," the girl said. "But I'm tired, I don't want to."

"So?" his wife said to him. "What do you want to do? You want to take it easy at home a little today?"

"No," he said, flipping the blanket off. "I have a hearing in court at eight thirty."

"Mommy," the girl said. "When are you going to brush my hair?"

"Give your hair a rest, okay? I'll brush it in a minute. So, do you want me to make you some coffee before I go?"

"No, no," the lawyer said, sitting on the edge of the bed and trying to limit his movements to the bare minimum so as to stave off the headache that had already announced itself. He looked over at the rabbit-shaped alarm clock and said, "You guys should get going. You're late. I'll head out after you."

"Okay, take it easy," his wife said and kissed him on the lips, a kiss the lawyer felt was genuine, not forced or apologetic or meant to conceal. "I really love you," she said before leaving, and the lawyer gently nodded his head, to the extent that the headache allowed.

Water, first of all water, the lawyer thought as he walked up the stairs. He drank straight from the bottle, as he always did when no one was around. Then he called Tarik, who was on his way to the office. "I have a hearing on the Marzuk case at eight thirty. Please go down to the courthouse and ask for a continuance on account of illness. I'll be in the office at nine. I have to take care of something first. Oh, and Tarik, we're interviewing the new interns this afternoon and I may need you there. Could be you'll be the only one there. Interview them yourself and choose yourself a bride at the same time, okay?" the lawyer said, laughing.

The lawyer made Turkish coffee and added milk and sugar. In the mornings he took his coffee with milk, which had an immediate effect on his bowels. He took the cup of coffee down to the study, lit a cigarette, and checked the *Haaretz* headlines online. Then checked to make sure that he had everything he needed, realized that he had forgotten *The Kreutzer Sonata*, left the cigarette in the ashtray, and went to his daughter's room to get it. He was on page thirty and had been using the note as a bookmark.

Mornings in Jerusalem are cold, even in summer, which is why the lawyer had a gas-operated water heater installed in the house, ensuring that the shower water was hot as soon as it was turned on. He found the right temperature and then stood beneath the wide veil of water cascading from the eight-inch shower head. He brushed his teeth, shaved his face, washed his hair. Looking up at the shower head, washing soap off his body, he was struck by a long-forgotten childhood memory. He saw his mother boiling water on a gas stove on a cold winter night and he saw his brothers, naked, freezing, and his mother approaching with a pot of warm water, ladling it over their heads with a brass cup, one at a time, and then scrubbing them hard, an expression of great suffering on her face. Her children had to be washed every day, they would go to school clean, even in winter, even if it meant suffering. When the boys were done they shared a single towel. Then came their little sister. His mother washed her in a little tub, supporting her neck with one hand and washing her with the other, shampooing the fine strands of baby hair.

There were a dozen white shirts hanging in the closet, all starched and ironed, each paired with a tie of his wife's choosing. His pants were hanging on special hangers. He picked out a pair of black slacks, chose a shirt, placed a tie around his neck, and decided he'd tie it later. Putting on his shoes, he called Samah.

"Hi, Samah, good morning. I'm running a little late. Something came up. Yes, I know, I spoke with Tarik already. What else is on the agenda for today? Okay, I'll be in by nine. Wait, just a second, that ID number you gave me yesterday, do you still have it on you? Yes, exactly, Amir Lahab. Send the number to our guy in the court system and ask him to find a current address, please. And tell him not to take his time this time. Be assertive with him. Tell him I don't want to wait until tomorrow. Okay, great, can I bring you a cup of coffee? Oh, and Samah, do me a favor and keep this between us."

The lawyer's carefully laid plans began to go awry as soon as he got into his car and fielded a telephone call from his wife.

"Where are you?" he yelled toward the speakerphone.

"At work. I just wanted to see how you're doing. Did you leave for work already?"

"Yes, sure, is everything okay? Is something wrong?"

"No," she said. "Everything's fine. I took the kids in, everything went smoothly. I'm heading into a meeting now and I won't be able to use the phone so I figured I'd give you a call before it started, see if you decided to stay home."

"No, no, I'm in the car."

"You on the way to court?"

"Court?"

"You said you have a hearing at eight thirty, remember?"

"Oh, right, sure. I'm on my way to the district court," he said, and immediately felt that she was checking to see whether he was tied up and if he might beat her to the punch and file first.

"Okay, so I'll give you a call later?"

"Yeah, yeah, 'bye."

The lawyer felt like he was choking. He cranked up the AC in the car and opened the window. Was it possible that his wife was smarter than he was? Craftier than he was? She had never before called him in the morning to see how he was doing, to find out where he was and whether he'd made it to court or not. He envisioned her standing outside the Israeli civil court for family matters, which opened at eight thirty, fully aware, as was he, that her financial future hung in the balance. "She's never called me in the morning before," the lawyer said out loud. "Never asked me about my fucking job. So why now? And the kiss? And the sweet talk in the morning? Since when does she touch my forehead to see if I'm running a fever?"

The lawyer, waiting in traffic, cursed the car ahead of him. He had to stop himself from leaning on the horn. Maybe she was just trying to soothe him. Maybe she was just shaken by the fact that he'd found the letter, maybe she was afraid he didn't believe her? And with good reason. He imagined her laughing out loud, in a voice that wasn't even hers.

"I just talked to him," he heard her tell the man by her side. "He's on the way to court, nothing to worry about. He bought the whole story, doesn't suspect a thing."

The lawyer tried to find a shortcut and turned off Hebron Way toward Talpiot. He wasn't sure where to go — to family court, to catch her in the act? But what would he do then? Laugh? Cry? What would he do when she tossed him that scornful look, proud for having beaten him? She'd be safe there. What could he do to her in front of all those policemen and courthouse security guards.

And maybe the best thing was to simply go to the Sharia court this instant and file for divorce there. But that wouldn't help either. If she was already at family court then it was over, the civil court system had jurisdiction. The lawyer decided to drive by her work to see if her car was parked outside. That way he could continue on with his plan. "Just a little wrinkle," the lawyer mumbled to himself. "Just a little wrinkle."

He replayed the brief conversation with his wife. What were the noises he'd heard in the background? He wasn't sure. Was there that kind of din in the family court already at this hour? Did he even hear much noise? Actually it had been completely quiet. Was her office completely quiet? Where did she work on Sunday morning anyway? At the clinic? Or the office? What an idiot. What an ass he'd been all these years. He didn't so much as have his wife's number at the office. Now he knew why she always called the office and not his cell: so she'd know exactly where he was at any given moment. "No," he'd heard her say, "it's because I never know when you're available."

The lawyer tried calling her back on her cell. At the very least this time he would make a point of listening to the background noises. But what would he say? Would he ask her if she wanted to meet for lunch? That would be unprecedented. What would he ask her: Where are you working today? Why did he want to know that? The lawyer couldn't come up with a convincing reason and, at any rate, she didn't pick up. *A meeting;* the lawyer smiled and told himself he had married someone with a superior mind. The first thing he would do was look for her car outside the social services office in Talpiot. She went in to that office at least twice a week, of that he was certain. If not, then he'd go to that fucking mental health clinic of hers. And if he didn't find her car there, either? Well . . . He honked at the car in front of him.

CORPSE

Pushing the key into the lock, I hoped that nothing had changed. The weekend edition of the paper waited beside the door, wrapped in a plastic bag, covered in dew. I picked up the paper, shook off the drops, and opened the door.

Ruchaleh was on the couch, awake, looking terrible. Her eyes were puffy, her gaze was fixed on the ceiling, and there were two empty bottles of red wine on the table. The sun had risen but the blinds were still shut and the only light in the room came in from the kitchen. I said nothing. I stood in the entryway and waited for her to turn toward me. There was no need for me to go up to the attic. Something clearly had changed. Moving slowly, Ruchaleh turned and looked at me. Then, making a great effort, she smiled and moved her head up and down, again and again.

"Do me a favor," she said, "and don't stare at me with that pitying look."

I froze, even though what I wanted to do was run to her and hug her and tell her that I loved her. I wouldn't care if she said something like, *I can't stand histrionic people,* or *What a pathetic Arab.* I wanted to fall into her arms, console her, be consoled, receive a warm hug, and hear her whisper in my ear, "Don't worry, Mommy's here," in a voice that would soothe all my fears.

"What are you doing standing there like a golem?" she said. "It's over, it's done."

"It's just beginning," I found myself saying, completely unsure of what I meant.

"I can't stand," she chuckled, and then she was quiet for a moment before adding, very softly, almost apologetically, "Come here, you little dunce." I walked over to her and she hugged me harder than ever before and she wasn't even taken aback when I lay my head on her chest. She hugged me as though I were hers, and I, on my knees, on the floor, burying my head in her chest, tightening my grip, tried to make myself more and more hers. I didn't look up but I knew she was crying. She groaned in pain and her body shook. "What are you doing crying like a little kid?" she asked me in a wavering voice, stroking my hair. I knew she was silently saying, "Stay here, stay here with me." I stayed until she fell asleep and only then did I break her embrace.

"*A'rib?*" the man in charge of burials in Beit Safafa asked over the phone.

"*A'rib*" I answered in Arabic. Stranger.

"So then it will be a small funeral," he said.

"There will be no funeral," I said.

"You have permission for burial?"

"Yes, I got it from the hospital."

"You know where to bring him?"

"No."

"You know the small mosque near the cemetery?"

"I'll ask."

"Okay, bring him there," he said. "Ask anyone in the village and he'll direct you there. Everyone knows where the cemetery is."

"Okay, thank you very much."

"Allah *Yirachmo*," *God have mercy*, said the man to whom death was a livelihood.

Equipped with the signed certificate of death and the ID card, I set out in Ruchaleh's car for the morgue at Shaare Zedek, where Yonatan's body was being stored. An older nurse looked at my paperwork and made a feeble attempt at empathy.

"How are you taking him?" she asked.

"Ambulance," I said right away, and she nodded.

"Should I order one for you?"

"Yes, please."

"Okay, you can wait over there," she said, pointing her chin in the direction of a small waiting room. Then she picked up the phone and began to dial.

A small TV, resting on a metal arm that protruded from the wall, showed soundless footage from the government channel. Two stern-looking men spoke to one another. One,

who looked like the guest, was religious, with a black yarmulke, a thick beard, a white shirt, and a black jacket. The
man who looked like the host wore a knitted yarmulke and a
blue dress shirt. His beard was trimmed and sculpted. Every
once in a while a few passages from the Bible appeared on
the screen and then disappeared. The two men were visibly
excited, waving their fists, punctuating with their hands,
making expansive gestures, smiling at the camera, twisting
their faces into occasional grimaces, underscoring again and
again their wonder at the potency of Biblical verse.

"Shalom," the Arab ambulance driver said to me in halt-
ing Hebrew, perhaps on account of my clothes and perhaps
on account of my physical appearance.

"Shalom," I responded, rising to my feet.

"You're accompanying the body, right?" he asked with
no preamble and no superfluous attempts at commiseration.

"Right."

"To Beit Safafa?"

"Yes, to the small mosque near the . . ."

"Yeah," the driver said, handing me a copy of some
paperwork, "I know the place. I'm from there. You going
to follow me?"

The driver lit a cigarette on the way to the ambulance,
giving his younger assistant time to walk over to the stretcher
and the enshrouded body and push it toward the ambulance.
The driver opened the back doors and the younger man
pushed a button on the stretcher and shoved it into the
ambulance, the legs of the stretcher folding into the track.

They drove slowly, and I followed. For some reason I
felt a burning desire to take photographs. It seemed to me
like the only reasonable way to pass the next few minutes,

behind the lens of a camera. To press, swivel, document, hide, distance myself from the events. But even if I had brought the camera with me, I doubt I would have had the nerve to use it. On Army Radio a famous Israeli singer spoke about his experiences during the past week, softening his voice, making it sound thoughtful, trying to enliven the banal conclusions that he had reached regarding his life.

"This next song has accompanied me during sad and happy days alike," he said after he had finished his little speech and before he let the music speak for itself.

The ambulance entered the village and immediately drew the attention of the locals. Kids on bikes trailed behind the ambulance and pedaled furiously in their attempts to over-take the two-car convoy. The driver opened his window and told them something, probably that nothing exciting was happening, that this was just the body of a stranger being brought to burial, not someone from the village. A crowd tumbled out of the small mosque near the cemetery. The men stopped and stared at the ambulance and waited to see what was going on. I berated myself for forgetting that there was this little thing called Friday prayers and that it was the absolute worst time for a clandestine burial. I parked behind the ambulance and stayed inside the car. The driver turned around and threw me a look. Three men, one of whom seemed like the man in charge and the other two his helpers, came up to the ambulance driver and shook his hand, smiling. They exchanged a few words and looked over at me. A few of the worshippers came over and spoke with the men, whispering, and once they realized that it was not a villager who was being brought for burial and their curiosity had been satisfied, they left and went to report back to their friends that there was nothing to see.

I got out of the car only after all of the worshippers had dispersed. The driver's assistant pulled Yonatan out of the ambulance and wheeled him toward a small room adjacent to the mosque, the two young men from the burial society trailing behind him.

"He can go to hell," an elderly man said to me in Arabic as I stood there. "Who's going to pray for this dog?"

"Shalom," the man in charge of the burial service said to me in Hebrew. "Don't worry about it, we'll take care of this. You staying here?"

"Yes," I said, not understanding exactly what was happening.

"He has no family members?"

"Not that I know of," I said.

A little kid on a bike circled around us and yelled in Arabic, "How long are they going to bury collaborators here? How long?" The man in charge barked at him to get lost. "Sure," the kid yelled. "What do you care? For you it's good business. You couldn't give a damn."

"Get out of here, now," the undertaker yelled, "or the first place I'm going to go after I'm done here is your father's house. Get out of here."

The kid pedaled off and the ambulance driver laughed and said the kid was right. "They've turned our cemetery into a garbage dump for foreigners," he said in Arabic, and the undertaker looked at him apprehensively. "Don't worry about it," the driver said, looking at me. "He doesn't understand a word, this one." The stretcher was brought back to the ambulance and the driver and his assistant shook hands with the undertaker, bid him farewell, and drove off.

"You're not a family member, right?" the undertaker asked me.

"No."

"So, what is this, your job?"

"Yeah, among other things," I found myself responding.

"You know how this works?"

"No."

"The boys are washing him now. Then he goes into the mosque for a brief prayer and then we bury him. The grave has already been dug." He pointed to a far-off corner of the cemetery. "Everything's ready. You want some coffee?"

"No," I said. "Thank you."

The washing ceremony was brief. The two young men emerged with the body in a wooden coffin and hurried into the mosque.

"Just a second," the undertaker said to me and jogged over to them. No prayer for the dead had been recited, of that I was sure. The coffin hadn't been inside the mosque for more than a minute and the two men were coming out, carrying the coffin, walking briskly across the street that separated the mosque from the cemetery.

"Who died?" asked a driver who'd stopped his car.

"A foreigner," the undertaker said. "*Allah yirachmo*, a foreigner. A foreigner."

The man drove off and the undertaker turned to me. "That's it, they're burying him," he said. "If you'd like, you can leave a little something for the young men."

"Yeah, let the little fucker pay," one of the young men said as he walked with the coffin toward the grave. His partner laughed.

"Shut up," the undertaker yelled at them, his face showing sorrow and disappointment.

"Of course," I said, and I took two fifty-shekel notes out of my wallet.

"Thank you very much," the undertaker said, parting from me quickly and walking toward the cemetery. I heard him say, "You're making me look bad," to the two men as they lowered the coffin into the ground. I got back in the car and started the engine. From afar I could see the heads of the two young men bending down to the ground and the undertaker directing them with his hands. I imagined that they had laid out the usual five blocks and that they were placing them on the body and then filling in the ditch with sand, spade by spade. I sat there and watched them work. One of the young men spat into the grave and laughed.

UNDERGROUND PARKING

The lawyer parked his car in the lot above King George Street. It was nearly nine in the morning. He turned off the engine and stayed in the car. The lawyer was scared. Where had all of this come from? He was afraid that this uncontrollable feeling would destroy his life and his career, make him lose his clientele and his livelihood. What was he worth without them? A month or two without any good cases and his life would start to unravel. The salaries,

the mortgage, the car payments, taxes, shopping, his son's
nanny, his daughter's school. The lawyer could see his life
begin to crumble. Why had she done this to him? Didn't
she see that he'd been working like a mule to support them?
He was always apprehensive that a young lawyer would
come up and knock him off the top spot, but who would
have thought that he'd be undone by matters of love and
betrayal? Instead of showing up in court and representing
an important client against charges of unlawful possession
of a firearm, he was out and about on the streets, prowling
around for his wife's car like a jealous teenager.

There were five floors of underground parking at the Ministry of Social Affairs' west Jerusalem office in Talpiot, and
the lawyer drove slowly along the avenue of parked cars,
eyeing each and every one.

Having not found his wife's car, he made a U-turn and
started back to the ground-floor exit. As he approached
daylight, his phone announced two messages. The lawyer
looked at the screen and saw that he had missed two calls
while underground. One from Samah and one from his wife.
He called his wife but once again she did not answer. The
lawyer left Talpiot and drove toward the mental health clinic
where his wife worked two or three days a week. What did
she do there exactly? he wondered as his phone rang again.

"Is everything all right?" she asked. "I saw you called
but I couldn't answer because I'm in a meeting and my phone
is on silent. I just stepped outside. Is everything okay?"

"Yeah," the lawyer said. "What kind of meeting?"

"A staff meeting."

"At the mental health clinic?"

"Yes. There's a staff meeting every Sunday. We present cases. If everything's okay then I'm going to go back in. You sure everything's okay?"

"Yeah, everything's fine. I'm just stuck in traffic."

And still the lawyer drove to the clinic to look for her car. But even when he saw it, he felt that it was possible that his wife had deceived him and that she had parked there and then taken a taxi. He tightened his grip on the steering wheel and exhaled. He was sweating. He tried to loosen up, stretch his muscles. He was not thinking logically anymore, he seemed to be losing his mind.

There's no reason for this, he told himself, there's no reason to act like this. Your life is fine. Your life is in order. You are heading into an office that is humming with work; you will always have clients. Your caseload and your income have gone up each year. Clients don't just melt away, nothing has changed.

"He's dead," Samah announced when the lawyer walked into the office.

"Who?"

"Your guy."

"What? That's not possible," he said, putting down the little cardboard tray and the three cups of coffee. The phones rang.

"Lawyer's office, please hold," Samah said, laying the phone down on the counter. She pulled a piece of paper out of the fax, handed it to the lawyer, and got back on the phone. "Sorry for the wait, how may I help you? Hello, Abu

Ramzi, how are you?" Samah looked at the lawyer and he shook his head, making clear that he could not take the call. "No, I'm sorry, he's not in the office right now. He's in court. Yes, of course, I'll give him the message. 'Bye."

The lawyer sat down on his office couch and looked at the fax from the population registry. Amir Lahab, born in Tira, 1979. The lawyer took out the note Samah had given him with the ID number she had received from the outpatient clinic in east Jerusalem and made sure that the numbers matched. According to the population registry, this Amir Lahab had died on Thursday, a little over a week ago. What kind of coincidence was that? Now, while he was searching for him, the guy just happens to die?

Impossible, the lawyer thought, something is wrong. There's no way he's dead. Just yesterday he had spoken with the man's mother, who did not seem to suffer from mental illness, and she had said she had spoken to him over the course of the past week. The lawyer leaned back on the couch and ran his hands back and forth through his hair.

"What's wrong?" Samah asked, coming into the room with the lawyer's cup of coffee.

"Nothing," the lawyer said. "Nothing."

"Did you know the deceased?"

"What?" It took him a moment to understand her question. "Oh, no, no. Listen," he said, sitting up straight and pulling two books out of his briefcase, *One Hundred Years of Solitude* and the one featuring the work of Egon Schiele. He flipped through the first pages of the novel and showed Samah the signature, *Yonatan*. "Scan this page, please," the lawyer said, "and this one," he said, showing her the signature on the art book, "and send them to the graphologist.

Tell him it's very urgent. And that there's no need for an official report."

Samah took the two books. "What should I ask him?"

"What? Oh, ask him to compare the two signatures. Circle the name *Yonatan* on both of the documents."

Once she'd left the room the lawyer looked around for the telephone number that he'd gotten from Meissar, the mother from Jaljulia. What would he say to her? *Did you know that the son you spoke with last week is dead?* The lawyer wanted to check the ID number, ask if there was anyone else from Jaljulia with the same name, but he knew those kinds of questions would make her suspicious and would not likely be answered.

"Hello?"

He heard her voice and hung up the phone.

GARBAGE CANS

On Thursday, after the shiva, Ruchaleh packed a big suitcase full of clothes and moved into a hotel room until she could find herself an apartment. Selling the house was a chore she left for me to take care of. "Leave whatever you leave, take whatever you take," she said when I dropped her off in front of the hotel.

She had probably been waiting for this moment just as I had, played the day-after scenario in her head thousands of times. She knew exactly what had to be done, knew which suitcase to take, which clothes to pack. She had not shown any sign of hesitation when she walked out of the bedroom with her suitcase and took five books off the shelf in the living room—books she may have chosen years ago—and then walked into her study and back out again with a bag slung over her shoulder.

I think I may have thought about this moment more than Ruchaleh, and I was sure that when the time came, after months of nightly planning, I would get things done on autopilot, briskly moving from chore to chore. But on the way back from the hotel I felt myself start to lose my train of thought and everything that had seemed so clear started to blur.

When I got home I called the real estate agency that Ruchaleh had decided to work with. Upon hearing that there was a private house in Beit Hakerem going on the market, they insisted on sending someone that same day. I had to be very firm with the real estate agent and tell him that the earliest I could see him was Sunday, though I reassured him that I would not speak with other agencies in the meantime.

Ruchaleh had said I could stay at the house as long as there was no buyer but I knew I would never be able to sleep there alone, not even for one night, without her and without Yonatan. *Sterilization*—that was my code word for the initial first step. No trace, I said to myself as I started emptying the attic drawers and dumping the contents into garbage bags.

I tried not to look at the contents of the desk drawers, which I knew so well, but rather to pull each one out, dump everything into a bag, and move on without pause. There was no time for contemplation. Diaries, pictures, report cards, drawings from kindergarten, letters. I still wasn't sure if these things should be shredded or burned.

Having finished the desk I moved on to the closet. I pulled the two gym bags my mother had bought me off the top shelf and stuffed my old clothes inside. After five years of neglect the clothes looked pathetic. They're not mine, I tried convincing myself, and I shivered. They're not mine. I brought the blue sweater to my face and sniffed it; that is not my scent, I said to myself, and I used the sweater to wipe away the tears, scratching them off my face, and then I shoved it into the bag.

The plan was to lay the old clothes outside next to the garbage cans, as all of the neighbors did, donations to the Arab garbagemen. These bags, though, I thought, might look suspicious to the neighbors. They usually left their belongings in see-through bags and not in old canvas gym bags that could look suspicious. I unzipped the bags, dumped their contents into the garbage, and then folded the bags and tossed them in, too.

I packed my new wardrobe in a suitcase that I had bought earlier in the week and, since I had promised Ruchaleh that I would leave the attic empty, I took all the things I didn't want, threw them into garbage bags, and put them out on the curb. The eggshell mattress, the wheelchair, the ventilator, and all the rest of the medical supplies were to be picked up the following day by the Yad Sarah organization. They were delighted to hear that I was interested in donating all of the furniture in the room, too.

Noa was in class when I arrived at her house but she had left me a key, just as she'd promised, right under the mat. Despite Noa's love of music, all she had was a little compact stereo with poor sound so I brought her Yonatan's stereo and his electric guitar, presents for allowing me to stay with her until I found a place of my own.

After dropping everything off at Noa's, I went back to the house to pack up the CDs and the books. The bag with the stuff from Yonatan's drawers, I decided, should be thrown out somewhere else, far away.

TWO-HUNDRED SHEKEL NOTES

"I'll be back in five minutes," the lawyer told Samah, who was holding the phone in one hand and sending the graphologist a fax with the other. On the way down the stairs he bumped into Tarik.

"So?" the lawyer asked.

"Good news! In the end the prosecution were the ones who were reprimanded."

"You didn't have to ask for a continuance?"

"No, the police never even managed to bring in the accused."

"Great," the lawyer said, smiling a genuine smile. "All right, I'm headed out for five minutes. Your coffee's waiting for you, probably already cold."

The lawyer was happy he hadn't had to ask the court to reschedule the hearing. He took it as a sign. Maybe everyone was not against him and maybe the luck he had always had had not run out. Just one tiny little inquiry and then it's over, the lawyer promised himself. One more thing and then I'm putting this entire thing behind me. I don't care if this Amir is alive or dead; if his mother spoke to him or not. Enough. After I look into one more thing I will go back to believing in my wife's version of events.

"Oh, good morning," the lawyer said to Meirav when he saw her behind the counter of the used bookstore reading the paper.

"Good morning," she said. "What's up? What are you doing here on a Sunday, in the morning no less?"

The lawyer laughed and hoped he sounded credible. "You're right," he said, looking around for Yonatan's boxes, "something is up."

"What?" Meirav asked.

"On Thursday I came in and bought *The Kreutzer Sonata,* you remember?" He showed her the book.

"Yeah, I remember. What about it?"

"It's a great book. I just wanted to ask if you knew who sold it to you?"

"Sure," she answered. "I was the one who was working when all the stuff came in on Thursday. Why?"

"Do you think you could give me, I don't know, the person's number or e-mail or something?"

"No, sorry. We're not allowed to give out the numbers of sellers or buyers. If it's something important and you really need his info, you better talk to the owner."

"I understand," the lawyer said. "It's kind of like attorney-client privilege or something, right?"

"The owner's pretty strict about it," Meirav said. "He's worried people are going to steal his clients or, even worse, his sellers."

"Okay, fine," the lawyer said, opening the book. "The thing is, Meirav, that while I was reading I found these between the pages of the book." He produced a pair of two-hundred shekel notes.

"Oh," Meirav said, looking confused.

"I think these might be Yonatan's," the lawyer said, watching her face for a reaction.

"Yeah, they must be." She typed something into the computer. "I'll call him and tell him to come pick it up."

"Hi, is this Yonatan?" Meirav said into the phone. "Hi, I hope I'm not disturbing you. My name's Meirav and I'm calling from the used bookstore. We met on Thursday when you brought the books in, remember? No, no, everything's fine, it's just that someone found two two-hundred shekel bills in one of the books. Yeah. So I was thinking, I don't know, maybe we could send it over to you or you could come by and get it." Meirav was silent, she nodded her head and looked at the lawyer. Then she said, "I don't see why not, it's your money."

The lawyer gestured to Meirav that he would like the phone. She said, "Just a second, the customer who found the money wants to talk to you. Just a second," and she handed him the phone.

The lawyer took a deep breath.

"Hello, Yonatan?" he said, his voice rising at the end to form a question.

"Hello," said the voice on the other end of the line. The lawyer could hear noise all around him.

"I bought *The Kreutzer Sonata* a little while ago and . . ." the lawyer's voice wavered.

"I know, it's okay," the other man said. "It's fine. I don't want the money. Do whatever you want with it. Give it away, take it, give it to the store, I don't care."

"I understand," the lawyer said, wondering what to say next. It sounded to him like the voice on the other end of the line had left the noise and was searching out a quieter place. "The thing is, aside from the money, I also found the note."

"What note?"

"A note in Arabic, and that's why I'm here."

"Sir," the other man said impatiently, "I don't know what you're talking about, and I'm heading into a class so I'm going to hang up now."

"Do you know Arabic, Yonatan?" the lawyer asked, looking over at Meirav, who was starting to fidget, apparently regretting ever handing the phone to the lawyer.

"Why do you ask, sir? Who are you?"

The man's response told the lawyer that he was on the right track.

"Yonatan," he said, this time more forcefully. "Do you know someone by the name of Amir Lahab?"

"Who are you?" The lawyer could hear the fear in the man's voice. "Can you please tell me who you are?" the man said, practically begging.

The lawyer decided to end this part of his investigation. "So, should I bring you the money when we meet up?" he asked.

"Why should we meet up? I just told you that I don't want the money. What do you want from me?"

"No problem," the lawyer said, smiling at Meirav. "No problem. I'll bring the note, too. Okay, have a good rest of the day. They have your address? Great, excellent. Okay, see you soon." The lawyer hung up the phone without waiting for a response. He looked at Meirav and grinned. "What kind of person says no to cash?"

"He wanted it?"

"Of course," the lawyer said. "He sounded really busy,

though. He asked that I take it over to his house. Sounded like a nice guy. And he definitely has good taste in books."

"No doubt," Meirav said. "There were some amazing books in there."

"Okay," the lawyer said. "I'll head over there. Could you tell me how to go? What's the shortest way to get there?"

"To 35 Scout Street?" she asked, looking at the computer screen. "The best thing to do is take Bezalel Street all the way to Herzl and then make a left."

"Great, thanks a million."

A SIGN AND A BELL

The lawyer was feeling pleased. He'd taken care of everything he'd set out to do. His wife was at home with the kids. How could he have thought, only earlier that morning, that she had beaten him to the punch and filed first for divorce? The matter of her car and the five floors of the parking garage also brought a smile to his lips. True, he hadn't yet found an intern. Only two out of three had shown up and neither had made a particularly good impression, especially not on Tarik.

"Both goody two-shoes," Tarik had said after the interviews. "So what, so they have good grades? They're both spoiled little girls who've never seen anything outside a textbook and don't know a thing about how the world works."

"So we'll wait for next week, there'll be more candidates," the lawyer said, laughing. "And yes, they really weren't very kind on the eyes."

He was also pleased that he was close to finding the answer to the riddle. And now, on his way to Beit Hakerem, that was all that remained of the whole sordid affair: the riddle, the challenge. He had seemingly forgotten about his wife's involvement in the matter and now only sought to find out who Yonatan was, who Amir was, what the two had to do with each other, and how the whole thing had happened.

It's possible that the lawyer was tickled by the notion that Amir and Yonatan were actually a couple. If that turned out to be the case, he'd be delighted. If it turned out that his wife, before he had come along, had been in love with a gay man, it would make him the happiest person in the world. In his mind the old picture of the tough, tall, muscular Arab with the giant cock turned into one of a dainty little porcelain-faced faggot dancing with his wife at the party. It was true that in public the lawyer had never said anything against homosexuality and, in fact, took pains to publicly say that every person is free to choose whomever he or she wants to spend their lives with. He also railed against the persecution of homosexuals in Arab lands and in Iran and said that this type of treatment was a sure sign of social and cultural malaise, a fundamental lack of openness among the Arab and Islamic communities. And yet the notion of his wife dancing around with a gay man filled him with an undeniable giddiness.

The lawyer slowed down and looked at the numbers on the houses. He parked his car outside of 34 and looked across the street for 35. A small gate led to a garden and a large house. There's no way a social worker could afford this place, the lawyer thought as he waited outside the front door, thinking that the house looked a lot more like a family home than the pad of two young gay men. The neighborhood was quiet. No cars came down the narrow street and, other than the barking of dogs and the whirr of cars on the nearby avenue, the lawyer did not hear a thing. On the front door there was a wooden sign with the name Forschmidt.

The lawyer knocked softly with his fist on the wooden door. In his hand he held *The Kreutzer Sonata,* his wife's letter, and the two two-hundred-shekel bills. No matter who opened the door, the lawyer had decided to be straightforward. To tell the truth and to ask for answers. I bought a book that Yonatan sold, he rehearsed, and in the book I found a letter in my wife's hand. I was wondering why that was. Just curious. What's more, she said she had written that note to a colleague by the name of Amir Lahab. The lawyer knocked again but there was no response. He hit the bell, listened to its muffled ring inside the house, and waited for some time until the door opened.

MEETING

"Shalom," I said to the man at the door, sure he was the real estate agent. "Please, come on in, you're a little bit early but that's fine."

"I think you might have me confused with someone else," the man said, still standing at the door.

"You're not the real estate agent?" I asked.

"No," he said and a huge smile spread across his face. Now I started to notice the Arabness of his look and his accent, and I knew without a shadow of a doubt that this was the voice from the bookstore earlier in the day. "You're Yonatan," he said, with only the trace of a question.

"Excuse me," I said, "but who's asking?"

"No one," he answered, still smiling. "Just a lawyer who's looking for Yonatan."

"Why, what did he do?"

"Nothing," the man said. "He didn't do a thing. I believe, though, that I bought a book that he sold." He raised *The Kreutzer Sonata* up to eye level as though it were an important piece of evidence. "I found a few hundred shekels inside and I said that I simply had to return them to him."

"Thank you," I said. "If you'd like I can give them to him."

"So, then you're not Yonatan?" he asked.

"I don't see why it matters, sir," I said.

"It doesn't matter," the lawyer said, pulling a folded white piece of paper from the book. "But I found a note in the book, too, and it seems to be a bit more personal than money, so I thought I would hand it over to Yonatan in person."

"I'm Yonatan," I said impatiently. By now I was sure that the unexpected guest was an Arab.

"Please forgive my audacity," he said, as though performing before a packed courthouse, "but could you please show me some ID?"

"Sir, I have no idea who you are. You come to my house with an old book and some story about money. I don't care about the money and I don't care about the note. I don't want to show you my ID and I don't want to continue this conversation." I held the door open and only a lifetime of good manners stopped me from slamming it in his face. I waited for him to leave, but perhaps I already knew that this was the first stage of what was going to be a long conversation.

"Your name's Amir," he said sharply in Arabic.

"What?" I said, trying to stick to Hebrew. "Who the hell are you? What do you want from me?"

"I know who you are," he went on in Arabic. "I visited with your mother in Jaljulia yesterday. I wonder what she'll think when she discovers that her only son is dead."

I stood before the lawyer, said nothing, and watched as he produced a pack of cigarettes and a lighter.

"You smoke?" he asked in Arabic.

I nodded and took a cigarette.

"*Tfaðal*," be my guest, I said, and motioned him into the house, looking to see if anyone had witnessed our conversation. "You can smoke in here."

He lit my cigarette and kept his unlit, clenched between his lips.

"Who are you?" I asked when he was seated on the couch. I had taken Ruchaleh's usual spot and was feeling uncomfortable.

The lawyer's gaze flitted around the room, taking in the books. "You know what," he said, "I've always dreamed of having this kind of book collection. You want to sell it?"

"They're not mine," I said, trying to force him to get to the point, to stop gloating.

"And what about this one," he said, knocking on the table where he'd set down *The Kreutzer Sonata*. "Is this one yours?"

"Please," I said, "just tell me who you are and what you want."

"Like I said, I'm a lawyer, but I'm here not as a lawyer but as Leila's husband." He stopped and looked me right in the face.

"Who's Leila?" I asked, furrowing my brow, and I could tell immediately that he was relieved. His muscles seemed to slacken and he leaned back and lit his cigarette.

"You once worked at the outpatient clinic in east Jerusalem, right?"

"Yes."

"Well then," he said, flattening the note out on the table, "the whole thing started with this."

I looked at the note, written in a very feminine and beautiful hand. "What is it? Where's it from? That was in the book?"

"Yes," the lawyer said. "That was in the book."

"Okay," I said, picking up the note, "what does that have to do with me?"

"She wrote it to you, did she not?"

"Who?"

"Leila, my wife."

"Who's Leila?" I said again, insisting that I did not remember.

"She worked with you at the outpatient clinic in Wadi Joz. You remember?"

"No, I don't remember anyone by the name of Leila who worked there," I said, traveling back to those days, to the clinic, to Wadi Joz, to the social worker I was supposed to be. "It was all boys there if I remember correctly, no?"

"There was a Leila there, too. She was an intern."

"Ohhh," I said, surprised, even though the lawyer did not seem convinced. "Yes, yes, I remember. You're right.

Wow, Leila. A student, right? We even once did a house call together in the Old City. How is she?"

"She's well," the lawyer said. "The question is how are you?"

"What's that supposed to mean?"

"That means that I'm glad you were able to jump-start your memory and now I am going to need you to answer a few questions before I leave."

"What kind of questions?" I asked.

"Questions like how did this note, written in my wife's hand, which you claim not to remember, wind up between the pages of one of your books. And also, if you would, please enlighten me as to when all of this happened." There was something firm and resolved in the lawyer's look, something that showed me how distraught he was. He was sure I'd had a relationship with his wife and I knew I had to tell him the truth — otherwise everything I'd accomplished would go down the drain and I'd find myself answering the questions of real investigators, incriminating not only myself but those dear to me.

I took a deep breath and started to tell the story.

I don't remember the note or how it made it into that book, but I do remember the book well. It's one of the first books I read here, at Yonatan's place.

"When did you leave the clinic?" the lawyer asked.

"Over seven years ago. And I didn't leave, I fled."

"Do you have an exact date?" the lawyer asked.

"No, not exact, but I'm pretty sure it was in January, seven years ago." I could tell that the date I provided set him at ease, apparently because it added up with his own arithmetic.

"You have to believe me that I really don't know a thing about your wife. At the time I was struggling with a few different things. I didn't know if she was married and I didn't care. I was in a very different place then, you see."

"No, I don't see," the lawyer said, without even mentioning whether they were married at the time.

"I don't know what this note is about. I don't even remember it. I don't even know if she wrote it to me or it just ended up in my book. Maybe she wanted to thank me for the house call. I really don't know. All I remember is that one day I left them a resignation letter and I fled the office. I ran away from everything. Maybe this note was in the incoming-mail box, maybe it was on the table, maybe I just shoved it into my bag by accident."

The lawyer began moving around in his seat, looking anxious. "What about the party? Or do you not remember that, either?"

"I'm not exactly sure what you want to know or why you want to know it. What party?"

"I want to know everything, Amir," he growled. "And you want to know why? Because I found this note, which, as far as I'm concerned, is a love letter written by my wife, in a book that belonged to someone by the name of Yonatan. I want to know who this Yonatan is and how he's connected to my wife and to you. Where is he, Amir?"

He was not going to leave without the whole story. He'd stay until he heard the whole thing. And the truth is I already started to feel myself wanting to tell. I wanted to tell someone everything that I had been through during these past years — the lies, the impersonations. To tell all, from the day I graduated and arrived at the house on Scout Street. All the things I couldn't tell my mother or Noa or anyone else in the world. And maybe I also felt that he would understand.

I fought back the sob welling up inside me, took a deep breath, and started from the beginning.

"Yonatan's dead," I said. "I buried him a week ago."

EPILOGUE

The lawyer looked at his watch and saw that it was already five thirty. He left the office and walked down the stairs and out to King George Street. Would he make it to the bookstore today? It had been several weeks since he'd last been. The lawyer wavered for a moment and then decided not to take any chances and headed back to the parking lot. He didn't want to be late for the Thursday salon and dinner. This evening, he was pretty sure, they were going to meet at the accountant's house, or was it the civil lawyer's turn? He could not remember what they were to discuss, only that the gynecologist's wife had festively announced the topic at their last meeting. No harm done; his wife probably knew. Of course she knew. Soon she would call to remind him to get a good bottle of red wine and some fine chocolate for the hosts' kids.

Not that the lawyer lacked reading material. He still hadn't even had the chance to read through all of Yonatan's books. Truth be told, he hadn't read any of them aside from *The Kreutzer Sonata*. He praised the novella, told Tarik, Samah, and the rest of his Arab friends that it was "an amazing work of art," knowing full well that there was no chance in hell that they'd read it. His next book was *Life: A User's Manual*—a thick and impressive tome by some

French author whose name the lawyer had forgotten, and even though he was never really able to focus or follow the plot, he forced himself to read a few lines before sleep, mostly because, from what he'd learned on the back cover, the Frenchman who'd written the book was so important that he'd had a planet named in his honor.

The lawyer, promising himself a new book the following Thursday, hurried off to his car. He had to buy wine and chocolate and shower and get dressed for dinner, but before all that he had to make it to Bezalel. He wanted to see Yonatan's show.

Why was he going? the lawyer wondered as he lurched down the steep and narrow Hillel Street. He had not been invited to the graduating class's year-end exhibition but Yonatan had mentioned it once or twice during their subsequent conversations and it seemed to the lawyer that he wanted him to come. But why did he want to go? In the morning, at Oved's Café, he'd heard the art history professor telling a friend that he'd seen some "extremely compelling" works at Bezalel's year-end exhibition, including one outstanding project by a graduating photography major. The lawyer, sure the professor was referring to Yonatan, felt the jealousy begin to bubble.

Why was he so jealous? After all, the lawyer believed Yonatan's story. He believed him even when he said that he didn't remember Leila's note and that he could hardly recall her name. But the fact that she might have had a relationship with a talented, perhaps successful artist rattled him nonetheless.

All things considered, the lawyer thought as he lit a cigarette with the electric lighter in the car, Yonatan's revelations had only improved his relationship with his wife. After their initial meeting on Scout Street, the lawyer had come home full of love and lust for his wife, so much so that he decided to alter his sleeping habits and return to her bed.

"We have to force the kids to sleep in their rooms," he had told his wife as he took his daughter down to the ground floor and moved his son's crib into his room. The feeling was wonderful: he desired his wife, fell back in love with her, and, despite the discomfort, even insisted on spooning before sleep. When their daughter came upstairs crying in the middle of the night, the lawyer insisted that she return to her room. His vigilance lasted for several nights. After that he gave up and let his daughter back into the bed and resumed sleeping in her room downstairs. What can you do? he thought. With all due respect to love, I sleep much better alone.

What would he say if he met Yonatan at the exhibition? Walking toward the art academy, the lawyer tried to formulate the sentences that would explain his presence. But why did he even need to offer an explanation? The show was open to the public. They would surely speak in Hebrew, only in Hebrew. He could say to Yonatan, *I remember you mentioning the opening and art has always interested me so I decided I'd swing by,* or he could mention that he had heard about the exhibition from a friend, a professor of art history, and had decided that he couldn't afford to miss it. After all, he also liked art, especially the work of a certain Egon Schiele.

The lawyer's apprehension quickly changed shades, turning into a desire to know what "Yonatan" was like in public, among his friends, among the artsy crowd in attendance, and to see his reaction when he saw the lawyer—whether he blushed when he lied, whether his lies were transparent, and whether this charade was something he could really pull off.

The lawyer walked through the gates and onto the campus and stood before a sign that pointed the way to the different exhibits—plastic art, visual media, ceramic design, architecture, and other shows that did not interest him in the least. He looked for the arrow that pointed the way to the photography exhibit.

There was very little foot traffic in the photography wing when he got there. Each time he heard steps along the hard floor, the lawyer spun around to look for Yonatan. There were different-sized photos hung on the walls of the open classrooms and along the halls. The lawyer tried to walk slowly and lend himself the air of someone just taking in the arts even though what really interested him was the little white rectangle next to each photo, where the student's name was presented.

The lawyer, looking for Yonatan's work, toured the halls and the classrooms, gazing at landscapes and rotted-out buildings and portraits of people who glared at him, generally in the nude. There were also plenty of unclear photos, cut in the middle or blurred or splotched with color. He walked into the classrooms and, if they were empty, he made do with a glance at the name of the student presenting. If there were others milling around that particular exhibit, then he forced himself to make a round, eyeing the pictures at a hurried stroll.

The third room he entered was Yonatan's. All it took was one glance and he was set at ease: these were not the photos that the art history professor had referred to earlier in the day. There was no way that these old photos, in black and white, were outstanding or compelling. He himself had already seen more interesting photos in that day's paper.

"To my mind," the lawyer heard an older woman whisper to her partner, "this young man's work is the most interesting of all."

"Yes, he's a real talent," her authoritative partner said. "What's his name?"

Please, no, no, the lawyer prayed before hearing the woman say, "Forschmidt, Yonatan Forschmidt."

The lawyer looked very carefully at Yonatan's prints, the faces along the wall. He felt he had to understand what had so impressed the elderly couple, for whom art exhibitions were surely a way of life. He breathed in deeply and started to examine the expressions on the people's faces, the wrinkles, the pupils, the sad smiles, every last one of the details that Yonatan, that bastard, knew how to zero in on. They really are impressive, the lawyer thought, looking at the close-ups of the children, teens, women, and men. The lawyer, who was always proud of his ability to discern between Arab and Jew at a glance, had a hard time determining the ethnicity of these people.

He looked at his watch. He still had some time and he lingered in front of the prints and thought of the best way to express his enthusiasm to Yonatan, if he should bump into him. All told, there were twelve prints on display, eleven of which were portraits. Suddenly the lawyer was drawn to the twelfth one, which was positioned apart from the rest, in the corner, as though someone were hiding it from him.

The photograph was of a naked back, the arched back of a woman on the edge of a child's bed. He approached the picture slowly and felt his heart rate rise as he drew nearer to the woman's bared back. Ashamed of what he was doing, he looked over his shoulder to make sure no one was coming. This picture, also in black and white, had been taken in a rather dark room, and he imagined that Yonatan had trained a soft yellow night-light at the woman's back. The complexion of her skin, her hair—trailing down the nape of her neck in a few scant ringlets—were of an indiscernible shade.

Again he made sure that he was alone in the room and then took one more step forward, so that his nose almost brushed against the print. He stared hard at the spot where the woman's behind touched the bed, at her scapula, her spine, her neck. Suddenly he put a hand out to caress the naked woman's hips. He could have sworn they were Leila's.

A GROVE PRESS READING GROUP GUIDE
BY LINDSEY TATE

Second Person Singular

Sayed Kashua

ABOUT THIS GUIDE

We hope that these discussion questions will enhance
your reading group's exploration of Sayed Kashua's
Second Person Singular. They are meant to stimulate
discussion, offer new viewpoints, and enrich your
enjoyment of the book.

More reading group guides and additional information,
including summaries, author tours, and author sites
for other fine Grove Press titles may be found on our
Web site, www.groveatlantic.com.

QUESTIONS FOR DISCUSSION

1. Begin your discussion of *Second Person Singular* by considering how contemporary Jerusalem affects and shapes the characters' lives. Does the city—with its distinct neighborhoods and its rich mix of people from different ethnic and religious backgrounds—ultimately liberate or entrap its inhabitants?

2. This novel sharply observes the role of identity in human lives and relationships. Discuss how Kashua questions what identity means, how identity is formed and measured, and whether or not it's possible to change identity.

3. Consider the dichotomy central to the lives of the novel's Arab Israeli characters: their insistence on the importance of their past, combined with a desire to fit into modern Israeli society, without being defined by their cultural heritage. Does Kashua sympathize with their position? How does the phrase "immigrants in their own land" apply to this discussion? (p. 10)

4. The nameless narrator appears to live an enviable life as a big-shot lawyer with an attractive wife, two children, a large house, and a foreign car. Whom does he attempt to impress with this lifestyle, and to what extent has he succeeded? Does his lifestyle match the reality he aims to project?

5. Consider his thoughts about his children's schooling: "All of a sudden the lawyer started to feel that they were sending their children like spies into the heart of a foreign culture" (p. 40).

6. What future does he imagine for his children? What are his hopes for them?

7. Read the paragraphs (p. 49-53) in which the lawyer finds the love note written by his wife between the pages of *The Kreutzer Sonata*, and discuss his reactions to her supposed infidelity. What does his incensed inner monologue reveal to the reader? Is he surprised by the emotions and reactions that reside in him? What do they suggest about his identity?

8. Discuss the book's title—why did the author choose it? How might it fit the theme of identity? Why is the novel partly written in the third person, and partly in the first person? Why do the narrators remain unnamed?

9. Find examples of Kashua's sense of humor throughout the narrative, and his portrayal of absurdity in domestic situations. How does humor help him to navigate his novel's serious subject matter?

10. Discuss the loneliness and dislocation experienced by Amir, the social worker, as he transitions from student life

to professional life, and moves out of his dorm and into the world. Why does he choose to stay in Jerusalem despite its hardships, instead of returning to his home village? Why does he refuse to claim his father's land from his relatives? What is he searching for, or moving away from?

11. Why does Amir resign from work? What does it reveal about him?

12. Compare the excitement of Amir's life as a student in Beit Hanina with the carefully maintained artificiality of the lawyer's life. What are the main differences between Amir and the lawyer in the first half of the novel? How do they mirror each other?

13. In the midst of Jerusalem's hectic bustle, Yonatan lies in a vegetative state, his promising life paused. As an Ashkenazi Jewish Israeli, what does he represent to Amir? What are the differences between Amir and Yonatan?

14. Find instances of the self-loathing that Amir feels about his lack of sophistication and his lack of a Western education. Consider how this sense of failure impacts his relationship with Yonatan. At what point does Yonatan transform from someone who instructs Amir through books, music, and photography, to someone Amir can inhabit? Does Amir make a conscious decision to take over Yonatan's identity?

15. How does Amir's action parallel the lawyer's journey for a new identity? Who ultimately changes more—Amir or the lawyer?

16. Discuss the role of Ruchaleh, Yonatan's mother, in the novel. Discuss the complicated emotions she feels toward her son, and the way these emotions manifest in her relationship with Amir. Was her attitude toward/ treatment of Amir surprising?

17. Consider the following statement about Ruchaleh: "She had nothing but scorn for tradition, nationalism, religion, roots, roots trips, and sentences like 'He who has no past, has no future'" (p. 290). Did Yonatan's attempted suicide shape these thoughts in any way? What would she have said to the lawyer and his wife at their dinner discussion on nationalism in education?

18. The novel questions to what extent one can truly know another person. Amir learns very little factual information about Yonatan, and he does not press Ruchaleh for details—thus forming a subjective image of his patient through his possessions. How well does Amir know Yonatan? In attempting to uncover Yonatan's story through his books and his music, how does Amir attempt to discover himself?

19. For both the lawyer and Amir the social worker, the ultimate success is to slip between cultures, not to be singled

out as Arab. Is Kashua critical of this loss of nationalism? Or is he a sympathetic observer? Would the other characters agree with Ruchaleh's observation that "Man was only smart if he was able to shed his identity" (p. 290)?

20. What does the lawyer's sister mean when she states that Leila is "not like us" (p. 144)? Why is that statement so appealing to the lawyer? Does the description of younger Leila match that of married Leila? How has she changed? How much has she been changed by the passage of time, and how much as a consequence of her story being told through the eyes of two different people?

21. Find examples of the lawyer's inner conflict with his sense of self. What do his shifting opinions and ideas indicate about his character? Why is he "not willing to be the only joker in the group" (p. 243)?

22. Talk about the function of photography in the novel—as a means of making sense of the world, and of highlighting perception. Amir hoped to "take the kind of sharp, detailed pictures that revealed the entire world of the stranger on the other end of the lens" (p. 197). Why is this ability important to him?

23. "I can understand the desire to want to be judged for who you are and what you've done and not your nationality or your ethnicity" (p. 215). Discuss the characters' motives throughout the novel in light of this statement. How

does it explain their actions, their hopes, their desperate search for a sense of belonging without feeling guilty? How does it oversimplify the complicated issue of straddling two worlds?

24. What does the future hold for the lawyer? Will his life change because of the "love letter?" Will Amir become "free, loose, full of dreams, able to think about love. Like those . . . who felt no need to apologize for their existence, no need to hide their identity" (p. 304)?

SUGGESTIONS FOR FURTHER READING

Dancing Arabs by Sayed Kashua; *Let It Be Morning* by Sayed Kashua; *Panther in the Basement* by Amos Oz; *Sharon and My Mother-in-Law: Ramallah Diaries* by Suad Amiry